Praise for Faith Hunter's Soulwood Novels

"Rich, imaginative and descriptive. H_____ _____ __vel in her Soulwood series _____ _____ _____ ___ plot coupled with the b_____ _____ ___ __ _y an unforgettable read. _____" ___ews

"I love Nell and her _____ _____ _____ ___ead about their adventur___ _____ ___ ___ Book Club

"Faith Hunter does a masterful job . . . and has created a wonderful new heroine in Nell, who continues to grow into her powers." —The Reading Café

"Once again, Hunter proves she's a master of the genre."
—Romance Junkies

"*Blood of the Earth* by Faith Hunter is the best first installment of an urban fantasy series I've read in about a decade. Highly recommended." —Rabid Reads

Praise for Faith Hunter's Jane Yellowrock Novels

"Jane is a fully realized, complicated woman; her power, humanity, and vulnerability make her a compelling heroine."
—*Publishers Weekly*

"Readers eager for the next book in Patricia Briggs's Mercy Thompson series may want to give Faith Hunter a try."
—*Library Journal*

"Hunter's very professionally executed, tasty blend of dark fantasy, mystery, and romance should please fans of all three genres." —*Booklist*

"Seriously. Best urban fantasy I've read in years, possibly ever." —C. E. Murphy, author of *Stone's Throe*

Also by Faith Hunter

The Jane Yellowrock Novels

SKINWALKER
BLOOD CROSS
MERCY BLADE
RAVEN CURSED
DEATH'S RIVAL
THE JANE YELLOWROCK WORLD COMPANION
BLOOD TRADE
BLACK ARTS
BROKEN SOUL
DARK HEIR
SHADOW RITES
COLD REIGN

The Soulwood Novels

BLOOD OF THE EARTH
CURSE ON THE LAND
FLAME IN THE DARK

The Rogue Mage Novels

BLOODRING
SERAPHS
HOST

Anthologies

CAT TALES
HAVE STAKES WILL TRAVEL
BLACK WATER
BLOOD IN HER VEINS
TRIALS
TRIBULATIONS
TRIUMPHANT

FLAME IN THE DARK

A Soulwood Novel

Faith Hunter

ACE
New York

ACE
Published by Berkley
An imprint of Penguin Random House LLC
375 Hudson Street, New York, New York 10014

Copyright © 2017 by Faith Hunter
Excerpt from *Skinwalker* copyright © 2009 by Faith Hunter
Penguin Random House supports copyright. Copyright fuels creativity, encourages
diverse voices, promotes free speech, and creates a vibrant culture. Thank you for buying
an authorized edition of this book and for complying with copyright laws by not
reproducing, scanning, or distributing any part of it in any form without permission.
You are supporting writers and allowing Penguin Random House to continue to
publish books for every reader.

ACE is a registered trademark and the A colophon
is a trademark of Penguin Random House LLC.

ISBN: 9780451473332

First Edition: December 2017

Printed in the United States of America
1 3 5 7 9 10 8 6 4 2

Cover art by Cliff Nielsen
Cover design by Katie Anderson

To my Renaissance Man,
who keeps me relaxed through months of writing.
You make life worth living.

ACKNOWLEDGMENTS

Teri Lee, Timeline and Continuity Editor Extraordinaire. Where have you been all my life?

Misty Massey, Overseer of the copy edit!

Mindy "Mud" Mymudes, Beta Reader and PR.

Let's Talk Promotions at ltpromos.com, for getting me where I am today.

Lee Williams Watts for being the best travel companion and PA a girl can have!

Beast Claws! Best Street Team Evah!

Mike Pruette at celticleatherworks.com for all the fab merch!

Lucienne Diver of The Knight Agency, as always, for guiding my career, being a font of wisdom when I need advice, and for applying your agile and splendid mind to my writing and my career.

Cliff Nielsen . . . for all the work and talent that goes into the covers.

As always, a huge thank-you to Jessica Wade of Penguin Random House. Without you there would be no book at all!

ONE

I walked the length of Turtle Point Lane near Jones Cove, my tactical flash illuminating the street and the ditch, trying to keep my eyes off the lawn and runnel of water and mature trees to the side. *I should be in the trees, not here in the street, wasting my gifts on asphalt.* I hated asphalt. To my touch, it was cold and dead and it stank of tar and gasoline.

But the K9 teams had dibs on the grass and were already in the backyard, the mundane tracker dog and the paranormal tracker dog, with their handlers, and lights so bright they hurt my eyes when I looked that way. As a paranormal investigator, I had to wait until the human and canine investigators were finished, so my scent didn't confuse the Para-K9s. Standard operating procedure and forensic protocol. But that didn't mean I had to like it.

Armed special weapons and tactics team—SWAT—officers, on loan from the city, patrolled the boundaries of the grounds, dressed in tactical gear and toting automatic rifles. Knoxville's rural/metro fire department patrolled inside the house along with uniformed cops, suited detectives, and federal and state agents in this multiagency emergency investigation.

The PsyLED SAC—special agent in charge of Unit Eighteen, and my boss—had put me to work on menial stuff to keep me off the grass and out of the way until the dogs were completely done. As a probationary agent, I did what I was told. Most of the time.

My steps were slow and deliberate, my eyes taking in everything. Crushed cigarette butts stained by yesterday's rain, soggy leaves, broken auto safety glass in tiny pellets, flattened aluminum cans in the brush and a depression: an energy drink and a lite beer. A gum box. Nothing new, from the last twenty-four hours. I was surprised at the amount of detritus on a street with such upmarket houses. Maybe the county had no street sweeper machine, or maybe the worst of the filth ended up hidden in the weeds, hard to see, making the street appear cleaner than it really was. Life was like that too, with lots of secrets hidden from sight.

I had already searched the entire street with the psy-meter 2.0, and put the bulky device in the truck. There were no odd levels of paranormal energies anywhere. A small spike on level four at the edge of the drive, but it went away. An anomaly. The psy-meter 2.0 measured four different kinds of paranormal energies called psysitopes, and the patterns could indicate a were-creature, a witch, an *arcenciel*, and even Welsh *gwyllgi*—shape-shifting devil dogs. I had nothing yet, but I needed onto the lawn to do a proper reading. I'd get my wish. Eventually.

I searched the area around a Lexus. Then a short row of BMWs. I took photos of each vehicle plate and sent them to JoJo, Unit Eighteen's second in command and best IT person, to cross-check the plate numbers with the guest list. The air was frigid and I was frozen, even though I was wearing long underwear, flannel-lined slacks, layered T-shirts, a heavy jacket, wool socks, and field boots. But then, along with uniformed county officers, I'd been at the grounds search for two hours, since the midnight call yanked me out of my nice warm bed and onto the job at a PsyLED crime scene. Field examination was scut work, the bane of all probie special agents, and we had found nothing on the street or driveway that might relate to the crime at the überfancy house on a cove of the Tennessee River.

To make me more miserable, because I had drunk down a half gallon of strong coffee, I had to use the ladies', pretty desperately. I stared at the Holloways' house, trying to figure out what to do.

"I just went to the back door and knocked," a voice said.

I whirled. I'd been so intent that I hadn't heard her walk up. A young female sheriff's deputy grinned at me. "Sorry. Didn't mean to startle you," she said.

"Oh. It's okay." But it wasn't. I was jumpy and ill at ease for reasons I didn't understand. There were woods with fairly mature trees all around, water in the cove nearby, and well-maintained lawns the length of the street, all full of life that should have made me feel at home. Instead I was jumpy. All that coffee maybe. "I'm Nell. Special Agent Ingram." I put out my hand and the woman shook it, businesslike.

"You don't remember me," she said, "but we met at the hospital during the outbreak of the slime molds back a few weeks. You gave me your keys and let my partner and me get unis out of your vehicle. I never got the chance to thank you. May Ree Holler, and my partner, Chris Skeeter." She pointed to a taller, skinny man up the road.

"Your mother escaped from God's Cloud of Glory Church, like I did," I said, referring to the polygamous church I grew up in. "I remember. Her name was Carla, right?"

May Ree grinned at me, seeming happy that I remembered. "That's my mama. Hard as nails and twice as strong." She indicated the dark all around. "Us females always get it the worst on these jobs. The male deputies can just go in the woods, but it isn't so easy for women. The caterer let me in to use the bathroom. Even gave me a pastry." May Ree was short and sturdy with a freckled face, brown hair, and wearing her uniform tight, showing off curves. She had a self-assuredness I would never achieve. Her hair was cropped short for safety in close-combat situations, but her lips were full and scarlet in the reflected glare from my flash, and she was fully made up with mascara and blush, even at the ungodly hour. "Go on. And if they offer you something to eat, bring me another one of those pink iced squares. I missed supper."

"I will. Thanks," I said. If I couldn't get her one I'd give her a snack from my truck when I came back out, presuming the bread wasn't frozen. Still moving my flash back and forth, covering my square yard with each pass, I walked from the street, up the drive, and to the back door, where I snapped off the light. I thought about knocking, but I had learned it was easier to apologize than to get permission. Not a lesson I had learned at the church where I was raised, but one I had learned since coming to work with PsyLED. I might get fussed at or written up, but no one would punish me for an infraction, like the churchmen did to the churchwomen.

Opening the door, I slid the flash into its sheath and stepped inside. The warmth and the smell of coffee hit me like a fist. I unbuttoned my jacket so my badge would show and blinked into the warmth. My frozen face felt as if it might melt and slide off onto the marble tile floor. I breathed for a few moments and tried to unclench my fingers. My skin ached. My teeth hurt.

The arctic front had no regard for global warming. It had hit, decided it liked the Tennessee Valley, and decided to stay. This was the second week of frigid temps. Snow I liked. This, not at all.

Once the worst of the personal melting was done, I looked around. The kitchen was empty, a room constructed of stone in various shades of gray on the floor and the cabinet tops and the backsplash. The owners must have taken down a whole mountain to get this much polished rock. The ceiling was vaulted with whitish wooden rafters and joists. Cabinets with the same kind of treated whitish wood rose ten feet high. A ladder that slid on a bronze rail was in the corner. The stove was gas with ten burners and a copper faucet over the stovetops, which looked handy unless one had a grease fire and thought to use water to put it out. There was a commercial-sized coffeemaker with a huge pot half-full, two big, double-glass-door refrigerators, and a separate massive two-door freezer. I spotted the small powder room off the kitchen and raced into it before anyone could come in and tell me to get outside and use the trees.

I was one of maybe twenty-five law enforcement officers and investigators from the various law enforcement branches and agencies called in to the shooting at the Holloway home. The FBI was here to rule out terrorism because a U.S. senator had been at the private political fund-raiser when the shooting started.

PsyLED—the Psychometry Law Enforcement Division of Homeland Security—was here because a vampire had been on-site too. The fire department was here because there had been a small fire. The local sheriff's LEOs were here because it was their jurisdiction.

Crime scene investigators were here because there were three dead bodies on the premises, though not the senator—he was shaken up but fine. The grounds search was because the shooter had come and gone on foot. It was complicated. But dead and wounded VIPs meant a lot of police presence and a shooting to solve, especially since the shooter got away clean.

When I came back out, the kitchen was still empty and I decided a bit more of the "ask permission later" was called for. Most anything was better than going back outside to search the road and paved areas for clues into a crime I had not been informed about. Two automatic dishwashers were running softly. The pastries were taped under waxed paper, including little pink iced squares. May Ree would be disappointed. There were four ovens, and all but one was still warm to the touch. I inspected the planters under the windows. At first glance they appeared to be full of herbs—basil, rosemary, thyme, and lemongrass—but the leaves were silk. Which was weird in a kitchen that looked as if someone loved to cook.

Trying to look as if I belonged, I wandered through a butler's pantry, complete with coffee bar, wet bar with dozens of decanters and bottles, and wine in a floor-to-ceiling special refrigerator. Beyond the butler's pantry, stairs went up on one side and down on the other, proving that the house had multiple levels, not just the two obvious from the outside. Picking up on the smell of smoke and scorched furnishings was easy here.

I stayed on the main level and meandered into a formal dining room on one side of the entry. There was more stone here too, and wood in the vaulted ceilings. The twelve-foot-long dining table was set for a party, though I didn't recognize any of the food except the whole salmon and the tenderloin of beef. It seemed a shame to let the food go to waste when May Ree was hungry, but there was blood on the floor in the doorway, leading from the back of the house to here. Since there was blood, the food itself might be evidence, so I kept my hands to myself and stepped carefully.

I had seen EMS units racing away as I drove up, so I knew there had been casualties, but seeing blood was unsettling. My gift rose up inside me, as if it was curious. Not trying to drink the blood down, not yet, because I wasn't outside, my hands buried in the earth, but more like a mouser cat who sees movement and crouches, trying to decide if this is something worth hunting.

A formal living room decorated with a Christmas tree and presents and fake electric candles in the windows was on the other side of the entry. It had real wood floors and a ten-foot ceiling with one of those frame things set in the middle to give it even more height. Maybe called a tray ceiling; I wasn't sure. Life in the church hadn't prepared me with a good grasp of architectural terminology. The entire room felt stiff and uncomfortable to me, maybe due to the fact that all the plants were fake. Fancy tables, tassels on heavy drapes, carved lamps, furniture that looked showroom-fresh. This wasn't a place to kick up your feet.

The room was full of people in fancy dress, and oddly, I knew two of them, Ming of Glass, the vampire Master of the City, and her bodyguard, a vamp I knew only as Yummy. Yummy flashed me a grin, one without fangs, which was nice, but she mouthed, *Opossum*, at me, which was a tease I didn't really need. I mouthed back, *Ha-ha. Not.* Yummy laughed.

All but three of the partygoers in the room looked irritated—two vamps and a human. Vamps tended to expressionless faces unless they were irritated or hungry, both of which were a sign of danger. The human was sitting on an ottoman, and he looked devastated, face pale, his tie undone, a crystal glass in one hand, dangling between his knees. I figured he was the husband of one of the dead. There was blood spatter on his shirt and dark suit coat. A man who didn't belong in the expensively dressed crowd stood beside him, taking notes. A fed, I figured as I slipped away, before I got caught, to wander some more.

I passed uniformed and suited LEOs here and there, two I recognized as local and one unknown wearing a far better-fitting suit. Probably another fed. The firefighters left through the front door, big boots clomping, and gathered on the street. Two crime scene techs raced into the room off to the side, carrying gear. No one paid any attention to me except to note that I had a badge on a lanyard around my neck. I hooked my thumbs into my pockets and moseyed over, probably a failure at looking as if I belonged.

The action was in the game room and the stench of fire grew heavier. Inside was a pool table, comfy reclining sofas, and a TV screen so big it took up most of the wall over the fireplace. On the opposite wall were antique guns in frames behind glass. Cast metal that might have been machine parts was protected within smaller frames. What looked like an ordinary wrench was centered on the wall in a heavy carved frame as if it was the most important thing hanging there. People commemorated the strangest things.

There were also lots of old, black-and-white photographs of stiff-looking people wearing stiff-looking clothes. Their hats and the way the women's clothes fitted said they were rich and pampered. The men's mustaches and thick facial hair made them look imposing, at least to themselves; they had that self-satisfied look about them, the expression of a hunter when he was posing with a sixteen-point buck. However, their expressions also made them look like their teeth hurt. Dental care was probably not very common back whenever these were taken.

Standing in the doorway, I spotted Rick LaFleur, the special agent in charge of Unit Eighteen, talking to Soul, his up-line boss, the newly appointed assistant director, and another woman. If body language was a clue, the PsyLED agents were arguing with the African-American woman in the chic outfit. She wore the tailored clothes as if they were part of her, as much as the scowl and the aura of power. I figured she was the new VIP in charge of the Knoxville FBI. They were too busy to pay attention to me, so I strolled in. Saw things. Smelled things. Touched things with the back of my hand, here and there.

The gas logs had been on, but were now only warm to the touch. A game of pool had been interrupted and balls were all over the tabletop. The solids were mostly gone. One cue stick lay on the floor in two pieces. Drinks of the alcoholic variety were on every available surface.

The entire room smelled of fire, the sour scent of a house fire—painted wallboard and burned construction materials, lots of synthetics. The stench was tainted with what might have been the reek of scorched flesh. Icy night air blew in through the busted windows; blackened draperies billowed. Charred furniture and rugs spread into the room from the window. The fire seemed to have started there.

There were bullet holes on the wall opposite the windows. And there was a pool of blood on the floor. A body lay in the middle of it. She had taken a chest shot. Dead instantly if I was any kind of judge. There was no taped outline. No chalk outline. Just the blood and the body, still in place.

I stared at her. The victim was middle-aged with dyed blond hair and blue contacts drying and wrinkling, shrinking over her gray eyes. She was wearing a pale blue sweater top and black pants, three-inch black spike shoes. Diamonds. Lots of them. There was blood spatter on the wall in an odd outline, as if someone had been standing behind her. Blood on a chair and small table. Blood on a shattered glass on the mantel near her. That bloody pool beneath her was tracked through by the shoe prints of the people who had tried to save her. There was a lot of blood.

My gift of reading the land—and feeding the land with blood—was less reticent now, more focused. Hungering. But I had been working with it, trying to harness it, and I stroked the need like the hunting cat I compared it to, flattening its surface, pushing it into stillness. Proud of myself that I had the strength of will to not feed my hunger and the earth beneath the house, I turned from the body.

By now, the crime scene had been captured in photos and video and cell cameras and drawn out on paper by hand. Multiple redundancies. Crime scene techs were still working, but oddly, there were no numbered evidence markers in the room. I had to wonder why. Maybe they had been placed there, then already removed as CSI gathered up the physical evidence.

I approached the broken windows. Outside, a coroner's unit waited, lights not flashing, not in an upscale neighborhood. The EMTs and their vehicles had left with the wounded, three, I had heard, one critical. Farther beyond, a media van waited, a camera on a tripod and a reporter in front of it, filming for the morning news. In the dark of the driveway, where the cameras couldn't get a shot, two uniformed figures lifted a gurney with a body bag into the coroner's van. There was already one gurney inside. Three dead, three wounded at this scene.

The window glass was shattered, in pellets all over the floor. It reminded me of the automobile glass outside, but this was clear and the vehicle glass had been tinted and well ground into the asphalt.

The cloth blinds were burned and tattered, the drapery seared. The walls were scorched all around them, and up to the ceiling. A table by the window was mostly shattered charcoal and candles had melted across the surface. A blackened glass was on its side. It looked as if the shots had smashed the glass, spilling the alcohol and toppling the lit candle. I guessed that the fire had spread quickly, but I wasn't a fire and arson investigator. I knew to keep my opinions to myself unless asked. Opinions went into the evidentiary summary report in the "Opinion" box, where they were mostly ignored. They weren't facts.

I slipped out before someone asked me what I was doing. Next door was the master bedroom. Master *suite*. Yes, that sounded right. It was full of people. Instead of pushing my luck, I slowly went up the staircase onto the second level.

On the second floor were six bedrooms and four full baths. Counting the servants' powder room, the en suite in the master, and the two guest powder rooms on the ground floor, that was a lot of bathrooms. I had grown up in a house that technically had more square footage and more bedrooms than this one, but it was nowhere near as fancy. The Holloways' home was luxurious, what T. Laine probably called "new-money decadent." They probably paid their decorator more than the yearly income of most American families.

I traipsed back down, hearing T. Laine's and Tandy's voices from the master suite. T. Laine was Tammie Laine Kent, PsyLED Unit Eighteen's moon witch, one with strong earth element affinities and enough unfinished university degrees to satisfy the most OCD person on the planet. That was how she had introduced herself to me. Tandy was the unit's empath, who claimed his superpower was being struck by lightning.

I'd wandered around as much as I could without entering the master suite, but I was nosy, so I stood just outside that door, taking the excuse to see, hear, and learn what I could before being banished back into the cold by Rick. Who was now standing in said master suite. He was in front of the window, facing the door and me, being dressed down by a well-suited FBI-agent-type in an expensive suit and tie, regulation all the way. Rick's black hair was too long to be regulation, his black eyes were tired, and his olive skin looked sallow. Rick had aged in the last weeks, though he looked a bit better now that he had learned how to shift into his black wereleopard form and back to human. He frowned at me, but didn't interrupt his conversation.

"This isn't one of your magic wand and broomstick investigations," the fed said. It was said in the tone of an older kid to a young one, insult in each syllable, in a local, townie accent. "This was an attack on a house party and fund-raiser with some of the biggest movers and shakers in Tennessee. Super-wealthy business and political types, with their fingers in every financial pie in the nation."

Toneless, Rick said, "With all due respect, there were

witches and vampires at the party. The strike could have been aimed at the Tennessee senator, Abrams Tolliver, as you *assume*, or at Ming, the closest thing Knoxville has to a vampire Master of the City, with whom he was speaking."

I knew of the Tollivers. Rich, powerful people who made their money when the Tennessee Valley Authority stole the land of all the state's farmers and changed the face of the South. The men of God's Cloud preached about the entire Tolliver family going to hell, and maybe taking up their own special circle right next to the devil himself.

"Or just the fully human victim, or one of the human homeowners, which is far more likely. This is not your case," the suit said. "This is a joint FBI, ATF, and Secret Service investigation, not some trivial magic case."

"You are incorrect," Soul said. I stepped quickly to the side, because the assistant director of PsyLED was standing behind me and I was blocking the door. My heart started beating too fast, and my bloodlust rose with my reaction. I pushed down on it, anxious about its agitation, but not worried enough to leave the house.

"You need to return to the living room with the other guests, lady," the suit said. He sounded frustrated. And unimpressed at the vision Soul presented, all gauzy fabrics, platinum hair, and curves.

"On the contrary. I am exactly where I belong, young man."

"Who the hell are you? If you're law enforcement, where is your badge and ID?" he replied.

The room fell silent. I covered my mouth and moved inside quickly, along the wall, to keep them all in view. Soul walked slowly closer to him, silvery gauze waving in a rising wind that wasn't really there. I didn't have the same kind of magic as Soul, but I felt her power on my skin like small sparks of electricity. *Arcenciel* magic was wild and hot, a shape-shifting ability that defied the laws of physics as scientists understood them. It wasn't common knowledge—in fact, half of Unit Eighteen didn't know—that Soul was a rainbow dragon, a creature made of light. But even without that knowledge, if the suit didn't know a stalking predator when he saw one, then he needed to spend more time in the wild, to hone his survival instincts.

"What. Did. You. Say?" Soul asked.

"Hamilton!" a woman barked. "What the bloody hell."

It was the woman from the game room, the African-American woman who wore the power of her office like a crown and robe. Her ID was clipped at her collar and her name was E. M. Schultz.

Soul didn't turn to her, keeping her eyes on the suit and saying, "I've been on conference call to PsyLED director Clarence Lester Woods, the secretary of Homeland Security, and the director of the FBI, as well as the head of Alcohol, Tobacco, and Firearms. This is a joint investigation between four, not three, branches of law enforcement. You may address me as Assistant Director, PsyLED. And your services are no longer needed at this crime scene." She turned her head as if looking for something.

In a tone that wasn't quite a question, not quite a demand, she said, "Special Agent Ingram?"

I jumped. Soul kept on talking. "Take Mr. Hamilton outside. Give him your flashlight. Teach him how to do a perimeter grounds search. Then come back in here. I need your services."

I was staring at Hamilton, his name touching down in my mind, in the place designated for it. Chadworth Sanders Hamilton, his father's second son from his second wife, named for his mother's grandfathers. And my third cousin, by way of Maude Nicholson, my grandmother. My distant cousin from the townie side of the family. I'd heard he had graduated from the FBI academy at the top of his class and come back home to make his mark. This embarrassing dressing-down was likely not the mark he wanted to make.

I held up a hand to identify myself and silently led the way to the kitchen. There, I found foam cups, poured coffee from the coffeemaker, and put them on a tray with napkins, a bread knife, and a spoon. I could practically feel the embarrassment and fury emanating off Hamilton as I worked, my back to him. At least the anger would keep him warm for a while. And there was no way I was going to tell him that we were related when he was so furious. Maybe later. Maybe . . . Carefully, tray balanced, I left the warmth of the house, my cousin on my heels, not offering to help with the load. I didn't know if that made him a jerk or just oblivious, but so far, my cousin was not making a very good impression.

Outside, I flashed my light three times, handed it to Hamilton, and said, "Forty-eight hundred lumens. Battery will last another two hours before it has to be recharged. One yard squares, from the middle of the ditch to the middle of the lane. This'll be the third pass so it should be pretty clean."

"What's up, Ingram?" May Ree asked, joining us at a jog. The other deputies followed, and so did three SWAT officers, until we had a small crowd.

"Coffee," I said, unnecessarily, as they reached in for the cups. "Keys." I placed them in May Ree's hand. "There's a loaf of bread in the passenger seat of my truck and a jar of jam. Bring the knife and spoon back in when y'all are done. I'll get some fresh coffee out here as soon as I can." May Ree dashed down the road to my car. I continued to the others, "This is Hamilton. Probie. Looks like he came out without a coat, so he'll be cold."

"It's all right, kid," a deputy said. The county cop was six-six easy, and had a chest like a whiskey barrel. "We've all been stupid from time to time." Several officers laughed.

Hamilton flinched and burned hotter, probably thinking about the dressing-down he'd just received, not the coat he'd forgotten. Probably furious that he'd been called "kid" by a county cop, someone an FBI officer might look down on, in the hierarchy of law enforcement types. But he kept his mouth shut. He looked pale in all the flashlights and totally out of place, underdressed in his fancy suit.

The deputy continued, "I got an extra jacket in my unit. It'll hang to your knees, little fella like you, but it's clean. Hang on, I'll get it." He too jogged off.

I didn't laugh at my cousin's expression at the words *little fella like you*.

Hamilton accepted a cup of coffee. And the coat. And a slice of bread and jam. I waited until the cups were gone and Hamilton was wearing the borrowed coat and starting on the road. He was all but kicking the pavement like a kid. I hadn't told him who I was, that we were distant cousins. My grandma Maude had been disowned when she married into the church. I doubted that Hamilton knew I existed.

Back inside, I figured out how to work the coffee machine and got coffee gurgling, found a gallon-sized carafe, a table-cloth, more napkins and foam cups. When the coffee was ready, I took the tray back outside, placed the tablecloth on the hood of a county car, the tray atop it, and went back inside, where I made another trip to the powder room and put on fresh lipstick. The assistant director of PsyLED wanted me for something. That made me nervous. I had learned that lipstick gave me false courage. False was better than no courage at all.

I made my way through the house until I found Rick, Soul, and a seated man in khakis and a golf shirt, in a small room on the second floor. The room was no bigger than a closet, a tiny space dedicated to the Holloways' security system, two vacuum cleaners, brooms, push mops of various designs, and lots of cleaning supplies. I slipped in behind Rick and leaned against the wall so I could watch the security video beside his shoulder.

It was a nice system. I had studied most commercial brands and a couple dozen government kinds while in Spook School, the PsyLED training facility. This was an integrated one, with motion detection sensors that triggered the outside cameras and automatically downloaded all video to the system. Later someone had to go through all the captured images and delete the homeowners' dogs, wildlife, and the occasional teenager sneaking into or out of the house after hours. Currently there were four images on the big screen.

"There are four cameras with views of the outside," the khaki-clad man said, "but there's no sign of the shooter's approach to the house until here." He stopped all the video and pointed to the image on top. "He or she seems to be able to bypass all the cameras until he stops, where he—for convenience we'll say 'he'—appears as a vague shape outside the windows of the game room."

The shape was little more than a smear of movement, not really visible on digital, as if he somehow disrupted and blurred the images. Magic could do that. So could some types of disruptor equipment the military was working on in R&D. However, by the blurred images, it appeared as if it was a lone assassin. The image on the screen started moving again.

"Exactly eight seconds after he appeared on screen, he started shooting, and, unlike the man—or woman—wielding it, the weapon is easily visible as a fully automatic M4 carbine." The video progressed to show the attacker shooting.

"M4?" Soul asked. "How did he get an M4?"

"Don't know, ma'am," Khaki Man said. "The M4 carbine is heavily used by two branches of United States armed forces as the primary infantry weapon, it's currently available on the open market, and it's legal in Tennessee, so it isn't impossible to get one."

I dredged through the day of class we spent on military weapons and remembered that the M4 was replacing the M16 rifle in most Army and Marine Corps combat units. Sooo . . . Except for the way the shots were fired, the attacker could be military. Or the weapon could be stolen. Or purchased on the commercial market. He could have gotten it most anywhere.

"All right," Soul said.

Playing the footage again, Khaki Man said, "There were four three-second bursts, moving from the shooter's left to his right, combined with one extended magazine change, which takes place here." He stopped the security video with each statement, and pointed as the shooter changed out magazines. "Then he started shooting again and repeated the four three-bursts. Then he took off."

To me, the attacker's motions, though blurred, looked masculine.

"One thing of note. Shooting through glass is tricky. Well-trained shooters usually put a single shot through the glass first, then take out the targets. Inside," he continued, "the female falls. Two other victims fall, here and here." He pointed again, though the images were badly blurred, the outdoor camera picking up little inside. "People take cover. Rounds topple the candles, which ignite tablecloths. Fire leaps to the draperies, races over the furniture and up the walls, then follows the oxygen outside through the broken windows." He showed us footage of the fire blazing out through the broken window.

"Then the shooter is tackled by a security guard, Amos Guerling. Amos said he could see the gun, but not the person. You can see here, the flash of flame when Amos was burned, deep second or maybe third degree on his upper arm and left hand, with visible and significant muscle damage. Source of the flame is unknown at this time, though ATF and the fire department are checking for accelerants on Amos' clothing. Assassin then seems to disappear into thin air. Our security people put out the fires, inside and out, with extinguishers and began emergency medical treatment on the victims."

"What branch?" Soul asked.

"Beg pardon, ma'am?"

"What branch did you serve in? All the men and women who work for ALT Security Services are former military."

"I see you do your homework, ma'am." Khaki Man spun in his chair. He was tanned brown, the color of a hickory nut in fall, with close-cropped dark hair and greenish eyes. The name tag said his name was P. Simon. "Green Beret, ma'am. Four active tours in the Middle East."

"Where and when?"

"Classified, ma'am."

"Of course." But I could tell by her tone that Soul would find out in case the man was involved with the shooter on the wrong side. If this shooting was an inside job, the security team would be the first suspects.

"Can you tell me what the dogs found, ma'am?" Simon asked.

"No," Rick said. "Sorry. Need to know."

Soul glanced at Rick before speaking. "The Canine Unit's findings will be released to the press shortly. I think we can divulge this now. The standard crime scene K9 dog was able to track a suspect across the back lawns, across the tip of the cove, to Lyons Bend Road, where the trail disappeared. We have officers going door to door to see if a vehicle is missing or if an unfamiliar vehicle was seen parked somewhere. The paranormal K9 dog gave scent signs only for human scent, giving no signs for nonhuman species." The paranormal dogs were trained only to known paranormal types, so Soul wasn't giving much away. She went on, "Despite the shooter's disappearing act there is no indication of magic used at the scene of the crime nor at the scene of the perpetrator's appearance and disappearance. He used a mundane military weapon and he scents human."

Simon said, "It's obvious by the camera distortion that he used some kind of an obfuscation spell over himself. Therefore not human. Ma'am," he added.

Proving that whatever classified jobs he'd had in the military, he knew how some magic affected digital tech. Obfuscation spells were fairly new, having been around only three years or so.

"And that places this under our jurisdiction," Rick murmured.

"Discussion is taking place at high levels about who will take lead on this case," Soul said, her voice calm.

By *discussion*, I knew she meant arguments. Every branch of law enforcement wanted this case except the sheriff, who had too much political acumen to want anything to do with a United States senator, three rich dead VIPs, multiple wounded, and vampires.

"Ingram," Soul said.

I jerked upright, away from the wall where I had slouched, and said, "Yes, ma'am." It was time for whatever job Soul had for me. Her eyes flashed darkly in her olive-skinned face and she smoothed her platinum hair, twisting it in its long, curling coil.

"K9 is finished. CSI has completed their outdoor work.

Walk the grounds. Sit for a while. Look things over. Tell me what you find."

"Yes'm." I turned and hightailed it out of the security cave and outside. I was being told to use my gift, to read the land. As I fled the house, my gift crouched and licked its lips. Metaphorically speaking. Not in reality. Or that was what I told myself.

I buttoned my jacket as I walked to the truck again, getting out the psy-meter 2.0 and my faded pink blanket, and then back to the window where the shooter had stood. Turning, I viewed the grounds and the drive and the darker smear of the cove. The air smelled icy and rivery—that peculiar odor of the Tennessee River at normal levels—and my nose felt frozen. My breath was a white cloud in the security lights. Somewhere nearby, an owl hooted. Farther off, a dog barked, distressed.

The K9 dogs and handlers were gone. SWAT was gone. The coroner's vehicle pulled away with the woman's body as I watched. The lights illuminating the backyard went out, which made me smile. Rick, or maybe Soul, was making sure no one could see me when I went to work. I saw Hamilton walking back from the street up the drive, my flashlight still brightening his way. He didn't see me, and went on inside. Three sheriff deputies' cars pulled away. Two couples and a group of five guests left, walking down the road for the cars parked along the verge. Three of the BMWs left too. Overhead, the sky was still black, but it wouldn't be long until it shifted into the gray of predawn. I closed my eyes, letting my night vision return. I breathed the air and let my body relax. It was easier to read the land when I wasn't hyped up. That was JoJo's term for excited and nervous—*hyped up*.

I set the folded blanket on the grass and calibrated the psy-meter 2.0. I did a quick scan of the area under the window and then across the yard, getting only small psysitope spikes on level four. Nothing definitive. Not even anything I could point to and say, maybe. And when I checked a second time, they seemed to be fading, reading slightly lower on the scale than before. Anomalies?

I wouldn't be determining the species of creature just now, but that couldn't be helped. I turned off the unit and sat on the blanket. Blowing out a breath, I placed my hands down, palms open, on the lawn and pressed down. Scratched my fingertips into the thick grass until I touched the dirt below. Instantly the discomfort I had been feeling all night eased. *This* was where I belonged. I breathed for a few minutes, letting my body settle and my gift quest free. Down. Into the earth. With a job to do and earth to read, my bloodlust settled too.

Grass leaves, crisp and dormant, the roots thick, well fed, and satisfied, was the first thing I read. It had been grown as sod and placed atop soil that had been enriched with mushroom compost and a good mix of supplements. Roots of trees, shrubs, and plantings intertwined. Insects and grubs and earthworms were hibernating. Down into the ground, I quested. Deeper. Rocks were here, the rounded stones of a much larger river bottom. Limestone below that, holey and shattered. The first water table was only a few yards deep.

I pulled back and let my interest settle on the grass. Plants didn't tend to notice things outside of rain, abundance or lack of nutrients, abundance or lack of sunlight, fire, seasons, and the phases of the moon, so I didn't expect to sense anything. But I did.

I found a path of damage. It trailed from the trees near the cove, to the window and back. Both paths crossed a runnel that fed the water in the cove. The path of wounded plants extended beyond that, all the way to the asphalt. I rechecked with the psy-meter 2.0, which showed next to nothing, now.

The shooter had left a trail. One only I could follow.

TWO

The grass was dying, its leaves injured, the roots failing. The shooter had damaged them all. By next week the path he—it?— took would be brown and dead. There was no way that the shooter was human. But I had no idea what it was and that was the first thing that Rick and Soul would want to know. If I could identify the type of paranormal creature it was, that might place the entire investigation into the hands of the PsyLED team. Without that, no federal agency would consider relinquishing control.

I stood and carried the psy-meter back to the truck, where I locked it in, and then took my blanket into the darkness, toward the trees, following the trail of the . . . whatever it was. Every place where its feet touched down was dead. To the sides, spreading out, was less damage, but I didn't think that grass would survive either. It was a type of injury I could follow even without having my hands in it, yet the dormant grass didn't even know it had died, as if passing away in its sleep.

I walked through the yard, my fingers freezing, my toes frozen. My cheeks felt even colder, and I realized that I was crying, crying for the death in the ground. I reached the trees at the back of the property and moved deeper into them, into the darkness. The roots along the shooter's pathway were wounded, but I thought the trees would survive. All but one little scrub oak. It was maybe five feet tall, only a few spindly branches to either side, and it was nearly dead.

I spread my blanket out and sat next to the oak. I cupped my hands around the base of the tree, so that the outer pads

FLAME IN THE DARK

of my hands touched the ground, my fingers on the bark. Sinking into the tree, I felt along the pathways up and down it, the starchy sugars and oils and organic molecules that spoke of life. The ruined limbs were at the outer edges where the thing had brushed by it, touching it with the death in its body. I could trim them back but it wouldn't help. The roots were damaged in ways I couldn't even understand. I tried pushing life into them, tried to heal the small tree. But it was ruined. It was dead. I sat back on my backside.

I understood why people cut down healthy trees. I understood the concept of trees as crops and building materials, of trees as being removed for habitations and business buildings. But killing for the sake of killing—even trees—was an alien concept to me. And this creature—the shooter—was a killer. A killer by nature, perhaps? A killer by its cellular composition? It appeared that it killed just as it breathed, by body chemistry, or by instinct, by predisposition and reflex. I knew it but I couldn't prove it. I didn't know what the shooter was. But the death of the tree made me weep.

I wiped my cheeks, feeling the chapped skin. I didn't question why I cried more over a baby tree than I did over the woman the shooter had killed. Surely the woman with the gray eyes deserved a greater grief. I would have to look at my own biases, but later, when I had time, after this long night was over. Wiping my face, I stood. Gathered up my blanket. And continued after the killer. I followed the death of plants through the woods, ignoring the scratches of nearby limbs, the vines and shoots and roots set to trip me, reaching down to the roots, trying to support them all, to the end of the cove, where I stopped. The destruction led directly into the water.

I thought about following the trail in, but a stupid image of a crocodile coming out of the water to chew me up stopped me. I knew there were no crocs or alligators this far north, but knowing wasn't believing. Instead I walked to the end of the cove and down the other side about twenty feet. He had probably tried to throw off tracker dogs, but good dogs didn't get fooled so easily. Neither did I. The dead earth was simple to spot. Easy as pie, I picked up the trail and followed it out of the neighborhood.

By the time I stumbled out onto the main road, I was exhausted. I had given too much of myself to the land and to the dying sapling. I crossed the ditch and sat down hard, the frozen earth penetrating through my pants instantly. I shoved the blanket under me and huddled into my coat, hands in my pockets, where I discovered a pair of gloves I hadn't known I carried. That was stupid. My fingers were so cold they ached bone-deep. I pulled the coat high on my neck and huddled down, searching for body warmth that seemed dangerously lacking.

Down the road, I saw bright lights coming my way. A car, slowing.

I was alone. On a county road before dawn. I should be afraid. I should open my coat and have my hand on my service weapon. But I was mad. And if anyone tried to hurt me right now, pulled over in a car and tried to abduct me, I'd drain them into the earth and feed the land. And feed myself. And that thought was scary. When had I thought about replenishing my own energies with the life force of another? A dark pit opened up in me, full of dread dreams and fear.

The car stopped and the door opened. "Nell?"

It was Occam. I blinked against the glare and squinted at him. And remembered him asking me to dinner only a few weeks or so ago. The dread and fear spread. We had never addressed that invitation. We had gone on as if he had never spoken, never asked. But I remembered. And I was apprehensive and fretful at what dinner with the wereleopard might mean.

"You okay, Nell, sugar?"

"Not really." He started toward me, and I barked, "Don't touch me!"

Occam stopped, backed slowly to the car and behind the door. "Come on. Get in the car. I'll take you back to the house. Rick should never have sent you out alone."

"Why? 'Acause I'm a woman?" I asked in my strongest church dialect, indignant.

"No. Because this is a dangerous situation and we should be working in pairs."

I thought about that. If I'd had someone with me, would I have spent less of myself trying to save the sapling? Probably. I'd have been smarter because I'd have been thinking more about humans and not so much about trees. Occam stood by his car, letting me think. In a more townie accent I asked, "Where've you been all night?"

"In the office off the master suite, questioning the party-goers," he said, his Texas accent stronger than usual, deliberately calming, soothing. "Bunch a self-entitled snobs. Useless in a firefight. Two of 'em wet their britches."

A chuckle burst out of me. Dark cop humor, bloody and coarse, but it helped newbies to adjust, to view death and horror impersonally. My laughter faded away. Yes. I had needed a partner. The wearies pulling at my muscles like claws, I stood and dragged my blanket with me, trudging to the passenger door. I got in to find the heater blasting on full. I pulled my gloves back off and held my hands to the vents as Occam's fancy car took us back to the house.

I watched him as he parked in the drive, his blond hair swinging, his amber eyes looking fully human. He glanced at me and away. As if sensing my mood, Occam said nothing, just got out of his fancy car, taking my blanket and putting it in my truck before he followed me inside the house and went back to whatever he had been doing before he came to check on me.

Standing in the cramped space of the security system, I made my report to Rick and Soul.

"Can you prove he—it—wasn't human?" Soul asked.

"Empirical evidence in a few days," I said, speaking in my work accent. "Maybe. But not scientifically."

Soul heaved a sigh she might really need. I wasn't sure if her species needed air the same way humans did. Maybe they breathed through their pores or had holes in their rib cages or something. "I'd like you to speak with Ming of

Glass and her bodyguard. See what you can get out of them. When you are done, they may leave, with our thanks."

I stood, flatfooted, meeting Soul's gorgeous and slightly amused eyes. At her side, Rick looked as surprised as I felt.

"Ummm. Don't you think there might be someone better than me to talk to a vampire?"

"No," Soul said. "You are precisely the right person to address the issue of paranormal beings who've committed first-degree murder and/or hate crimes with the highest-ranked vampire in Knoxville. And it will be an opportunity to rebuild bridges that you set fire to when you referred to all Mithrans as smelling 'maggoty,' I believe?"

I blushed hotly, and the last of the chill flushed out of my body. "Ohhh. You think she knows—"

"I am quite certain that she knows. Your reaction to Mithrans has made all the rounds. Go make nice with the head of Clan Glass. Rebuild some bridges. She's waiting on you upstairs in the office we are using as an interrogation room. Go on," she added when I stood there. "Take Tandy with you."

I left the room, which had suddenly grown too close and lost all oxygen. Tandy was outside the door, his reddish brown eyebrows lifted. Like Occam, I hadn't seen him all night.

"You heard?" I asked. "That you're supposed to go with me to question the vampires?"

"No. But I felt. What happened?"

Tandy was the unit's empath, which meant he could tell what other people were feeling—humans and paranormals both. The gift had been forced on him by Mother Nature when he was hit by lightning three times, and the reddish Lichtenberg lines that crossed his pale skin like the veins in leaves were a lasting legacy. I told him what had happened and about my punishment as we climbed the stairs to the second floor. He didn't laugh, which was nice. He handed me a folder containing several printed papers, including the questions that had been asked of all the party guests and two floor plans of the crime scene room, one with Xs for where everyone had been standing. A dozen more. There was no time to memorize any of them. I shoved them back into the manila folder.

My thoughts were rattled and I pulled what I could remember about proper protocol with a powerful vampire to the forefront of my memories. I needed excellent manners, a calm attitude, and the ability to play conversational chess, thinking ahead a dozen moves or so. And if Ming had ordered the shooting? There was nothing I could do.

Vamps were policed by their up-line boss, which in Knoxville meant Ming of Glass. And Ming could be judged and punished only by the Master of the City of New Orleans, Leo Pellissier, her up-line master. Or any vampire who managed to challenge her to a blood duel. Or any non-law-enforcement human who got close enough to stake her and managed to survive. The position of vampires as regarded by law enforcement was hazy.

"Nell," Tandy said. "You'll be fine. Just remember: be polite, and never, ever meet her eyes."

"That's good advice," I whispered and cleared my throat when the words came out like busted gravel. We passed through the bedroom and into a sitting room, where Tandy opened the door on the far side. The small room beyond was set up as an office, decorated with heavy draperies, heavier rugs over wood floors, dark wood wainscoting, a leather sofa, two leather armchairs, and a desk the size of Minnesota. Well, not really, but it was huge, oversized for the small office.

Ming and Yummy were sitting in the armchairs, Ming upright as a board, Yummy stretched out, with a leg over the chair arm. The blond vampire looked relaxed, but her position shielded Ming from the doorway and allowed Yummy to roll down to the floor in the event of an attack. The position would fall below any gunshots and give her plenty of room to strike and take out an opponent. As a vampire, she had the speed to cross the distance and take out a human shooter in an eyeblink. And bullets wouldn't hurt her anyway unless they were silver. Ming was positioned to roll under the massive desk, into relative safety.

Tandy paused near the desk and the recording device

centered on it. I stopped to the side of Ming, carefully not between Yummy and her charge. Tandy said, "It's standard operating procedure for us to record this conversation. Do you have objections, Ming of Glass?"

Ming waved a hand, the motion languid. "I have no objection."

Tandy pushed a button and stated the day and time, the address, and the location in the house. He said, "Special Agents Thom Andrew Dyson and Nell Nicholson Ingram, with Ming of Glass and one member of her security. Would you state your name, miss?" he asked.

"No," Yummy said.

Tandy went red. I wanted to giggle, and all the fear drained out of me. The vamps were playing games with PsyLED. I decided it was not the right time to engage or I'd be playing the game they wanted to play, not one of my own. There are things a girl learns listening to the squabbles of an extended family. Timing is one of them. "Ming of Glass," I said. "I'm honored to speak with you. I'm Special Agent Nell Ingram of PsyLED."

As if to remind her, Yummy said, "Maggots, my master."

"This is the one, then?" She turned black eyes on me and it was like being hit with a paralysis spell. I froze. Like a rabbit in the gaze of a hawk, I didn't want to move. At all. Ming was Asian and old, even as vampires go. Vampires tended to show less expression as they aged, and the term *inscrutable* fit them all. With Ming it was inscrutable, unfathomable, and indecipherable times three. Usually. Right now, her tone held a warning of some kind, and I broke into a sweat. Which I knew she could smell. Nervous sweat, even the giggly kind, was a foolish thing in the presence of an apex predator. It spoke of prey, and I knew I had lost face already.

I stepped behind the desk. Sat. Sighed. "I ask forgiveness for all insult, Ming of Glass. None was intended." I opened the folder. It was supposed to be a sign that the topic of maggots was ended. "I'd like to ask—"

"Do you feel maggots in our presence at this time?" Ming interrupted.

I thought about timing and vampire games. I'd studied some in Spook School. Sometimes letting them swim on the line worked. Or truth. I was better with truth. And wood. I gripped the wood desktop and sank my fingernails into it, shoving past the finished surface into the grain, damaging the fine furniture, but touching bare wood. It was soothing. The tree had been large, old, and beautiful. Teak. Even dead, it was full of power I could use. I drew on the remembered life in the dead tree and I stared her straight in the eyes. Mithrans aren't used to humans doing that, especially humans who had dealt with them before. Like law enforcement. Vamps mesmerize with their eyes. Instead, Ming blinked. "Not exactly, ma'am," I said. "Only when I walk where Mithrans have walked for a long time, on wood or on the earth, and with my bare feet, do I feel the presence of their undeath."

Ming stared back at me. Hard. Nothing happened. "And are your feet bare now?" she asked.

"They are not," I said, knowing that when this line of questioning was turned from speech to text and entered into the official record, I'd be teased about it. Which Ming surely knew.

"And the maggots?" she pressed, her tone arch.

Ming of Glass was pushing me, testing me the way a cat did a mouse she might eat, except she was bored and the mouse was a game. My voice hardened and I let a little church into my words. "I stepped in a dead possum when I was a child, barefooted, in the woods. It was cold and slick and crawling with maggots. That sensation stayed with me. I insulted Mithrans when I mentioned that at a time when I was rattled, insecure, and unwise. Again, I offer apologies."

"Accepted. But before we continue, did you feel maggots in the yard where the shooter stood?"

She was asking if the shooter was a blood-sucker. I took in a breath, putting the questions together with the events of tonight. She was asking if there might be a strange vampire in town gunning for her. Or someone in her ranks trying to take her out, outside of vampire protocols. Or trying to stir up trouble for the head vampire in Knoxville. I had heard of

vampire wars. That would *not* be happening. PsyLED was
putting together a protocol for dealing with that sort of
situation—blood-suckers rampaging in the streets—and
rumor suggested that the protocol involved killing vamps on
sight. Which I was sure Ming did not know. "There were no
Mithrans in the yard. May we proceed?" I asked, keeping
my expression wooden and my scent pattern muted.

"Of course," Ming said, no hint of amusement in her tone
now, and her eyes hard as steel.

I released the wood of the desk and handed the paper that
was traced with the floor plan of the game room to Tandy
and indicated Ming. He carried it to her. I said, "Would you
both please show Special Agent Dyson where you were
standing at the time of the shooting?"

I set the other sketch, the one with the positions of the
people already in place, on the desktop and scanned the list
of questions. Tandy handed the sketch back to me, with two
fingers marking spots near where the first round had come
through. I compared them to the locations given by the other
guests. It matched the locations where someone else had
placed them both. It also suggested that the shooter had been
aiming at them and missed.

"Mithrans have much better eyesight than humans," I
said, "and a much better sense of smell and hearing. Did you
see, smell, or hear anyone outside the window prior to the
onset of shooting?"

"Nothing," Ming said. There was something pleased in
her tone, as if she liked either the question I asked or the
exchange we'd just had. Maybe she was less inscrutable than
I thought.

Yummy shook her head. "Me neither. I was watching the
people inside the room. We didn't bring outside security,
depending on the team hired by the Holloways. That won't
happen again."

Ming said, "We will not insult a host with such actions."

"With all due respect, my mistress, Cai has already said
otherwise. You and your primo will have this discussion, not
you and me."

"You are cheeky," Ming said, but she didn't sound upset about that. Maybe Ming liked cheeky. I filed that away for future reference.

I said, "And to whom were you speaking at the time of the first shots?"

"The party was a fund-raiser for Senator Abrams Tolliver and also an opportunity to make business deals. I was speaking to Senator Tolliver himself when the first shots were fired, though my body was between him and the window." Which again insinuated that she was a target.

"Would you walk me through the sequence of events from just before the first shot until the police came?" I asked.

"I was speaking to the senator. I heard a shot. I moved. My security did not deem me as moving fast enough nor far enough away from the violence. She lifted me and moved me faster." Again there was a wry tone in Ming's voice. In ordinary circumstances, ones without emotional components, Ming's voice gave away more than her expressions. "She deposited me in the butler's pantry. *On the floor.*" Ming turned her gaze to Yummy.

Yummy looked back at her and, without emotion, said, "You are welcome, my mistress."

This meant that Yummy could move faster than a master vampire. That was interesting. I wished I could remember Yummy's real name. Yummy was the nickname given to her by Jane Yellowrock, the vampire hunter who worked for the vampires in New Orleans. I couldn't remember anything else about Yummy, except that she had been part of Jane's team the night Jane raided the compound of God's Cloud of Glory Church to find and save a kidnapped vampire.

Yummy continued, almost as implacable as Ming herself, "There was a fire, my mistress. Mithrans are flammable."

I nearly choked on the "flammable" comment. Yummy went on.

"You were safe where I placed you. Cai is pleased." From Yummy's tone, that subject was now closed. Cai, Ming's primo blood-servant, was the ultimate authority and Yummy reported to Cai, not Ming. More interesting.

Ming met my eyes again and said, "I remained on the floor until I was helped to my feet by a properly deferential human. I do not know his name but he was wearing a black shirt with brown pants. A name tag hung from his shirt. He assisted me into the kitchen and inquired after my health. He informed me that my scion was injured and was in the dining room. I proceeded there, fed her, and healed her." She looked at Yummy again. "She is insufferable."

"I am," Yummy agreed. "I am also your hero tonight."

There were a lot of subtexts in this conversation. I pulled it back to the line of questioning and addressed my next question to Yummy. "Is that your blood in the entrance to the dining room?"

"It is," Yummy said, her eyes on her mistress. "The shots were still striking the house. I shielded two women with my body and got them to safety. I was injured during that time."

"You could have been killed," Ming said.

"There was no silver in the bullets. I am strong, healthy, and well fed by my generous and kind mistress," Yummy drawled, locking eyes with Ming. "I healed well enough to bring others into safety and have them call the cops."

"How many others?" I asked.

"Ming, the first two women, three men, and two more women. Then the shooting stopped."

"Did you, at any time, see anyone who might have assisted the shooter?" I asked.

"No," they both said, more or less in unison.

"Did you hear anything that might suggest that someone inside was part of the attack?"

"No," they said again.

"Did you smell anything non-human or peculiar before, during, or after the shooting?"

Both hesitated but didn't glance at each other. "Possibly peculiar," Ming said, after a moment that stretched too long. "But the river and cove are heavy with scent. Human party-goers wear a disgusting amount of perfume. The fire was odorous."

Yummy said, "Nothing out of the ordinary."

"Have there been any threats against you or the Mithrans of Knoxville?" I asked.

"Nothing out of the ordinary," Yummy repeated. Ming said nothing.

"Will you provide documentation about any of the *ordinary* threats to PsyLED?"

"Yes," Yummy said, turning away from her mistress' eyes.

I finished with my final question. "Ming of Glass. Are you aware that you were standing beside the senator and directly in front of the woman who died? That the first shot is believed to have missed everyone, deflected by the window glass? That you moved in the fraction of a second before the second shot? And that it struck the victim?"

Ming turned her gaze to me, pinning me to the chair. I felt like a bug on some collector's insect board. Holding this gaze was a lot harder than holding her ordinary gaze. This one made my skin want to crawl. "She died because of me?" Ming asked. "Because I moved? I was the target?"

"We haven't ruled that out." I scanned several pages and looked back up, having learned case details for the first time. "Her name was Margaret Clayton Simpson. Did you know her?"

"I knew her grandmother. My clan does business with her husband, with his son, and with a Clayton uncle. I have a scion by the name of Clayton, whom you have met. I did not know Margaret personally except by name and to shake her hand. She feared Mithrans. I do not force my presence on such humans."

Yummy said, "I knew her name. That's it. We're leaving. I have to get my mistress home before dawn, and we'll just make it." They both stood and I followed only a half beat behind them.

"Will you contact us if you think of anything more?" I pulled a card from my pocket and handed it to Yummy, who leaned in and accepted it. "Thank you for your time, Ming of Glass."

"You are welcome, Special Agent Ingram."

They turned to leave and Yummy said over her shoulder, "Later, Maggots."

Tandy smothered a laugh. I said, "Ditto, Yummy."

The blond woman flinched just the tiniest bit.

"Yummy?" Ming asked.

"I'll explain later, my mistress." Yummy tossed a glare my way and preceded her blood-sucker master out of the room and down the stairs.

Tandy turned off the recorder and fell into the chair vacated by Ming, laughing. I gave him the same glare Yummy had given me.

"Don't," he said, holding his hands in a gesture of surrender. I could hardly believe this was the same man I had first met, when he was fresh out of Spook School and fighting to stay sane in the presence of multiple people with conflicting emotions.

I huffed out a breath. "Okay. Were they telling the truth?"

"More or less. They have a very complicated relationship."

I gathered up the papers and stacked them neatly in the folder. "Tell me something I don't know."

"You're hungry and sleep deprived and grieving. People died here, but I don't think you knew them. Who are you grieving for, Nellie?"

Tears welled up in my eyes. I walked from behind the desk and toward the door, which Yummy had left open. "An oak sapling. Never mind. I'm making my report to Rick and going home." Which I did.

I walked into my cold, dark house just after dawn.

Moving on muscle memory alone, I put winter wood into the firebox of the wood-burning cookstove that also heated my house and my water, topped off the hot water heater mounted on the back, and turned the mousers out into the cold with orders to catch mice and rats. They stalked off, ignoring me except to give me dirty looks. Clearly I was a bad mama. The water was tepid, but I showered off the long night, redressed in the flannel pajamas, wool socks, and slippers I had thrown off when the call came in about the shooting, and wrapped up in my faded pink blanket before joining the cats in the icy morning air outside.

I sat on the intertwined roots of the sycamore and the poplar, roots that looked as if the trees were holding hands, fingers interlocked. I called them the married trees and sitting here, upon their clasped hands, was the first place where I had communed with the land of Soulwood, my land, long before I knew what I was doing.

Eleven years ago, I had come to this farm, escaping the leader of God's Cloud, who wanted me as his junior wife or concubine. To get away from Colonel Ernest Jackson, a pedophile and sexual predator, I had accepted a marriage proposal as junior wife, from John Ingram and his only remaining wife, Leah, and moved away from the church compound, away from my family, away from all I knew, to nurse Leah as she died. It had been a good bargain. I was twelve years old. A few years later I legally married John. Our arrangement was completely without romance, a business proposition that had left me with the land after John sickened and passed away. Thought of in such bald terms it was a horrible thing to have to do, but at the time, it had been like salvation shining down from heaven.

When I agreed to marry into the Ingram household, I hadn't known I would inherit anything, and this small patch of land and these two trees was all I felt I could claim. It was where I'd gone when nursing duties for Leah had gotten to be too much, where I came even now when I wanted solace. I tucked my blanket around me, placed my palms flat on the frozen ground, and breathed out, letting the tension flow away.

I could hear the faint click and hum of the windmill that powered my pump and sent water into the cistern. Could smell smoke from my fire. The faint and faraway stench of polecat or skunk. Both should be sleeping but perhaps a hungry hunting fox had risked the scent-weapons for a chance to eat.

I sank down, through the bare ground, into the roots of the trees. They were sleeping, the whole woods, all hundred fifty acres that bordered the flatland around the house, up the steep hill, and down into the gorge. All of it was in winter sleep, dormant. Perhaps dreaming, if the Earth and her plants dreamed. It was warm, deep in the darkness of the land. And the soul of the woods reached up to me, as if taking me by the hand. The woods embraced me. And I sighed out my misery, putting one hand to my belly to rub away the anxious feeling, the rooty scars deep inside, hard and unyielding. The woods didn't understand why I was sad, but they didn't care either. They wrapped me in their calm and peace and I let the long night go.

Much later, when the sky had grayed and whitened and blued, and the sun had risen over the hills, I pulled back from the sleeping land and turned my attention to Soulwood's problems. I nursed a failing patch of muscadine vine, and told the land it was a good thing to send water up to the spring above the house. I searched out and checked on the pregnant bear that was hibernating in a split in the rock not far from the spring. Bolstered the health of the asparagus I had planted above the windmill two years past. I had forgotten it, knowing that when it was ready to put forth enough shoots to eat, I'd remember. But now some kind of grubs had been chewing on its roots. I sent a pulse of energy to make them trundle away from the easy food source.

When I had done all I could to nourish the land, and I couldn't put it off any longer, I turned my attention to the boundary between Soulwood and the church compound, to the dark, hollow place where the foreign entity once known as Brother Ephraim had carved out a space for his soul. It was still there. A little larger. A little more vile. A little more entrenched than before. The place he had carved out beneath the ground of Soulwood was dark and virulent, like a pocket of pus growing beneath perfect flesh, preparing to attack the entire organism.

Brother Ephraim watched, silent. He had been my enemy and the enemy of my family for years. He had been an evil, cruel, horrible man who used religion as an excuse to hurt women. When he came on my land to hurt me, and had bled on Soulwood, I had fed him to the earth. That was my own special gift, to take the body and soul of humans and feed them to the land, to nourish it, to support it.

I had fed Soulwood twice, the first time when a man had tackled me in the woods and tried to have his way with me, to get both my body and the land that came with it. I hadn't known the first man's name, had never even seen his face. But he had died fast and his essence had fed my land, making my trees grow strong and swiftly, so much that the forest now looked like old-growth trees.

I had thought taking Ephraim would be the same. But either my land had rejected him or Brother Ephraim had found a way to keep his consciousness intact, because the old pedophile and sexual predator was still here, an infection that I hadn't yet figured out how to kill.

The last time I had studied him this intently, he had attacked me, a psychic attack that had been enough to kill me, had my land not deflected the hit. Soulwood had fought back, had protected me. This time, as I watched him, Ephraim did nothing, though I knew he was aware of me, aware and watching me back, planning something horrible and violent, some way to kill me or, worse, some way to trap me with him in his tiny cell.

More thoroughly, more minutely, I examined the cave-like place he had carved out of my land. It was separated from Soulwood by a membrane that was much thicker than before, soil that he had compacted, soil that he had sterilized. I feared that he'd learned how to do that from me. His one physical assault against my land, I had sealed off by salting the earth at the point of entry. The land there looked a lot like the land now around his hidey-hole. It made it hard to see what was happening on the far boundary, shoved up against the church lands. But I slid my consciousness around to the side and pressed to the very edge of Soulwood.

The membrane on the far side was thinner, less structured than the membrane on my side. The membrane near the church was stretched out, sending long tendrils through the land, deep, and down the cliff face onto the church grounds.

Well, well, well, I thought. *You'uns is trying again, ain'tcha. Trying to reach that vampire tree. Trying to do something evil. I know it. I just don't know what you're planning yet.* I reinforced the cell walls that encapsulated Brother Ephraim on that side, thickening them, hardening them, making them as impervious as I could. Studying their construction.

Because I was lying to myself. I knew what Ephraim wanted. He wanted to contact the tree in the middle of the church grounds. The tree was part of his plan to bring harm to me. And the tree might actually have the ability to hurt me and to help Brother Ephraim.

The tree had once been an oak, but thanks to contact with my blood, it was now a devil tree, a vampire tree, growing vines and thorns and erupting rootlets from the ground, roots that tried to grab little girls' and boys' feet and pull them in. Tried to stab any adult who intervened. It killed pets—puppies and kittens. It wanted blood, had, ever since it tasted mine. It acted like a depraved and evil tree, but I had the feeling that the vampire tree had a purpose, needs, and desires. I had tried to give the tree a job, thinking that was all it wanted, but instead of doing what I encouraged it to do, the tree was still growing wild and acting out, killing or trying to.

The last time I'd been on church grounds, the tree was nearly twenty feet around, with serpentine roots like bark-covered boa constrictors petrified in place, leaves like some prehistoric succulent, and four-inch thorns. It had eaten a bulldozer. Had destroyed a concrete block fence. Had resisted burning, chain saws, explosives, and herbicides. I needed to figure out what it wanted and how to contain it. It and Brother Ephraim. Until I figured all that out, I once again choked off Ephraim's little tendrils with my reinforced wall. No way was I letting the tree that had once had access to my blood merge with my enemy.

Satisfied that I had done all I could to contain Brother

Ephraim, I pulled away from the boundaries of Soulwood and back into myself to discover that I had become a daybed for the cats. Torquil was in my lap, curled between the blanket and me in a warm nest. Jezzie was stretched across my shoulders. Cello had made a hammock of the blanket at my elbow and stretched out and twisted like melted taffy in what looked like an anatomically impossible position.

I shooed them away, gathered up my blanket, and went inside. The house had warmed and I turned on the slow-moving overhead fans to move the air around. The cats streaked ahead of me and ignored me when I told them they had a job to do outside. They leaped onto the bed and burrowed under the covers. I did not want to sleep with cats, but I was too tired to make them obey me and put them back outside. I turned on my brand-new electric blanket and crawled in.

And really, with three cats warm and purring, my new bed had never felt so good.

THREE

I was up at noon to let the cats out, add wood to the stove, and tumble back into bed. And I was up again at three, the sunlight peeking through the blinds. I wasn't sure what species I was, but my kind didn't do well with lack of sleep, unless that lack of sleep was spent in the woods communing with the trees—and even that had its own consequences. I started coffee in the new Bunn coffeemaker, brushed my teeth, washed my face, and checked my . . . well, they weren't fingernails. Not anymore. My nails were slightly green, thicker at the nail beds than they had been, thinner at the tips, where they flattened out and spread into leaves—green leaves with distinct veins and curling tips. As part of my morning—afternoon?—ritual, I clipped my leaves. It had become part of my daily grooming habits, one that was even more necessary after time spent communing with the woods. I also clipped the leaves that tended to appear at my hairline at the nape of my neck. I liked the way they felt against my skin, but they tended to creep people out—a new phrase for me. Had I left my hair long, they wouldn't show, teaching me that some seemingly simple decisions often had long-term consequences.

While gooping up my hair I caught a glimpse of my eyes in the mirror. They were greener. I had noticed a color change a few weeks past and it seemed to be accelerating. I wasn't sure I liked the color, and it too creeped out some people, but there wasn't anything I could do about it.

I dressed in one of five mix-and-match outfits that worked for the office and the field, refilled my one-day gobag, and checked my messages, an act that had become SOP—

standard operating procedure—since Unit Eighteen became part of my life and the cell tower went up at the highest point of my land. There were six e-mails and double that many texts, one that had come while I was sleeping and informed me of a meeting at headquarters. I was likely to be late for that unit briefing. I had somehow slept through the group text, slumber claiming my brain and not letting go.

As a probationary agent, I wasn't supposed to miss meetings, so I tossed some of my homemade granola into a plastic sealable bag and grabbed a carton of milk—which had horrified my mama the last time she was here. Good churchgoers drank only milk they took fresh out of the cow or goat, but I didn't have time to care for animals or barter for essentials, so packaged and processed foods had entered my diet.

I was out the door roaring down the mountain in my Chevy pickup in minutes and was only a bit late to the meeting, even without turning on the new lights and siren mounted inside the cab and up on the roof. Rick had barely introduced the case, and was giving a summary of the particulars, when I thrust myself into my chair.

"Thank you for joining us, probie," Rick said.

I didn't much like apologizing for things I didn't do on purpose. Traffic and sleeping and horrible work hours seemed good reasons to be late, but I wouldn't say that unless pushed. And telling him I was late because I had to clip my leaves seemed . . . unnecessarily comedic. I held in a grin and nodded.

"Something amusing to you, probie?" he asked.

"Not a thing. You'uns was sayin'? 'Acause I'm alistenin' with all my ears," I said in church-speak.

T. Laine coughed into her hand, covering an aggressive jaw, as if trying to hide a laugh. She said, "Our Nell's learned snark." Her dark eyes sparkled, a sure sign I was going to bear the brunt of her wicked sense of humor.

"Nothing to learn, Tammie Laine," I said, knowing she hated her first name. "All churchwomen learn how to speak the truth in ways that keeps them from getting the back of some man's hand."

"Ouch," she said.

"Mmm," I said back.

"To continue," Rick said, "we have three dead and three injured from a shooting at the home of Conrath and Carolyn Holloway. The party was a fund-raiser for the political VIPs of East Tennessee . . ."

I tuned him out except to listen for anything I didn't already know. I'd learned early on that repetition and more repetition was a big part of any investigation. There were good reasons for that, but it was still boring.

Occam's head dipped; his hair swung forward. He was watching me with hooded eyes, unblinking, concentrated. He didn't have to say a word for me to know what he was thinking. He'd sink his claws into any man who gave me the back of his hand. It warmed me all over, but it was a bit intense and I dropped my gaze. It settled on the coffee urn on the table and the metal travel mug in front of me. Someone had painted green leaves all over it. T. Laine? Tandy? Somehow it felt like Tandy's work. That warmth inside me spiked. I knew a gift when I saw it. And then I realized that all our mugs had been artistically enhanced. Occam's had a stylized spotted leopard on it. Rick's, a black leopard and the letters *SAC*. JoJo's showed a caricature of her, wearing a red turban and dozens of earrings of every sort. T. Laine's showed a hand holding a gray stone with a full moon behind it, for her moon gift magics. Tandy's showed clouds and huge lightning bursts, which was kinda mean, as being struck by lightning had given his skin the red tracery and his gift of empathy. Soul's mug was undecorated except for the letters *AD* for assistant director of PsyLED. But then, not everyone knew that Soul was an *arcenciel*, a rainbow dragon shape-shifter. That intel was need-to-know.

"Nell?" Rick asked. "Woolgathering?"

I thought back to what he had been saying.

I said, "There was nothing in the land that I recognized. I included in my report about the dead plants and the sapling. Ming of Glass and Yum—her assistant—asked if the shooter was a vampire. It wasn't. I have no idea what species it was except that it—he—I'm going with he—wasn't human."

"So you were listening," he said.

"Not actively. I was hearing but not listening. There's a difference."

Rick shook his head. He looked tired, like he needed protein. Or like I made him tired. That was actually a possibility, since I had claimed him for Soulwood as part of healing the curse on his soul and body. His olive skin was paler than usual and his black hair seemed streaked with more silver each time I saw him. Oddly, his white shirt needed ironing and his pants looked like the same pair he had worn at the Holloways' the night before, which meant he hadn't been home to sleep or shower or anything. I got up and found a protein bar in the drawer by the sink. Tossed it to him. He caught it, looking from me to the bar, and dropped into his chair with a soft, drawn-out sigh. "T. Laine?" he asked, opening the package, taking a bite.

T. Laine said, "I hung around the feds as much as I could. There was no sign of magical use in the house or on the investigators. All human, all the way. The feds didn't want to talk around me, so I put in earbuds and pretended to play with my phone. But in reality I was wearing the new MMs."

Rick looked interested. MMs were micro mics, a device dreamed up by JoJo. They looked just like earbuds but amplified noise like mega hearing aids. When hooked to a cell with the proper app, the ambient noise could be filtered out, so that the wearer could hear and record any conversation the wearer wanted. Sometimes. Sometimes not. JoJo was still working out technical problems. MMs were likely illegal. They were certainly not something that could be used for evidence gathering, but they were handy when you wanted to be sneaky. JoJo had made two sets of the MMs, and T. Laine had one, Rick had the other, though he probably already had better than human hearing, being werecat. "And?" he asked.

"Nothing from the feds. There's some kind of ambient hum at the Holloways'. Maybe part of the security system. But I did get something from the security team when I went by the master suite. The hum disappeared there, and the guy in charge of the team? He has a drug problem, a gambling problem, and two girlfriends. And a wife. I gave the info to JoJo."

We all turned to Jo, who said, "Deep background in process. Peter Simon is a former Green Beret, injured in a nonmilitary exercise, I guess you'd call it, while on leave. He was jumping out of a plane and his parachute didn't open correctly. He survived the landing and made it through rehab, but he was on Oxy for about six months and it looks like he never kicked the habit. The addiction is what drove him out of the service, put his marriage into trouble, and gave him two ladies on the side. One may be his dealer. The other is pregnant with his baby."

"Making him a target for coercion or blackmail," Rick said. "What about the gambling problem?"

"Occam has that one," JoJo said.

"Tennessee's gambling laws are some of the toughest in the country, and so Simon has no legal way to indulge. We got a warrant for his electronic history and he has a bookie named T.J., just the initials, and nothing in the system on that name or any correlating name with those initials. It's gonna take time and more time to do an electronic probe and analysis on all the particulars. I'm willing, but the feds have the people and the system in place to do a full electronic forensics workup. And they don't know about this angle yet."

"He's human. Giving this to the right federal agent, in the right way, could give us some negotiation room if we need it later," Rick mused. "Clean up the file and send it to me. I'll make a call."

Occam nodded and started tapping on his tablet.

"Tandy?" Rick asked.

"Everyone has secrets," Tandy said slowly. "It's not hard to read past the natural protective emotional barriers of most humans and paranormals, but unless the interviewer asks the right questions"—he looked around the table—"the emotional reactions are not exactly easy to interpret. *Everyone* we interviewed at the party had secrets. That said, I didn't pick up on guilt that might be related to the shooting."

I had tuned in to Tandy's report as he spoke. Only weeks

past, the empath had been a bundle of nerves and emotional pain. The not-so-secret affair with JoJo was doing him a world of good.

"But you did pick up on other guilt?" Rick asked.

"Several who were currently having affairs, one who was feeling guilty about something at his job, maybe embezzling. Several with substance abuse problems. Three with anger issues. One couple with domestic abuse issues. I amended the reports on each of them and Jo is checking them out."

"Jo, dig deeper into all the things Tandy picked up. If you can substantiate it, then make sure the domestic abuse is turned over to whatever agency can best address it," Rick said. "If the embezzlement is likely, see it goes to the DA for consideration of further investigation. The affairs, substance abuse, and anger issues are out of our bailiwick unless they indicate a tie to the shooting. That all, people?" When no one spoke up Rick said, "You all know your assignments. Go. Stir the nests. Keep your eyes open."

Once the meeting was over, the others took off into the field to continue follow-up interviews, visits to the city morgue, and higher-level meetings with the FBI and ATF and assorted law enforcement organizations. The probie had no such fun assignments, and JoJo was too important at IT operations to be wasted on basic field drudgery, so the two of us were relegated to the office.

I spent the late afternoon in my little cubicle reading over the speech-to-text interviews and correcting mistakes. JoJo continued digging through a surface background check of all the partygoers tapped by Tandy, to see if anything pointed to problems that might have resulted in a crime of passion or crime of profit. And once those exciting and dangerous (not at all) assignments were done, JoJo and I began to create a working, searchable bible of the crime, the people who had been injured, the party guests, the caterers, and the security personnel, with strong concentration on Peter Simon, the head security guy, the one with the substance abuse problems, woman problems, baby problems, and problem problems.

It was boring and tiresome, but listening on earbuds while reading the transcripts on an electronic reader did give me time to water all the plants I had started in the office and stick my fingers into their soil, giving them a little boost to make them thrive. In front of each window I had planted a mixed assortment of plants, and we now had access to spinach and three varieties of lettuce, a dozen varieties of basils, mints, chives, thymes, and other edible herbs. Rick had grumbled that I was using the office as a greenhouse, and since he was right, I hadn't argued. But I needed the fresh greens to offset the impact of fast foods on my system, and the others had quickly learned how to augment their own meals with the fresh stuff, and asked for tomatoes, cukes, and squash. I wasn't sure how I'd grow all that with the limited light in HQ, but the fresh food sounded wonderful.

An hour after sundown, I made black China tea with lemon mint and brought mugs and the carafe to JoJo with my notes. She didn't look up but sipped her tea, which was made to her specifications with lots of sugar and no cream. "Mmmm," she said on an exhale. "I wondered if you were going to stop farming and start working today, you lazy girl."

She was teasing me. It had taken a bit of time to learn that insults and what the team called snark were actually bonding friendship rituals. I still wasn't good at responding to it, but now I knew what it was and my feelings didn't get tangled up in the repartee. "I was checking the reports. I found only a few errors so far and most of them are mine. Clementine doesn't like my accent." Clementine was the name given to the new voice-to-text software, which was much easier to say than CLMT2207.

JoJo blew a laugh through her nose. "Yours and mine both, chicky. I think the designer was British and male. Black and female weren't on his radar when he input his 'regional pronunciation, intonation, and enunciation modulations.'"

I held in a grin at the quote. "Hillbilly was even less on his radar. Still, I think the new software is pretty good."

"Anything that keeps me from being the unit's transcriptionist is good by me." JoJo—who was really Special Agent Josephine Anna Jones—stretched in her chair, throwing her arms up and arching her spine. PsyLED agents didn't tend to follow regulations in dress or hairstyle, and JoJo was less amenable to rules than most. Today she was wearing red and pink—red beads in her wrapped braids; red leggings under a flowing pink skirt; layered dark pink, skintight, tank-style tunics that flared below her waist; and a short, dark red jacket. Her shoes were black. If for some reason JoJo had to go into the field, the skirt would come off, field boots would replace the shoes, and she would be ready to go. "What else did you find?" she asked.

I almost told her that the mints were happy today, but JoJo would just roll her eyes. "Everyone at the party has interlocking business and personal relationships that sometimes go back generations. They attend the same churches, are either right wing or left in their politics and theology, vacation at the same places, and bank at the same institutions. Their vacations are lavish. They routinely cheat on their spouses. They divorce often, and those divorces are spectacular and vicious, the custody battles brutal. They make money together, they politic together, and they marry into each other's families. It's almost incestuous." And I would know, coming from a church where the bloodlines were mapped out for generations to keep us from marrying our own cousins. "You?"

"More of the same. Nothing that points to a specific reason for murder, terrorism, or even political assassination. There's been no recent chatter about anyone looking for a hired gun, and nothing on the terrorism boards, international or homegrown. So we still don't know who the real target was."

"The Holloways' blinds and draperies were open, so if there was a specific target, all the shooter had to do was take a hunting rifle and a deer stand, ratchet it up into a tree, and take a single shot," I said, "or several if he wanted to confuse the objective. This was messy. It feels like terrorism."

"Look at probie drawing conclusions." She pointed at me as if showing me off to a crowd. We were alone. I wasn't sure I understood, but she added, "Not bad, girl. I'm leaning that way too. Evidence that obviates that conclusion?"

"The eight seconds we noticed on the video before he started firing," I said. "He took time to study the scene, choose his target, raise his weapon, aim, and make a limited fire to take out people with the first rounds. And he had a rate of fire upwards of seven hundred rounds per minute and a caliber of ammo that would punch through brick walls, enough to take out everyone at the party if he'd wanted to. It's been suggested that he—we're guessing male—wasn't used to the weapon or wasn't a good shot. Or had another agenda."

"Yeah. Not bad at all, Maggoty. Get back to work."

I shook my head. The nickname Maggoty had made its way into the official reports. It was embarrassing, though there was nothing I could do about it.

A piercing wail came over JoJo's computer and her attention snapped back to the multiple screens. "Get your gear," she said. "We got another one. Knoxville PD just got a ten-eighty-one code. Multiple shots fired into a restaurant. Secret Service is on-site, which means the senator was there. Sending the address to your tablet and your cell." Her voice rose to follow me down the hallway. "Abrams Tolliver's family is inside. His security team is pinned down. Wear your vest! Take an AR-15 and a comms unit. More info as I have it."

"I'm not certified yet on automatic rifles," I yelled back as I grabbed gear.

JoJo cursed and said, "Take one anyway. Give it to one of the team when you get there!"

"Got it!" I shouted and checked out an AR-15 from the weapons room and added it to my gear.

"Be safe!" JoJo shouted.

I grabbed my gobag and was out the door into the dying light of day while the last words were still dying on the air.

I had requested use of an official vehicle, but the request was taking forever making its way up the chain of command, and so I was still using my old truck for official business.

The C10 didn't have speed, it didn't corner well, and it drank gasoline like a Saturday night drunk did liquor, but it did have three things going for it. It wasn't a vehicle that people saw and thought, *Cop*, it was reliable, and the heater put out hot air like an industrial furnace. It was already warm inside by the time I reached the end of the street and turned on my jerry-rigged blue lights. My new PsyLED car would be here in a day or a week or maybe a month. With official vehicles it was hard to tell. But when it came, I'd have an ugly but city-smart vehicle to drive while on business, and the truck could be for farm activities, as it should be.

Pierced Dreams was the only four-star restaurant in Old City Knoxville, and the location was not good for armed response. East Jackson Avenue completed its evolution into West Jackson Avenue at the intersection with South Central, which was a hub of the Old City revitalization. The intersection was not a perfect ninety degrees, but a skewed crossing of angles, with nearby access to I-40, Highway 158, and Hall of Fame Avenue, as well as industrial sites and multiple railroad tracks. The Tennessee River cut the city in half and it was always close to anything in Old City, not that the river was any sort of getaway route, not with RVACs and drones and such. But the shooter could get away easily by car, motorbike, or bicycle or on foot. Or take hostages. Or hold law enforcement or the populace in place, pinned down, and take them out at his leisure.

Into my comms unit, JoJo said, "More shots fired. And a fire alarm is going off. One report says flames are visible inside Pierced Dreams. Another says flames are shooting up from a nearby building. Rural/Metro Fire and KFD are all en route. This is an active shooter scene. Repeat. This is an active shooter scene."

"Copy," I said. I took corners too fast, hearing sirens converging on Old City, seeing the city's blue law-enforcement lights interspersed with the red flashing of other emergency units and the Christmas decorations on buildings and streetlights. Leaving the rest of the city with a decreased policed presence. If there was a second incident, things could get difficult. Law enforcement concentrated in one area was a major concern. A few well-placed bombs and the city could lose a large percentage of its officers. It also gave criminals the opportunity to commit crimes in other parts of the city, places with less coverage.

My headlights bounced across the greenery as I took a turn too fast. My heart was speeding up, my breath growing fast and shallow. I forced my breathing to slow down and tried to relax my shoulders.

"Info coming in," JoJo said into my earbud. "Feds are on-site. Uniforms are on-site. We have two civilians down and two security personnel stationed outside not answering comms. According to Secret Service, Abrams Tolliver is among those inside, uninjured. I do not have a name for the SAC. Repeat, do not have the SAC."

The SAC was the special agent in charge, the person coordinating law enforcement and making demands. Secret Service superseded the FBI, the state police, and the city police. And PsyLED unless we proved that the suspect was a paranormal, and that hadn't happened. Since it hadn't been backed up by a reading of a known paranormal creature on the psy-meter 2.0, and all I had was a possibly anomalous spike, my reading about the shooter from the Holloway party was *opinion*. If Ming of Glass hadn't been involved in the first shooting at the Holloways', I doubt we'd have been part of it at all, but mundane human LEOs hated to deal with the blood-suckers. That I could deal with. Not knowing who the SAC was complicated matters because it said that the chain of command had not been established.

"More info," JoJo said. "Tonight was also a fund-raiser event, and I have the guest list. Scanning and comparing to last night's event."

"Copy," I said, taking another corner too fast.

JoJo said, "Meanwhile, we have Occam heading that way as part of the fed contingent, ETA one minute, and T. Laine and Tandy coming in from the medical examiner's office, ETA seven.

"Occam, you copy?"

"Copy. Arriving on-scene now with feds. I was liaising with them when the call came in." The sounds of shouting and sirens came through Occam's comms system. "Don't know which way our people are coming from, but enter from the west. City streets are being blocked off by uniforms. Staging area is on West Jackson, half a block from Central. According to on-site security, there were multiple shots fired. No shots for the last two and a half minutes. No sign of the shooter or shooters, but it's getting dark, so we may have missed something. Activating vest cam. JoJo, you getting this?"

"Acquiring direct video upload now. Feds are sending up an RVAC, people. Tandy and T. Laine, you copy?" JoJo asked.

"Copy on active shooters, staging area, and RVAC. ETA four if traffic holds," Tandy said, his voice tense. I hoped T. Laine was sending out soothing vibes. The empath on a meltdown at an active shooting scene would be a problem.

"My ETA is thirty seconds," I said. I took yet another corner too fast, seeing blue and red lights just ahead, grateful for the RVAC. Remote-viewing aircraft were small, quiet, and easier to control than drones. The lack of wind, the presence of city lights, and the location made them useful tonight. They could buzz rooftops, clearing them for shooters, drop into alleys and take a look with infrared and low-light cameras, and follow unknown subjects from above. They were freakishly expensive and if the shooter spotted one and shot it down, there would be no replacement until next year's budget. But better a dead plastic toy than a dead human; I didn't care how many got trashed.

My talents were pretty useless in the inner city. If I recalled, there was nothing green within blocks. The closest green would be the artificial berms near the loops of major roads.

"People," JoJo said. "We got some major players at both events—the party last night and the dinner venue tonight. Abrams Tolliver and his brother Justin Tolliver and their wives. Justin is one of the überwealthy. He is heavily involved in, and financially supports, the state's political scene. He also runs the family finances, a wheeler-dealer in real estate development and hedge funds. He's got so many enemies it's easier to figure out who doesn't hate him. Mayor Morning was present both nights. Ming of Glass, the vampire VIP, is on both guest lists. Ming justifies our presence. I see Matilda Johnson, Irena Hastings, and Samuel L. Clayton. Johnson and Hastings are big in the arts scene and Clayton is a local preacher and political up-and-comer. All three are on to-night's guest list but were not on last night's." She paused and added, "I see here that Clayton is not attending because of his sister's death at the Holloways' party. That would be Mar-garet Clayton, deceased. There may be more last-minute inclusions or cancellations, names that didn't make it onto tonight's guest list as compiled by the Secret Service and just sent to us."

I pulled onto West Jackson, wondering if the original tar-get was Abrams Tolliver or one of the others or more than one of the others. This was getting sticky. I rolled down the truck window and held out ID to the uniformed officer at the bar-ricade. I followed his pointing finger to parking in the staging area. "I'm on-site in official parking," I said. "Occam? What's your twenty?" His "twenty" was his location.

Occam said, "I see your POC POV. Park at the back of the lot where it adjoins the train tracks. Approaching you now."

"POC POV" was "piece-of-crap personally owned ve-hicle." Occam was making fun of my truck. I pulled into a parking spot between a van for EMTs and the special op-erations team—SWAT—patted the dash, and cut off the engine. Occam tapped on the window. I opened the door and slid to the ground.

Shots sounded. Two, close together, followed by a third. Before the first two echoed, I was on the pavement under-neath Occam. Fear blasted through me. Fear of being held down. Fear of being *controlled*. Memories of fighting for my life. *I could take his life* . . . Bloodlust slammed through me. On instinct, I elbowed him in the gut, rolled, and hit his jaw with the heel of my other hand. A fast two-strike reaction. Spook School training. Fighting my need. "Get off me!" I yelled, kneeing him hard.

Occam *oofed*, breath leaving his body fast.

I could have his life for the land . . . I hit him again.

He rolled over. Out of my reach. "Do not . . ." I caught a breath. Forced down the craving, the want, the blazing desire to kill, to take his blood and his life and his soul for the earth. To save myself. I found my feet and backed away, moving in a crouch, into the shadows of early evening, hiding. Heard sirens taking off and tires squealing as if chasing a car. I shivered hard and took another breath. "Do not ever . . . *ever* . . . attack me. Again."

"Holy shit." He groaned, still on the ground half under my truck. Curled in a fetal position. "Ohhh. Why'd you do that?"

I ignored him and tried to replay the shots and the echoes. I estimated them coming from a distance. More cop cars chased away. No more shots were fired. "The unit's AR is behind the seat," I said, "if you want it."

Occam shook his head no and made a little gagging sound. I locked the truck cab.

"Are you Special Agent Ingram?"

I flinched. Whirled. Pulled my service weapon. All at once. A female uniformed cop stood near me, crouched low between vehicles, as if to avoid shots fired. I swallowed a pillow-sized fear clogging my throat. I was breathing fast, my pulse beating in my temples and the back of my neck. I pushed down the bloodlust and managed to speak almost normally. "I'm Ingram."

"Ming of Glass just drove up. She deman—*requests* that you speak with her."

If the vamps were here, it was now officially night. I bent and picked up my comms gear and my bullet-resistant vest and reseated my ten-millimeter. Occam was watching me as he rose from the ground, not quite all cat grace. His nose was bleeding where I'd hit him. The blood-need reared up in me, almost as if it was a separate consciousness, a demon of deadly desire. I squeezed it down, forced my shoulders to relax. Surprisingly, the lust inside me complied, if only enough not to kill.

Occam wiped his nose on his jacket sleeve. If he reported the blow I'd be in trouble. But he was grinning, a satisfied, intense smile that suggested something I couldn't interpret. His blond hair hung over his eyes and his jaw was fuzzy with a two-day beard he hadn't had last time I saw him only hours ago. The beard was a result of shifting to his cat and back to human. His cat was still close to the surface, but not so close that his eyes glowed. Yet.

A thought squirmed in the back of my mind like a worm on a hook, that female cats often fought a male as part of mating rituals. Which was not an idea I wanted to contemplate. I shoved it aside.

"Where did the last shots come from?" Occam asked the uniform as I geared up. Our eyes met and slid away. Met and slid away. Nervous, I reseated my Glock GDP-20 in the hard plastic holster with a faint click.

"Shooter in a car. Drive-by. Handgun. No casualties. They already got him." To me she said, "If you'll follow me. And keep your head down."

I was still fastening my vest as we wove through the lot, our feet silent on the pavement. I caught snatches of conversation between cops as we jogged:

"Twenty-five rounds located so far. Most in the restaurant's wall."

"Way more casings in the street than twenty-five."

"No shit?"

"Way more."

"Witnesses're in the empty building next door."

"Two bottles of perfectly good vodka hit and shattered."

"I hear the vodka set off a kitchen fire."

"Singed the hair off a cook but didn't touch her scalp."

"Ten-ninety-ones are to stay in place until CSI and the MEs are finished."

"Medical examiners are *here*?"

"I know, right? Weird."

Ten-ninety-ones were dead bodies, in Knoxville PD radio codes. The stink of gunfire and burned hair and scorched building fouled the air. I looked around for fire trucks and decided the trucks must have pulled up to the restaurant from the back, from the street on the other side. EMS units were lined up in the roadway, uniformed officers standing guard at the door to the restaurant, visible in the glaring headlights. Heavily armed SWAT officers were inside and out. Shadows flickered on the walls and the asphalt, oversized, bulked, armed.

"Over here." The uniformed cop jerked on my sleeve, pulling me against a marked vehicle. She pointed to a black limo across the street. "In that one." It wasn't a long limo, but a short one. The vehicle looked heavy, as if armored. "Don't expect me to get any closer to the fangheads," she said. "I like the blood in my veins where it belongs. Maintain cover position until we clear the street and the buildings."

"Thanks," I said, "and I feel the same way about vampires. But you don't say no to Ming of Glass." Crouching, I stepped off the curb into the street and raced over. The chauffeur got out, hunkered down like I was, and opened the back door. I did not want to get in that limo, sit on that leather, touch anything with bare skin. The thought of dead possum and maggots wiggling on my bare feet nearly made me gag as I ducked inside and sat, hands in my lap, my eyes adjusting as the door closed on me with a solid *thunk*.

"Special Agent Maggot," a familiar voice said.

"Fanghead Yummy," I said. Which was totally impolite, not that I cared as much as I might once have. Except that the inside light came on and Ming was sitting beside the blond vampire. "Ming of Glass," I said, not apologizing, though the words *I'm sorry* wriggled in the back of my throat like a squirrel in a trap, trying to get out. Mama might fear vampires, but she would be polite to Satan himself. I'd be polite, though I had a momentary vision of Mama meeting the devil in the middle of an ice storm, the Angel of the Morning hovering on bat wings at the end of Mama's shotgun.

"You find us amusing?" Ming asked.

I blurted a half-strangled laugh. "No, ma'am. I just imagined my mama meeting, *ummm*, you."

"Your mother fears Mithrans?"

My laughter died. "My mama survived her worst nightmare. Now she don't fear nothing. You called me over here?" It wasn't exactly true, but it sounded good.

"Do you feel maggots in my limousine?"

I thought about lying, since I'd already insulted the chief blood-sucker in Knoxville. "Not through my clothes. I thought you were inside Pierced Dreams when the shooting took place."

"I was just arriving. I was delayed. If one of my kind was behind this shooting, is there any way you or your fellow nonhuman police officers could tell?"

"The cats aren't trackers. They're sight hunters. We don't have our own K9 paranormal dog. We don't have a werewolf on the team, and that would be the best nose were-critter."

"If I flew a werewolf in, could it—could *he* track this shooter?"

"I doubt it. Too many scent patterns." I paused.

"You have thought of something," Ming said.

"Maybe." I frowned. It would be against regulations. But PsyLED didn't always go by regs. And Jane Yellowrock had a tame werewolf . . . "Hmmm."

"Tell me what you are thinking," Ming said, her voice full of velvet persuasion, a vampire mesmerism.

I looked her in the eye. "Really? You'un gonna try that on me? 'Cause it don't work."

"So I see." Ming sat back against the leather, making it sigh like flesh still alive. She motioned to Yummy. "Go with her. Provide assistance as needed. PsyLED will bring you back before dawn." Ming looked at me, her eyes intense, giving a final little push with her voice and her mind. "*You* will bring her back before dawn."

"I'll be glad to give Yummy a ride, but if traffic stalls us on the highway and she burns up, you'un're paying to have my truck fumigated. I hear it's mighty hard to get out the burned vamp stink."

Yummy made a strangled sound that might have been laughter.

Ming's eyes went wide and then she burst out laughing. She was still chuckling when Yummy followed me out of the limo into the exhaust-laden air and the too-bright lights. "Girl, you are either stupid or you got big brass ones," Yummy said.

I decided that no reply was the wisest reaction this time. Not that I'd been wise for the last few minutes. Occam appeared at my side, ushering us into the shadows cast by streetlights against the ornate brick wall of a building. He was walking fine now, as he took in Yummy as part of his constant scan of the street and buildings and law enforcement rushing around. Around us, Old City's Christmas decorations glowed, a festive red and white this year. To me he said, "Uniforms and feds found the greatest concentration of casings. They think the shooter stood in the greenspace there." He jerked his chin to a couple of winter-leafless dogwoods and evergreen plantings at the edge of a roofed overhang. "There's some land. Rick wants you to get a read."

The patch of earth was maybe ten feet by twenty. "That little bit of land? You'uns—you're kidding."

"Nope. I got your blanket outta your truck." He held out my faded pink blanket and I took it, uncertain for two reasons. I had locked my truck, and the blanket suggested that Occam either had a key or owned and knew how to use a slim-jim. And I didn't like reading city land. It was usually dead land.

Yummy leaned into Occam and breathed deeply. I realized she was taking his scent. "Wereleopard. I am still eager to taste you."

Occam turned his eyes from me to her and said, "No. Again. No."

Yummy laughed and her voice took on that persuasive tone, low and liquid. "You might change your mind. Such liaisons have always been things of pleasure and joy."

I wondered if that meant that Yummy and Occam had ever—

"Come on." Occam turned his back on her in a catty insult, speaking to me. "I got a camera for you to work with."

Yummy's eyes lit up in what must have been relish at the insult. As if she found Occam even more interesting and delightful prey now than before.

"Nell? *Camera*," Occam said.

The camera was a ruse to keep the humans among us from having a fear reaction at a paranormal person. I was listed in Unit Eighteen as an undifferentiated paranormal, meaning that I wasn't among the short list of paranormals with known powers, gifts, and disadvantages—like vampires catching fire in sunlight. Yummy knew I wasn't human because she had seen me communing with the land once. And because she knew Jane Yellowrock. Reading the land in such a public place might tell everyone everywhere that I wasn't human, and . . . well, I hadn't told my mama or daddy yet. So holding a camera was a ruse.

Keeping to the semiprotection of the brick wall, I followed Occam down the street to the winter-bare trees. And the ten-by-twenty plot of land was revealed to be the brick-paved outdoor eating area of a restaurant, one with cement planters for the trees and greenery. There were rounds everywhere, each marked with a numbered yellow evidence marker. Tables and chairs were overturned; drinks were pooled and reeking of alcohol. There had been people eating out here when the shooting started, outside in the cold, which was just stupid to my way of thinking. But there was nothing for me to read, no land in sight. I looked at Occam and crossed my arms over my chest. Yummy was watching the byplay with the same kind of amusement that a human might display when watching monkeys in a zoo.

Occam looked around. Sighed. "Right. Okay. I see." He handed me a camera. "Try anyway."

I threw the blanket back at him and sat on the cement edge of a planter. Placed the camera on the ground prominently in front of me as if it had a purpose. I dug my fingers through six inches of mulch and stuck them into the soil. It was good-quality potting soil mixed with topsoil. There was a nice concentration of nutrients. One spot where some stupid human had dumped in a cup of coffee. I boosted the tree, just in case the winter was long and cold, and withdrew my hand. "Nothing. But why do they think the shooter stood here? The rounds probably popped off the roof." I looked up. So did Occam and Yummy, who pursed her mouth.

She laced her fingers together, bent her knees, and said, "Come on, cat. I'll boost you up and you can pull me up. Maggot can wait down here."

I spotted Rick in a group of suited men and women, mostly Secret Service and feds. "I'll be eavesdropping over there." Occam didn't acknowledge my comment. Without looking, he took a running start and bounded into Yummy's hand. The vampire tossed him up and forward and he touched down on the roof with cat grace. In his cat form that leap would have been easy all on his own.

Yummy backed up and raced in, leaping onto the planter and pushing off with one foot. Occam reached out over the edge and grabbed her arm, pulling her up. They collided, fell out of sight, and hit the roof. There was little doubt they had landed flat, together. Yummy laughed, the sound delighted. Teasing. Sexual.

A strange feeling opened up in my middle at her laughter. I was pretty sure I had never heard laughter like that before, but I knew what it was and what it meant. The strange feeling in my rooty middle went wide and empty at the sound, sad and betrayed. Until Occam said, "*No*," his tone cold and full of threat. "Look away from me."

The vampire made a pouting sound. "You take all the fun out of the hunt. Now put away your toy before we have an incident."

"Put away your fangs first."

The frozen tone of his voice eased some of the odd emptiness inside me. If there had ever been something between them it was long gone. I heard nothing else until the sounds of them rising reached me, and they walked across the metal roof. Then I heard them repeating what sounded like the "hands and push"/"leap and catch" being replayed as they attained the roof of the two-story building next over, one that shared a wall with the restaurant with no land in front.

My attention returned to the shooting scene and when I breathed, the air was heavy with diesel exhaust. All the emergency medical vehicle engines were still running. I turned and moved toward Rick, through the law enforcement officers and crime scene techs, all milling around, all with jobs to do. I was almost to the street.

Shots rang out. I dove to the pavers behind the planter. I caught a blur of movement from the corner of my eye on a roof. Either there were two shooters or the shooter had repositioned catty-cornered across the street. He—or they—had us pinned down. But then the movement was gone. Had someone been targeted? Or was the shooter just creating confusion so he—it?—they?—could get away?

My heart was slamming in my chest. My breath was fast and shallow. I was terrified. Had I mistaken clouds in the sky for a shooter?

High up, I caught a distorted shape against the skyline, an amorphous form bending over a long rifle, aiming down. Three shots sounded. Three more. These three hitting emergency vehicles with the injured inside.

FOUR

Cops ran everywhere. Screams. Shouting.

"JoJo!" I shouted into my comms. "Active shooter on the roof of—I can't see the business name. Multistoried building on South Central. There's a white plaque in the brick, like an original name. It might start with a *C*, and the word *Building* after it?"

"Hang on. I got your position." I heard soft tapping. "You safe? You look like you're out in the open."

I realized JoJo was following us in real time on the interactive map. "I'm behind a planter," I said, lifting my head. "But there's a cop in the street. She's four feet from me. She's hit. Bleeding. I'm gonna—"

"Stay put," JoJo warned.

"But—"

"Stay put. That's an order."

On the other side of the street, two paramedics and a cop rushed into an emergency medical van, bodies low, crouched. Even over the sound of the EMS engines, which were still running, I could hear the girl in the street panting. Blood trickled between the tiny rocks in the pavement. I could feel it. Almost taste it. Bloodlust rose in me, hesitant, uncertain, but . . . interested. There was no land to feed here. Thank God, no land to feed. "Jo," I said, "she's—"

The ambient noise on the comms system altered. "Attention, all law enforcement personnel," JoJo said. "The shooter has been spotted on the top of the Carhart Building."

The EMS unit made a sharp turn at her words. More shots rang out, pinging into the vehicle. Ramming right through the body of the oversized van and burying themselves in the street. The engine gunned and the van rolled into the street, in front of the downed officer, the engine block between the wounded woman and the shooter's position. The three responders fell out the rear door to the asphalt, keeping low. They pulled emergency supplies from an oversized red kit. Went to work on her.

"Thanks, Jo," I said. I was panting hard.

"Not me. EMS did that all on their own. You got eyes on the shooter?"

Scraping along the brick pavers, I reversed my body position so I was facing the other way. The angle of the van's emergency lights now gave me more shadow protection, but if the shooter had low-light or infrared-vision goggles I was toast. I pulled myself along the bricks on my elbows, in between two other concrete planters, and angled myself so I could see the top of the Carhart Building clearly, as fully as I could at night. "Nothing," I said, "except SWAT is converging there. If the shooter is still inside he's caught.

"Is Occam okay?" I asked. "He's—"

"On the roof with a vampire," JoJo said. "I know. RVAC has eyes in the air."

"That was fast."

"City just had a multiunit emergency response exercise. They got this one nailed."

One of the paramedics in the street got back in the EMS unit and it moved again, this time turning at a sharper angle to the Carhart Building. Yummy landed on all fours beside me, like a praying mantis. I squelched a squeal and Yummy laughed. She was enjoying this.

Without even thinking, I reached out, grabbed her shirt, and yanked her to me. Her face was two inches from mine. All vamped out. Fangs down, eyes bloodred with huge black pupils. "That cop got injured," I said, "protecting this city and your'n boss. How 'bout you'un get in there and give her some blood instead of playing games?"

"Take your hand off me, little female."

"No."

Yummy's eyes went even wider. Surprised. She tilted her head in one of those creepy inhuman moves they do and looked at the EMS unit. The driver was scrunched down in his seat, making a small target; the other two responders were loading the wounded officer into the back of the glorified ambulance. "JoJo," I said, "tell EMS that a vampire is about to join"—I stretched my own head to see the number stenciled on the van—"Unit Two-Fourteen, to offer her services as blood donor."

"Copy that," JoJo said.

"I'll pick you up at UTMC," I said to the vampire.

"I'll be thirsty," Yummy snarled.

"I think the appropriate response is 'Cry me a river.'" I let go of Yummy's shirt. "Move."

The vampire shot away from me with a pop of sound and landed at the back door of the EMS unit. And then she was inside and the vehicle was backing down the street. I maybe shoulda felt bad about talking to Yummy that way, but short of staking a vamp, talking mean was about all that might get them to pay attention.

"You scare me sometimes," JoJo said.

"Oh? We saved a vamp's young'un not so long ago. Call the Clayton vampire and get some more blood-suckers to the hospital," I said. "Tell them they owe us."

Occam joined the conversation from somewhere, his voice calm and amused in my earbuds, and said, "Do it. But tell them they owe the *city*. Not us. Tell them it'll be good PR."

"Mmmm," JoJo said, her tone saying she didn't like calling the vamps for favors of any kind.

"Copy that," Rick said. "And ask nice."

I jumped. I'd forgotten he was around tonight.

"Yes, sir," JoJo said smartly, indicating she still didn't agree but she could blame her supervisor if problems resulted from vampires feeding cops. Rick chuckled, the sound like dry leaves scattering before a slow wind.

Occam appeared between the planters, near my feet. He

hadn't jumped from above, so he must have come down from
the roof elsewhere and cat-crawled to me. "Did I hear you
just threaten a blood-sucker, Nell, sugar?"

"Special Agent Ingram," I said, tapping my earpiece with
a fingernail, reminding him we were being recorded and
every word would be transcribed.

"Right." Occam gave me a cat grin, all self-satisfaction.
"Wish I'd seen that, Nell, sugar."

"We got two RVACs in the air now," JoJo said. "And local LEOs just obtained footage from traffic cams showing
an armed figure fleeing the scene, heading south on South
Gay Street. Obtaining the images now. Stay in position.
SWAT is clearing the Carhart Building."

Occam said, "The Mithran and I cleared the roof and
building at our nine."

"I'll let the local LEOs know."

In the wake of the EMS unit pulling away, two others
backed out, each carrying injured. Occam cat-crawled higher
into the tight space, close enough for me to feel his were-
warmth as he lay on the pavers beside me. Close enough for
me to be uncomfortable, though he never indicated he was
aware of anything untoward in lying on the ground so close
to me. It was odd. And oddly comforting, to have a fellow
agent in the cramped space with me.

Fellow agent. That was what I thought of him? A small
part of me questioned whether it was just any agent or Occam
himself that created the comfort. Occam and I had unfinished business between us. Or I thought we did. He had asked
me out for a date, nearly a month ago, for a dinner that had
never happened. The memory of that invitation surfaced and
I blushed for no reason I could fathom. I had thought about
that invitation off and on and figured he had changed his
mind since he never mentioned it again. I couldn't decide if
I was relieved or insulted or disappointed, but since I didn't
date, not ever, I had settled on relieved. But I still thought
about it, mostly at night before I fell asleep. Thinking about
it now made me break out in a hot sweat and made me sud-

denly cranky. I wondered if the werecat could smell my change in physical state. And that made me *more* cranky.

However, I didn't want to look at those questions, not in the middle of a shootout, and so I shoved my feelings away and turned my attention back to the actions along the street. We waited, not sure if it was safe to move yet. Not talking, just sharing the narrow gap, holding position.

"Okay. Got the images from the traffic cams," JoJo said. "Looks like either the same shooter from last night or a similar creature. Fuzzed features. Male gait. Seems to be carrying an M4 carbine, just like last night. Looks like we have a single shooter, at events where the senator, his rich brother, and their wives are."

"Where's the shooter now?" Rick asked.

"They don't know. He took a turn through an alley and vanished. The alley has access to buildings on either side, to their roofs, to a parking lot, and to three streets front and back. Two minutes after he vanished, a black SUV pulled into traffic. Then a Mercedes and a beat-up truck like Nell's. Two motorcycles, probably Yamahas, sped past traffic cams. And a bicycle. They're clearing the buildings and the parking lot, but my personal opinion is, they lost him."

The next hour ticked by slowly, sharing the space behind the planter with Occam while the SWAT officers in tactical gear and the uniformed officers cleared every single building up and down the street. It was almost pleasant, even though the brick was cold and I was freezing. And I was thirsty. And I had to go to the bathroom. And Occam was lying so close. Not that he did anything untoward or unpleasant, but . . . I had never been so close to a man for so long. Not even when I was married. Marital relations between John and me had been fast and mostly unpleasant and most nights I had then slept elsewhere.

"I wish we had coffee," he muttered after an unconscionable amount of time.

"And some of that cold pizza on the 'All' shelf of the refrigerator in the break room," I fantasized.

"Who brought Elidios' pizza in? It's all the way out on Callahan and Central Avenue Pike."

"I'd guess Rick. He doesn't sleep much," I added, "except on the new moon."

Occam swiveled his head to watch me in the darkness. "And you know that how, Nell, sugar?"

I shrugged. It was part of the claiming/healing. I just knew things about Rick sometimes, and when there was no moon, he slept hard and deep.

Occam let it slide. "You never ate at Elidios' Pizza?" When I shook my head no, he said, "The unit should go there for supper one night."

I made a noncommittal sound and Occam turned his attention back to the streets and the wait that was both boring and too full of turmoil. When the city police had determined that the immediate area was safe enough to move, I crawled to my feet, left Occam lying there, and entered the closest restaurant, begging the use of the bathroom and something to eat. Anything they had left over. The restaurant manager, two cooks, and three waitpersons had been hiding in the kitchen, and they opened the place up just for the emergency responders, offering sandwiches and reheated soup, food that they claimed would be thrown out anyway. It was pretty good eatin', according to the officers who came in for something warm. But to a girl raised in the church, where women knew how to cook, the bread was slightly stale and the soup needed bay, thyme, and black pepper. I didn't say that, though. I knew about gift horses and minding my manners and I was hungry enough to eat that gift horse.

Once I had used the facilities and stuffed soup and a sandwich in my mouth, and Occam had eaten three hoagies with double meat, we went our separate ways, Occam to take Rick some food and work with him on perimeter and rooftop examination, as well as the pattern of physical evidence. Crime scene techs showed up and began the collating and collection process. I traced up and down the street with the psy-meter 2.0, catching small spikes on level four again. So the readings hadn't been erroneous. Our shooter creature, whatever he was, had a definite pattern. It suddenly hit me. I read a low-level four. But . . . I didn't spike. So this thing wasn't a whatever-I-was. Relief, and maybe a little regret, moved through me like a slow tide.

I sent my new info to JoJo at headquarters and then crossed the street and entered the relatively warm room the city police had commandeered for questioning witnesses, where two FBI agents, T. Laine, and Tandy interviewed the bystanders and the people who had been in the restaurant. I watched through the door until the questioning was over and the last haggard couple left the room for the cold of night, followed by the PsyLED agents. They stopped when they saw me.

T. Laine said, "No one saw anything except the chaos that erupted when the shooting started. Questioning so far has been an exercise in futility." T. Laine had perfect teeth, and had lots of schooling—most notably she had some training in large-animal veterinary medicine, which came in handy with Unit Eighteen's werecats.

I looked at Tandy for his assessment. He looked pale and there were dark circles under his eyes. His reddish hair was mussed up as if he'd been running his hands through it.

"No nudges on his truth-o-meter," T. Laine said, "but he's tired, and we have the bigwigs to talk to next."

"Too much fear in such a small place," he said. "Panic has a smell and a taste, and—" His words cut off as he swallowed.

"Go take a break," T. Laine said. "Get hydrated. Nell can help me with this one."

A tingle of excitement raced through me, but I squished it down. "There's water, coffee, and food across the street. The manager stayed on after he officially closed up, just for law enforcement."

"Yeah, thanks." Tandy walked away.

"Bigwigs?" I asked.

"The Tollivers. The senator and Justin, the rich brother,

and their wives." She sent me a knowing look, her dark eyes amused. "Excited, probie?"

"As a dog with his tail stuck in an electric fence."

T. Laine shook her head and said to me, "Come on. Grab a water. No telling how this will go. We'll have Secret Service and feebs and God knows who else in there with us."

The room was short on space, short on heat, and short on amenities. It had a five-foot-long folding table with a lamp on it and a few chairs: two for the couple, one for the questioner, and three against the wall, out of the way, so the interviewed would see only the primary interrogator. The rest of us were supposed to stand. The air inside was stale, laced with the stink of the fire and scorched coffee.

There was also a plastic-wrapped case of water and a stack of legal pads, as well as the recording equipment, which consisted of a futuristic mic—a four-inch, freestanding handle topped with a metal circle and a wire through it, hardwired to a box about the size of a pack of playing cards. T. Laine had her cell out to record. So did the others. I didn't bother.

An African-American woman in a trench coat, pants, and low heels walked into the room and I had no doubt this was the Secret Service special agent in charge of the crime scene. Behind her, and similarly dressed, strode another woman, one I recognized from the Holloways' house investigation. Stevens? Stoltz?

They both placed tablets and pads for notes on the table and looked around at us, taking everyone in. The second woman's eyes didn't so much meet mine as bore a hole into my brain. I had made a reputation for myself when I took down the Knoxville FBI chief as a paranormal serial killer, and some feds didn't like me much. The first woman spoke. "For those who haven't met us, I am Special Agent Elizabeth Crowley, Secret Service. This is Special Agent E. M. Schultz, FBI. I will be leading this discussion. Not interrogation. *Discussion*. The Tollivers are neither persons of interest, nor are they suspects. They are an elected government official and his wife and they are distraught. They are terrified. This will not be questioning as usual. If you have a question, you may ask it after Schultz and I have completed our questions. You will be polite and respectful and show proper deference. Is that clear?"

I nodded. T. Laine nodded. Everyone nodded. I had a feeling that anyone who disagreed would have been put out of the room with extreme prejudice. The SSSAIC was scary. She picked up the mic, clicked it on, gave the date and time, and introduced herself. "This is Elizabeth Crowley, Secret Service. I am joined by . . ." She held the mic to Schultz, who gave her name and rank. Crowley then pointed the mic at T. Laine, who said, "PsyLED Special Agent Tammie Laine Kent."

Crowley went around the room and ended with a finger pointed at me. "PsyLED Probationary Special Agent Nell Nicholson Ingram."

Crowley looked back and forth between T. Laine and me, as if memorizing our faces and putting them together with a mental dossier she was keeping on each of us. "Anything I should know from your agency before we begin?"

T. Laine shook her head no. I raised a hand the way I had in grade school. "Ming of Glass seems to be afraid that both attacks were actually aimed at her."

"The Master of the City of Knoxville?" Crowley asked.

T. Laine's fingers jerked out in some kind of warning, but I couldn't interpret the gesture.

"No, ma'am. Ming of Glass is Blood Master of Clan Glass, but there is no MOC. Knoxville falls under the territory of Leo Pellissier of New Orleans."

I could see things taking place behind Crowley's eyes, but I couldn't interpret them either. "I see. And Ming of Glass. She was here?"

"Yes, ma'am."

"And you let her leave?"

Oh dear. "Ummm . . ." Now I could interpret T. Laine's finger wave. It was a *Keep your mouth shut* signal.

"We'll talk after." She pointed at the suit closest to the door. "Bring them in."

They brought Senator Tolliver and his wife in, and I focused all my senses and abilities on them. The senator looked younger than his age, his face taut and firm, with minimal wrinkles at the corners of his eyes and around his mouth. A self-important, condescending man, hiding behind a façade that was usually friendly, interested, but that façade was cracked now, and arrogance was peeking through, making his eyes hard and dark. His nose was slightly hooked, nostrils a little too thin to be called handsome. The senator's wife, Clarisse, was younger than he, her face pale, her mascara smudged, as if she had been crying. She wore her hair in a dark, short bob streaked blond, and had blue eyes. She held on to the senator's hand under the table and he leaned to her, saying quietly, "It's almost over. We'll be home soon."

She touched her mouth, an indication of nerves, and said, "I'm just worried about Devin."

"The Secret Service are with him. He's in good hands." Her husband smiled. "He's probably asleep. And if not, then he's beating the pants off them at some video game."

Clarisse laughed shakily and touched his shoulder. She seemed like a china doll woman, easily breakable or maybe already broken and glued back together so the porcelain face was what the public usually saw, and not the hurting, fractured woman beneath.

"You can do this," he whispered.

Her face changed; she gave a practiced smile to her husband and then to Crowley, the perfect doll-face mask back in place. The senator studied her a moment, then nodded to proceed.

"Thank you for helping us with the timeline," Crowley said. "It's very important to the investigation and I appreciate the care and effort it must take after two such violent and horrifying situations."

"I've never been in a firefight before," Clarisse said. "It happened so fast."

"What time did you arrive at the restaurant?" Crowley asked.

I listened with half an ear and turned my attention to other things, like the hallway just beyond us, where a stretcher, covered by a white sheet over a formless shape, was rolled past. I was glad Clarisse wasn't looking.

"Who was your waiter?" Crowley asked.

"I don't remember," Clarisse said. "Do you, dear?"

"Mark? Luke? I remember it was one of the gospels. I'm usually better at names," Abrams said, sounding self-deprecating, as if to indicate his bravery and confusion.

"Where were you seated?" Schultz asked. "Could you see out into the street?"

"No, we were seated side by side, facing the kitchen," Abrams said. "The chef is supposed to be quite amazing. We had just placed our order and were talking small talk and business."

"The waiter was bringing our soup. He had just stepped from the kitchen. The tray full of soup bowls exploded," Clarisse said, her eyes growing wider, her fingers touching her mouth again. "Then the man across from me jerked." Her fingers pressed hard against her lips and she spoke through them. "He was just getting ready to stand, leaning forward and up. His head went bloody and blood splattered all over the woman behind him. People started screaming. I started screaming." Her eyes filled with tears and I realized that she was wearing colored contacts, the eyes beneath them gray and not the pretty blue she showed to the world. I remembered the contacts on the corpse's eyes at the Holloways' house. Was there a connection? With contact lenses? No. That was foolish. Clarisse wiped her eyes, smearing the mascara even more. "Can we please go?"

"I think we're done here. I need to get my wife home," Abrams said, standing, giving a politician's smile, one that said several things at once. The most obvious was that he was too important to deal with the kind of questioning suffered by the hoi polloi and that he had been far more patient than he had to be. "I can come in tomorrow to give a statement. My wife will be writing hers and sending it in by e-mail. I have your card. If there are problems with that arrangement you can certainly speak with my attorney."

"Of course, Senator. Thank you for staying and talking to us. If we have further questions we'll be in touch, but I can't imagine that will be necessary," Crowley said smoothly. "Stevens, see them safely to their Secret Service escorts and then to their car, please. Make sure they get away safely. And see Justin Tolliver and his wife in."

"Yes, ma'am," a suit said and opened the door. "This way, Senator, Mrs. Tolliver."

"My brother and his wife had to leave," Abrams Tolliver said. "Babysitter complications. He said to call and he'd come to you at your convenience." Abrams held out a hand to Crowley. "Our cards with office and private contact information."

"Thank you," Crowley said, though it was clear she was peeved that someone had left her interrogation site.

When they were gone, Crowley turned off the mic and looked around the room. "Comments?"

"One," I said. "He had a crust of mud on his shoe. It was a dress shoe. Fancy. He was in the city. Why mud?"

"Anything particularly odd about the mud?" she asked, as if humoring me.

"Not a thing," I said, "if he was a farmer. He'd been in a car and a restaurant, not a field."

"Nell," T. Laine said.

"What? You think she's gonna bite me?"

"Speaking of biting, why did you let Ming of Glass go?" Crowley asked smoothly. It was a cop question, slid in when not expected, hoping to get a reaction.

"Because she wasn't in the restaurant when the firing started. She drove up later. She waited around for a while in case you needed to talk to her, but then she left. I've got her number if you need to talk to her." I held up my cell.

"You have the Master of the—" She stopped. "You have the number of Ming of Glass in your personal cell phone database?"

"Her security guard, actually." Whose name I didn't know. Calling her Yummy would be embarrassing, but the

SSSAIC didn't ask for it. "I wouldn't call in the daytime. That's like poking a sleeping lion with a stick."

"I'll keep it in mind." Crowley stood and gathered her belongings, her face expressionless, her emotions indecipherable. "Include that information in your report," she said to me. To the others, she said, "You are all dismissed. I expect reports in my e-mail by ten a.m."

We all filed out of the room and into the cleanup.

There were three wounded and one dead, not counting the officer, lots of rounds fired, and no one had seen anything. I scanned the files being put together by JoJo and recognized none of the victims' names. Worse, with the exception of the presence of the senator and the expected presence of Ming of Glass, Jo could find nothing that tied any of the dead or wounded to each other or to the people at the Holloways' party. The worry about assassination or domestic—or paranormal—terrorism was still a very real possibility.

Near dawn, JoJo said into my earpiece, "Nell, I got a vamp calling, saying she needs her taxi driver at University of Tennessee Medical Center. She asked for Maggot."

"Ha-ha," I said. But I slid off my chair and jogged to my truck. I gave her my ETA and once again appreciated the superheater in the old Chevy.

Yummy opened the passenger door, looked over the interior, and said, "You have got to be kidding."

"Nope. You could call an Uber."

Her face scrunched in distaste; she slid in and closed the door. "Hell, Maggot. Can't you afford a new car? Doesn't PsyLED provide you a car? Does it have a radio?" She punched the buttons and twisted the knobs.

"Probably. Eventually. And yes. But it stopped working last week. Buckle up." I slid her a sideways glance and pulled into the light five a.m. traffic as she complied. "No working radio. We'll have to talk," I said.

"About maggots?"

I laughed. "About life. Tell me about yourself."

"I'm sure you have a dossier on me. Read it."

"My time's valuable." I let my words glide into church-speak. "You'uns ain't important enough to me to read it."

Yummy burst out laughing and twisted around in the seat so her legs were splayed, one knee angled at me. "I like you, Nell."

"Hmmm."

"You're not gonna say you like me?"

"My mama taught me to be polite and to not lie. Those two things aren't always mutually agreeable."

Yummy laughed again and dropped her head against the back window with a soft thud. Her very pale blond hair swung and fell still. "I was born the first time in 1932 in a little town in South Louisiana. I was turned in 1953 by a vamp named Grégoire, who said he loved me and that we should be together forever. He looked fifteen but in the sack he was truly immortal." Yummy glanced my way. "He could do things with his mouth . . ."

Yummy was testing the waters, seeing how far she could go. I had learned quickly that no reaction was the best reaction when dealing with paranormal creatures, especially the predatory kind. I didn't react, just eased through a green light and up behind an early school bus.

Yummy went on. "Sadly, when I woke up dead in 1960—early by Mithran standards—Grégoire had moved on emotionally and sexually and was sleeping with young men and the Master of the City of New Orleans, Leo Pellissier, a former and once-again lover. In the intervening years my brothers went to war and never came back, my father died of a heart attack working in a paper mill, and Mama remarried and moved away." Yummy's accent had changed as she spoke, taking on a twang I didn't really recognize, maybe Frenchy Southern. An accent that was biscuits and gravy with hot sauce and alligator sausage or something. It was slightly like Rick's when he was tired or angry, but softer, more melodious. She went on, now sounding a little sad, and I had to wonder if she knew she was giving so much away, or if she just needed to talk and didn't care what she exposed about herself. "Instead of being head-over-heels in love, I was part of the Clan Arceneau blood family. But I was alone, a blood-sucker of little consequence, living with fangheads I didn't much like and what amounted to human slaves. I was a small fish in a large fishbowl full of predators, all with bigger teeth than I had."

She looked my way again and I pretended to be wholly focused on the street and the lights ahead. "I wasn't interested in group sex, in making new slaves, or in helping to run a vamp's household. So I learned to fight and went to war, as much as women were allowed to in Uncle Sam's army back then. When I got back, I took on all comers until I killed one of Grégoire's favorites and he sent me to Ming of Glass. I've been here ever since."

That was a lot more than I expected her to tell me. I made a soft noise as I digested her story.

"Your turn, Maggot."

I grinned at the windshield and quoted her. "I'm sure you have a dossier on me. Read it."

When she stopped chuckling, Yummy said, "I like you more and more, Nell Nicholson Ingram. Okay. How's this? You were raised in God's Cloud of Glory Church, became a common-law wife to John Ingram at age twelve, and nursed his wife Leah until she died. Then you married him legally and nursed him until he died. You inherited all his land, which shared a boundary with the church, against which you led a war of ignoring and attrition for years. During that time, you educated yourself at the local library and recently got a GED. You joined PsyLED this year. You graduated in the middle third of your class at PsyLED training school and would have graduated higher had you received a traditional education. As it was, you classified as an expert marksman with two weapons, when you finally took the weapons qualification course, top of your class in poly sci, and bottom of your class in interpersonal interactions."

"Not bad," I said. Every special agent had to qualify for weapons, and requalify at regular intervals. It wasn't as rigorous as the military's qualification, but it was thorough and I hadn't been certain where I had positioned in the class or what my final ranking would be. My certificates had come in the mail less than a week ago, and I was proud of them. That Yummy knew all that meant the vampires were capable of doing, or buying, deep background research on federal agents. That was something I'd have to think about later. "I'm not good at flirting or making small talk, but I bake good bread and make excellent soup and have even better survival skills."

"Now that we're done showing off," Yummy said, "and since you aren't about to let me feed on your soft, beautiful neck, how about pulling over and let's get breakfast." She pointed to an IHOP. "I'm paying."

"Deal," I said, swinging the wheel and popping into the parking spot. "It's nearly dawn and it's your skin that'll be burned crispy, but I'm hungry enough to risk you dying again."

"Ain't you just the sweetest li'l thang."

I grinned at her as I slid from the warmth into the cold and slammed the door. "I may not have fangs, but I can still bite."

Yummy on my heels, I thought that my mama would have a conniption fit if I was ever dumb enough to tell her I'd had breakfast with a fanghead. Especially since I wasn't hungry. But making friends with a paranormal creature who could fight might be smart. If friendship was actually happening here. I wasn't yet sure.

It was after dawn when I used the inconspicuous keypad to enter the unmarked door between Yoshi's Deli and Coffee's On and into the field office of PsyLED Unit Eighteen. As I entered, I gave a halfhearted wave at the very conspicuous roving surveillance camera over the door, and waited until it closed behind me before I slogged up the stairs into the

PsyLED offices. I was so exhausted my knees wanted to buckle.

I dropped my gear on the desk in my cubicle and stuck my fingers into the soil of the plants lining the window. A feeling of completeness rushed over me, feeling much like waves rolling over a beach, not that I had ever seen such a thing in person. I'd been close to the ocean when I went to Spook School, but it wasn't someplace I wanted to go alone. The videos I had seen of the Atlantic made me think of isolation and aloneness and abandonment.

The soil and the mulch and the compost in my plants had the power of the ocean, but without the loneliness and isolation. They were all from Soulwood and connected me to my land instantly. The soil felt a little too dry and I made a mental note to water the plants. As I withdrew my fingers, I brushed them over the herbs, and the mixed scents of three kinds of basil, lemony thyme, and oniony chives filled my nostrils. I locked away my gun and found the coffee machine with my eyes closed.

I pretty much slept through writing my report and the debriefing that followed. And later I could never have explained how I drove all the way to my house and crawled into my bed.

I woke when one cat leaped to my outside bedroom windowsill, yowling that it was time to come back inside. I stumbled out of bed, let the cats in, and fed the mousers dry kibble. Still half-asleep, I added scrap paper to coax the coals alive in the skin-temp firebox of the Waterford Stanley wood-burning cookstove. Living off the grid was time-consuming, never-ending, hard work. Fortunately, thanks to muscle memory and repetition, I could do most of it in my sleep. When I had some flames, I added kindling, hot-burning cedar, and slow-burning oak to the firebox and adjusted the dampers. Topped up the water heater on the back of the stove, testing the warmth with my hand. It was still warm, but not hot. I fumbled around and made a whole pot of coffee in the

Bunn and scrambled some eggs while bread toasted and water heated. I did not want a tepid shower.

I ate standing in front of the stove, my wool socks doing nothing to keep my feet warm. The house was frigid, another one of the drawbacks of living mostly off the grid. I had been thinking about buying a small electric space heater, but the watt-hours usage might not be worth the speed of the warmth. The stove would eventually heat the house to bearable without depleting the solar panels. At least that was what I told myself today.

Carrying a second cup of coffee to the bathroom, I showered. It wasn't a long luxurious shower, not with the size of the hot water tank, but it was at least hot. I checked the calendar to make sure it wasn't a church day, as I had promised Mama I'd come to services on Sunday, and dressed in work clothes. Still caffeinating my body, I repacked my gobag, put a load of clothes on to wash, and drank a third, and then a fourth cup of coffee, while I rubbed down a few venison loins with oil and my own spicy recipe meat rub before I put them in a Dutch oven on the hottest part of the stovetop. Awake enough to slice veggies without carving off a finger, I added veggies and diced potatoes. Satisfied that I'd have food to eat and a warm house when I got home, I finished a few housekeeping chores, made more coffee and poured it into a thirty-ounce travel mug, put the cats on the back porch for the night, and locked the door.

I was halfway to PsyLED when my cell jangled and JoJo's voice said, "Justin Tolliver's house is burning. Sending address to your cell. Lights and siren. LaFleur wants you there ASAP."

I pulled off the road, slapped the lights in place, turned on the siren, and set the cell to give me directions to Tolliver's house. I drank coffee all the way there, knowing for sure that caffeine was a gateway drug to crack. Had to be. Mama would be horrified if I ever let that slip.

The sun was setting over the bend of the Tennessee River when I pulled up to the mansion, parked, and slid to the ground. The rear of the place was engulfed, flames flinging themselves out the windows and doors and the holes in the roof created by the firefighters. The roar and crackle of the fire, the rushing of water through the fire hose, the thrum of diesel generators, all created a rush of heat and noise unlike any other.

I had never seen such a huge inferno and found myself struck still and speechless as the fire's heat and might reached out and gripped me in its raging fingers, scorching my face even out in the street. Glowing embers and stinking ash fell from the sky, burning. I tossed my good coat back in the truck and pulled a hand-me-down on instead. The heavy coat had belonged to John, my husband, and it hung on my too-slender form, but it was something I didn't mind getting burned, and it had a hood, which I raised over my hair as I watched the scene. I reseated my weapon in the holster, made sure my badge was in view before I locked up the C10.

Three fire trucks were on-site, pulled up in the grass, two pumping water in through the roof holes, one watering down trees nearby to keep the fire from spreading. Firefighters strode through the ruined lawn, each wearing heavy gear and oxygen tanks and fire-blackened yellow coats.

Feds were on-site too, as was P. Simon—the former Green Beret ALT Security guy, from the Holloways' party—and Rick, his silver-laced black hair sparkling. A group had gathered beneath the protection of the wide arms of a fir tree. I looked around and saw a small sign that read ALT SECURITY. It was interesting that a man with so many personal problems was at the site of another situation involving the Tollivers. I sent that info to headquarters and heard back instantly that ALT was the highest rated private security firm in Eastern Tennessee. All the rich and famous used them for protection and security. Before I left the truck I sent back a two-word text. *Still strange.*

I jogged over to them. There were three uniformed men from KFD and two feds, both from previous crime scenes, Chadworth Sanders Hamilton and E. M. Schultz. There was also a small group of four civilians, Justin and Sonya Tolliver and their two children. The smallest child wore what looked like pajamas with bunny slippers and a blanket wrapped around him. The massive fir tree was dripping wet from a drenching by the fire hose, but offered protection from the falling ash.

I was joining a debriefing in the middle. One of the fire department uniforms was saying, "Preliminary testing indicates that an accelerant was present near the back of the house, probably gasoline."

I turned my eyes to him, blinking against the dark, my retinas burned by the flame, my mouth firmly shut. These were the bigwigs at this investigation and I didn't want to get myself thrown off the scene.

He continued, "It's too early to definitively call it, but I suspect arson."

"I think that assessment is premature," Justin said, his voice clipped and precise, sounding like a lawyer, even in his shirtsleeves and damp pants and house shoes. He scrubbed his head with both hands, leaving his hair standing up in tufts, staring at the house with eyes that looked too large, too full of emotions that I couldn't decipher. "The lawn care company kept supplies under the back deck. I never saw a gasoline can, but it's possible they left one there."

"Sir," the fire investigator started.

"No." His hands slid down his face, past his nose, which was hooked like Abrams', nostrils too narrow for his face, a Tolliver feature. "Not until you have something more conclusive than just a hit on gasoline."

Sonya leaned against Justin, crying softly. He didn't lift his arm to wrap around her. Instead he dropped his hands from his face and gripped his wife's shoulders, setting her aside as if she was in the way. There was trouble in this marriage, I thought. And I wondered how much the house had been insured for and if one of them had seen a divorce lawyer recently. And then wondered how I had changed so quickly from churchwoman thoughts to law enforcement thoughts. I'd never have considered such a thing only a few months past.

Justin said, "It could have been electrical. Maybe a short in an outside outlet. And if there was gas under the porch, then the can got hot from the fire. It probably burned and splashed flaming liquid up the walls, right?"

Even I knew Justin was being foolish. He had been present at two shootings and now his house was on fire. He had to sense that he was, perhaps, a target.

"Gasoline doesn't act like that, sir," one of the fire department's uniformed men said gently. "Special effects on TV and movies are often wrong."

Special Agent Hamilton smirked at Tolliver. So far, my distant cousin had shown no particularly good character traits. I had a feeling that I was not going to like him even if I ever got to know him better.

I looked back at the burning structure just in time to see a partial roof on the back of the house, maybe a porch roof, fall in. The crash shook the ground, jarring up my legs and spine. The embers shot high, the flames finally freed to feed on the air, ravenous, destructive. I knew how that fire felt. If I ever let my bloodlust go, it would feel that way—explosive, ferocious, violent.

Sonya walked away from her husband, closer to the fire, as if mesmerized. Justin followed, the flames reflected off his skin, glowing golden.

Schultz turned, her gaze following the Tollivers' actions, her face to the fire, her dark skin gleaming. "This house burning like a torch might be a crime of opportunity, a fluke of timing." Softer, so it didn't carry, she asked, "Are the Tollivers getting along?" No one replied.

Rick said, "Ingram? Thoughts about this fire?"

I flinched just the tiniest bit, then raised my hands to lower my hood, taking the time to evaluate Rick's question and think how I wanted to say this. "Since Justin Tolliver was at the scenes of both shootings, coincidence, while possible, seems unlikely. Even though there's a different MO here, there's a good chance it's tied to the Holloway crime scene, and the restaurant even if only by copycat or opportunity."

"How high?" Rick asked.

"I'm not a mathematician," I said, keeping my words toneless. "This is just common sense, using reason and probability."

I hoped that was what Rick had wanted to hear. However, if I was right, and killing Justin or Sonya was the objective all along, that meant that Ming, the witches, and Senator Abrams Tolliver could be cut from the possible list of targets. And with no absolute proof that the assailant was a known paranormal creature, the Secret Service and PsyLED both would probably pack up and go home. Until we had a witness, a clear video, or a tissue sample that could be analyzed, there *was* no paranormal.

"What can you tell me?" Rick asked me. It was a hint to go read the land.

I pulled my flash from my pocket and nodded to the group. "I'll check the grounds with the psy-meter. Mr. Tolliver?" I called out. "Your wife needs a hug." I spun on the grass and left the group before Rick could tell me to mind my own business.

The Tollivers, Justin and Sonya and their children, had a good three acres, which was a large patch of ground this close to inner-city Knoxville and Sequoyah Hills. I stayed out of the way of the fire crews, and under the dripping forest of trees and shrubs on the boundaries of the property. There was a shed in back, with an old flatwater kayak leaning against the wall. It looked recently used, clean, and not covered with yard dust, as it might if it had sat for a while. Beside it, there were a pair of wading boots, a tackle box, and what looked like a fishing rod, broken down into easy-to-carry segments. At the back of the shed, the psy-meter 2.0 showed the telltale spikes at level four. Spikes that led toward the house. I caught Rick's eye and held up four fingers. I knew he'd see them in the dark. Cat eyes. He gave me a minuscule nod.

I put the expensive device away and got my blanket. It was faded, frayed, an ugly pink thing, but I liked it. It made me feel good about reading the land, as if I brought part of Soulwood with me each time I sat on it.

I stopped several times to try to read the ground, but the fire had woken the plants. Usually when I read flora, I got nothing, because plants were sluggish thinkers, slow to recognize anything of humankind other than the fire that came in our wake and the destruction of chain saws. But this was the ancient enemy of life. Fire was the destroyer. All I got from the plants I touched was, *Fearfirefearfire,* from everything: from the grass, shrubs, the old firs and oaks; the warnings had spread from plant to plant. At the back of the property, behind the shed where I had first found the level four psysitope spikes, I finally found something other than fear sizzling through the flora. I found several spots of death when I placed the blanket down and sat, hidden by shadows and winter-bare flora, put my hands into the earth, digging my fingernails down for a light read.

The plants in a narrow opening between two maples were beginning to die, exactly the way the plants had died at the other house. Standing again, I traced the passage of death. Sliding into the dark undergrowth between the trees, I switched off the flash. Tucking my coat under me, I sat in the shadows and placed my hands flat on the ground, digging my fingertips into the soil beneath. The roots were dead. Here was the spot the assassin had come in by. I got up and brushed my hands off. Using the flash, I followed the trail back through the woods, along a rivulet creek that fed the Tennessee River, to a tertiary road, where I lost the trail of dead plants. Tracking my way back, I fingered the plants, tearing off leaves and small stems and digging out rootlets. They looked and felt dead, but also smelled, very faintly, burned. Had I missed the scent at the Holloways'? It had been much colder that night. I had been exhausted. Hungry. It was possible I missed something.

Back at the house, standing in the overhang of trees, I studied the yard, where I'd felt a second patch of dead. It was near the garage, where the Tollivers seemed to park their cars. I needed to go back to the Holloways' and smell the plants at the first crime scene.

Rick caught my eye across the lawn and I nodded slowly,

hoping he understood what I was saying, that it was the same attacker. He nodded back curtly and gestured me over. I made my way along the edge of the property back to the small group. "So," I asked, "gas?"

"Yes and no," said a man in a fire department uniform and a winter coat. "Gasoline was recovered from the gas can under the porch, but the can was below the worst of the heat and didn't explode. Didn't contribute to the fire at all. From the way the fire started—on both stories at the same time—and the way it spread—inward from both levels and fast—I'd say the structure was targeted with a flamethrower, but we didn't get a hit on known accelerants except the gasoline. If the sprinkler system hadn't come on, some of the family, particularly the kids, might not have gotten out alive. The fire ate right through their rooms."

Sonya Tolliver sobbed, gathered her children close, and herded them toward a big SUV. She opened the door with the keypad and climbed in with the children, shutting the door on the fire and the unwelcome information. Her husband looked us over and then fled after his family.

When the vehicle door closed, Rick asked me, "Ingram, what did you determine?"

"It's the same attacker," I said. "Or the same species as the previous attacker, a paranormal."

"You can't know that," Schultz said.

"In a couple of days, the plants in a specific trail are going to start to die. If you want, I can mark it off for you once the fire department is finished. At the Holloways' house, I detected the same kind of trail. There should be dead plants along it now. Go look."

"And how do we know *you* didn't create this 'trail'?" Hamilton asked, his eyes hard, piercing me through the smoke-filled air that swirled our way. This man, like other law enforcement officials, knew that Unit Eighteen was composed of mostly paranormals. Although he probably didn't know what I was, it was a good guess that I wasn't human. My cuz didn't like paranormals. Which just ticked me off something terrible.

I narrowed my eyes at him and drew on my churchwoman accent. I had learned that deliberately using it seemed to throw people off their game, as if they didn't quite know how to relate to me. Oddly enough, it had become part of my arsenal. "Are you'un asking me if I am the unknown suspect who shot the people at the Holloways' fund-raiser party?" I asked, squaring my shoulders and advancing on him. "Are you'un asking me if I have a flamethrower? Are you'un jist trying to cause trouble, or are you'un trying to make me, specifically, mad? I'm jist curious, since you'un's bein' an *ass* an' all."

Rick coughed, but I had a feeling the choked sound was laughter stuck in his throat. It also let me know that Hamilton was being difficult to all the paranormals, and not just me.

Schultz said, "Hamilton, do you have a problem with Special Agent Ingram? If not, back off, probie."

Hamilton shoved his fists into his suit coat pockets and took a step back, but he was staring back and forth at Rick and me. Hamilton was looking more and more like a paranormal hater and had decided to dump me in with the weres and witches on PsyLED Unit Eighteen. Or maybe he was another one who hated me for exposing his former boss as a shape-shifter and cannibal, when they'd had no idea. That seemed to have left a bad taste in a lot of FBI agents' mouths.

Schultz went on as if nothing rude had been said on either side. "So either Justin Tolliver was the primary target all along, or the entire family is under attack."

"Politics or money?" Rick asked.

"Both?" She looked at the house. "First I'll get Hamilton to pull records: financials, political contributions, life insurance, marital problems." She glanced at the SUV where the Tollivers had taken refuge. "Follow the money."

"I agree," Rick said. "This means we'll have to guard the senator and his entire family at work, home, governmental buildings, travel, and school."

Schultz made a rude sound and said, "I'll call it in. We need more people until we stop this guy." She studied Rick. "Can you, you know, smell anything?"

"You mean like smoke?" Rick asked, an amused glint in his eyes.

"Something humans can't pick up?" E. M. Schultz shrugged, her gaze taking in the lean wereleopard. "House is damaged, too hot to work up right now, but U-18's investigatory technique goes about things a bit differently, I've heard."

"Sometimes," Rick acknowledged. "And underneath the stench of burning wood, brick, synthetic fibers, wallboard, shingles, stone, and a dozen other household stinks, I do smell something odd. Not magical, not were, not anything I can put my finger on. But if it comes to me, I'll call."

Schultz tilted two fingers into a chest pocket and removed a card. "Business and personal numbers. Anytime."

I watched Rick take the card, his eyes alight, but when Schultz glanced back at the house, the flirty glow in his gaze faded fast, into something bitter and grieving. Weres can't have sexual relations with humans without passing along to them the were-taint, which was an automatic death sentence carried out by grindylows—the cute but deadly judge, jury, and executioner of the were community. Not that many humans knew all that, likely Schultz included. Which meant that if I was interpreting the little scene correctly, Schultz wanted to date Rick and he couldn't date her, but wanted to, and maybe flirted by instinct. Even outside of a polygamous church, romantic and physical relationships weren't easy.

I scowled, my mind envisioning Occam, the way he had looked last time I saw him, blond hair floating, scruffy beard. And for some reason that image hurt me on a level that made no sense, except that Occam couldn't have anyone either. Unless he and Rick wanted to get together . . . And I didn't see either of them wanting the other.

Unless . . . My body and mind stilled. I wasn't human. That meant that Occam and I could—

"Nell?"

I flinched, looked up into Rick's black eyes, and realized he had been talking to me for a while. The other agents were gone and it was just Rick and me under the trees. "Ummm. Yeah?"

"The feds will be providing protection for the senator and his family, and Justin and his family, and they have requested a paranormal LEO on-site. That means that our unit will be doing double duty, tracking the assassin and providing body detail."

I tilted out my thumb in a gesture that meant, *Please continue.*

"The senator's house is a huge chunk of real estate, with a six-thousand-square-foot main house, a guesthouse, three pools, and tennis courts, in Sequoyah Hills, on Cherokee Boulevard. It backs up to the Tennessee River and is well protected from all sides. The feds intend to move all the extended family onto the property."

I tapped my cell and checked the time. It was a little after four a.m. The night had flown by as I read and communed with the grounds. "You want me there?"

"You can go home. I want you to sleep today if you can and take the night shift tonight, nine to nine a.m."

"Good, I'd like to sleep me some sleep."

"Go. I'll send Senator Tolliver's address to your cell. Be on time."

"Copy," I said and made my way to my truck. I could barely keep my eyes open on the drive back home. But I didn't make it home before my cell rang and I knew instantly that my morning nap was about to be tampered with. "Good morning, Mama," I said, tiredly.

"Nellie girl, I'd be most appreciative if'n you'un would drop by for a bit. Breakfast in half an hour?"

"Mama, I—"

"We'uns having French toast and waffles and eggs and bacon. Thank you'un, pum'kin. See you in a bit."

The connection ended. I didn't know what Mama wanted or what she had up her sleeve, but I knew it was likely something sneaky. Probably several somethings sneaky. Manipulation was an art form among the women in the church. Knowing I should go straight home to my bed, I put on the blinker and turned toward the church lands.

FIVE

My ID was sufficient to get me onto the compound of God's Cloud of Glory Church and I turned off the C10's lights as the truck crawled forward. Holding my flash out the driver's window I searched into the shadows on either side of the road, looking for fresh shoots of the vampire tree. It was too dark to make out anything in the gloom of a cloudy dawn, in the darkness beneath the scrub pressing up against the twelve-foot-tall fence that surrounded the church grounds.

Dissatisfied with my perusal, but unwilling to abandon the heated air and search on foot, I rolled the window back up, put the lights back on, and took the most direct route to the Nicholson house. The fact that the most direct route bypassed the vampire tree was just happenstance. Mostly. It was still there. Still creepy.

I parked the old Chevy beneath the trees in front of the three-story structure that was home to my extended family: my father, my mama, her two sister-wives, and all the assorted sibs and half sibs. Before I could get out of the truck, the door was yanked open and Mud, or Mindy as the rest of the family called her, threw herself inside and hugged me so hard I thought I might break in two. "I missed you'un," she mumbled into my coat. Before I could respond, she reared back and said, "You'un stink like fire. Not like a campfire, but like garbage burning."

I dropped off the seat, to the ground, and said, "I was at a house fire. Part of my job."

She narrowed her eyes and studied me like she might an unfamiliar beetle she found eating basil in the greenhouse.

"Did somebody try to burn a family out? Was they witches?" Her voice dropped. "Did they burn her at the stake?"

"No one got burned. No stake. All house fires stink really bad. And in the real human world, witches don't get burned at the stake."

Mud made a sound of disagreement that was remarkably like Mama's and took my hand, pulling me up the steps to the porch. "Breakfast is on. You'un comin' to church with us this morning?"

"No. Just breakfast and then home."

"You'un fallin' away? The mamas say you'un's fallin' away and driftin' into sin."

"I have a job. And no, I'm not falling into sin. But I don't worship at God's Cloud anymore."

"You'un going to church somewheres else? 'Cause if'n you ain't going to church then you'un's falling into sin. Sam said so."

"Did he now?" Sam was my older full sib and a bit of a worrywart. He also didn't always know when to keep his big mouth shut. "I'll speak to Sam. Let him know I'm not falling into evil and damnation." Except I'd killed two men . . . so maybe I was.

Mud shoved open the door to the house and dragged me inside. The roar of voices hit me in the face like a huge fluffy pillow, warm and soft and smothering. I hung my winter coat on the wall tree, smelling bacon and waffles and French toast and coffee as I followed Mud into the kitchen, where she pushed me onto a bench and brought me a cup of steaming tea. "Mama, Nell worked all night putting out a fire and she needs to sleep so don't nobody be giving her no coffee. It'll keep her awake."

Instantly I was bombarded with questions from the young'uns about fires and the exciting life of a firefighter and when did they start letting some puny woman fight fires. And then I had to explain about not being a firefighter, but that women could do any job a man could except produce sperm to father children.

At that point I was called down by Mama Grace, Daddy's

third and youngest wife, who said, "Nell Nicholson Ingram, I know you'un ain't been gone so long as to have forgotten what conversation is and is not appropriate for the breakfast table. Hush you'un's mouth."

Mawmaw was coming in the front door and heard the final part of the conversation. "Let the girl talk," she said. "That's biology, and biology is schoolin'."

"Thanks, Mawmaw," I said.

"Though at this age," she added, as she fell on the bench beside me, "I'm of a mind to say something more. Coffee, please, Cora," she said, interrupting herself. Staring around the table at the females present, she continued, "While menfolk are handy to have around to do the heavy lifting, any smart woman can figure out how to do things on her own if necessary. And Nell has a point about the role of fathering children."

I sat still and listened as the young teenagers at the table dove into an argument about women's rights and women's role in the family, politics, business, and the world in general. The boys started demonstrating muscles and their sisters told them to act like adults and then suddenly Mawmaw was quoting Archimedes about using a lever to move the world. Which digressed to Archimedes running around naked in public when he discovered new mathematic principles. And then the young'uns in the main room started singing the alphabet song, followed by a song about Moses in the Nile, followed by a song about numbers that I had never heard before. I didn't even bother asking Mawmaw about her great nephew, Hamilton the FBI jerk.

I let it all wash through me, absorbing it and remembering the good things that came from growing up in God's Cloud. As awful as some parts had been, growing up a Nicholson had not all been bad.

Mama plunked a plate in front of me stacked with French toast and a half dozen strips of maple-cured bacon. Melted butter ran down the yeasty, egg-soaked and drenched, French-style bread, mixing with blueberry honey. My mouth watered and my throat made some sound of amazement and Mama said, "Eat. We'll bless it when your'n daddy gets here." Then she upended a cup of her homemade whipped cream on top of the fried toast and I dug in. Oh yeah. Being a Nicholson was some kind of wonderful when it came to eating.

I was mostly done, groaning with the pain of a too-full stomach, yet still scraping my spoon across the plate to get the final dregs of deliciousness off it, when there was the slightest hint of change in the ambient noise. In a flash, the teens scattered, some outside to chores, others up the stairs. Mama Grace, soft and rounded, as if her body had been lined with down-fill, set a pot of stinky herbal tea at the head of the table and herded all the littlest young'uns up the stairs too. My own mama, Mama Cora, dished up a plate of waffles and set them beside the herbal tea. She removed my plate and poured me more China black tea. Her lips were tight. Her face was pinched. Something was up.

And then I heard the faint *thunk*ing. Without even turning around, I knew. I knew why I had been asked to breakfast. I knew why everyone had gone running. They had set me up. I glared over the rim of my cup at Mama and she ducked her head, not meeting my eyes.

I swiveled on the bench and watched Mama Carmel, daddy's senior wife, help Daddy from their room behind the kitchen, to the table.

Daddy looked pale enough to win a contest with a corpse, and sorta yellowed too, what the church midwives called jaundice in babies. He had lost at least another ten pounds, leaving his face saggy and his work clothes hanging on his frame. His hands carried a faint tremor. Daddy still had not been to the surgeon who put him back together after he was shot, when the group of shape-shifting devil dog *gwyllgi* tried to take over the church. Whatever was wrong inside him was getting worse. "Morning, Nellie," he said, easing into his chair with a pained sigh. "God's grace and peace to you today."

My eyes flicked back and forth between the mamas again in accusation and then I glared at my father. "I'd say the same thing back to you'un, but you'un don't deserve it."

My father reared back in his chair. "What did you say, young lady?"

"I said, you'un don't deserve God's grace and peace, since you'un clearly been throwing it back into the face of the Almighty for weeks and weeks." Daddy opened his mouth and I stood up from the table so I could use height for intimidation. Tactics from Interrogation 101 at Spook School. Stuff I'd never expected to have to use on my own father. "You used to tell us to make use of all God's gifts and not ignore them. Not ever. That ignoring gifts was a sin. And yet, God sent you to a surgeon after you got shot, and gave you the gift of life so's you could continue to love and be loved and do God's will. That was a gift. And yet you'un throwing that gift back in his face. I'm rightly ashamed of you, Daddy."

Daddy opened his mouth, and then closed it. Things were happening deep in his yellowed eyes, too fast to follow. His mouth opened and then closed tight, opened again. He looked like a beached carp, not that I was gonna say that. I had pushed as much as I was likely to get away with. After way too long, Daddy tilted his head to me and looked me over. Me in my work pants and dark suit jacket, bulge of my weapon in the small space between shoulder, armpit, and breast. He looked over at his wives, not a one of them looking at him. He made a disgusted sound, deep in his throat. "So that's the way of it now? My womenfolk ganging up on me?"

I thought about telling him I was no one's "womenfolk," but Daddy needed to see his surgeon and maybe that was more important than me standing up for myself. At least right now.

"Coffee, Cora, if you please," he said. He pushed away the cup of herbal tea and accepted the cup of coffee, taking his gaze back to me, his interest particularly heavy. He sipped, still staring as he set the cup down on the table with a soft tap. "Carmel, if you would be so kind, make an appointment with that doctor."

I didn't dare look away from him, at the faces of the mamas, but I could practically feel the elation in the air. If churchwomen danced, they'd be do-si-do-ing right about now.

"You, Nellie girl," Daddy said, "will *never* speak to me in that tone again."

I raised my chin, knowing it was challenging, but I was a churchwoman no more. Not a woman to be cowed by a man, even my father. I had gotten what I wanted. Now to nail it all down. "You'un act you got sense in your'n head and I won't have to."

One of the mamas choked and started coughing. Daddy glared at me, his lower face hidden by his mug, his sickly eyes glaring. "I reckon we won't be talking about your'n future after all this."

"What about my future?" I demanded. "I got me a good farm, good land, a good job, and good friends. I got family here and a life out in the world and that's the way I like it."

"But you'rn alone, Nellie girl. And the mamas got a young man they want you to meet."

I blinked slowly and turned my gaze to my mama. I had been set up all right. I had been set up in two different ways at the same time: to harangue Daddy into seeing a doctor and try to get me back into the church.

"You'll like him, Nell," Mama said, taking a step back at whatever she saw on my face. She put a hand to her reddish brown bun in a gesture that looked nervous and firmed her lips. Mama was a stubborn woman and she pushed through. "His name is Benjamin Aden and he's Sam's age. You been gone a long time, but you'un might remember him as a little'un. He's one a Brother Aden's boys, college educated now, with a degree in renewable farming practices or some such. He's a modern kinda boy and he only wants one wife. And he's coming for coffee."

At that moment, a knock sounded on the door. And Daddy grinned as he lifted a big forkful of waffles to his mouth. He looked a lot better than he had only moments past. Amusement at my discomfort seemed to agree with him. Getting back at me for my insolence probably made him even happier.

Mud threw open the door and cold air raced past, stealing the heat of the house. "Mama! It's Benjamin and Sam!"

I stepped away from the table as the two entered, Sam sturdy and self-contained, peeling out of his jacket. And Benjamin, who pulled off a toboggan to reveal dark hair over deep blue eyes, a full mouth, and a strong jaw. He was *pretty*. Taller than me. Wearing traditional church-style clothes, but store-bought: plaid shirt over T-shirt; newish jeans that had been ironed to a sharp crease. He had smooth skin and a look about him that said he'd be capable and quiet and kind.

They came across the room and I realized I was still standing, shoulders hunched, wearing smoke-stinky work clothes. Pants. Jacket. My service weapon under my jacket. My hair in a short bob, not bunned up like a proper woman. Tired. No makeup or lipstick left on my mouth, and not sure if that was a good thing or a bad one.

I was horrified at the thoughts I was having. As if any of that mattered. It didn't. I was the woman I wanted to be. Yet my eyes darted around as if looking for a way out that wouldn't require me to address Benjamin.

Daddy called the men to come on over, and then called for coffee, sounding hale and hearty, as if he wasn't actively dying from the damage inside him. Asking . . . asking the womenfolk to serve the menfolk. Just the way it always used to be. Just the way it always would be in the church. That realization somehow settled me, and my shoulders went back to their proper position instead of up around my ears.

"Set a spell, Nell," Mama said, replacing my cup with a fresh one and pouring a pale tea. This one smelled of chamomile, ginger, and vanilla.

I brought my gaze back from the men, who were settling around the table, being served. Served by the *women*.

"Don't you dare be rude," Mama hissed at me. "He's a nice boy. You be nice too."

I started to tell Mama off. I wanted to storm away. But Mama looked at me with pleading in her eyes and I could do neither one. I blew out a breath. T. Laine would call this effed-up family dynamics, the *effed* word in place of the regular one because they knew I didn't care for it much. And she would be right. Worse, it wasn't Benjamin's fault that Mama had set this up.

Benjamin was the eldest son of Brother Aden. I liked Brother Aden and I adored his second wife, Sister Erasmus. I could be polite.

But that didn't mean I had to just sit and take this. "It's mighty warm in here," I said as I pulled off my work jacket and draped it across a nearby chair back. I turned back around, my gun and its weapon harness in plain view, along with my badge clipped to my belt. The house went dead silent. I leaned across the table and held out my right hand. "Hi, Benjamin. I'm Nell. Good to meet you." Only a beat or two too late, Benjamin took my hand and shook it. I released his hand, which was warm and strong and tough-skinned. I lifted my long legs back across the bench, one at a time, the way men did, instead of the way a woman did—sliding in or sitting and lifting knees demurely over, skirts decorously tucked. Into the silence, I took a sip and said, "Thank you, Mama. The tea is wonderful. Just what I need after a long night at a fire investigation."

Mama's eyes were big as saucers. Daddy looked as if he'd been hit with a big stick right up across his noggin.

Benjamin, however, looked intrigued. Maybe even fascinated. His big baby blues latched on to me and his full lips lifted into a slow smile, the corners curving up first, then his eyes crinkling. "It's a sure pleasure to meet you, Nell Nicholson."

"Ingram," I said. "Special Agent Nell Ingram, of PsyLED, Unit Eighteen."

"Ingram," he said back, as if committing it to memory. His eyes were a peculiar shade of blue that I figured would change with the light and with his emotions. His lashes were long and darker than his hair, and I had a feeling that he smiled often. A contented man.

Benjamin said, "I'd heard that Sam's widder-woman sister was with law enforcement. Accomplished. Competent. I didn't know she was such a beauty too."

And darn it if I didn't blush like a tomato. And hide behind my tea mug like I was twelve years old.

Benjamin flashed a set of straight teeth at me in a broader smile and swiveled his body to the head of the table. "Sam tells me you'uns got a new tiller, Brother Nicholson. What brand?"

The talk and all the attention fell away from me. I listened with half an ear and sipped my tea. Fifteen minutes after Benjamin and Sam arrived, I stifled a yawn, mumbled my good-byes, and got up, gathering my jacket and coat and hurrying from the Nicholson house. Outside in the bright dawn, I yanked on my winter coat and opened the car door.

Mud was curled up on the seat wrapped in a blanket that she must have brought from inside. Her hair was reddish like mine, still long and unbunned, saying that she was too young to be considered for marriage or concubinage, and for the menfolk to give the child a wide berth. She turned bright eyes to me. "You gonna marry Benjamin and move back home?"

I climbed in, pushing her small frame across the seat and shutting the door. I turned on the truck and eased away from the front of the house so I could make a fast getaway if needed. I turned the heater on high and parked on the side of the street, leaving the engine running. I had to be careful what I said to my sister, because Mud was just like me, whatever I was. Undifferentiated paranormal of some kind. And no way in hell would I allow her to be married in the church. I turned in the bench seat, bringing up my leg and leaning against the door.

"What's home, Mud?"

She squinched her eyes at me, thoughtful. "You mean like the address? Or 'Home is where the heart is'? Or, maybe home like the church compound? Or home where I'll marry and have babies?"

"None a them. My home is a lot of things. It's Soulwood—a plot of land that I claimed with my sweat and blood. Home is Unit Eighteen, a place I can work and be of use in the world, a place where I have value. Home is family I can come visit, but not be tied to. Home is *choice*. A chance to grow.

To learn. Home, meaning my life and where and how I'll live it. That's what home means to me, Mud."

"You don't wanna have babies?"

It was odd that Mud had picked up on that small part. "Not particularly. Or at least not now. I want the choice to determine when and where and if I'll have babies. Myself. Not some husband telling me what and where and when. If I have babies, I want it to be something that a husband and I choose together."

"Like birth control?" She leaned in closer and whispered, "I done heard that Imogene Watkins and her man is on birth control. And that if they take in another wife they'll make her use it too. That's a sin, ain't it?"

I said, "Mud, are you smart? Book learning smart?"

"Yep. Smartest girl my age."

"Smarter than the boys your age?"

Mud frowned as if comparing herself to men was a new and unexpected possibility. "I figger I am. What's that got to do with home?"

I knew this conversation was going to come back and hit me like a nail-studded two-by-four, but I had to say it. In for a penny . . . "Here on church grounds, living in God's Cloud, you will never be able to explore that intelligence. Chances are you will never go to college. You will never travel. You will never—"

It hit me, hard and fast as that two-by-four. I reached out and took her hands in mine. "You will never put your hands into any soil but that allowed by your husband." Mud's mouth fell open in dismay. "You will have baby after baby, sharing a home with one man and several women and lots of children. You will plant only with other women in the greenhouse. You will never be able to claim trees or land and feed it with your soul, sharing back and forth."

Mud whispered softly, "You'un can do that too? We'uns're really the same thing? The same kinda people?"

"Yes. And I can, maybe, help you learn how to control your gift. How to explore it. If that is what you want. But not if you stay at God's Cloud. Not if you live here. Not if you make church land your home instead of the whole world your home. You will have to choose what home is to you. You. Not the mamas or Daddy. You. You have to decide what you want."

"I ain't got no money. I can't buy no land."

I smiled. "If you want land, we'll get you land. But you have to decide what kind of life you want."

"And if I want babies and a husband and land too?"

"That would be your choice."

Mud pulled her hands free, rose to her knees, put her palms to either side of my face, and guided my head closer. She kissed me on the cheek, released me, opened the passenger door, and slipped into the day, the blanket around her shoulders flying in the cold breeze.

I wasn't sure what I had accomplished. Teaching a child to be free wasn't a matter of telling her once and being done. It was a long battle of opportunities offered and worldviews explored. And if this conversation came back and caused me trouble, then . . . I'd deal with it. I put the C10 in gear and headed out of the compound.

But all the way home, fighting sleep, I kept flashing back to the way Benjamin's eyes crinkled at the corners. And then instantly I'd see a vision of Occam, his too-long, shaggy blond hair swinging against his scruffy jaw, his brown-gold eyes watching me. And as I maneuvered up the mountain to Soulwood, I realized that Occam did indeed watch me. A lot. A real lot. Like a cat with his attention on prey.

The venison stew on the stove had filled the house with enticing scents, but I was too tired to care. I gave it a good stir, added wood to the stove, took a tepid shower to wash off the fire stink, and fell into the bed.

I woke to knocking at the door and I pulled a robe over my pajamas, picked up a shotgun, and went to the front of the house. It was Occam and I didn't like the way my heart leaped at the sight of his silhouette in the front window. I broke open the weapon and set it aside, unlatched the door, placed my body and face into the crack, and scowled at the wereleopard. "You ain't never heard of cell phones? People use 'em to announce visits, so that other people are dressed and presentable when guests arrive."

Occam held up a box of Krispy Kreme donuts and said, "The 'Hot Now' light was on. I got twelve." Pea climbed up to Occam's shoulder and sniffed the air, her black nose fluttering, her neon green coat catching the red sunset, turning an odd shade of olive brown. The grindylow showed up at the full moon, when the werecats were the most unpredictable, and also whenever they were about to have personal interactions with non-were-creatures.

My scowl went darker. I pointed to the box. "Still hot?"

"Pretty much."

"Bribe," I said.

"Totally, Nell, sugar."

"Okay. But you don't tell my mama I let you into the house while I was in my unmentionables." I shoved away from the door, swiped the donut box, and opened it on the way to the kitchen. The sweet dough was utterly wonderful and I stuffed a huge bite into my mouth and chewed. Without turning around, I closed my bedroom door on Occam and dressed in a hurry: navy pants, sturdy black field boots, a crisp white shirt worn tail out, with a belt around the waist. I also strapped on my weapon harness and grabbed a clean dark jacket. Presentable, I swiped another donut on the way to the bathroom, ignoring Occam, who said, "You'll ruin your dinner."

"You ain't my mama or my daddy, cat-man." I shut the bathroom door. Between bites, I washed my face, brushed my teeth, gooped up my hair, and put on some makeup. Work makeup, I told myself. Not Occam makeup. But it made my eyes look bright and kinda sparkly. I stopped at the entrance to the kitchen.

In the main room, Occam was stretched out on the couch, his cell in one hand, an empty bowl and spoon at his side. He had eaten some of my venison stew and made himself a cup of coffee. He looked all cat-graceful, and the term

languid came to mind. And *serenity*. As if he belonged here.
I felt my cheeks heat again. They were doing that a lot. To
cover my reaction and the blush I said crossly, "I see you
made yourself at home. I hope you liked the stew."

"Nell, sugar, it was amazing. Next time I bring down a
deer, I'll take an extra one and drag it to your door."

He was talking about bringing me a dead deer during the
full moon. In cat form. A deer I'd have to butcher. An act
that sounded a lot like a mating ritual for a big-cat. I scowled
at him. "No, thank you. I can skin a deer, but it takes all day,
working alone, without the proper tools. I got friends I can
buy venison from for the cost of the processing. You eat what
you kill. Just dispose of the remains in an appropriate location an' don't foul my water sources."

"Yes, ma'am," Occam said, sounding relaxed and Texan
and . . . extremely, extraordinarily manly. Macho even,
though I had never, ever used that term to describe a male.
The muscles of his arm bunched when he lifted a hand up
and shoved two couch pillows behind his head.

Torquil, the white mouser cat with the black helmet-
shaped head hair, had settled into his lap. Without looking
away from his cell, Occam petted the cat, his fingers long
with prominent knuckles. He looked . . . Not kind. Not peaceful. He looked a little dangerous. A predator in his den. Even
with a cat on his lap. Jezzie jumped to the sofa back and
walked along it, watching cat and werecat with predatory
interest. Occam's blond hair caught the light and his muscles
shifted again, just a bit, with the movements of his fingers.

I had a flash of curiosity, about what his fingers might feel
like if they touched my skin the way they stroked the cat. I
shook the thought away as totally unseemly and unacceptable.

Casually, or as casually as I could manage with the inappropriate thoughts I was having, I walked to the table, looked
at the donuts, and asked, "What's up?"

Occam looked up from his cell and gave me a grin that I
could only call rakish. It made me take a breath that was too
deep and somehow filled with electricity. I looked at the
donut in my hand as he pocketed his cell and rolled up from

the couch. He took a step toward me, the cat nestled in his arm. "Nell, sugar, I've been patient. I've been understanding of our cultural differences."

"Mmmm," I said, which meant nothing but was a noise Mama used to make when she was half listening. The donuts were fantastic. I wondered if I would be guilty of the sin of gluttony if I ate one more. And if I should care. I took another.

Occam took another step toward me. "Nell."

My head came up fast and I forgot all about donuts. There was something in his tone that stole all my interest.

"I've given you time to think things through and cement your position in the unit. I've done all the things T. Laine and JoJo said a cat needed to do to let you be comfortable with me."

My eyes went wide. *Lainie and Jo had done* what?

"But I'm done huntin'. Done stalking. Done being patient. I've said it before, and I'm saying it again. I want to take you to dinner, Nell, sugar. I want to date you."

My hand was still holding the donut, paused halfway to my mouth, which hung open. Slowly, I closed my mouth and set the ring of uneaten fried dough on the table. Jezzie bounded across the tops of the furniture to the table and batted the donut to the floor. Pea jumped after it, a neon green flash. I didn't even care.

"What?" My voice croaked and I cleared my throat, but I didn't repeat the word.

"I want. To take. You. To dinner," he repeated, separating the words just enough to make sure that I understood them. "On a date. Casual, easy, something simple but tasty. I was thinking maybe the French Market Crêperie or Chesapeake's. Tonight. It's a weeknight so we should be able to get in without reservations on your way to work."

"I—um. I thought you had changed your mind," I said, my voice sounding odd as I remembered the two of us, lying on the concrete in the dark, between the planters. He hadn't said anything then and that would have been a good time to renew a discussion of dating. Or maybe not, with bullets

flying. It had been weeks since he'd asked for that date. Was
I supposed to bring it up next? Was there a date protocol I
didn't know about?

I remembered his eyes on me from time to time in the
office. "Ummm," I said, my thoughts flashing. What was I
supposed to do? "I'm a widd—" I stopped. Remembering
my family's house, the boisterous happiness of domestic
clatter. And Benjamin. Suddenly oxygen deprived, I took
another breath and this one quaked slightly as it went down.
Occam tilted his head, watching me, analyzing me, one hand
still soothing Torquil, standing in front of me, otherwise
motionless, waiting.

His expression made me analyze myself, my own feelings.
I *was* feeling something. Unfamiliar somethings. Curious.
Interested. Resistant. Stubborn. Vulnerable. And suddenly
thinking about Benjamin, the man Mama surely wanted me
with. And how he would know and understand my odd
quirks of reticence, my lack of sophistication. How he would
be patient and kind and funny and fit into the old life I had
left behind with such ease. How he would never push me.
Would keep me sheltered. Protected. In a home on church
lands. That wasn't what I wanted. Benjamin wasn't what I
wanted. But . . . I was aware of who he was and what he
represented in terms of safety and effortlessness, of who he
was as the man introduced to me by my family. Sam's friend.
Someone I had met from the past. Someone who represented
familiarity and simplicity. Someone easy. *Someone safe.*

Occam represented something totally different. A date.
A future that was absolutely unknown. And he had taken
advice from T. Laine and JoJo to back off and give me time.
Time I thought meant he wasn't interested anymore. That
had probably been the wrong advice.

"Nell, sugar?"

I blinked and my eyes burned. I'd been staring so long
they had dried out. Beside Occam on the reading table was
a library book that had been there over a week. There was
a thin layer of dust on top. It had been suggested to me by
Kristy, a librarian and my friend. It was a book by a psy-

chologist and it dealt with victims of polygamy, incest, child marriage, sexual slavery, and rape. It was hard reading. I hadn't gotten very far in it. But I had learned that abuse victims often formed negative patterns of thinking and feeling and living, and could sometimes be lured back to what the author called "unhealthy lifestyles and situations." I blinked again. *That was why I was thinking about Benjamin.*

"Ohhh," I said. From a strictly intellectual standpoint, I understood that my own confusion and reticence to fully enter the nonchurch world was pattern based, but that didn't make the patterns go away.

"Ohhh," I said again. "Ummm." This time I cleared my voice. "A date? You sure? Like normal people?"

"Nell, sugar, you and me, we ain't normal. We're paranormal. Übernormal."

"You and me? What's Pea say?"

He pointed. "She's right there. Ask her."

I looked at the grindylow, who had finished off the donut. She leaped to the tabletop and bounded to the Krispy Kreme box. Her five-fingered hands, vaguely raccoon-shaped but with opposable thumbs, struggled to open the box top. "Donuts are bad for you," I said.

The grindy chittered at me, sounding as if she was telling me to mind my own business. She pushed the top up. With one hand-paw, she scratched the sugar from the edge of the box and lifted it to her mouth, where she licked it off. Her tongue wasn't red. It was an odd shade of green. Had it been that color before?

"Is it okay for me to date Occam?" I asked her. At the words a hot blush shot through me. "Would I get the weretaint if we . . ." I swallowed, not able to say the sex word. ". . . dated?"

Pea looked me straight in the eyes and chittered. She abandoned the donut box and trotted to me, where she stood on her hind legs and stretched up with her front hands. I took her up in my arms and she sniffed my mouth, around under my ears on both sides, and up under my hair, where the leaves grew when I read the land. Her fur tickled; her nose was damp and cold. She made odd, high-pitched mewls and moans that might have been some kind of language. She spun in my arms and leaped across to Occam, covering far more distance than her limbs and build suggested she could. She scampered up Occam's chest, shoving Torquil off her perch, and sat on the werecat's arm, nose to nose. She chittered again, and then leaped back to the table, giving her total concentration to the donut box and its sweet contents. She extended a single steel claw and speared a donut, pulling it out onto the tabletop, where she bit into the sugary dough, leaving a narrow, V-shaped, toothy bite. Ignoring us. Leaving us to . . . what?

When I looked up from the table, Occam had moved. Silent. Predatory. He stood in front of me, far enough away for me not to feel like prey. But close enough to feel the heat of his body. Far too close. I raised my eyes from his chest, slowly, to his face. His lips were laughing and challenging, a hint of cat-gold in the depths of his eyes. His voice a purr of sound, Occam said, "Pea says you can't get were-taint if we . . . dated," Occam said.

A funny feeling sat on my chest, like an electric elephant, charged and heavy. The feeling began to spread out and up. And raced to my fingertips in a tingling uncertainty.

Occam moved closer. "Nell, sugar. I aim to kiss you now." He leaned in, slowly. One hand came up, even more slowly, as if he thought I might break and run. He placed the hand on my cheek, the body heat of the werecat warm. His hand was smooth, skin over bone with strong knuckles. His fingers caressed from the corner of my eye down. Across my jaw.

His eyes held mine. So close I could see the specks of gold and brown in his amber eyes. His breath feathered across my face, smelling of the sweetness of donuts. He moved closer. Closer still. His lips were almost touching mine. Almost. Not quite. He smiled slightly. "Nell, you act like you never been kissed before."

"I ain't—I haven't. Not like . . . Not like this."

Occam's pupils widened a little. Shock traveled through his body and hand to me.

I said, "John pretty much took what he wanted. He wasn't mean. He jist—*just*—wasn't kind or gentle."

"Hell, Nell." Occam's eyes darkened. "You never been romanced?"

I thought about the other books I had read. Romance novels. Books filled with passion. With need. With sex that both partners wanted. And I thought about Yummy and her interest in Occam. "No."

"Ohhh. Sugar." His hand slid around my head, to my nape. His palm cupped my head. Carefully, he stood so his body didn't touch me. His lips lowered the fraction of an inch. Touched mine. Warm, gentle. They slid across my mouth. Heated. Not chapped. Not demanding. Not hard.

I smiled against his mouth. And leaned in to the kiss. Something like electricity leaped from Occam to me. Electric heat spun through me. Down my limbs to my toes and my fingertips. Like a flurry of snow caught in a whirlwind, if snow were made of sparks. Back up to my belly, where the warmth and charged flurries pooled, low down.

I breathed out a sound I didn't know I was going to make, half moan, half surprised pleasure. Occam's other hand caught my face, holding me tenderly between his cupped palms. His thumbs caressed both cheeks. I closed my eyes. His tongue licked across my lips. My mouth opened and his tongue slid along and inside my lips, across my teeth.

I touched my tongue to his.

He stopped. Froze in place for a heartbeat or ten. I slid my tongue along his, testing the texture and the shape. His tongue moved. Following mine like a dance.

My breath was coming fast. Fear and excitement trembled through me. My cell buzzed and I jumped halfway into the kitchen. So did Occam's. The werecat cursed softly, and we both pulled our cells.

I read the group text from Rick aloud. "Debrief in sixty. No exceptions." I didn't look up before I added softly, "So much for a date." The word felt odd on my tongue, as if it didn't belong there. Like the kiss. One not sanctioned by family or church or contract for marriage. *Negative lifestyle patterns.* I wasn't certain if I was relieved or disappointed. I touched my mouth. Looked up at Occam.

"Temporary delay, Nell, sugar. Temporary delay."

"But that was a very proper kiss." I felt my mouth form a surprised and satisfied smile as I turned to the kitchen.

I put the Dutch oven in the fridge, gathered up my gobag and coat, and followed Occam out of the house. Thinking. I could eat a meal with Occam. I could. I had kissed him. Not because I was supposed to, or had Daddy's permission to, or had wifely duties to perform, but because I wanted to. So. Dinner. Though I might not swallow a single thing. I might just push food around on my plate nervously. But I could sit at a table with him. I could kiss him again. Maybe.

SIX

The EOD—end-of-day debrief—was short and full of nothing much. While we ate pizza from the "All" shelf, Rick spoke. "PsyLED isn't lead agency for the investigations, but it's probably only a matter of time. So I want each of you to keep up with all interagency findings. First up is the fire at the Justin Tolliver home. Initial testing results are uncertain regarding accelerant on-site. However, consistent with the way the fire spread, investigators are still looking at the possibility of an accelerant-induced fire, deliberately set. I want the Tollivers' lives combed through. FBI has financials, offshore accounts, cumulative debt, life insurance, trust funds, extramarital affairs, friends, lovers, enemies. I want us to take their data and sift it. Find out if this is part of the restaurant shooting and the Holloways' party shooting, an accident, or just an opportunity taken by an unhappy spouse or family member or business partner.

"Pierced Dreams. JoJo? Casings? Physical evidence?"

JoJo punched a key on her laptop. "All the casings collected from the shooting sites have been tested for fingerprints and all were clean. The shooter used gloves from the beginning of the process to the end, likely nitrile, according to the tech who looked at them under a scope. Nitrile can leave swipe marks that cotton won't, and nitrile is more common these days for shooters, since it gives good tactile sensation. All the casings matched. Same gauge, same brand of ammunition, further indicating that we have only one shooter. None of this has been released to the media so unless someone at one of the hospitals talks about the caliber they pulled out of the victims, we're good on keeping this part of the shooter's MO under wraps." To Rick she added, "I'm putting on weight. You gotta stop picking up pie from Elidios'."

The SAC's face softened into an almost-smile and I realized how seldom Rick had actually relaxed since he got back from New Orleans on his last trip. I needed to call his ex-girlfriend and my only almost-friend who lived outside of Knoxville. There might be things I needed to know.

As if the near-smile had been her goal, JoJo said, "On to physical evidence. We have three cigarette butts from the Carhart Building, all the same brand, but recovered from a location that would make the shots fired difficult to make, about twenty feet from the nearest casing. I'm guessing that someone in the building takes illegal ciggie breaks up there, but the butts have been sent to the forensics lab for possible DNA evidence. A lot of fast-food wrappers and empty water bottles, a used condom, and two flip-flops, both of them left feet, one orange, one white with skulls on it, were also bagged from the Carhart roof. From the roof of the other building, Occam and his vampire partner recovered a tarnished key, three old marbles, a stick of pink chalk, a pair of men's underwear—briefs, size medium—an old faded ID, possibly a Michigan driver's license from the seventies—"

"Anything pertinent to the case?" Rick interrupted.

"Not a thing. But it's all gone to FBI labs for workup."

Rick thumbed through printed reports on his table. "What do we have on the number of threatening e-mails and letters and their writers provided by the senator's office and by Ming of Glass' personal assistant?"

Tandy said, "There were no overlaps between the two. No name appeared on both lists," he clarified. "No similar handwriting. No similar e-mail addresses. The feds eliminated four serious death threat contenders for the senator, and according to my research, one is in jail, one's dead, one's too disabled to be our shooter, and one's living in the Pacific Northwest, working in a marijuana bar and too stoned to want to travel. Fifteen others they eliminated based on lack of skill set. We eliminated another dozen based on them being human, wrong general body type (too tall, too short, major weight difference from the blurry images we have to date), or with alibis that checked out on initial inspection. We still have about twenty on the original list of possible suspects."

"And on Ming of Glass' list?" Rick asked.

"Hate groups. Nothing that looks like a lone attacker. More like big talking, but if they really did attack, it would be a direct ambush with numbers on the attackers' side. Nothing that looks like they would be willing to produce collateral damage while trying to kill fangheads. Humans First. DTF—Death to Fangheads. Homegrown hate and fear. And nothing that links the victims, according to the feds, who are following up on that angle."

I took another piece of the wonderful pizza and listened with half an ear. The meeting dragged on for another hour until Rick finally asked, "Anyone got anything else?" When no one responded, the meeting ended with Rick's orders. "All leave and time off is canceled until this is resolved and we have someone behind bars. All agencies are getting pressure from above to resolve it fast. Like yesterday. We'll be pulling twelve-hour shifts, sixteen to twenty if needed, as of tonight. At the start of your next shifts, bring gear to catch naps here if necessary. T. Laine picked up four air mattresses and if the case gets too demanding, we'll designate a room somewhere for everyone to crash."

I tried not to think about how we would divide up the sleeping space if both women and men needed to sleep at the same time, though I realized that was probably an outmoded notion of propriety under the emergency circumstances. And I realized that through the meeting, I hadn't thought once about Occam. Or Benjamin. Or the future as a lonely widderwoman. I sat a bit straighter. That was good. It had to be.

Rick stood, his movements more lithe than yesterday, more relaxed than last month, before he learned to shift into his black wereleopard. He was healing too, his body having put on weight, his face not quite so deeply lined this close to the full moon. He wasn't fully healed, but he was getting there. Rick leaned forward, his fingertips splayed on the table, his weight forward, pressing on them. "We'll be split into two divisions, each with a.m. agents and p.m. agents. One team member will be office detail, one will be field. Office agent will be in the office at all times, to collate information, co-ordinate efforts, and keep comms open. For the time being, one person will be with the senator and his extended family, including his wife and kid, his brother, his wife, and their kids, at all times, which means his house at night and his office by day. One person will liaise with the FBI team when-ever possible. There are seven of us—" He stopped abruptly. Paka, his faithless, backstabbing, wereleopard ex-mate, was gone. She would not be back if she wished to live. "Six. Seven with Soul, who will be coordinating with the feds and filling in as needed. It'll be tight but we can do it.

"I want JoJo in the office by day. Tandy, you'll pull office coordinator on night shift. Occam, I want you to collate reports tonight, but cut it short. You'll be with the senator by day, and T. Laine can spell you or split the assignment when the family isn't all in one place. Nell, you'll have to start early tonight and work long. I want you to ride by the Holloways' house and check the dead vegetation left by our shooter, then go by Justin Tolliver's and check for similar readings there. Make it fast. You're first on night shift at the senator's home, and he's on the way there now with a mo-torcade. I've sent you the GPS and address. Read the land if you can without making it obvious. I don't want you to take heat for being a para. Main purpose? Get a feel for things so you can spot anything new, anything that changes." He held up a hand when I started to protest. "I know grass doesn't spot anything new, doesn't understand changes, short of fire and chain saws. I get it. Read it anyway. Confirm a baseline."

"Yes, sir." Even I heard my tone. It wasn't as respectful as it should be. The thought that I had been rude to Daddy and enjoyed it a bit too much flashed through my mind. The thought that I had kissed Occam flashed through too.

Rick frowned at me. "Is there a problem, probie?"

"No, sir. Except that we're stretched thin, since before you left for New Orleans. A little help might be nice. Why not ask Soul for a few people from Unit Twelve or Unit Fifteen? Especially if you think you're going to be sent back to NOLA for the vampire Sangre Duello."

Around the table, the team members were suddenly bent over tablets or taking notes by hand on pads. I frowned at them, trying to figure out what I had said.

Rick had grown up in New Orleans, knew it like the back of his hand. He and Soul had been sent to NOLA when a ship full of European vampires had attempted to debark from a cruise ship without proper or official papers. There had been bloodshed and political ramifications. And—though it hadn't hit the media yet, and was something I knew only because I had access to Jane Yellowrock, a source not regulated by my low security clearance—the Master of the City of New Orleans was about to go up against the European emperor in a blood duel—Sangre Duello.

In the middle of the tense silence, I realized that no one in Unit Eighteen had ever spoken of the vampire war or the European vampires or NOLA around Rick. It was clear he had come back to Knoxville a quietly grieving man. He'd been sent packing by Yellowrock. She hadn't been his first love, but she had, perhaps, been his most significant. It was complicated. The Sangre Duello was a sensitive subject, most of which was above my pay grade. And I had just galloped into all those complications like a barrel rider on a fast horse.

Stiffly, Rick said, "Soul is aware of our staffing situation. We'll get help if this goes on much longer."

"Ummm. Okay?"

T. Laine rolled her eyes and took a slice of pizza, muttering something that sounded like, "Family dynamics suck."

Without meeting Occam's eyes, I escaped the meeting.

Two hours later, I pulled in and checked out possible parking at the senator's home. Sequoyah Hills was where the movers and shakers of Knoxville lived. If your home was on Chero-

kee Boulevard, the address itself said you had old money and
political ties. The senator's home, like his brother's burned
one only a few miles away, backed up to the Tennessee River.

I parked on the grass, got out, and gave my ID to the
guard, who was a local cop, working after hours—heavy,
about five-ten, with brown eyes. I almost remembered his
name, but it wouldn't come, and his name tag was hidden by
the lapel of his winter coat. But I had met him when he pulled
guard duty not that long ago, in a neighborhood full of slime
mold and dead animals. Sharing territory with cops from
different levels of law enforcement can be difficult. He had
been easy to work with, and gestured me onto the grounds
with, "We looking for a fanghead or a witch?"

"Why would we be looking for a vampire or a witch?" I
asked, not sure from his tone if he was a paranormal hater.

"They sent *you*." He shoved his hands into his pockets
and led me down the drive.

"Ah." That made sense. Paras were PsyLED's area of
expertise. "Neither. Not sure what we're looking for right
now. Except dead plants."

He looked around the yard and said, "Everything's dead."

Midway, I stopped and he stopped with me. "Not dead.
Dormant."

"There's a difference?"

We both took in the well-manicured but brown centipede
lawn and the expensive imported plants. The inner borders
of the property had been landscaped with river rock and
planted with dozens of varieties of grasses, including feather
reed grass, fountain grass, little bluestem, and purple millet,
in an appealing array of heights and colors, with three bird-
baths, and with birdhouses nailed to the trees everywhere.
The bare branches suggested mostly maple varieties close
in, with tall, skinny conifers behind them to provide a shield
from the neighbors' yards. Beneath and around the trees at
the garage I spotted low hostas, sedges, and rounded mounds
of winter-dead flowers, most in winter-dormant phase, protected by mulch. There was a rose garden that encircled a
bow-windowed breakfast room, through which I could see

a number of kids and three men in the black of ALT Security, as well as a man in a suit, guarding. I made a note to look at JoJo's file on ALT employees again. I turned around and around slowly, taking more in.

The main house was spectacular—three stories with a round turret-like thing on one side, river rock and brick construction, added on to several times, remodeled often. The garage held six cars. The drive and walkways were made of river pebbles in white concrete. I walked around back to see a lap pool on the left, a hot tub on the right, and a much bigger, heated pool in the middle, with water slides, swing ropes, and brightly colored inner tubes floating on top. The tennis court was on the far side of the house.

The guesthouse was on the river side of the pools, but situated to not affect the view from the house, and looked exactly as described, with three small bedrooms and a big, open living area. Security lights illuminated the grounds; more light poured out through the windows. It looked as if Justin and family were living in the guesthouse.

The landscaping was stunning, with all the grasses at different heights and the outer windbreaks made of fir trees in irregular rows: Douglas, Fraser, noble, and balsam, some native to Tennessee and some not, but scattered to look like a natural fir forest. The grasses were equally local and imported and of varying heights. It was pretty, but it was the kind of landscaping that made security a nightmare. The firs and grasses gave privacy, but also provided cover for an attacker. Or an attacking army.

"Yes. There's a big difference. Have the K9 dogs been over the property?"

"Just left. You gonna tell me what we're looking for?" There was just enough tone to imply that I might be keeping secrets, the kind that could get a fellow officer killed.

No one had said not to talk to cops, but I knew to be circumspect. And cautious. "Our attacker is human-shaped. Impossible to see clearly on security cameras, so some kind of magical shielding might be involved. Or not. He— assuming a male from the way he moves—may or may not be working alone. But there is a possibility that he kills vegetation. Maybe not all the time. Maybe it's coincidence."

"But you don't think so," he pressed.

I shrugged. I had been by the Holloways' home before I came here, and also by the burned hulk of the Tollivers' house. There were trails of dead vegetation in both places, along with crime scene tape and private security guards walking the perimeters, avoiding the dead zones by instinct. They just looked wrong.

On the way to the senator's home, I had also taken a roundabout way, across the Gay Street Bridge and motoring down West Jackson Avenue and South Central. There were dead plants all up and down the street. I had reported it to Rick, who had fallen silent. We had no idea what we were dealing with, and if we didn't know, then we didn't want to scare the public or the local law with guesses or half-baked theories. Yet.

"Did the dogs spot anything?" I asked.

"They acted odd. I don't know much about dogs, but one, a springer, kept sitting down. That mean anything?"

"Probably," I said. "Maybe it'll be in the morning reports."

"How does he kill plants? Herbicide?"

I stared around at the grasses and the trees. So far as I could tell, nothing was dead here. I sighed and looked at the officer. "I haven't been told anything about the methodology." That wasn't a lie but it wasn't the truth either. I knew the shooter wasn't using herbicide. "If I learn anything pertinent that's more than just guesswork, I'll share if they let me. You'll look for dead plants and tell me if you see anything odd. Deal?"

The officer mulled that over, while checking the perimeter. His eyes moved back and forth, avoiding the lighted areas that might decrease his night vision. Former military. I could tell without asking. He swiveled back to me. "Deal."

I extended my hand. "Nell Ingram." Not Special Agent Ingram. Just my name. That made it personal.

"Phil Joss." We shook.

"I need to read the property with the psy-meter. Okay by you?"

"Have at it, lady." He walked away, a heavy man swaddled in a heavy coat, on protection detail on a cold night. I wondered if anyone would bring us coffee.

Not sure how Phil Joss felt about paranormals, I decided to hide my lack of humanity. I placed my blanket on the brown lawn, opened the psy-meter 2.0, which I had already calibrated, and placed my cell phone beside it, open to take notes. I held the machine's wand up to the north. And was hit with a spike, strong, potent. Level four shot high, redlining. I leaped to my feet, attracting Phil's attention. And then the spike of energy was gone.

"Ingram?" he asked as he sprinted over, his weapon in one hand, held down at his side.

I shook my head and held the wand to the north again. Nothing. Not a blessed thing. I checked to the east, south, and west. Nothing. "I don't know. I got a spike, but it's gone. I'm going to walk around the property. Take measurements all over."

"Hang on. I'll get someone to go with you. He's a rookie, but he's better than nothing." Phil's tone suggested that the rookie was not *much* better than nothing, but he was what we had. He removed his radio and said, "Culpepper. To my twenty."

"Roger that. On my way."

Less than a minute later, a tall rangy kid with a shock of hair the color of new pennies walked up, covering a lot of ground with each step. "Joss. What's up?"

"This is Ingram. PsyLED. She needs cover while she takes paranormal readings. You stay with her and keep watch. Try to keep her from getting shot. And yourself too." The last part sounded like an afterthought.

Culpepper seemed to think so too, but he pulled on the

hem of his jacket and tilted his head until his skinny neck popped. "On it." He looked at me, waiting.

I indicated the driveway with my head and said, "Let's start at the drive and work counterclockwise around the perimeter. Then we'll decide where to go next."

Culpepper nodded and I tossed my pink blanket over my shoulder, made sure my weapon was secured. Then I led him back to the front of the property. I was making decisions, setting up game plans, and that was wrong. I was a probie. I got the scut work. The jobs no one else wanted. In dangerous situations I wasn't supposed to be senior agent on-site. But here I was, senior PsyLED agent where evidence suggested that a bad guy might be. I had learned that the things I was taught in Spook School weren't always practiced in the real world.

Back at the street I checked the machine against Culpepper, who was purely human. Then I started walking, watching the readings, waiting for a spike.

Culpepper asked, "Why counterclockwise?"

Not taking my eyes off the levels, I said, "If there's a witch working on-site, walking clockwise, also called sunwise, might activate it." From the corner of my eye I saw him flinch. The rookie had no idea he could set off a witch working. I held in a sigh, still talking, taking a chance to educate the kid. Who couldn't be more than twenty—only three years younger than me, but oceans apart from me in experience. "Widdershins, or counterclockwise, also called lefthandwise, is less likely to blow up in our faces. Keep an eye out."

His hand on his weapon—as if that would help against a spell—Culpepper followed in my footsteps. He moved in jerky uncoordinated jolts and lurches, as if he expected to be attacked at any moment. He was especially twitchy beneath the fir trees and in the tall grasses, so at least he knew where physical attacks were likely to originate.

I didn't get a single spike on the psy-meter 2.0. As the minutes passed, I began to wonder if the machine was broken.

I checked it against myself and got a low level four reading, so that part was working. I needed to run full quality control on it by testing it against weres and witches. Maybe a vampire, if I could get one to come by.

But since there was only one vampire I might feel halfway willing to call, and Yummy would probably scare the human cops, I decided against calling anyone. When I finished the perimeter search, I said to Culpepper, "I need to read the land while sitting on the ground."

He looked at me quizzically and said, "Okay by me. I'll wait over there." He pointed to a nearby tree and moved to it, light-footed as a hunter after deer, now that the threat of a spell attack had been ruled out. A lot of local boys hunted. I'd bet my pink blanket that Culpepper had been born into a hunting family.

I found a comfy spot, out of the way of the security lights, and began to check the ground, my way, by reading the land. Sitting on the blanket, the psy-meter open in front of me as if I were still using it, my hands in the soil, I found nothing dead or dying. No indication that one of the creatures had been on the property at all. Not anywhere. I sighed and sat back on my blanket.

"Hi."

I nearly flew off the ground. Spun around, going for my weapon. The form of a woman was limned by the security lights.

"I didn't mean to startle you." It was Sonya Tolliver, in her robe and house shoes. Culpepper was still in place, his back to me, checking his phone. *Idiot*.

I let go of my service weapon, remembered how to breathe, and caught the strong smell of perfume that the cats had mentioned. It wasn't unpleasant, but there was a lot of it. I said, "Nell Ingram, PsyLED, ma'am."

She didn't introduce herself, but she probably knew that no one on the grounds needed her to. She said, "I can't sleep."

"I can see how sleep would be difficult. You've had a bad few days."

"Yes," she said, her voice growing sad. "It's been difficult. I suppose it always is when someone loses everything they hold dear."

I didn't know what to say to that so I stayed silent.

"I saw you. At the fire. You told Justin I needed him."

"Ummm. I've been known to have a big mouth, ma'am."

Sonya Tolliver laughed, a despondent sound. "But in this case, accurate." She reached up and pulled her hair around, tugging it out of the collar of her robe. It was long with reddish tints. "He used to be there for me. We used to be there for each other. Now he's . . . distant. My husband is involved with work and . . ." She looked into the night. "I hope it's only with work."

I remembered the questions about the stability of the Tolliver marriage and what a burned house might mean to the finances of a distressed relationship on the verge of divorce.

Sonya looked out over the property toward the river at the back. "We used to go fly-fishing together. Camping. We'd pitch our tent on the bank of a stream, light a campfire, fish, and eat the catch if the season was right. And s'mores. We used to love s'mores. S'mores by moonlight." She walked a few paces past me, staring at the back of the property and the river. I could hear it, lapping softly, a faint splash of fish or muskrat jumping. "Then the children came. Camping became a lot more difficult. And now we seem to have grown apart. We haven't been camping in years."

She fell silent, and I tried to figure out how to keep her talking. "I was married. John died a few years back." I went to stand near her. "No children." She didn't reply. "John was older than me. There wasn't much leaning on each other at all until he got sick. Then I was his nurse. And he passed."

"Are you alone now? No husband? No boyfriend? No family?" Her tone said she found that thought unfathomable.

"Family nearby, but I live alone," I said.

"Do you like it?" She turned to me, finding my face in the dark. "Living alone? I can't imagine how I'd ever live alone."

"I like it okay. I like the quiet."

Sonya made a thoughtful sound in the back of her throat and we fell silent. "Are we in danger? Well, I know we're in danger. But . . ." She pulled her robe even tighter. "Are they going to get to us? What if they use a drone or a long-scope rifle like in that movie?"

I didn't know what movie she meant, but I said, "We're doing all we can to keep your family safe, ma'am."

"Thank you." Sonya turned and walked back to the guest-house. I heard the door close.

Culpepper was nowhere to be seen. So much for backup.

The night was long, frozen, and coffeeless. And tedious, mind-numbing, and boring. When the hours moved along toward dawn, I picked up my blanket and went back to my car, where I wrote my report about speaking to Sonya, while yawning, and listening to country music on a local radio station.

I was stumbling on my feet the next morning when Occam showed up, arriving early, just after sunrise. I was so tired I didn't even care that he wanted to date me. That we had kissed. I just plodded to his fancy car and checked the psy-meter 2.0 against his were-energies. I decided that the machine was working, but couldn't rule out that it was giving false positives, which was no help at all. I grumped that out, gave him my notes, and trudged back to my truck, exhausted, frozen, and annoyed. This case was likely to bore me to death.

Unfortunately for my exhaustion and state of mind, Rick pulled up before I left. I glared at him when he tapped on my truck window, but rolled the glass down and turned off the noisy truck. "What?"

He chuckled softly. "Long night?"

"No coffee. Humans are scared of their own shadows. Psy-meter is acting strange. And I'm sleepy." *And Occam kissed me. Wants to date me.* Not said.

Occam trotted up, his gait long and lean. "Morning, boss. What's up?" he asked.

Speaking softly enough that his voice wouldn't carry out of our small group, Rick said, "The dogs indicated that a paranormal creature of unknown species was at every one of the incident sites. I got a good whiff of the Tollivers' pillows at their burned house. The master suite was in a protected area away from flames and water damage. Justin smells human. His wife, Sonya, wears a lot of perfumed products, but underneath it all, she doesn't smell human. Not quite. I've never smelled that scent before, but I'm betting that she's a para of unknown species."

My sleepiness took a hit of adrenaline and I woke up fast. I had talked to Sonya. And just before that, the psy-meter had spiked. But I hadn't actually measured Sonya with it. My mind raced through the possible ways that Justin's wife might have fired on the Holloway party while being a guest, burned her own home, and shot up Old City. She had been placed in the dining room at the Holloways' when the shooting started. She was with Justin during the Pierced Dreams shooting. She was home with Justin eating dinner when the fire started and had been with her family for a good forty minutes prior. "There's no way she could have done the attacks. And we've all agreed that the shooter looks and moves like a man," I said.

"Partner?" Rick asked.

"We weren't present when the FBI and Secret Service spoke with Justin and Sonya," Occam said. "I doubt we'll be allowed to bring them in for questioning."

"We need to be careful," Rick said. "We've got law enforcement overlap, political complications, and pressure from up-line to not upset the applecart. Funding is a never-ending issue, and Abrams Tolliver is a big proponent of funding PsyLED. We don't want to offend him by bringing in his sister-in-law."

"Or outing her," I said, "if she's still in the closet. Her husband may not know."

"If we have to arrest her, that might offend the senator," Occam said, with a bit of insolence in his tone. "But if we don't arrest her and her alleged partner shoots him, that might offend the senator even more."

"So, let's posit that Sonya Tolliver is an unknown paranormal creature. Then maybe there are more of them," I said. "Maybe the same kind of creature is tracking and attacking the Tolliver family." I thought of the church and the way the churchmen had chased me. "Maybe she got away and they want her back. Or maybe they are protecting her. Or maybe lots of things."

Rick had been checking our perimeter, his eyes traveling but his head unmoving. Satisfied we were unobserved, he withdrew his hand from his jacket with an odd, dull, crinkling sound. He was holding a gallon-sized plastic zipped bag, the air smoothed out, a wad of cloth inside. A pillowcase. Rick had stolen Sonya Tolliver's pillowcase. "Get a good whiff," he instructed Occam.

The werecat took the bag, hitched his hip against the truck as if to get comfy, opened the bag, and ducked his head to it. "Hooo," he said, making a face. "Musky. That's pungent." He passed it to me.

I stuck my nose in, expecting to get an awful scent as part of the boys' "Here, this stinks—you smell!" game. I caught a hint of body odor and something a little like pond water. I thought back to the house and the grounds. There had been fishing equipment and the kayak behind the shed. "I smell river water. The river is close enough that the scent shouldn't count. There's nothing here that reminds *me* of the assassin."

"Your nose ain't any better than a human's, Nell, sugar."

I shrugged and passed the zip bag back.

Rick said to Occam, "If you get a chance to read the senator's house, I want you to sniff around. In case there are paras passing as human living there too."

"Yeah, that's gonna go over real good with the Secret Service. 'Hey, you, Texas boy werecat,'" Occam said in a passable nasal Jersey accent. "'What da hell you doin' sniffin' da senator's laundry?'"

Rick didn't laugh. "Don't get caught. Nell's right. If Sonya really is a paranormal, and still in the closet, then we might have an intra- or interspecies war brewing. The senator is working for pro-paranormal legislation. We need to keep him safe. And if someone in his family is paranormal and he knew it and didn't reveal it to the Senate Ethics Committee—"

"He could lose his position, which would hurt paranormals everywhere. It's to our benefit to keep him alive and healthy. Got it, boss." Occam winked at me and walked away.

I looked back and forth between the two werecats, absorbing the possible ramifications of the senator's family having a paranormal. In the middle of an internal or external war. Or launching a war. Or . . . Or I was too tired to think. I turned on the truck and the heater, and went home. Somehow I made it home alive, which meant Mama musta been praying for me because I'm sure I slept the whole way.

It was three p.m. when I woke to the sound of banging. I half fell out of bed, grabbed my shotgun, and stumbled to the front of the house, where I spotted Mud through the window, on the front porch, no coat, arms crossed over her chest, and three cats weaving around her legs. I put the gun away, located my service weapon hanging in its holster and shoulder rig on a kitchen chair, to make sure they were secure, and opened the door. The cats ran in, silent, twitchy, irritated. I'd left them out all day. "Mud?"

"You'uns need a dog."

"A dog," I said, feeling as if I'd missed something.

"To bark. To tell you'un when company's here." She looked at me as if I was stupid.

"I had dogs . . ." I stopped. The churchmen had killed my dogs, leaving the dead bodies on my front porch, about where Mud was standing. If I looked closely at the grain, I could still see the blood. Was Mud too young to know that? I decided not. "The churchmen killed them as a warning that I had to come back to the church and marry in." When she only frowned at me and hunched her shoulders harder, I asked, "Why are you here without a coat? And how did you get here?" I leaned out to verify that there was no car in the drive, no dust hanging in the air. "What happened?"

"I walked over the hill. It's gotta be some ten miles," she hyperbolized. "And your'n tree happened," she said.

She had to be talking about the vampire tree. The one that used to be an oak. When I got shot the tree had access to my blood and recognized my imminent death. The oak had healed me. Had changed me somehow. And my blood had changed it, making it . . . something more. Something scary.

"It killed another dog," Mud said, leaning in toward me, pugnacious, truculent. *Truculent* was one of Daddy's words. "It was a *puppy*," Mud shouted. Tears gathered in her eyes, welled up, and spilled over, down her cheeks. "One a the Jenkinses' puppies. Mama said I could have it. And your'n tree *killed it!*" She screeched the last two words. Tears splashed on her dress.

And . . . I realized her hair was up. Bunned up. High on her head. Like a woman grown.

"Ohhh," I whispered. "Oh no." I held the door wide and Mud rushed inside. I stared out into the glare of day. My mind blank. Empty.

Mud had started her menstrual cycle today. That was the only reason she would have her hair up. According to the way the church used to be run, that meant Mud was now old enough to enter the marriage market. *Mud was only twelve.* Had the church changed enough that she would be safe? Were the church elders still marrying off young girls in what was legally and morally statutory rape? Would Daddy say no? Defend her? Daddy was sick. What if he died? Who would protect the young Nicholson girls?

Moving woodenly, I closed the door. Followed Mud into the house, my feet icy on the wood floor. I put wood in the firebox, on top of a few glowing coals. Put on water to heat for tea. Wrapped an afghan and a warm blanket around Mud on the couch and tucked it in tight on her legs. Gave her one of John's old handkerchiefs. It was soft and neatly folded, frayed around the edges. She blew her nose, honking like a goose. I almost reached out and touched her bun, the way I might touch a thorn that could prick me. Jerked my hand back and raced to my room, threw on clothes. Trying to think. Trying to figure out what to say. What to do. The tree. The puppy. Mud with her hair bunned up.

I pulled on wool socks. For the first time in forever, I put my hand on the wood of the floor and said a prayer, to God, this time. Not to Soulwood. Asking for wisdom. Trees, no matter how ancient, weren't good with words. Maybe the Divine would be better.

SEVEN

I sat on the couch next to Mud. Pulled the blanket over my feet. Caught a glimpse of my fingernails. I had leaves growing out of the tips. I curled my fingers under. I had read the earth a lot lately. It had been two days since I'd clipped my leaves. I reached back to my hairline at my nape and encountered the peculiar sensation and shape of leaves sprouting there too. They were small yet. I could hide them. For a short while.

"Mud. Did you see the tree kill the puppy?"

She sniffled and wiped her nose again, holding herself stiffly away from me. "Yes. Dagnabbit," she said, cursing in church-speak. "It reached out and stabbed him with a thorny vine. And squished him until he stopped screaming. Stopped breathing. And then it raised him up and dropped him in the crook of a branch. Leaves"—she sucked in a breath that was more sob—"leaves covered his li'l body." She leaned to me at last and put her head on my shoulder. "His name was Rex. He was a bluetick hound. A runt. Too little to hunt." She blew her nose again. "Rex was gonna be my dog—*my dog*—'acause I became a woman today.

"And I got an offer of marriage."

I didn't stiffen. Didn't alter anything about my posture. But my voice was grating and hoarse when I asked, "Who offered for you?" A twelve-year-old *child*. I'd find him and I'd feed him to the land, even if it meant claiming the church compound and everyone and everything in it.

Mud didn't answer.

Marrying a twelve-year-old child was statutory rape. The

state was supposed to have stopped the practice when they
raided the church. There was supposed to be ongoing oversight. Girls were supposed to be safe now. "Mud?"

"Daddy wouldn't say. He jist told him I was too young.
That they had to wait till I was fourteen to come courtin'.
And sixteen to marry." She looked up at me, her hazel gray
eyes worried, her tone stark. "Sixteen is the age for marriage
in Tennessee, with parental consent, and even though we'uns
is still gonna have sister-wives, the church is gonna abide by
the age law from now on."

"Fourteen is way, way too young for courting," I said,
"and sixteen for marriage is abominable. You shouldn't have
to deal with men until you're eighteen. Or older."

"I know. I been thinking. 'Bout what you'un said. That if
I stayed in the church, I'd never put my hands into any soil
but my husband's. That I'd have baby after baby, and have
to share a home with bunches of people. That I wouldn't be
able to claim trees or land. Or feed it with my soul, sharing
back and forth. I'm not completely sure what you'un meant
by all that. But . . . but it sounds wonderful. And I want to
be able to have it."

I tightened my arm around her and eased her close to me.
"Have you . . . sat with a tree and talked to it? Taking its
peace and sharing its power? Deep underground?"

Mud took a slow breath and whispered, "Yes. Is that a sin?"

"No. It isn't a sin. Have you claimed land on the compound? You do that by—" I stopped abruptly, trying to remember how I had claimed the small plot of land behind the
house where the married trees were, the roots of the huge
poplar and massive sycamore intertwined. I used to cling to
them when I was tired or distraught, sharing and communing with them, back and forth. I had a feeling that they were
mine long before I claimed the whole land that was Soulwood. Had I bled on them?

The memory ripped up from the deeps of my mind. Dark
and full of grief. Fast, like flipping through a picture book
and seeing a story play out on the turning pages. It stole my
breath.

One awful night, as Leah lay dying, her breath stopping and starting, her pulse fragile and faltering, I had cut myself on a knife in the kitchen. I had wrapped the finger in a cloth and run outside, crying silently, though not because of the slice on my hand. Crying because my world was changing again and I was afraid. Crying because Leah was dying and I couldn't help her. Crying because I was a young girl facing death all alone. I curled on the roots and dug my fingernails into the ground, sobbing myself into exhaustion. I fell asleep at the married roots. As I slept, the cloth on my wound came loose and I bled onto the roots. The small smear of my blood had made the trees mine. That first claiming of two trees and a small patch of land, that had been an accident.

I had shed blood in other places. At the vampire tree. At the gate where I had wanted the tree to move to. My blood had claimed small patches of land in many places and I had deserted most of them.

Those small claimings had been completely different from the way I had claimed Soulwood. Feeding my attacker to the woods had made all of Soulwood mine. That was the blood of a sacrifice mixed with my will.

I had killed for my land. I was a soul stealer. That death, that feeding, had been my choice. And now, like an addict, I often thirsted for more blood to feed to the land.

I was a monster. I knew that. But if Mud was never put in danger, if she was never fighting for her life, could she have land, yet not feed it the life of another? Could she be a keeper of the land without being a killer? How would I keep her from creating a vampire tree? From becoming what I was, from doing what I did? Blood. Sacrifice. Polygamy. Interwoven bloodlines for two centuries had made me what I was, had given me my gifts.

My blood on the compound had made the vampire tree mutate, had made it mine. I had claimed it and changed it and then deserted it. And if Mud had claimed Rex the way I had claimed Paka and other sentient beings, then had the tree taken a sacrifice from my bloodline? Did any of this even make sense?

The simple truth was that I didn't know what I was. Didn't know what I could do. Didn't know what any of the repercussions of any of my actions might be. I had blundered. I had done evil. And I needed to protect Mud from making any of my mistakes.

Blood. Sacrifice. Polygamy. Interwoven bloodlines for two centuries. My brain tried to wrap around concepts that were older than time. My mind whirled and stumbled and I felt myself flush. My finger-leaves curled in anguish. The church taught that females were pure until menarche—the very first sign of menstruation. That once that occurred, they became women, became impure, and had to be taken in hand by a man. They pointed to the New Testament, First Timothy, to claim that childbirth kept women pure, that they were saved by childbirth. They taught that the moon cycles were evil and proof that God cursed Eve for an unforgivable sin and, through her, down to all women forever. Women were taught to feel shame just for being women.

Animals knew when humans got the woman's monthly curse.

Did trees? Did my trees? Did the vampire tree waken when Mud came near?

"Mud."

My sister looked at me quickly, and I realized my tone had altered. Her name was wrapped in my worry.

I shook my head. "No problem. Just, well, did you bleed at any time when you were near the tree?"

Mud's eyes went wide and fearful. "Did I kill Rex?"

"No, sweetheart. But, well, the vampire tree got the way it is because I bled on its roots. And if you bled near it and it sensed *your* blood, and we're sisters, well, it might have tried to protect you from the puppy."

Mud scowled, and I had a feeling that it looked a lot like my own scowl. "I cut myself," she said, holding up her left hand. "I slid a potato peeler on my thumb. It was leaking through the bandage."

I took her hand and turned it to the light. The wound was

still leaking; the commercial-style, pale beige bandage was red all along the central pad portion.

"I did it yesterday. It was still drippy when I left the house to go to devotionals."

"And did you pass by the tree?"

Mud held the thumb up and studied it. "Yep." She pushed me away and scooted into the couch corner. "That was afore I became a woman grown." We fell silent, thinking about blood and being grown women and the strange tree.

"Your'n water's boiling," Mud said. "I want real tea, not some yucky herbal stuff. Mama Carmel done been making me drink some awful stuff on account a me being grown up."

I remembered Mama Carmel's feminine-soother concoctions from my own days in the Nicholson household. They had been pretty awful. "How about something with lemon and ginger?"

"And then you'un tell me about what we are. More'n you done told me last time we talked. 'Acause I'm thinking we'uns, you'un and me, we ain't human."

With those words ringing in my ears, I made tea with lemon and ginger and a handful of raspberry leaf, brought the pot in a tea cozy, on a tray with mugs, honey, cream, and spoons, to the low coffee table in front of the couch. I poured two mugs of the lemon honey tea and mixed my own, leaving Mud's untouched. In the church compound, a woman grown made her own tea. She was a child no longer.

Mud stared at me, the pot, the mug, and I watched realization dawn in her eyes. Slowly, she leaned forward and added a small splash of cream and a drizzle of honey to her cup. Stirred the mixture and leaned back, holding the mug. "So this is what it's like? Being a woman grown? I make my own tea? Kill my own puppies? And have this awful thing happen to me every month?"

Something in the statement made me want to smile, but my mouth felt frozen. "It's not so awful. Churchwomen aren't allowed to have relations with the men during this time. They aren't allowed to work in the greenhouse or garden or with the animals. I think this is the time each month that church-women get to sit quiet, to read books. To meditate and have time to be introspective."

"Edith called it a curse."

"Mmm. Not all our sisters or friends are very smart. Sometimes even the best women can be kinda stupid."

"So what are we?" That was Mud. Cutting to the chase. Demanding answers.

"I don't know. Not exactly. I do know that we can claim land with our blood. Maybe even accidentally. And that when we do, we become responsible for it. We become its caretakers."

"And you bled on the vampire tree. You'un's claimed it."

"And deserted it," I acknowledged. I knew on some deep-down level that my desertion had caused the tree to mutate. That fact left me mentally wringing my hands with guilt. My neglect had killed a puppy today. Taken back to its most basic beginnings, *I* had killed Rex. "To say that I didn't know what claiming it might mean, and didn't know that deserting it would make it bloodthirsty, is no excuse. We can make land healthy and fecund. We can make it grow crops or, seems like, we can make it spit out weeds and thorns. We do that by communing with it. And by bleeding on it. Little drops. That's how we claim it."

"Gross. The bleeding part. I get the talking-to-trees part. I been talking to plants since I was in diapers. So what are we?"

"I don't know. A friend told me I was *yinehi*, which is sorta like a fae." At her blank look, I said, "Like a fairy."

She looked down at herself. "Too big. Ain't got no wings. Can't fly."

I laughed, the sound unexpected and stuttering. "Good point. I did some more research, but I still didn't find us. I guess I need to expand my search parameters. Find out what we are."

"*Search parameters.* Townie talk. And when you learn what's what, you'll tell me, right?"

I nodded my head and cradled the lemon ginger tea, letting it soothe me. "Soon as I know I'll tell you."

"So how'm I gonna get land? And how'm I gonna *not* get courted in two years and married in four? And how'm I gonna be safe? I want land. It don't have to be as good as Soulwood. I can make it grow if'n I work at it, right? I want a place a my own. No husband and no children."

"You're too young to know if you really want children or not."

"Churchmen don't care what I want. They decide and the womenfolk follow. All exceptin' you'un. I want a real life. With the land."

"Mmm. I'm still trying to make up my mind about young'uns and I'm nearly twenty-four years old."

"Okay. I'll decide if I want a man and babies after I'm twenty-four."

I smiled. We both sipped.

"Why'nt you'un got no Christmas tree?"

I topped up our cups. "Well, sister mine, I've had no time to think about Christmas. Soon, though."

"You'un tell me when and I'll help you."

"Deal."

The three mouser cats raced down the stairs and leaped on the couch to curl on top of us and around us. The house warmed. And it occurred to me that . . . that maybe Mud could live here. With me. And that maybe I could give her a small part of my land. Like a land dowry. Or something. If Daddy would ever let her move in with me.

"You know you'un got green leaves growing out your'n fingers?"

I held out my hand, fingers splayed. "Yep."

"Am I gonna grow green leaves?"

"I have no idea, sister mine."

"I reckon we'll figger it out as we go, then."

"I reckon," I agreed, ideas and possibilities racing around in my brain like bumper cars, all filled with excitement and delight slamming into concern and fear. All the things that could go wrong. All the things that I might have to reveal to my family. The tree I had to corral and harness and direct. Brother Ephraim to kill. Again. And all that very soon.

* * *

My time with Mud was short, but I let her help me clip the foliage off my neck and away from my fingernails. She seemed to find it amusing, and giggled every time a leaf went flying. The laughter did us both good, but I was going to be late to work, and so I cut it short, gathering up my gear and herding the cats onto the back porch. Then I drove my sister back to the church compound, let her out, and watched her go inside the Nicholson house.

Not wanting to do it, but knowing I had to, I drove to the tree, parked, and got out, wrapping my coat tightly about me, shoving my hands deep into my pockets. The sun was setting, casting a red glow on the once-upon-a-time oak and dark shadows leaning long behind it.

The tree was no longer young and vibrant and full of life. It had dark, thick bark and abundant, swollen leaves, too thick and pliable to be a live oak or a deciduous tree. The leaves were more like the foliage of a succulent, with scarlet-lined veins that, when broken, dripped a red substance viscous as blood, gooey and oily.

The tree had grown wildly since I had used it to heal me. It now had the girth of an old-growth tree, bigger than five men holding hands could reach around, with branches that coiled and curled. Vines sprouted from the jointure of limbs and trunk, each covered with needle-like thorns. At the base lay the remains of a cement block wall, tumbled and fallen in shattered heaps, the wall the churchmen had constructed with the hope of keeping the tree confined. They had also tried chain saws, fire, herbicides, dynamite, and a bulldozer, which the tree had eaten. It was entombed inside the mass of leaves and vines and branches somewhere, the huge behemoth buried. This one tree looked like the forest of a child's fairy tale, one capable of burying a kingdom.

Around its base, at the wide dripline, roots had sprouted up new growth. It looked as if the tree was trying to grow an enchanted—or cursed—forest.

"You figured out a way to kill that thing?"

I didn't turn around at the sound of my brother's voice. "Hey, Sam. My last suggestion didn't work, I guess."

"Couldn't get close enough to cut it or blow it up. Thought about throwing a stick of TNT on it and hoping for the best, but I was afraid it might throw it back at us."

I breathed out a laugh, a sound a wereleopard might make. Chuffing. Tilted my head to Sam. He was standing to my left, at the back of the truck. Like me, he was dressed in winter layers, his hands in his pockets. A hand-crocheted toboggan in Mama's favorite blues was on his head. With each breath, he blew a cloud of vapor.

"What is it, Nell?"

I shook my head, watching him in my peripheral vision. "I need to do some thinking, brother mine. On the vampire tree. On a lot of things. When I got something to say or do, I'll let you know."

Sam pressed his fists deeply into his pockets, his heavy jacket pulling down. "When that time comes, am I gonna have to hold off the pitchforks and kerosene to keep some a the church folk from burning you at the stake?"

"Would you protect me, Sam?"

"Yes."

I nodded at the simple statement. "Why did you set Benjamin on me? Why did you surprise me like that?"

My brother shrugged. "You been gone a long time, but I still miss you, Nellie. I miss your spirit and your smart mouth. I miss the way you don't let nothing and no one stop you from doing the right thing. Even if you'un suffer for it. Daddy, he's been fighting the mamas for months about going to the surgeon. You'un stomped him and now he's got an appointment." The church-speak faded as he spoke. "The family needs you. The church needs you. We need you to lead us into the twenty-first century. Into the future. It's that or die." When I said nothing he added, "Church membership numbers were highest in 1954, at well over twelve hundred. Now church rolls stand at six hundred fourteen, with women leaving the church all the time. The church is dying."

I thought about that. Thought about the cycle of life and

death. Understood that all trees die eventually. All forests.
So do all civilizations, all organizations, and all churches.
Maybe it was time for God's Cloud to die, be chopped up
and fed into the fire of some new church. "I'll let you know
about the tree when I figure things out." Leaving my brother
staring at the mutated oak, I walked back to my truck and
drove away. Thinking that my brother was a hunter. And the
hunter in him had baited a trap well with Ben Aden and with
the plea to bring the church into the twenty-first century. He
meant everything he'd said, in the best way possible, but he
was still reasoning like a churchman.

On the way out, I slowed and studied the place where I
had told the vampire tree to move; the place where I had
dropped my blood to encourage it to move. All along the
fence were small growths, with dark bark and heavy, reddish-
tipped engorged leaves. Some of the growths had put out
vines that had begun to curl into the hurricane fencing. I had
a feeling that they would grow fast, winter or no.

I had made a bad mistake asking them to grow here.
Probably had made several more mistakes. I had to decide
how to fix them all. Probably like yesterday.

I pulled up at PsyLED headquarters on Allamena Avenue,
a newish road on newly developed land off Highway 62. It
was three stories of government-building ugly, with the two
top levels set aside for PsyLED, and for an eventual PsyCSI,
whenever the government got around to fully funding the
agency. The bottom floor was Yoshi's Deli and Coffee's On,
and I stopped for a coffee. As I entered, the girl behind the
counter smiled at me and said, "The usual?"

"Oh. Yes, please." I watched her making me a caramel
cappuccino and understood that I had, at some point in the
last few weeks and months, gone through a rite of passage
without even realizing it. *The usual.* I had a usual coffee at
a coffeehouse. Unlike God's Cloud of Glory, I had entered
the twenty-first century. I was a modern-day woman. Maybe

even a city girl. Knowing that didn't help much, but it did show that things could change.

My heart heavy and my mind full of thoughts that writhed like snakes, I carried my gear and coffee inside and up the stairs. I had a feeling that the EOD debriefing was going to be long and tedious.

JoJo said, "Financial update. Like everyone else with assets, the Tolliver family has money invested in the Tennessee Valley Authority. They also are heavily invested in four local small industries that make parts for weapons manufacturing companies, a video/PR/talent agency that handles the careers of several Tennessee sports icons and three big country singers, and a medical corporation called DNAKeys." She glanced up from her tablet. "Which is where it gets a little interesting." She looked back at her screen, her earrings swinging. "Social media conspiracy nuts suggest that DNAKeys is holding a vampire and wolves or werewolves prisoner on the premises *and* is doing animal experimentation that sounds like something out of a horror movie. Multiple social media sites have shared the accusations, specifying internal sources for the charges. I'm working to track down the sources so we can interview them.

"The claims got so bad the company asked the Cocke County Sheriff's Department to take a walk through the facilities eight months past. The investigators discovered no paranormal sentient beings. The detective I spoke with suggested that the conspiracy stuff could be kids or smear tactics from a political or business enemy. But basically he said no crimes were currently taking place on-site."

"Probably a waste of time, but send the address to our cells," Rick said. "Occam and I can check it out tonight." He meant in cat form.

I glanced at the corner of my laptop screen as we all worked through reports and files and updated everything pertinent, checking the phase of the moon on the little icon there. The full moon was only days away. I looked up at JoJo and her tight lips indicated that she knew why the cat-boys wanted to go skulking around in cat form. Things always got kinda crazy around PsyLED in the nine days of the moon. There was a quote about moon tides for were-creatures, though I had no idea who had said it originally. It was part of were-lore. *The urge to shift and to hunt waxes strong three days out, abides the three days of, and wanes three days after. Nine nights of pleasure and nine days of hell.* We were getting close to the craziness.

Rick continued, "The sheriff was invited in. We haven't been, and we don't have probable cause to get a warrant. But we can get close enough to get a good sniff, just to rule out weres and vamps."

"Uh-huh," JoJo said, typing furiously. "If the sheriff missed something and you get close enough for werewolves to catch your scent, things could get dicey. I respectfully suggest that you put this plan of action on the back burner, boss."

Rick tilted his head in a gesture that said, *I hear you and I'm ignoring you.* "PsyLED's mandate is any and all crimes committed by, perpetrated on, or related to paranormal creatures. We'll go in downwind."

Tandy, who had been awfully silent, said, "We know that several werewolves were never captured after that recent were-taint outbreak in Asheville. Law enforcement has been working under the assumption that not all the infected persons were caught. If you go in downwind, and stay several hundred yards away, you should be okay. However, it might be smarter to send in an RVAC. And safer."

JoJo raised her eyebrows at Tandy, shooting him a look I couldn't interpret. But then, the two were probably in a sexual relationship, hiding it from Rick, in opposition to PsyLED standard—but not enforced—protocol, and outside of proper marriage.

Proper marriage. There was a holdover from the church teachings of my youth. These days people didn't get married to have sex; they just went ahead and did it. And in the church they married only to have sex, in the past with underage girls. It was evil. If I dated Occam I'd be in the same situation as Tandy and Jo. Now that I was out of Spook School, dating a coworker wasn't *exactly* forbidden, but it wasn't smart either.

Rick said, "Nell, I want you to go back, again, to the Holloway home, to Justin Tolliver's burned house, and then to the senator's home. I want you to read the earth for two reasons. One, to specifically search for paranormal energies *other than* the assassin who burns things. All we have is the anomalous reading on the psy-meter 2.0 and the scorching or chemical burns to the land, and there isn't anything in the histories or mythos that pinpoints a creature who does that. We need more to go on. Read deeper. Find us something to work with."

I didn't sigh, but I wanted to. Being a paranormal investigator might sound exciting on the surface, but it really wasn't. It was a lot of repetition, of going over the same evidentiary ground (literally, in my case) over and over again. It was paperwork, rereading paperwork, comparing paperwork, and a whole lot of brainstorming and interviews. I was getting tired of going over the same ground, but that gift was why I was part of PsyLED. Rather than share my litany of complaints I repeated, "Other paranormals. Like what? Witches? Vampires? Weres?"

"Anything. Any magical signature that doesn't belong. And then you pull night shift on the senator's grounds."

"Okay. If we're done, then I'm outta here." At Rick's nod I grabbed my bags, taking off for my trusty rusty truck.

I ran a few errands and then started my investigation with Justin and Sonya Tolliver's burned home, where the security guards and one lone FBI agent—not my cousin—gave me access to the grounds. It was impossible to smell anything other than the ruined house, stale water, and the heavily scorched lawn, but the trail of the assassin was clear and unquestionable, brown and burned trails through the grass. The guards had seen nothing and no one since the fire except for scaring off some kids out exploring, with beer, the night before. They had raced off before the guards could get a vehicle tag. Not that the uniforms had tried very hard to catch a few drunk kids.

I did a quick read on the dead grass and on the living lawn, with the psy-meter 2.0 and with hand-in-dirt, and texted my impressions to JoJo. I found nothing new—no weres, no witches, no vampires, no unexpected paranormal signatures. Feeling the night and the long guard duty ahead, I drove to the Holloways' house. The ruined windows had been replaced, the crime scene tape was gone, and a neat For Sale sign was out front. Not that I blamed the family for moving.

Even without putting hands to soil, I could tell that the ground around the repaired house was dead along the trail used by the assassin. Dead under the window where he stood to fire the gun. Dead through the path to the road in back. The only advantage to an additional read was the ability and opportunity to pinpoint exactly where the shooter left the land for the road. And where he disappeared. That and the fact that here, where the overriding stench of house fire was not present, the dead grass and plants smelled very slightly scorched, more certainly a chemical burn, rather than a flame burn. The smell was odd but not definitive of species origin, not anything I could pinpoint from Spook School class, Paranormal Physiology 101 or even 202. Nothing recognizable. And the psy-meter read baseline normal. I made a mental note to get a cat nose out here to sniff around.

To avoid comments from the lone guard patrolling the grounds, I went to the edge of the lawn at the back of the property, near the stand of trees, close enough to see the dead sapling in the security lights. I placed my old pink blanket, folded, on the ground, then sat and stuck my fingers directly into the dirt at the base of an undamaged tree. I sank my consciousness lightly into the ground.

Where I found maggots. Instantly they crawled and wiggled up my fingers to my wrists.

I yanked my fingers out, shot to my feet, and danced away. My breath came fast. Tingles ran up and down my whole body. My stomach roiled and I thought I might gag.

My most fearsome maggot memory squelched under my

bare foot again, as intense as the day it had happened, when I stepped into that dead possum, covered with maggots. They slimed onto my bare foot and wriggled. I had screamed and screamed.

The only other maggoty memories were vampiric in nature.

Standing a good ten feet away, I forced calm into myself with some deep breathing exercises and then forced myself to pick up my pink blanket and carry it back to the C10. I dropped the blanket into the back and sat in the cab, the heater on high, cleaning my hands with baby wipes, which I had discovered were essential to any investigation. Though the baby-scent fragrance was awful, it did help to clear my head. Rick had sent me here to check for paranormal presences. I had found one. But what if it wasn't from a bad guy, the shooter?

When I was less panicked, I found Yummy in my contacts and punched call.

She answered with, "Well, if it isn't Maggoty."

More than you know, I thought. "I want to know what you or one of your pals has been doing at the Holloway house, hiding in the edge of the woods."

There was a hard silence and I thought my cell might have dropped the call. I wanted to say, *Hello?* But I needed to appear strong and that one interrogative might ruin things. After a good few *Mississippi*s, Yummy said, "You are able to detect that a Mithran has been to that house?"

"Yeah. Walking the edge of the property. Standing long enough in one spot for me to sense it. You wanna tell me what you folks have been up to out here?"

Yummy blew out a breath, one I know she didn't need, and so it was either muscle memory, emotion, or for effect. "I policed the grounds last night, searching for the attacker, trying to sniff out if it was a Mithran."

"And what did you smell?"

"The attacker smells neither like Mithran nor like cattle," she said, her words precise.

It took a moment for me to understand that she meant the

shooter didn't smell like a vampire or human. Vampires drank humans, so they ended up thinking of them as food sources and pets, hence the *cattle* term. It was as insulting as my *maggot* term. I decided to ignore it. "Why do you keep asking—worrying—if the shooter is a vampire?" I heard a soft uneven tapping on Yummy's end, like a fingernail or pen against a hard surface, as if she was thinking.

She sighed again. Definitely for effect. "A small group of Europeans carried out an attack against the Master of the City of New Orleans. There's been a retaliatory challenge to the European emperor, Titus Flavius Vespasianus, a challenge of Sangre Duello."

That wasn't news, nor was it surprising that she should know so much. The surprise came because she shared it so freely. "I'm aware of that. Go on. There's gonna be a fight."

"We await the schedule. If Leo Pellissier loses, then all the Mithrans within the borders of the United States and Canada are at risk of extermination."

That bit was news to me, but Yummy was on a roll, so I let her talk.

"There've been whispers that others of the Europeans came ashore during the attack, and found shelter and safety. Rumors that they *called* those they sired or bound. Mithrans have gone missing."

"Some of yours?" Yummy didn't reply to that one. "And you think they might come after you and Ming of Glass, to harm or kill."

"It's not an impossibility."

I debated telling Yummy what we knew about the arson and the shooter. Vamps were flammable, much more so than humans, so the likelihood of the attacker being vampish was not very high. However, she had told me about the situation in New Orleans and her fears for the Knoxville area. Rick would call it quid pro quo. "For your ears only. Would it help if I told you, without question, that the attacker is *not* a vampire?"

"You're so certain?"

"Yep. There's no maggots at any of the sites except yours."

Yummy gave a low, mocking laugh. "I'm not sure if I'm happy at the information or insulted at the comparison."

"Whatever it is, he, she, or it burned the foliage everywhere he moved, with what reads like a chemical burn. You ever hear of a creature able to do that?"

"No. Chemicals strong enough to kill foliage might damage a Mithran's flesh. I have access to Ming's records. I can do a search."

"Couldn't hurt. Might help. If we knew what it was, we might know where to search. Might know when to expect another attack."

"If I find something pertinent, I will call."

I almost said thank you, but that might put me in her debt. I settled on, "Any information you might provide could prove useful."

Yummy laughed again, her tone telling me that she knew exactly why I had phrased it that way, and ended the call.

I wrote a report on my laptop and sent it in. If I failed to mention Yummy and her information about the Mithrans, well, I could consider the vampire a confidential source because nothing she'd said impacted the case at this time. I felt a little guilty, since Rick had told us to share anything about paranormals, but I squished the guilt down, and then ignored the guilt that came from ignoring guilt.

Satisfied, I put the truck in drive and motored on over to my assignment for the night, at the home of Senator Abrams Tolliver. I read the earth there too, and it told me nothing it hadn't before, except that no maggoty vampire had been stalking the premises.

The investigation went on all night, and I kept up with it on my government-issued encrypted cell phone, reading files and reports, in between walking rounds with the feds and the Secret Service. While on dinner break, sitting in the truck with the heater roaring and a cup of coffee steaming on the dash, I ate a sandwich I had picked up at a supermarket and read deeper into incoming reports.

Arson had been confirmed at Justin Tolliver's house, though the type of accelerant had yet to be determined. Rick checked out the paranormal scents and told me things smelled odd but not definable or species specific.

My reading of the land notwithstanding, the attacker had been deemed *possibly* paranormal, the *possibly* keeping PsyLED from assuming charge of the case. Based on the possibility, however, PsyLED would have a bigger investigatory role. PsyLED and the FBI were still operating under the auspices of the Secret Service, and for now, we had access to files not compiled by us, cooperation still taking place.

At least one of the Tolliver family was also deemed likely a paranormal. Justin's wife Sonya had been outed, though none of the Tollivers knew it yet. Nor did the feds or the Secret Service. Soul was holding that information close to the vest for now, since Sonya wasn't a suspect.

PsyLED's focus had currently shifted to the research facility, DNAKeys. Which seemed like the wrong way to go to me, because interest in the facility was based on the rumored presence of paras in captivity, not on physical, direct, or circumstantial evidence. But my opposition to DNAKeys as an investigatory focus was a gut feeling based on precisely nothing. I didn't include that in my comments on the report.

I reopened my notes for tonight's readings and into the "Comments" space I typed, *Ground at Holloways' and Justin and Sonya Tolliver's feels wrong. Damage is beneath the surface, not on top, as it would be if chemical or physical agents had burned the ground and plants. This has nothing to do with vampires or were-creatures.* I thought about adding the words *in my opinion*, but that urge was church-think left over from my upbringing as a woman in God's Cloud. My readings were not opinions. They were fact. So I hit enter and read on.

JoJo had discovered that there was a fire at DNAKeys fifteen months past, one answered by the East Tennessee Rural/Metro Fire Department. That was when the tales of the creatures imprisoned there began to surface, probably gossip spread by the responders. I doubted that the paid firefighting employees would chatter, but maybe a volunteer had gossiped. Surely Rural/Metro had a roster of volunteers. Since the forest fires of 2016, most rural departments had a list they kept on hand.

I texted the office and asked for someone to obtain a roster of volunteers at the stations that had answered the fire call at DNAKeys. Tandy texted back that JoJo had already acquired it. I didn't ask if it was obtained legally or if she had found a backdoor and acquired it on her own. Hacking was illegal, but so easy, according to our IT specialist. Tandy sent me the list and on it, I found two names I knew.

Thaddeus Rankin Sr. and Thaddeus Rankin Jr., or Thad and Deus, father and son, who had put in the windows on my house. Volunteer firefighting sounded exactly like something the two would do. I texted HQ that I would be stopping by the Rankins' place of business as soon as my schedule permitted. Tandy texted back that I could leave the night shift in the hands of ALT Security and the other government guards. With PsyLED now in an improved investigatory position, my talents could best be used elsewhere, and Soul wanted an initial interview with the Rankins tomorrow. Meantime she had another job for me.

I walked the grounds again and said good-bye to the guards before heading back to HQ to prep and organize for a nighttime op.

EIGHT

It was the operation I thought to be foolish: Rick and Occam were going to approach the DNAKeys research facility and scope out the place with cat eyes from tree-limb level. The whole idea was stupid, but a probie couldn't say it to the SAC, or to the man who had asked her to dinner.

Rick finished the op instructions with the words, "Nell, you're to pull backup, manage comms, and be an extra ear. Here. Try these." He held out a set of binoculars attached to a strap system shaped to fit a human head. Rick was holding up the unit's brand-new low-light, IR-vision binoculars. "You'll be the first to use it."

My heart did a funny little leap. A probie never got to be first on anything good. Last week we had all watched the how-to video for the expensive headgear, which had taken a big chunk out of the remaining budget for the year. The goggles, made with a redundant dual-tube design that could withstand all kinds of weather changes and temps, had an automatic brightness control, bright light shut-off circuitry, and a spotlight/floodlight built-in IR illuminator. The binocular-shaped gadget would allow me to see clearly even in areas with no ambient light. Like, the middle of nowhere in the middle of the night.

I gave Rick a grin suitable for him giving me a fully equipped greenhouse, took the contraption, and started to put it on. He stopped me with a raised hand, amusement in his dark eyes. "Night vision, remember? Go to the locker room, kill the lights, and adjust it to fit."

I had to change anyway and grabbed both my small gobag

and my large, four-day gobag on the way to the locker room, where I adjusted the straps and the eyepieces and familiarized myself with the location of the small knob that turned from off to on to IR. According to the video I had watched, the night-vision goggles were pretty much idiotproof.

Satisfied, I tucked them into my small gobag and changed clothes. PsyLED provided desert night camo like the military used, and the cost had come out of my pocket, but I had never worn the clothing, and Rick hadn't told me I had to wear it tonight. I dressed in blue jeans, layered dark gray and charcoal patterned T-shirts, and my hooded winter coat, with field boots. All black is visible in low-to-no light, and the paler clothes would give me some light-protection, out in the middle of nowhere. The jeans would protect my body and save my nicer work clothes should I have to hike in somewhere.

I checked my weapons, making sure I had two extra magazines, one filled with hollow-point rounds, one with silver plating. Just in case. Under the coat, I put on the shoulder holster rig instead of the lower spine holster, which was less than comfortable while driving in the truck. Back in the break room, I ate a quick slice of pizza left over from someone's supper. I wasn't stealing; it was on the fridge shelf marked ALL. I refilled my insulated coffee mug and when I heard Rick and Occam departing, followed them down the stairs to the street. It was two a.m. and the guys had been awake for close to twenty hours. They were sniping at each other the way cats would if cats could talk.

"You'll follow my lead up to the—"

"Why should I follow your lead, Hoss? I've been a werecat longer than you have. I've actually hunted wild hogs, and those babies have tusks this long." Occam held out both hands a ways apart. I let the outer door close behind me and didn't look up to see his expression. "They can rip open a predator's gut in a heartbeat. You, my kitten friend, are the probie here. You have hunted exactly two full moons and brought down exactly four *deer*. Sweet little Bambis. With help from me, let me remind you. I should take point."

From nowhere, a grindylow leaped onto Occam's back, her neon green coat looking yellowish in the outside lights. "Ow," Occam said, grabbing her and tossing her to Rick as they walked.

The SAC caught her in midair and placed her on his shoulders without missing a step. He blew out a breath in a cloud and cocked his head, catlike. His eyes were glowing green in the parking lot's security lights. The shadows of the men lengthened and shortened as they walked. I followed. When Rick spoke it wasn't to the grindy, which he petted almost in a reflex, but to Occam. "I'm a black wereleopard. My melanistic coat is perfect for night hunting. Your spotted one is more visible."

"I'm more sneaky." Occam opened the driver's door of his fancy car. "When you're in cat form, you're thinking like a cat in the wild, not like a human, and your cat's out of control. Not a good thing on an op."

"I'm SAC." Rick got in the passenger side, tossing the grindy to the dash.

"Which means jack nothing, Hoss. I'm better qualified and you know it."

"We have protocol—" The car doors closed. The engine roared and they drove away. Leaving me standing there alone in the parking lot.

I put both fists on my hips and huffed in disgust, watching their taillights, my small gobag over my shoulder. I turned and waved at the very obvious security camera over the door to HQ, knowing that Tandy had seen the entire exchange. Upstairs, the lights in the office blinked off and back on. The fact that I had been abandoned had been acknowledged. Tandy was probably all worried about me. If it had been JoJo she would have been laughing so hard she'd snort coffee. I had seen that happen. Had to hurt.

I got in my truck, punched the address into my cellular GPS, and pulled into the street. I had driven a mile when my cell rang. It was Occam. I scowled at the cell and let it go to voice mail. Twice. On the third try I punched accept and said, "What?"

"Nell, sugar. Where are you?" Occam sounded properly quiet and deferential. "We left you in the parking lot. I'm sorry."

An apology went a long way to fixing things, but I had been raised with men who treated women with less respect than they did other men. "Yes," I said. "You did. And I got in my truck, and I turned it on, and I am driving. Alone. I am perfectly capable of arriving at the correct GPS on this, my first level-two nighttime op. I will see you there." I hit end.

JoJo and T. Laine would both say I was being bitchy. And then they'd high-five me and say, "Give 'em hell, girl." A woman had to stand up to men, even in this new, modern world. Women always did. And never more so than with alpha males who seemed to have a cat rivalry of some sort going on. I just hadn't thought it would be Occam who made me defend myself this time. Tears prickled my eyes, and ruthlessly I squashed them. *That* was stupid. I would not cry because men acted in human character and in cat character.

I took a right and headed toward Millertown Pike, and then Rutledge Pike, also known as Highway 11 West. As I drove, I thought about Benjamin and what would have happened had he been in Occam's place. He'd have asked me to bring him a cup of coffee and maybe have a good dinner waiting for him when he got back. The likelihood of him even thinking about me going on any mission was low to none. A woman's presence on such a mission would have been considered valueless. Occam just forgot about me. Or his cat did.

Men. Dang 'em all. My hands tightened on the wheel and I followed the cell phone's directions out of Knoxville.

DNAKeys' research facility was out of town, down a narrow, privately maintained, paved road on the far side of House Mountain State Natural Area. There were no streetlights this far out of town and no visible security measures, but there was also no gated entrance, so the lack of obvious security measures was likely occult—not meaning paranormal, meaning hidden. Occam's fancy car—a 2015 Ford Mustang two-door Fastback GT with all the bells and whistles—was parked in the dark off the side of the road and down a little-used driveway with an overgrown For Sale sign in the weeds, about a mile from the turnoff to the facility. I pulled in behind it, turned off the engine and the lights, and closed my eyes, letting them adapt to night vision. As I waited, I set my comms earbud in my ear, adjusted the mic, and hooked the comms system at my waistband. When my vision was more attuned to the night, I got out, carrying my flash, which I didn't turn on, and walked around the fancy car.

The men were nowhere to be seen, which meant they were changing shape or were already hunting. They hadn't been that far ahead of me so I was betting on shape-shifting somewhere out in the dark. I sniffed and listened to the night, taking in the smells and the sounds. A little exhaust. My coffee. Something musky. The wereleopards, most likely. I heard no sounds except what might be the far-off hum of cars. In the distance were city lights. Closer were security lights, which I assumed would be DNAKeys'.

I returned to my truck and sat, engine and lights still off, in the growing cold, sipping coffee from my insulated mug, strong and black. The caffeine was a drug, too bitter to be a froufrou drink, too strong to be my "regular." I waited, my senses straining into the dark, kneading my rooty middle, literally putting my fingers on my non-humanness. The cold seeped into me, and I pulled the pink blanket over me. I had rescued it from the truck bed and it no longer felt like maggots.

If this had been Soulwood I could have put my hands in the earth and discovered the cats' location easily. Out here, so far from home, the land wouldn't even know I was alive, especially in the dormant season. Trying to read the land would be harder. A lot harder. And I'd grow leaves that I would then have to prune. I shoulda brought me a good book.

The first indication that the men had shifted was a *thump* that rocked the truck and Occam's cat face pressed against the windshield, staring at me, lips pulled back, showing me his fangs. He hissed. My only reaction was to grip my cup so hard I feared I might bend the metal handle. I wanted to jump or squeal, or both, which I presumed he had intended. Occam's cat was mischievous. I narrowed my eyes at him, knowing he could see me clearly in the dark. His lips lowered to cover his teeth and he stared at me, white whiskers touching the windshield.

Occam was a pretty cat, all gold and dark brown, his golden eyes lined with black like an Egyptian king's with kohl. Deliberately, I sipped my coffee and stared back at him, giving as good as I got. Maybe better. He snorted, blowing twin spots of condensation on the glass. He lay down, belly on the warm hood, his huge, dappled body vanishing in the night, his face close to the glass.

He didn't shift his gaze away.

I was being hunted. I scowled at the cat and set my coffee in the mug holder, pulled on the headgear, drew my service weapon, and set it on the dash. Occam now appeared as a greenish spotted killer, haunches and tail hanging off the truck. "Take that, you dang ol' cat," I muttered. Occam blinked. Looked at the gun on the dash. At me. And turned away, giving me the back of his head. He flopped his head down flat on the hood. In cat-speak, it was a complete dismissal and a refusal to consider me anything but a bore, and certainly not a threat. It made me want to laugh or shoot him, or both, but I refrained. "Tit for tat," I said, knowing he could hear me through the windows. "Don't push it, pussycat."

Occam chuffed and started purring. I could feel the vibration through the truck body. He was having fun. The grindylow joined him, and started grooming Occam's fur, her long, improbable steel claws combing and probably trimming as she worked.

About ten minutes later, there was a second *thump* and a black big-cat joined him, a comms unit strapped around his neck, but otherwise hard to see in the night. My hood bowed, so I tapped on the window and waved them away. They ignored me. I tapped my mic to turn on the recorder and said, "Night op." I gave the date and the location by address and GPS coordinates. "Time is three twenty-six a.m. Occam and

Rick LaFleur at recon. Nell Ingram as backup." Without glancing my way, Rick nudged Occam. The two cats, with the grindy riding on Occam's back, slid to the ground and vanished, leaving the truck rocking and the hood returning to normal. Dang cats.

I adjusted the mic into a more comfortable position and holstered my weapon. Drank down most of the coffee. When the cold started to creep in, I got out of the truck, crossed the road to a tree I had seen when I reconnoitered Occam's car, and sat on the low branch. I adjusted the fit and the gear until I could see and hear and talk with ease and played with the headgear, switching back and forth from IR to low light.

I identified a small herd of deer moving along the hillside, their bodies reddish on IR, heated against the colder earth, and when I flipped the knob to low light, greenish. Later, two large dogs raced down the road, well fed and enjoying a night of freedom, possibly escapees from chains or small pens, from the way they played and loped and chased each other. They never saw or smelled the deer. Or me. An owl flowed over the ground, silent as death, and dropped on a rabbit. Its squeal of pain and fear was quickly cut off as the owl carried it to a branch and started eating.

Feral cats hunted, small spots of color depending on which visual spectrum I used. Minutes passed. The excitement of playing with the new night oculars wore thin. The cold deepened. I prepared to be frozen and bored. One thing the long wait gave me was time to think and I realized that being left in HQ's parking lot wasn't a gender thing. It was totally a cat thing. If Tandy had been their backup, he would have been left standing there too. As slights went it was small, and only seemed big to me because, as T. Laine would say, it had pushed my buttons.

Ninety minutes after the cats departed, the sun was starting to gray the eastern sky and low clouds were dropping, fog rolling down the hillside like an avalanche and along the road like a vaporous flood. A car rolled past. Then another heading the other way. A school bus rumbled and squeaked on a parallel road beyond the trees. The human world was starting to wake up and head to work and school. We needed to be out of here.

I tapped the mic three times, taps Rick would be able to hear even with the comms hanging around his neck. The taps stood for: *LaFleur, report back to origination and insert point, ASAP*. It was a reminder that they needed to become human again, that there was work to do. I three-tapped again. There was no reply because Rick had turned off his mic. And because his cat didn't have opposable thumbs to turn it back on. And because his cat didn't speak English. There were a lot of reasons why he didn't respond, most of them amusing.

Moments later, on the hillside, I caught a hint of movement, red in the infrared range. Two slinky cat shapes were working their way down toward the road, strides lazy, in no hurry. I made my way to my truck and started the engine, waiting for them to shift back. I wanted to leave them as they had left me, but weres in the midst of shifting were vulnerable, and I knew better.

But that didn't mean I had to wait till they got dressed. The moment I saw a human shape in the low-light goggles, still naked and steaming in a greenish haze, I drove off, stopping once for fresh bakery bread and a bear claw that tempted me like a sweet devil. The claw was greasy, nowhere near as good as Mama's, and I was able to eat only part of it, but the to-go coffee was surprisingly tasty, much better than the burned sludge I expected.

I picked up a second coffee—my regular in the coffee shop—along with an egg and bacon on flatbread, which was wonderful. Upstairs, I checked in with HQ, where Tandy was turning everything over to JoJo, who had gotten up from a nap in the back room. T. Laine was typing up a report so fast the keys clacking sounded like castanets. Soul was in the break room making coffee, looking gorgeous and curvy and sophisticated, her teal and aqua gauzy skirts moving with the air from the heater vents. Or from her magic. Shape-shifting magic was different for each shifter species and *arceniel* magic was the least understood of all.

I was eating and inputting my report when Rick and Occam came in. Rick went to his office. Occam stopped at my cubicle, and I could see him reflected in the window where my plants grew, his body dark and indistinct against the rising sun.

"Nell, sugar?" he asked, sounding very Texan, the way he often did after a shift to his cat.

I hit enter and saved my report. Picked up my coffee and spun in my chair to face him. His blondish hair hung long. His beard was a postshift two-day growth and scruffy. His eyes were more-than-human golden. He was wearing jeans low on his hips and his T-shirt was faded and too tight, showing abs and biceps and deltoids. His arms were up, hands on the cubicle walls, balanced. "You still mad? We shouldn'ta left you."

"Not mad. Actually it kinda makes me feel all warm and fuzzy inside." His eyebrows lifted, wrinkling his forehead in confusion. "Makes me feel like I'm really and truly part of Unit Eighteen," I explained.

"I'm not following you, Nell, sugar."

"If I'd been T. Laine or Tandy or JoJo, you'd still have forgotten me. You were being cats, already focused on the hunt. It's the human's and witch's and empath's job to look after the werecats when you get focused on werecat issues. So forgetting me made me one of the team. You didn't think you needed to babysit the probie. Or the woman. I apologize for hanging up on you. I hadn't thought it through at the time."

"Day-um, woman." Occam looked half-impressed, half-fearful. "Just when I think I got you figured out you go and do something unexpected. So you ain't gonna be getting us back for forgetting you?"

"Oh, there'll be payback." I sipped and spun back to my laptop. "That's Unit Eighteen's way."

Occam snorted a laugh, all cat. A little intrigued. And I realized that I had, maybe, just flirted with the cat-man. A plant-woman flirting with a wereleopard. I felt a blush race up my throat into my face.

JoJo yelled down the hallway, "Gather 'round. Report!"

I picked up my laptop and stood, taking one step toward the hallway. Stopped in a sudden jerk. Occam hadn't moved. I was too close. I wanted to step back, but that would have been weak. I wanted to bull my way through him, but that would have been . . . dangerous. I wanted to cover my chest with the laptop. *Weak.* Wanted to hit him with the laptop. *Dangerous.* I couldn't think of anything to do that would be neither weak nor dangerous.

I raised my head and met his eyes, golden and glowing cat eyes. *Yeah. Dangerous.*

"Cat-boy," JoJo yelled again. "Get your butt in here and stop scaring the probie."

"Probie ain't scared," Occam growled. "Probie ain't never scared."

I thought that was the nicest compliment I had ever been given. A complete untruth, but nice that he would think I was brave when I was more often a worried, panicked rabbit, like the one eaten by the owl only hours past. I smiled, ducked my head, and pushed Occam out of the way, using my laptop to keep from touching him with my whole hand, though I felt his were-warmth on the backs of my knuckles. He resisted for just a moment and I pushed harder. He gave way and I walked past him, head high, laptop holding him away from me as I made the turn to the conference room. He followed. Cat-close.

His pursuit felt like the start to something new. I didn't know what, but I was feeling quite captivated by life and whatever it was sending my way. I also knew that if Occam had been a human male shadowing me this close, I'd have been scared. Worried. But it was a cat. It was Occam. And that was infinitely preferable.

In the conference room I took my seat and opened my laptop. Pea and Bean (the two grindys were too similar for me to tell the difference) raced up and around the tabletop, around the Christmas tree that hadn't been there yesterday. The grindylows were looking for treats, chasing each other. It was rare to see both at the same time, and I had no idea how they got around or how they knew when they were needed. According to official intel, no one knew that and speculation was rife. I just considered it their particular magic and let it go at that. Tandy gave them sunflower seeds, which both grindys adored. They settled at his place, rolling around like kittens playing. I figured they were still around because the weres had gone catty and were still acting catty, even in human form.

Rick stood at the far side of the table, leaning against the wall behind him, arms crossed over his chest, very alpha, in-charge, predator-ishy, without saying anything. The rest of the unit scattered into our regular places, not assigned seating, but the spots we had each gravitated to and semi-claimed.

Rick's eyes were still glowing greenish. I realized that he was too catty to lead a meeting and was still having trouble controlling his wereleopard. I had done the best I could to heal the magical attacks on his soul and his body, but I feared I had tied him to Soulwood. Or to me. And despite what Occam thought about my derring-do, I was too chicken to read Rick and see what was happening inside him.

Soul came to the room, standing in the doorway where she could watch us all. Or catch us if we tried to leave. Her eyes went back and forth between the werecats, evaluating. Neither cat glanced her way, ignoring her. She looked ignorable in human form but she had big teeth in dragon form. I hope the kitties remembered that.

JoJo gave the time and date, and every head turned to the second in command. JoJo was wearing black from head to toe today, topped by a black turban with a couple dozen braids hanging beneath it, her natural dark hair interwoven with blond and brown and red weaves. She was wearing three big earrings in each ear and none of them matched. One was a scarlet feather. She looked striking, stylish, self-assured, and amazing. Her eyes were on the cats as she spoke, evaluating but unconcerned. She also looked as if she could take on the cats and come out unscathed and still looking trendy.

Jo stated the name of every person present, but she didn't type anything. We were still using, or testing, Clementine, the voice-to-character software. A silence fell on the room. And grew. Waiting. Rick should have said something, but he stood against the wall, his French-black eyes greenish and unfocused. Jo looked to Soul, who ignored her, her own black eyes on the cats. Jo's mouth tightened and the skin at the corners of her eyes wrinkled. She looked annoyed, or maybe *cantankerous* was the correct term.

The others shot furtive looks at Rick. The grindys stopped playing and crouched. One was staring at Rick, the other at Occam. A feeling of discomfort grew in the room, and JoJo seemed to let it happen, the annoyed expression going vexed and stubborn.

I looked at Rick. At Occam. Occam was staring at me, golden eyes glowing. I gave him the back of my head, much as he had done on the hood of the C10. Cat insult back at him. He hacked in amusement and settled, the interaction seeming to calm him, to center him in his human side.

Slowly, Jo said, "Tandy and I found something." JoJo pursed her lips and shook her head slightly as if arguing with herself. She took a slow breath and said, "But first, Rick. Report on the DNAKeys' recon."

Rick's eyes tracked to her. He said nothing. The words came back to me. *The urge to shift and to hunt waxes strong three days out, abides the three days of, and wanes three days after. Nine nights of pleasure and nine days of hell.* And Rick had a nasty history with werewolves, who had tortured him. Had the visit to DNAKeys triggered something in him? I didn't know what was about to happen but—

"Rick LaFleur!" Jo snapped, slamming her palm down on the tabletop. "Report!"

Rick blinked. A grindy whirled and leaped across the room, covering ten feet in an instant, and landed on Rick's crossed arms, standing on them with her back feet and stretching up to meet him, muzzle to nose. She chittered at him, sounding mad. Rick blinked. The green glow of his eyes faded. He shifted position. Took the grindy in one hand and stepped to his chair. Sat. Moving like a human. We were all watching Rick, waiting to see what he would do.

He looked at Jo and said, "Thank you." Then he placed the grindy on the table and continued, "Our reports will be detailed, but as a summation, Occam and I both scented werewolves and vampires." His brows drew down and together, remembering or confused, I couldn't tell. He petted the grindy. She rolled over and batted his hand, the cutest judge and jury and executioner ever envisioned.

"There were other scents too, human and non, things we didn't recognize. There were cameras mounted in the trees at the periphery, and along a twelve-foot hurricane fence with razor wire coiled across the top. Inside the fence was a playground with balls and agility equipment. Just outside the fencing we saw lasers and other security measures, things human eyes might miss. Two guards, human, patrolled the grounds outside. There was something military in their bearing." Rick blinked and sat back. The grindy scampered back to Tandy and the sunflower seeds, which she stuffed into her neon green cheeks like a chipmunk or a squirrel.

"Occam?" JoJo asked.

"He covered it."

I didn't look at Occam. I had a bad feeling he was still staring at me.

"Okay," JoJo said. "Tandy. You're up."

Tandy punched a key on his tablet and said, "Just before shift change last night, JoJo found an unhappy DNAKeys employee on social media. One who has ties to two of the conspiracy theorist sites. She has a military background, a few documented mental issues in the past, and the skill set to target the owners and principle investors of DNAKeys."

Rick focused on the empath and a faint smile appeared on his face, starting in his black eyes. He looked fully human now that his human attention had been captured. "The people at DNAKeys missed that in a background search?"

JoJo said, "They're good. We're better."

"I had an interesting conversation with Candace McCrory during the course of the night," Tandy said, "posing online as Shaundell Mason." My head came up at that one. Tandy turned to stare at me, the overheads bringing out the reddish

Lichtenberg lines in his white skin. He finished, "Shaundell and Candace McCrory have set up a meeting for six p.m. tonight when Candace gets off work."

Shaundell Mason was me. Well, actually she was a fake identity set up with a full social media presence and a complete history, but all the photos in which Shaundell appeared were me, Photoshopped with red or purple or green hair and glasses and ripped black jeans and goth T-shirts. Shaundell was a member of the ASPCA and PETA, financially supported four rescue shelters, and fostered dogs, cats, and, once, a squirrel. She liked heavy metal music and had grown up in a restrictive, fundamentalist church.

"You want *me* to meet her?" I didn't believe that they'd let a probie meet with a source.

"She's your age, went to private school, father's a pastor from a hellfire-and-damnation church," Tandy said. "She's rebellious. Mad at the world. Your persona is all that and more. You're perfect for the meet. And you've been chatting for hours about saving animals that have been abused, closing down labs that use animal experimentation and exploitation."

Thoughtfully, Rick said, "Nell, if you dress the part and put on that red and purple wig, turn on that local church-speak, and tell her how much you hate church authority? You'll be perfect. You up for it, probie?"

I opened my mouth to say no, but instead I said, "Sure." *Sure?* Since when did I say *sure*?

"JoJo," Rick said, "you dig deeper. T. Laine, you're with the senator today. Watch for any signs of paranormal activity. Tandy and Occam, get some rest. Nell, go get some sleep. Anyone got anything else to add? Good. I want everyone here at four p.m., ready to roll, in place for surveillance at five. Meeting adjourned." Rick stood and left the room. Soul was no longer standing in the doorway.

Sure? I said *sure*. I stood, tossed my trash, and went to the locker room for a hot shower. Not having to wait while my water heated would save me time when I got home. It would be better if I could put on jammies and be ready for bed before I even walked in the door, but sure as shootin', I'd have a flat on the way home and have to change a tire in my pajamas. According to Mama, I'd burn in hell if I ever did something so irresponsible. Instead I slathered my homemade sandalwood-and-lavender-scented coconut oil over my body, and a mixture of hempseed oil, jojoba oil, and sweet almond oil on my face and throat, and put on clean undies with yesterday's office clothes. I paused, wondering how I smelled to the cats and reminding myself to never add catnip to my body oils. I'd seen the result of catnip on Rick and his faithless mate, Paka. I ran a little of the facial oil through my short hair before I dried it. I left off makeup, even though I looked as pale as Yummy. Gathering up my gear and both gobags, I pushed through the door to the hallway. And stopped short.

Occam was sitting on the floor in front of the door, his back against the wall and his legs stretched across the hallway. I didn't know if he was cat-claiming me or if he just felt calmer in my presence after the disturbing visit to DNAKeys. Either way I'd have to step over him. Which felt all kinds of wrong. No lady would—

I shot Occam a scowl that woulda set kindling on fire, hitched my bags higher, and stepped over his legs. Without stopping to see how he would react, I jogged down the steps to the outside. *Men.*

I drove away, ignoring Occam standing in the doorway. I had enough problems in my life without worrying about his catty self, this close to the three days of the full moon. Yeah. It was mighty awful sometimes. But I was tired of making allowances for cats.

Back home, I turned on the electric blanket that warmed my bed—a guilty secret I hadn't told Mama about buying. Wasteful, she would call it, when I could put heated rocks in a bed warmer in the bed with me. But I didn't have time for rocks to heat. I made up a fire in the cookstove and set a kettle on it for tea when I woke, then let the cats off the porch and inside. I fed them kibble and petted the ones who let me.

From my closet, I pulled out the threadbare jeans and the mismatched earrings and the thin, holey T-shirts. The scarlet and purple wig. The cheap high heels. Set them all on the bed. They looked perfectly awful on Leah's hand-stitched velvet wedding-ring quilt. I stripped down and put on flannel pajamas and fell in the bed.

I woke to my cell pealing. It was two thirty, my alarm chiming. The cats were curled around me, purring. I had shoved a pillow beneath my knee, and my face was half buried in another pillow. I was toasty, but the room was icy. I could hear sleet peppering on the metal roof two stories above me and on the windows at the back of the house. I was groggy from too little sleep over the last few days, but I had to get up. I had a wig and undercover clothes to get into. I had a job to do. I was going undercover in my first-ever meet and greet with what I hoped would become a confidential source. I was going to lie and cheat and fake with every word and every move. I was ashamed. And excited.

I turned off the blanket, crawled out of the warmth, and shivered in the cold. I added two oak logs to the firebox, thinking again about that electric heater I hadn't bought. I dressed in a hurry, the clothes warm from contact with the electric blanket. I stared at myself in the unfamiliar clothes, the ones bought for my undercover persona by JoJo and T. Laine on what they called a "girls' night out." I looked long and lean in the tight jeans and the tall heels, but also odd, half-finished.

So I made it worse.

I shoved my hair up under the stocking skullcap and situated the wig in place. Put on the earrings, one a real Cherokee Indian arrowhead wrapped in silver wire, the other a silver hoop big enough to catch on my clothes. I'd have to be careful not to hurt myself. I hadn't had pierced ears for long and I might snag the earrings and yank the jewelry through the earholes. I drew on heavy eyeliner in shades of green and purple with a thick band of black. Layered on the mascara. I added powder to make me paler. And pale lipstick.

I stared at the stranger in the cheval mirror. My new

height and the tight clothes made me look modelesque, though three-inch heels with crisscrossing straps were going to make it hard to walk in the sleet. I'd manage long enough to do the meet and greet. The colorful hair was a shock, but . . . I looked . . . I looked really good, actually. I looked *hot*. Which was a very uncomfortable thought.

I coiled my wig up into a bun and stuck hair picks into it. The picks had faceted onyx and skulls dangling from the ends. The multicolored hair looked better bunned up. Except for the sticks and the color of the wig, the hairstyle made me think of a churchwoman's bunned-up look.

It made me think of Mud with her hair up. For now, Daddy was keeping her safe, but I had to do something about her. Soon.

I shook my head and the earrings swung against my neck, which looked too long and skinny. I wrapped a colorful scarf around it and then tried on my winter coat, which seemed out of style with the outfit. I rooted around in the closet, among Leah's old clothes. I had never been able to make myself give away some things, even though I never wore them, and I remembered a quilted shawl made of velvet patchwork. She had made it at the same time she made the velvet quilt for the bed. I found it on a shelf and draped it around me. It looked splendid, perfectly matching the street-waif-meets-gypsy-fortune-teller look I hadn't realized that I was going for. I repacked my gobags with fresh clothing and with extra goop for fixing my hair after I removed the wig. I felt a car pull into my drive. If I hadn't been so busy, so distracted, or if I'd been barefoot, I'd have noticed it sooner. A knock on the door interrupted me and I sighed. *Occam.* Had to be. I'd had a bad feeling he would show here, wanting to chat before work. My gypsy-fortune-teller look was working.

I threw the shawl across my chest and strode to the door. Threw it open. To see Benjamin Aden standing there.

NINE

"Is Nell ho . . . Oh," he said. His blue eyes dragged from my sexy-sporty-strappy boots to the top of my colorful head.

Shame and horror and shock twined through me. "I'm going undercover," I blurted out.

Ben's eyes went wider if that was possible. "Nell, you look . . ."

I got a breath and the shock of icy air cleared my head. I narrowed my eyes at him. "Not like a prostitute."

He shook his head. "You look fantastic."

That was not the reaction I expected from a churchman. The cold air was stealing my meager heat and I stepped back to let him in. He shut the door behind him and I walked away, knowing my backside in the tight jeans was . . . moving . . . in front of him. I wanted to wrap up in the shawl to hide, but I tossed it on the couch. I wasn't a churchwoman. Not anymore. Except that I went straight to the woodstove, just like a good female in her homemade dress, and put a tea bag in a mug with the water I'd left heating. I put coffee on the Bunn, a strong French roast I knew a churchman would like. My tall heels clomped on the floor. I hadn't offered Ben a seat. I was equally mortified and electrified.

I got myself under control and turned back to him. "Have a seat." Not *Why'n't you'uns take a chair and rest a spell.* Not *Welcome to my home. Hospitality and safety while you're here.* Not the old God's Cloud of Glory sayings. The church and I were truly parting ways. At long last. My cell dinged with a text. I ignored it.

Ben looked squirmy and twitchy, standing by the couch,

looking everywhere but at me. Cello jumped up on the sofa and went to him for attention, sticking a demanding cat nose in his hand. Ben jerked away, his eyes wide. *There was a cat on the sofa.* Cats weren't allowed in most church homes except when there was a mouse problem. I stifled a giggle.

At the soft sound that escaped me, he flinched, but then he laughed and shook himself like a wet dog. He held out a basket in his other hand. I hadn't even noticed it. "Your mama suggested you might like some fresh eggs. She has some new laying hens. Easter Eggers and Ameraucanas."

I accepted the basket and pulled back the cloth that covered the contents. There were greenish and bluish eggs inside. I put the basket on the long kitchen table. One designed and built for a multiwife family with dozens of children. It was dusty. Unused. There were cat tracks across it. The floor beneath was dusty too, the result of a wood-heated house and a homeowner too busy to clean. Another sign I was following the yellow brick road to hell. My silence had gone on too long.

I glanced at Ben and away, fast. He was staring at me. "Please tell my mama thank you. And that I'll be over to see her soon." The Bunn stopped drizzling and I asked, "Cream? Sugar?"

"Black, please. Um, Nell, your hair—" He stopped.

A feeling like shame whipped through me. I knew what he had to be thinking. What any churchman would be thinking. "I'm not a scandalous woman."

His blue eyes widened. "I know that. I'm—"

"I'm a law enforcement officer." Still speaking, I placed the cup with a cloth napkin on the coffee table and turned back to the stove. "I have an interview with a girl who dresses like this. It's to make her feel comfortable so she'll talk. Like Paul when he went into the pagan temple and talked about the missing god. He didn't condemn. He started where they were."

"I know my Bible, Nell," Ben said, amusement in his voice. But he sat on the edge of the couch and tasted the coffee. "This is good."

"Thank you." I carried my tea to the armchair and sat. It

was totally inappropriate for me to have Ben Aden in my house, unchaperoned. Alone. Me, wearing sinful pants that showed off my feminine form. I fought a smile and sipped my tea. It needed to brew much longer, was weak and unsweetened. I sipped anyway, fighting the giggle that wanted to erupt from me. "My mama—"

"Sent me to see you. Away from family."

"She's matchmaking," I said, thinking that she woulda never done such a thing except that I'd been widowed and the social mores were different for widder-women. "Being devious," I added.

"Oh yes. She is. It's what churchwomen do whenever there's a single man looking for a wife."

Looking for a wife. I sipped my tea. Placed the mug on the table with a soft *thump.* "Ben, I like my job. I like my life. I love my farm. I'm not a churchwoman anymore." I was, however, babbling. "I ain't—I'm *not* ever going to live on church grounds and be part of a huge family. I don't even know if I want kids." I stopped suddenly. *I'm not human.* That was the important part. I couldn't say that. Some of the churchmen might still be desirous of burning nonhumans at the stake. It had happened before, long ago. A woman accused of being a witch, burned to death. *Mud. Esther. Priscilla. Judith. Mama. Or perhaps Daddy. Or my whole family, every man, woman, and child. It would be a midnight fire, source unknown, fast burning. The church would never call a fire department. Everyone inside would die.*

Ben's full lips moved in an easy smile that was slightly crooked, his teeth strong and white. "Nell . . ." It sounded like a caress.

I shook my head no. My cell dinged with another text. I pulled it from my pocket and cradled it in my hand without looking at it.

Ben said, "I love the land and the people. I don't love the lifestyle of four wives and forty children running around all over." Forty children wasn't an impossible number, if a man kept four wives and a few concubines all busy, but it made my frozen face crack a smile. "I came back to the church to

effect change. Along with Sam and his other friends, we
want to see the church move into the twenty-first century. I
want a wife who can help that happen."

I stilled. *Wife* . . . I'd been a wife. It hadn't been all bad.
John was an old man when he told me it was time to come
to the marriage bed. I was fifteen. I'd been an old bride by
church standards. John wasn't too demanding. A few times
a month. And it had kept me safe. Until he fell sick and died
and left me a widder-woman and landowner and far better
off than the churchwomen. John had left Soulwood to me.

Being in John's bed had been unpleasant, but I'd thought
it was worth it to be safe from the man who wanted to own
me. It was the kind of compromise women made all over the
world: sex and nurturing and nursing for safety. Prostitution
of a different kind.

"I don't know if we would suit," he said, "but I'd like to
get to know you better. I'd like to take you to dinner."

I had been staring into the distance, and whipped my eyes
to him.

Dinner.

His dark hair had fallen across his forehead in a long curl.
Too long by church standards. And Ben Aden wanted to take
me to dinner. Like Occam did. Occam who had kissed me.
Playing the field, JoJo had called it once when I was in the
room with her and T. Laine as they talked about men. *Dating.* "Oh. Umm. Oh." I looked around the house as if I had
never been there. Dusty. Cat prints. Lumpy brownish couch.
Tattered chairs. I hadn't noticed they were in such bad shape.
John's and Leah's things. So little that was mine. I didn't
know what to say to Ben.

Tears filled my eyes. Maybe fear. Maybe confusion.
Maybe lots of things. I blinked hard to push them away.
"Um." My cell dinged again. Then twice more with reminders for the first two. I held up the cell as if to show him where
the dings were coming from, or like a lifeline, and thumbed
it on.

The first text was from Mama, telling me she was sending
someone over with fresh eggs. Not even thinking that I might

be at work or sleeping off a night of work. No. Expecting me to be at home like a good churchwoman, because the idea of a woman with a regular job was beyond her world reference. Not mentioning Ben. Setting me up for matchmaking.

The second text was from HQ, updating me as to time and location for the op.

The last text was from Occam. It said, *Driving up your mountain. We need to talk.*

"Oh. Dear Lordy Moses," I whispered.

"What?" Ben asked, concern lacing his voice.

A car pulled up outside. Cello leaped to the floor and raced to the front door, as if knowing that a big-cat had come calling. *Mwor*ing loudly.

"This is about to be uncomfortable," I said, standing. "A coworker is here to have a chat." All truth. Not lying at all. "I don't know about dinner."

"Would you like to meet for coffee in the morning? Like normal people do? Somewhere in town?" Ben asked, bemused by my obvious and growing panic. A car door closed. The other cats raced to join Cello.

Were the cats moon-called yet? What would Occam do if—when—he met Ben? Occam who wanted to date me, and whose cat might perceive Ben as competition. My breathing was too fast. My hands were tingling. Soulwood seemed to roll over in the winter deeps and reach for me. *Oh no. I'd grow leaves.* A peculiar laugh stuttered out of me.

"Nell? Is everything all right? Can I help?"

I made that sound that might be considered laughter, the kind heard in a scary movie about ghosts in an old insane asylum. I sped to the door and grabbed up the cats and raced to the back door, where I shoved them onto the back porch, getting scratched in the process. Set the dampers to burn slow. Slung my gobags over my shoulder and my weapon harness over an arm.

Ben was watching me in befuddlement, and maybe some amusement. I heard Occam's steady footsteps on the stairs. All three cats started caterwauling at the door, wanting back in.

Ben looked back and forth between the front door and the loud cats and me. "Nell?"

"I'm okay, Ben. I gotta go to work." I sounded anxious.

"Nell?" He was getting worried. I'd heard that *protect the little woman* tone before. Usually just before a doting father pulled out a shotgun.

"Where?" I demanded. "Where can we meet for coffee or breakfast tomorrow? When I get off work." Occam knocked on the door, his lithe frame a darker shadow against the dim daylight of the front window.

Ben looked at the front door and at me standing with all my gear. I could tell he was itching to take the heavy load of gobags off my fragile shoulders. "Pete's Coffee Shop, downtown on Union?" he asked.

"I'll be there at seven."

"You sure?" He meant was I sure about my new visitor not being here to ravish me.

"I'm sure." I opened the door and tossed my two gobags at Occam. He barely caught them, but when he did, they seemed to weigh nothing. "I'll be right there," I said. And I shut the door in his face. Spun so my back was to the door. Ben was so close I nearly touched him when I turned. I pressed my spine to the door.

Ben's blue eyes were twinkling, but his face looked serious. He lifted a hand to the wig and touched the wobbly messy bun, as if to see if the colorful hair was real. "I'll see you in the morning, Nell." He took my shoulders in his hands and gently eased me out of the way. Opened the door, stepped out, and closed the door behind him. Closing me out of the conversation.

Oh. I should have gone out there. Should have stood my ground. Acted tough. I placed my ear against the door like a child listening in on a forbidden adult discussion.

"I'm Ben Aden."

Occam said nothing for a half dozen of my racing heartbeats. "Occam." There was a low half growl in his voice.

"You work with our Nellie?"

Our Nellie? That was church-speak, a way to cut off others that were interested in a churchwoman. It was also a claiming. I wasn't ready to be claimed, not by anyone.

"I work with Special Agent Nell Ingram."

That! That was better.

"Hmmm." There was a load of possible meanings in that one syllable. I feared that Ben was about to do something awful. Instead he said mildly, "Well. You have a good day, you hear. Weather's treacherous."

I heard Ben's farm boots tapping down the stairs. Heard his truck door close and the engine turn over. Heard the truck putter smoothly into the distance.

"Nell, you going to stand there all day or you going to open the door?" Occam asked.

I looked around the house. Thinking. The house would be fine unless I was gone more than a couple of days or unless the temperature dropped into the low twenties and stayed there a while. I took a fortifying breath and opened the door. Closed it behind me and locked up. I stuck my chin up and turned to Occam, who looked me over, much as Ben had, from toes to red and purple wig. My chin went up even higher. I threw the tails of the velvet shawl over me and adjusted my winter coat over my arm. "You wanted to talk. We can talk on the way to work."

"So I'm driving you in?"

"Might as well." I took the stairs to the ground, my strange heels making it hard to keep my balance on the sleet-slick steps. Over my shoulder I said, "If I'm not spending my off time sleeping on an inflatable mattress, someone can bring me home. Or I can take an Uber. Or maybe my Unit Eighteen vehicle will arrive. Miracles, anyone?"

"Or your boyfriend can drive you back?"

I ignored Occam and got in his car. The inside of the two-door Ford Mustang was still warm. I closed the door. And waited. Because Occam was still on the porch. Sniffing around? Taking in Ben's scent? Getting catty-possessive? Eventually he followed me and stowed my gear in the small trunk. And got inside. His long legs moved with a grace no human would ever achieve. The door closed, too softly, too controlled.

He started the engine and backed around, to pull down the dirt
road, down the hill, his long fingers clasping the steering wheel
gently, the way he might hold one of my cats.

The sleet had stopped but it had left a thick slick coating
on the road. He nursed the pedals. As we dropped elevations,
the sleet disappeared into a slush and then into water draining down the culverts and away.

"You seeing Ben Aden?" Occam asked long after we had
entered the bumper-to-bumper traffic of Knoxville's afternoon rush hour.

"That mighta been resolved if you hadn't arrived so pre-
cipitously."

"So this is *my fault*?"

"Ain't nothing nobody's fault, Occam," I said, sliding into
church-speak despite myself.

"So are you seeing Ben Aden?"

"I'm meeting him for coffee tomorrow."

"Did he bring you flowers?"

"No. He brought me eggs."

Occam slid his eyes from the traffic to me. "Eggs."

"Eggs. Sent by my meddling mama."

Occam relaxed suddenly. "Eggs." He shook his head.
"Coffee. Not dinner?"

"Not dinner."

"Then we'll have dinner tonight."

It was another way of claiming. I knew that. It shoulda
made me mad. Instead I laughed softly but shook my head.
"I got not one single idea how to take coffee or dinner with
a man, you stupid cat. Not one! It makes my stomach go all
sick just thinking about it."

"Food goes to your mouth, usually via fork or spoon, you
chew and swallow. Eatin' ain't that hard, Nell, sugar."

I blew out a laugh, feeling the unexpected tears gather
again. "Dating is more than just eating." I stared out at the
traffic and the fog that hung a few dozen feet above the road.
"At least Ben would know what I can and can't do for conversation and for fun and such like. He wouldn't ask me to

dance or play loud music or buy me a martini. I don't know how to be what you want me to be."

"Martini?" he said, sounding incredulous. "Who the hell said anything about a martini? I don't want you to be anything other than what you want to be, Nell. Question is, do you want to go back to what's old and safe or try what's new and adventurous? You want the easy way or the hard way? The easy way is to keep being a churchwoman. I'm new. I'm different. I'll be hard to date. And I'm not your church."

"Not *my* church. Not ever again *my* church."

"Then why are you talking to a churchman?"

"He ain't precisely a churchman. Well, he is, but he went away to college."

"And then went back inside? When he didn't have to?" Occam asked.

I thought about Ben's statement that he had gone away to school and then returned to the church so he could effect change from the inside. How much change? How much did a man grow and evolve his thinking patterns? I had lived away from church lands for over a decade and I still found myself falling into patterns of thought and actions that were church-bound. I remembered Ben's hands on my shoulders, the feel of them through my T-shirts. That had felt nice. It had been years since anyone had touched me. Except Occam, caressing my cheeks gently. I looked down at my lap.

I remembered the feel of John's hands touching me in the dark, under the covers. Rough and calloused. Nothing gentle about him, nothing tender or passionate. He hadn't been cruel. He had just been a man with his own needs, leaving me with the discomfort of my wifely duties. Ben would understand what I had been through. What I had done to survive. It was the way of women in the church. Would Occam understand if I flinched? If I pulled away?

Softly Occam said, "I know you ain't human, Nell, sugar. Does Ben?"

I firmed my lips and looked away. I had asked myself that question already. But no matter what happened in my life, I would not be pushed into a corner and forced to take something or someone I didn't choose myself.

When the silence had stretched too long, Occam said, "You'll have plenty of backup on the op, in the coffee shop, one inside and extra surveillance outside."

He was talking work talk, not the intensely personal stuff from only minutes past. I wasn't sure how to make the jump from dating to work. Occam didn't seem to have that trouble. I wasn't sure what I was supposed to say so I nodded but didn't look at him, fighting tears I didn't even understand.

"JoJo spent some time digging deeper into our source's social media history and discovered that our dissatisfied DNAKeys employee is probably a plant. Candace McCrory's ID is as fake as your own persona, an identity created to see who might be looking for info on the company. Look at the file, Nell. You need to see it."

I forced down my confusing emotions and turned on my laptop. I pulled up the file and the report in question and read Jo's summary. "Okay," I said softly when I was done. "Did Rick consider canceling the meeting when the fake-out was discovered?"

"Yes. But he called Soul. The up-line powers that be decided to keep it. Soul said there was a flurry of interest, as if the attention on DNAKeys had been a sign to someone. Soul is interested to see how it falls out." He went silent and drove for a while, weaving in and out of cars. "This could be a trap of some sort. You keep your wits about you, Ingram."

I blinked at the use of my last name instead of *Nell, sugar*. A name that meant important law enforcement work. That meant I was trusted to do that work in spite of my gender. Tears filled my eyes again, but I didn't turn to him. I didn't know what to say or do and doing nothing seemed a safer alternative.

I was sitting at a tall table in a corner window in Remedy Coffee, reading a book, a romance novel JoJo had insisted I carry as part of my undercover persona. She had placed the paperback book in my purse, which had come from her too. I didn't carry a handbag, especially not a huge, eggplant-purple leather satchel. Inside it, in a specially constructed holster, was my service weapon and an extra magazine. In the bottom of the bag was a small makeup kit, hand sanitizers, breath mints, a small bag of travel-sized hair products, a travel sewing kit, and a change purse. All that was JoJo's. Besides the gun, I had my cell phone and my small leather bifold ID wallet with my badge. And the wire. All hidden in special pockets.

This meet and greet was being recorded, videoed, and witnessed, with Unit Eighteen's SAC sitting at a nearby table, his black eyes focused on his work, tapping on his laptop, looking like a hip college professor taking a break. He was wearing a tweed jacket with leather elbow patches, a flannel shirt, and khakis. His hair, which grew fast when he shape-shifted, hadn't been trimmed since reconnoitering the DNAKeys' property, and it curled over his collar and around his ears, hung down his forehead in small ringlets. JoJo, who had approved his persona and his wardrobe, called him swoon-worthy. This close to the full moon, all I could see was his cat.

I used the darkening windows to check out the coffee shop and had a moment to think through all the coffee shops that had suddenly permeated my life. If I could get over my ingrained church reflexes I might actually become a townie—a city girl.

Turning the page in the romance book, I glanced around. I couldn't pinpoint anyone in Remedy who might be Rick's opposite number, a spy from the company, as no one seemed to be watching me. I checked my bun, repositioning the hair stick holding it in place. Stopped fidgeting. Deliberately checked my cell for messages. Waited.

I turned a page and glanced out the window. Occam was jogging around the block with a dog he had borrowed from someone, blowing breath in the cold air, the dog waddling, fat and bored. T. Laine was in a car across the street, watching through tinted windows. She had hoped for an unused

second-story window, but the building across Stone Street
NW had a blank façade. The other corner was a cemetery,
not a location conducive to surveillance. The location was,
however, perfect for a quick getaway on foot or bicycle.

I had gotten here early, spending the time reading and
rereading the texting and e-mails between Candace McCrory
and Shaundell Mason, my online persona. Actually Shaundra
Nell Mason, which JoJo had found amusing for some reason
when she originally crafted the ID for me. According to her,
I hated both my names and had combined them in college. I
liked dogs, bowling, and country line dancing, as well as au-
thors from the 1800s. Besides being a member of the ASPCA
with a lifelong desire to rescue and protect animals of all
kinds, I had espoused violence, if needed, to protect animals.
I loved books and was especially fond of Dickens, Emerson,
Thoreau, and Walt Whitman. Fortunately I had read all of
them in the years when Leah lay dying, and I loved Whitman's
Leaves of Grass. I was less fond of "I Hear America Singing,"
as it seemed to epitomize the church's way of life.

About the local animal shelters and ASPCA groups, I
knew nothing. If she tested me on them, I'd have to get
around that somehow. I had been pegged as an introvert so
maybe I could just act shy. But my main reason for being
here was to rule out Candace as part of any group who might
want to hurt the Tollivers from outside or inside their business interests.

Candace slid onto the tall bar chair beside me and put a
number on the table edge. I hadn't noticed her come in or
order, too busy thinking things through. I closed my book
and tucked it into my bag. We looked each other over.

Candace was a large woman, fond of fake fur—which
seemed odd in a person interested in animal rights—and
stretchy tees and those expensive furry boots young women
wore. And goth makeup with dyed black hair. She slid her
laptop onto the table and shrugged out of her fake-fur-lined
jacket. "God, it's miserable outside. Just frekking snow already," she demanded of the weather. "Candace," she finished, introducing herself.

I gave her a cautious smile. "Hi. I'm Shaundell, but I guess you know that already." Neither of us offered to shake hands.

"Easy to spot the hair. I appreciate you meeting me here. Sorry I'm late. Work was the pits today. You tried Remedy's espresso?"

I gave her a minimal shrug and pointed to my cup. "I like milk. Cappuccino or latte for me. But it's good. And the muffin was good too," I added, sounding helpful and timid, pointing to the plate and crumbs.

"Not for me. Just discovered I'm sensitive to gluten, can you believe it? I've lost a good ten pounds already but I totally frekking miss bread."

"Ummm . . ."

"So you can help the animals?"

Talk about a leading question. "Ummm . . ."

"'Cause I gotta tell you some are in bad shape. Starving. Hurt. They got one wolf cross that weighs less than sixty pounds."

"Red or gray?" I asked.

"What?"

"Red wolves are smaller. Sixty isn't bad for that breed. And it depends on the cross. What was it bred with? Breed a red bitch with a Chihuahua male and you can get anything." I knew next to nothing about ASPCA, but I knew dog and wolf breeding, so my words might cement me as an animal lover. Breeding was a passion among some of the men at the church. "And why do you think it's starving? Can you see ribs? Spinal processes? How about the hips?" None of this was why I was meeting Candace, but it might create a bond that would cause her to reveal something else. My classes in establishing covert relationships had indicated that such bonds were important.

Candace didn't answer and I pulled out my phone, accessing photos of starving dogs. On the right corner a small red light started flashing. Someone was trying to sync with my phone, likely the laptop Candace had brought in, and that was sitting only inches from my cell. But the PsyLED cell phone was heavily encrypted. If the automated attack was successful, the cell would make a soft ding and scramble itself.

I held out a picture of a starving dog. "Is it this bad?"

"Gross. No. I guess I'm worrying for nothing?"

"So they aren't starving. What is the company doing to the animals?"

"They're experimenting on them."

"How? Surgery? Cosmetics testing?"

"God yes. The whole place is a lab. They draw blood every week, do X-rays, scans, and when the animals die, there are autopsies. It's pretty gross."

I'd seen animals butchered for food. This city girl had no idea what she ate or how it lived or died. As a spy to draw me out, she was useless. I already knew I was better at this than she was. "What about werewolves? There's rumors in the ASPCA that DNAKeys has paranormals as prisoners."

"Yeah, they have a few. So what? They aren't human anymore. Weres're stark raving crazy and fangheads are dead."

Which wasn't exactly true. As a general rule, most were-creatures were only animalistic on the three days of the full moon. Werewolves were the exception to that rule. They were more cursed than the other weres and the females never fully regained their humanity, even on the new moon, but the males still maintained most of their humanity. Vampires were traditionally referred to as the undead, not dead, but I didn't offer any of that information. I nursed my cooling drink, catching sight of Occam and the waddling dog again. He stopped when another man approached and I watched as the other man took the leash and walked away. Occam tucked his hands in his pockets and sauntered on.

Candace's espresso came and she sipped. A look of almost religious ecstasy settled on her face. She sipped again with a long slurping sound, cradling the cup in both hands. But there was something false about the action that said this lack of manners was part of an act.

"What's DNAKeys doing with werewolves and vampires?" I asked finally. "Were-taint is contagious."

"They have a plan. Or two." She slurped again and launched into a list that sounded rehearsed. Were-experimentation was for creating supersoldiers, lab work done on the first floor of DNAKeys. Vampire experiments were searching for cures for cancer, for extending the shelf life of vampire blood so it could be used medically, searching for cures for Alzheimer's, leukemia, and bone and liver cancers. And the vampire testing was on the fourth floor. Conspiracy theories. Every conspiracy trope in the book. Was this meeting nothing more than a chance to secure access to my cell to check me out?

However, I had seen photos of the DNAKeys building. There was no fourth floor. I was about to call Candace on it when she grabbed my hand and squeezed my fingers. Hard. There was something stiff between our palms. "I gotta go," she said. "But if you can get help for the animals, I'd be really happy." She grabbed her laptop and left the building so fast I was left with my accusing mouth hanging open. Out the windows I watched as Candace hopped into the backseat of a passing car and drove away. I was pretty sure I had seen the gray sedan twice while we talked, but I wasn't certain. I glanced around and no one was watching me, so I stood and hid the espresso cup with my body. Using a paper napkin I picked it up and slid it into the oversized bag. For fingerprints.

Just in case I was being observed, I said aloud, "That was weird." I slung my eggplant-colored bag over my shoulder and walked out of Remedy and down the street, my head bowed against the misty rain.

Occam picked me up in his fancy car and we passed Rick getting into his own—a dull brown SUV with rust along the wheel wells. "That was weird indeed," Occam said, pulling into traffic and beginning a countersurveillance pattern through the dark. Dusk had come and gone quickly in the cloudy weather.

"Weirder than you know," I said, placing the cup into an evidence bag and starting a chain-of-custody form. "She, or someone in the coffee shop, was trying to hack my cell the whole time we were together." I checked my cell. The little light had stopped blinking and a green light told me the attack had been unsuccessful. I had to wonder what the hacker was thinking about a purple-haired woman with an uncrackable phone. I held out my other hand. "And she passed me a note."

"No kidding?"

"No kidding. Just like out of a spy movie."

"A bad spy movie," Occam said.

"I've only seen three, so I'm not one to judge."

"Only three spy flicks?" He sounded horrified.

"*The Accountant*, *Argo*, and *Mission: Impossible*—the first one."

"Nell, sugar, we gotta get you educated. In spy movies," he amended. "You did great in there, by the way."

I ducked my head to hide my blush.

"Read the note," he said.

I unfolded the note left by Candace. Who was a fake disgruntled employee, but had passed me a note just like a real disgruntled employee might. This undercover stuff was tricky, twisty, complex, and deceitful. And I liked it.

TEN

I read it aloud. "You passed the test. Meet the real girl at the main library on Church Avenue in thirty minutes. Mary Smith will be in the computer room. Red hair, red plaid coat."

"So Candace McCrory was a company plant like we thought? But she passed you a note to meet up with someone else? Why?" Occam asked.

"I don't know," I muttered. "Maybe she *was* an informer and *was not* an informer at the same time. Someone who believes all the conspiracy theories but is working for the company like a double agent? Or someone who likes playing games? Some of these animal rights people are scary. Not that fighting for animal rights is wrong, but . . ." My words trailed off. True and fanatical believers of *anything* could be scary. Churchmen. Churchwomen. Terrorists.

I finished composing a group text to JoJo, Rick, and Soul with the contents of the note. I finished the text with *Meet with the new girl? I know the library layout.*

Rick instantly sent back, *Yes. Occam as backup.*

I gave Occam the address and sat back against the seat, thinking, giving myself a good work-related reason to not look at Occam. He had called me Ingram. I liked that a lot more than I ever would have believed.

"It has to do with paranormal beings," Mary Smith said. I looked at her blankly. "The research on all the lab animals? It has to do with vampires and werewolves."

The blank look stayed on my face. I assumed that Mary

wasn't her real name. I had no idea who she was. The were-cats had mentioned smelling vampires on their reconnaissance of the research facility, but vampires and weres tended to live in a state of perpetual warfare. "Vampires and werewolves? *Together?*" I clarified.

We were alone in the computer lab, the on-again, off-again sleet keeping the regulars away. The room was chilly and we were both still wearing outerwear, Mary in a red plaid zippered jacket, me in my regular winter coat. She wore no makeup and had yellowed teeth that protruded in front. I wasn't sure the teeth were real, because she talked in an odd lisping accent, as if unaccustomed to the shape of her own mouth.

Mary nodded, her hands in her pockets, fists clenched, no chance of leaving fingerprints. "The director of the vampire and werewolf program is trying to genetically reverse engineer paranormal blood. He wants to find all sorts of medical applications for it for profit. He devised a cross-matching protocol back twenty years ago, looking for immune response. He has more lab data on vampires than the vamps themselves. He's sequenced the vampire genetic code, and now he's looking for all the differences."

The blank looks were working, so I gave her another one. I vaguely knew what sequencing a genetic code meant, but had no idea about the relevance to a company's R&D outcomes, possible future products, and profit margins. Nor did I yet know if the vampire research was real or a figment of her imagination. And I didn't know what it had to do with my cover about abused animals. "Okay. That sounds expensive and time-consuming. But I don't really care about vampires or were-creatures. I'm interested in rescuing animals."

"The company's intent is to find out if there are applications for life-extending and cancer-fighting and virus-fighting properties. Except this employee"—she pointed to herself—"thinks that there is another purpose. I'm not sure what, but I have ideas based on conversations I've overheard."

"Like what?" I asked, thinking about Candace's conspiracy theories. I was discovering that conspiracy theories gave me a headache.

Mary had freckles on her nose and her hair was cut short and worn like a red ball of curls. It looked good on her. Better than my multicolored wig did on me. Maybe that was why I had a headache coming on, wearing a wig.

"The second-floor researchers are experimenting on chimpanzees and pigs, with werewolf blood and vampire blood," she said. "Some super-secret DNA studies with genes implanted in human embryos—with an emphasis on curing humans of genetically caused diseases.

"The third-floor lab is working with vaccines against a virulent plague that hit the African Congo. The plague was kept out of the media"—she lowered her voice—"even though it killed every single human in two villages in the bush, striking and killing before anyone could get away. And the new Ebola vaccine doesn't work on this strain. DNAKeys is the only pharmaceutical company working on it, in conjunction with someone at CDC—though that's unofficial thanks to a funding cut. Keys is using vampire blood for that one, in a biosafety level four lab, which is nothing but a disease-infested prison. They're testing the Ebola under controlled circumstances on chimps and three species of macaques." Her eyes filled with tears and focused on me fiercely. "The doctors are giving the animals diseases and then trying to cure them, but none of them are staying alive for long and they are so sick. When the animals die, they cut them up. It's horrific. And there's more . . ."

She nattered on for several more minutes, talking about things that sounded like Internet urban legends and myths. I wanted to tune her out. I was doing a lot of that lately, and on one hand it seemed foolish to ignore possible witnesses and covert sources, but on the other hand, there was only so much conspiracy stuff I could handle.

"Okay," I interrupted, shoving my hands into my pockets, mimicking her body language. My Spook School interrogation technique trainers would have patted me on the back. My self-defense trainers would have given me a failing grade for hiding my hands, making sure there was no way on earth I could protect myself if Mary Smith—surely not her real name—attacked me. But it was cold, cold, *cold* in the computer lab. I didn't think the heat was on at all. Could computers freeze? "What else?"

"What else? Are you kidding me?"

"Not really. You told me that what the research lab is researching, and the results they're hoping for, could be good or could be bad. That's the way life works—good or bad. And you haven't said anything my animal rights group could get excited about without catching Ebola. We want to help, but not die a horrible death over it."

Mary sat back in her chair, nostrils flaring, hands still in her pockets. "No. You don't understand. DNAKeys has *goals* and they aren't sharing them. They want to end human lives or make humans unable to procreate, or maybe unleash the Ebola virus and wipe humans off the face of the planet. No one knows. It's all hush-hush research and testing, compartmentalized in various sections of the facility. And they have werewolves and vampires captive. *In cages*," she emphasized. "Like animals. *With* the animals."

Finally. That sounded like something of significance to PsyLED. I sat forward. "Okay. Lots of things going on. Paranormal beings in cages. Experiments. Got it. But there's government oversight, right?"

"No. Nothing. Even with the CDC interest and input, it's privately funded. No ethics rules are being enforced like in government-funded research facilities and pharmaceutical companies overseen by the FDA."

I nodded. "Okay. I understand."

My cell dinged. I pulled it from a pocket and glanced at the screen. The note was from JoJo, who was monitoring my conversation with Mary. The text said, *Plague is real. It's called Zaire ebolavirus 1.75 (EBOV 1.75). DNAKeys branched out to include researching strains of Ebola after the 2014 outbreak. Bet that's when they got themselves some werewolf captives with the hope that their blood might hold the cure.*

Mary looked as if she was about to bolt, so I gave an offhand shrug. "My roommate," I said, to explain looking at a text in the middle of a meeting. "She's stuck in traffic and she's got dinner. Okay, so maybe animal abuse. Maybe you can get me inside and I can see for myself? Then I could alert the local chapter about an ongoing abuse situation?"

"Are you crazy? No way!" Mary stood up fast.

My cell dinged again and I held up a hand as if to pacify Mary. JoJo had texted, *Justin Tolliver's wife Sonya and the senator's son Devin—motorcade just attacked. Limo in flames. Sonya presumed dead. Child saved by Soul. Get back here.*

I pocketed my cell. "Fine. I need to check some things, verify your claims. Can we chat again?"

Mary Smith walked away. Actually she stomped away like a petulant child. She hadn't touched a single thing; I had no way to obtain prints. As she left the room, she muttered, "Bitch."

I frowned. "What did I do?"

Ten seconds later, Occam stuck his head in the door. "You ticked her off, Nell, sugar. Whatever she wanted, you didn't give it to her. Let's go. We're wanted at HQ."

"I got the texts. Soul saved a kid from a fire. We got too many fires, Occam."

He pushed open the library's security door and we stepped into a shadow, looking around, making sure that Mary Smith didn't see us leave together. When we were reasonably sure that Mary—and no one else either—was watching us, we raced to Occam's fancy car and got in, out of the icy wind that had blown up.

"Fire. Yeah," he said thoughtfully, starting the engine. "Yeah. You're right. There is fire at every crime scene. The fires *seemed* natural, but fire is the single consistent factor at every incident. Fire is what makes this investigation a single, unified, cohesive case."

I thought back to the Holloways' party. "We thought the gunshots knocked over candles and started the fire. But what if they didn't? What if our shooter is a firestarter?"

Occam punched a screen on his dash and told the car to call HQ. It did. He passed our speculations to JoJo.

Over the tinny connection, Jo said, "Roger that. Running a search on that angle now. Checking the mythical creatures compendium with the addition of fire, hoping it's part of the existing mythos." We heard keys clacking softly and before Occam could sign off, she added, "FYI. Soul and the kid she rescued are at HQ; the others are heading in."

"We might beat them there." He peeled out of the parking lot, tires fishtailing on the thin layer of freezing rain. "ETA soonest depending on traffic." He ended the call.

Trusting in my seat belt to hold me in place, I snuggled my arms out of my sleeves and tucked my hands beneath my armpits to warm them. Occam's fancy new car had come with seat warmers and he adjusted mine to warm. This small service was mystifying to me, disorienting, bewildering. I tucked my chin down into my coat collar so I didn't have to look at him. I didn't have words to respond to all the strange feelings that were . . . not assaulting me, but hopping up and down on my heart.

I hated this. I had been a perfectly happy widder-woman—I snorted out a soft giggle.

"What?" Occam asked as he maneuvered around a corner and the tires sashayed back and forth harder.

My giggle went louder. I shook my head and giggled some more, saying, "Nothing." And then the giggles went away. I breathed out and felt some of the tension I hadn't recognized fade. "Nothing at all. Except that I'm happier now than before I joined PsyLED. I miss spending time in my garden. I miss time with my hands in the dirt and supporting my plants and herbs and veggies and trees. I miss time alone in my house. But I'm happier now. And that's weird."

"Not so weird, Nell, sugar," Occam said softly. "You got friends now. People who will protect you. Defend you. Stand with you. And you're getting your family back—on your terms. This is all good. It's stuff that makes for happiness."

I slid my eyes to the side and studied him. He was slouched in his seat, enfolded in layers that were all open down the front except the Henley T-shirt beneath. His hair was too long and swinging. His beard was always scruffy.

He was a cat-man. His body felt hotter than a normal human's. He would purr in his sleep from time to time. And . . . I liked him. Maybe too much.

I slid my arms back through my sleeves and scooted my hands under my thighs, squishing them between flesh and warm seat. Maybe smiling, just a little. "What about you?" I asked. "What do you do for family?"

"I spent twenty years in a cage as part of a traveling circus. Don't remember much before that. Went to school when I got away and then joined PsyLED pretty soon after. The job's my family right now. Hopefully that'll improve, and sooner than later."

I wasn't sure what the last words meant. But I blushed again, my flaming face hidden in the cold and dark of the car.

Back at HQ, we opened the door to the narrow stairway up to the second floor, and the stink of fire struck instantly. Occam stepped back outside, his nose wrinkled like a cat's snout. I didn't laugh. Much. I raced up the stairs, yanking the pins and the tight-fitting wig from my head, scratching my fingernails through my sweaty hair and scalp, pulling at the tiny green leaves growing at my nape, smoothing my short bob down over them. I'd have pulled the wig off sooner except I knew the sweat would make me colder. I slid my ID through the reader and straight-armed my way inside.

The stench of burned gasoline and scorched upholstery hung heavy and foul, polluting the air. Along with the smell of burned human flesh. Surely Soul hadn't brought a burned child here, one who needed medical attention.

I dumped my gobags in my office cubicle and made sure my weapons were locked up, then went in search of Soul and the child she had rescued. The little boy, whose name I didn't remember, was asleep in the break room, curled on the couch. Someone had found a blanket and it was tucked around him, but his collar and sleeves showed, singed and charred. I wanted to take him for a shower and give him a clean shirt, but that wasn't happening. Not in a law enforcement office where allegations of abuse might be made.

His face was coated in soot and streaked with tears, dried snot at his nose. His chapped lips made little fluttering sounds as he breathed. Brown hair curled over his head and he looked younger than the eleven years I remembered the senator's son being. Beneath the soot, his flesh was red, but not burned. No visible burns on him at all. Just that awful stench of . . . the burned body of his aunt. That was what I'd been told, that Soul had saved the boy, not his aunt Sonya. In his sleep, his hands clasped the blanket and he whimpered. My heart clenched and melted all at once. I had seen children cry themselves to sleep after some awful trauma. This little boy was sleeping the sleep of survival.

I went to the conference room, where the other members of the team were gathered. T. Laine vacated my chair, which I realized was positioned with a clear view of the break room doorway. I nodded to her that I'd keep watch.

Rick and Occam were standing together near the window, which was cracked open to allow in fresh icy air. The smell was rank and offensive. It would be overpowering to the cats' noses. As if to make up for the stench, T. Laine set a package of cinnamon sticks on the table, and turned on the Christmas tree lights. Neither helped much except to remind me that I hadn't bought or made a single Christmas gift. Usually by this time I had the Nicholson family gifts all made: jams and preserves and plants and floral fabric for dresses, plaid fabric for the men's shirts. Small store-bought items. Candy for the young'uns. I'd done nothing. And would start feeling guilty and get on the job of Christmas gifting as soon as this case was over.

As I slid into my seat, Soul glanced down the hall toward the break room and said quietly, "I thank everyone for being here. I know this case is exacting a toll on everyone. I'll try to keep this brief: the fire and the rescue and my impressions. Then, Nell, I'd like you to update us on the two interviews.

I know it will be in your report, but I'm interested in intuitions. I have a feeling we're missing something important."

I dipped my head in agreement.

"I was behind the senator's limo convoy," she said, "three cars back, when they came to a red light and stopped. I saw the fire explode inside."

"Inside?" Rick asked. "Not underneath and then up into the body of the vehicle?"

Soul shook her head and said to the group at large, "No. The fire originated inside. Then it burst out the windows. First fire. Then the explosion. I can only postulate that an instant of opportunity gave the aunt time to unlock the door and shove the boy out onto the pavement. The explosion caught him, burned his clothes and hair, but he escaped the worst of the blast and fire. His aunt, the driver, and the security detail were all killed."

But Soul was unscathed. Not a hint of scorching. I wondered how the feds and the Secret Service would take all this. I wondered if rainbow dragons breathed fire and smoke. As if she heard my thoughts she sent a smile to me, but spoke to the cats. "Do you have a sense of smell about the child?"

Both were standing in the window's draft and shook their heads, noses crinkled and brows furrowed. "Everything stinks," Rick said. "Just like the Tollivers' house fire but with diesel fuel."

Even more softly, Soul said, "And Justin and the senator? We know Justin's wife's linens had a peculiar odor. But when you were with them, did they smell of that same oddness?"

Occam shrugged. "Fire and smoke stink interfere with and overwhelm other scents, and we've had fire everywhere they've been. Fire was the clue. We just didn't put it all together until Nell did. Couldn't see the forest for the trees."

The last bit made me smile.

Soul murmured, "To me, this child does not smell human. I never got close to his family, or to the other Tollivers. However, you are agreed that at least Justin is human?"

"Justin Tolliver smells wrong," Rick said, "but not enough to trip my predator sense. I can't explain it but predators, meat eaters, smell of meat. This man smells of human, but also of fish and water and something musky. It could be scent transfer. His wife smelled worse but she wore perfume. Like body lotion and shampoo and perfume all in the same scent. Expensive matching products."

"Lots of perfume," Occam agreed. "So maybe Justin smells normal and the odd scent was from his wife?"

"The senator's wife wears too much scent, too," Rick said, comparing the two women. "Clarisse Tolliver may wear even more perfume."

"Or maybe the cats smell things when nothing is really there. We humans should get close to her," JoJo said. "After a shower or something."

"You women figure out how to do that," Occam said. "I got no desire to be arrested for busting into the senator's wife's shower and sniffing her. Rick stole a pillowcase. I'm not sticking my nose on a person."

"We'll know more about the fire after Arson finishes their investigation," Soul said to the unit. "But there was something odd about the initial flash of fire. There was a purple and orange blast of flame, just for an instant. I've seen many fires and explosions and this one was odd.

"Change of subject." She swiveled in her seat and said to me, "I can read your report later. I want your impressions of the two women you met today."

I frowned. "I grew up in a hotbed of conspiracy theorists. I can pretty much recognize the type whether they're right or left wing, religious or atheist. They all have a certain feel." I stopped, looked at T. Laine, and grinned. "A certain *vibe*."

"Listen to Ingram, going all new age, millennialist teenager," she said.

"And both of these girls had that vibe. But the first one started out fine and then at the end changed, got worried, fidgety. I got the feeling she was conflicted and feeling guilty about something." I shook my head. "That wasn't quite it. It's a lot easier to just be yourself, except some people don't know who they are and so for them it's easier to pretend to be someone else." T. Laine and Jo exchanged a glance I couldn't decipher. "But the girl posing as Candace McCrory was fully aware of who she was, but was pretending to be someone else and wasn't altogether happy about that. She was playing . . . I guess was playing several parts. Trying to be a lot of different things at one time."

Rick nodded, as if agreeing, watching me, listening. Evaluating. That was it. He was evaluating my performance. And he seemed pleased. I went on.

"The girl calling herself Mary Smith was earnest. She was a believer and full of anger and frustration. She was real. Why Candace sent us to Mary I don't know. But I will say that I have a feeling something is going on inside DNAKeys. Where there's smoke there's . . ." I stopped. "Well, you know."

Soul said, "I've listened to most of both interviews. It sounds as if some of the women's reports might have a basis in truth, but to what degree I can't speculate."

"Got something," JoJo said. "I just cracked DNAKeys' HR records."

"What did you just say?" Soul asked.

JoJo's head came up from her laptop; her spine went vertical as a two-by-four. Jo wasn't supposed to be hacking without a warrant. "Uhhh."

"CLMT2207," Soul said. "Strike the words beginning at 'Got something.' JoJo meant to say—" She gestured to Jo.

JoJo pulled on her earrings, a sure sign of nerves. "I just discovered information in an unsecured database. Right. That."

"Continue," Soul said, but there was a bite to her tone. I had seen her dragon teeth, but Soul was scary even in human form.

JoJo said, "Candace McCrory is really Evelyn McCrory. She has a history of paranoia and conspiracy fears. She's on antipsychotic meds, or maybe she's off her meds. Maybe the truth is a little less woo-woo and a little more cuckoo."

I shook my head. "No. I'd agree that Mary Smith was someone who needs meds, who might even have been broken somewhere along in her life. But not Candace. Underneath it all she was . . ." I held both hands in front of me as if holding a large vase between them. "Carrying a burden, but self-confident."

JoJo tapped her tablet for a moment and said, "Well. Pro-bie's right. The doctor treating Candace is the same as the doctor treating Evelyn. And he died in 2004."

"So besides creating a mock social media persona, DNAKeys went so far as to falsify and plant HR records for their double agent in two names? Both McCrory identities are false? Why?"

"*We* did it," I said. "Shaundell has school and work records and has donated regularly to the ASPCA and rescue groups."

Rick grunted. It sounded like a cat, all breathy and exas-perated. It had to hurt when the bad guys were just as effec-tive as the good guys.

"Elephant in the room," T. Laine said. I looked at her. I hadn't heard that one before. And she was looking at me. "Nell read humans back when we had a plague. Why not let her read the kid?"

My eyes slid to the doorway. "That was adults. Is it even legal to read a minor? No. It isn't right without his parents' permission."

"We sniff them," T. Laine said, "listen to them. How is this different?"

Soul tilted her head. Her platinum silver hair slid forward and she caught it with a hand and smoothed it, as if it was alive. "It is not illegal, evil, or against PsyLED protocols. Nor will it harm the child. Will it?"

I scowled at her. "This feels wrong. Churchmen think it's okay to do things to children too."

T. Laine's eyes went big and startled.

"Just a surface read," Soul urged. "Just deep enough for us to know if Devin is human."

Devin Tolliver. That was his name. And they wanted me to invade him. It made me feel squirmy inside and my rooty middle ached.

"Hello? Can I have some water?" a plaintive voice called.

The kid. Awake. I narrowed my eyes at Soul. She tapped

her ear, indicating that the child had been trying to listen to us. She made a shooing motion to me. I pushed out of my chair and stood, glaring around the table to show them that I thought this was invasive and a personal assault on the kid. Soul just shooed me on again, hands waving.

I turned on a heel and left for the break room. "Hey, Devin," I said, going to the sink. "I'll get you some water."

"Thanks. Can I have my cell and play some games?"

I poured water into a paper cup and carried it to the couch. The smell of fire was much stronger here, fire and gasoline and scorched hair and something musky and sour like burned flesh. Rather than pull up the upholstered chair in the corner, I knelt on the floor by the couch and gave him the cup. "Your cell was lost in the fire," I said gently, knowing he had lost much more than a cell phone in the fire that took his aunt's life.

"Oh," he said, and I couldn't interpret his emotional reaction to the mention of the fire. He wrapped his hands around the cup and lifted it to his mouth, drinking the contents down. He blew a breath and said, "Thank you."

"You're welcome. Devin, may I check your head for fever?" And I felt like a fiend. This was *wrong*. But if Devin was a paranormal, and if we could figure out what he was, then we might also figure out who was after the Tollivers and killing people. This was important. This was necessary. It was also a rationalization. I hated justifications. *Hated* them.

Devin nodded. I touched his head. It was unexpectedly cool when I had been prepared for sleep-sweaty and hot. I closed my eyes and let my consciousness flow down through my body and into Devin.

I was met with cool energy, gray and . . . It wasn't the right word, but he was chatoyant, as if a band of bright light reflected through him, the way light carried through stone. Or, better, perhaps, the way light carried through river water, reflecting on the dappled bottom, gold and green and gray and blue, with faint purple places, all glowing. I followed the light deeper.

I heard the word, "No!"

Devin jerked away from me and I cascaded back into the break room. Tumbled to the side, to the floor. Blinking up at the child.

"No!" he said again. "Stop that! You're a bad person." Heat blasted at me. Sizzling, ripping flame. I dove to the side. Rolled to my bottom, sitting on the floor beside the couch. Disoriented enough that I put both hands on the vinyl tile floor, to stabilize myself. "I'm sorry, Devin," I said. "I didn't mean—"

"Don't touch me!" he shrieked. Another blast, this one hotter. Scorching along my skin. Blistering, roasting. I screamed. Smelled burning hair and leaves. Burning *me*. I rolled away, to the far side of the room. Covering my head. Screaming. Noting in the instant when I closed my eyes and tucked tight that the flames were orange tinged with purple.

ELEVEN

The tingle of magic was everywhere—in the air, on my skin, in my hair, in the breaths I took. Blessed pure air, cold and rich and heavy with moisture and magic, flooded my lungs. I gulped and realized that I was crying. I was hurt. I was burned.

I fought to open my eyes, my lashes gummed together. I opened them a slit, intensely grateful that I could see through the tangled lashes and the tears. My hands were curled up near my face and the skin was weeping, blistered, and stinging. I blinked and looked around. I was in the hallway outside of the break room and T. Laine was sitting on the floor beside me. "It's okay," she said. "The fire's out. The kid's out. We're safe."

I was gasping, hyperventilating, and I knew it but I couldn't stop. T. Laine's face was creased with worry; Soul stood in the break room, standing guard over Devin, looking angry and guilty. And worried. And in shock. At herself? At something else? I had a fleeting thought that her emotions were turned inward and had little to do with what had just happened to me. Then that thought slid away with the pain.

"How?" I whispered, and my voice croaked.

"I keep my null weapons charged and on me at all times," she said. "Remember?"

As the unit's resident witch, T. Laine had the tools to stop most magical attacks and the ability to use them. "My hero," I whispered, straining to see into the break room.

The tile where I had been kneeling was smoldering, wisps of smoke still rising. I touched my head and encountered hair, happy it hadn't been singed. My face hurt and I touched my cheeks. They were burned, blistered, the pain more than I could define. "Ohhh. Oh, oh, oh," I whispered, blinking. And then I remembered what she had said: *The kid's out.* Null spells didn't knock people out. "You didn't hit him, did you?" My voice sounded less husky, but it hurt to talk.

Lainie smiled crookedly. "Just with a sleep spell. He isn't human, but he reacts to magic like one. Can I help?" She nodded to my hands and held up an amulet. "Healing. It'll take the pain out. Or it should. Now that you're growing leaves, I can't guarantee anything."

I stared at the amulet. It was a small moonstone wrapped in verdigris-stained copper. I wiped my nose with my wrist and gasped at the bolt of pain that ricocheted through me. "We could try. Probably should try. But I'd rather stick my hands in Soulwood dirt."

Her smile went more crooked and her expression was both worried and compassionate. My face must be more burned than I thought. It must be bad to make T. Laine try so hard to hide her distress. "We figured you'd say that, so Tandy's bringing all your plants in from your window boxes." Having a job to do was important to the empath when someone was feeling strong emotion. He must be suffering my misery almost as much as I was.

JoJo stepped from her cubicle and knelt beside me, holding a bottle of chilled water. I shook my head. "I'm cold," I managed. "Room-temp water, please?"

She switched it out and placed a blanket over me just as the shivers hit. I think I might have blacked out because someone touched my shoulder and I woke with a start that shocked pain through me like being tased. In the background I could hear cats snarling and screaming, Soul shouting, and maybe the sound of wind chimes, all cut off abruptly. My body stank of fire and pain, and . . . and I smelled rosemary. My eyes were stuck together again, but I got them open and focused blearily on the plants all around me. Without thought, I shoved my burned hands into the soil of two pots and *reached* for Soulwood.

It was here at my fingertips and yet so far away. I pulled

hard on the soil and the life in the plants. Instantly, the soil and the plants were desiccated, dead. I yanked my hands out of the pots and rammed them into two other pots. And then two more. Dropping into the soil and calling on Soulwood, so far away, the land sleeping the sleep of winter. It was dark there, shadowed and cold beneath the sleet that fell again. Two sets of pots later, and many dead plants around me, I felt a change.

In the darks on the horizon, a pale light came awake, deep and deep and *deep* in the earth. Stretching, curious, seeking me. And we . . . came together. Soulwood wrapped itself around me. The pain eased away.

The healing was the yellow of warm sun after an icy dream, the coolness of a mountain spring spilling down rocks, the touch of velvet moss along bare skin. It was the scent of pine in winter and the feel of roots reaching and spreading, seeking nutrients and water, and sharing life with me. I sighed and the breath didn't hurt. I realized it had been painful to breathe only when the pain vanished.

The pain in my face and hands flowed away with my breath, like water flowed down a hill, and deep into the earth of Soulwood. Deep and deep and peacefully deep, around rock, broken and splintered, through layers of rounded stone from some ancient riverbed. Home. I was home. The pain fled and faded and failed, waning like the moon. Peace. Healing. Soulwood.

I don't know how long I was there, but I knew the instant when Brother Ephraim awoke. I felt him stretch and twist and grumble. I focused on the place he had carved out of my home. It was as blackened as always, a place of death, of drought, of forest fire, but it coiled with scarlet snakes full of the poison of hatred and fury, and despite the absence of life as I knew it, despite the death layered atop death, it had life of its own—a life of twisted and bitter evil, sparking and sparkling and electric.

Ephraim stared at me, his charged hatred snapping like whips, hissing like snakes, but he didn't move. There was something about that snapping heat and antilife that seemed important, something I needed to guard against. But before

I figured it out, lightning struck at me, through the ground, through the deeps. Black light blasting at me.

I raised a wall between us, pulling on Soulwood. But the lightning was faster. It struck me, midchest. Midbrain. A blinding electric heat/light, boiling, roasting, tearing into me like the child of lightning and laser. I went blind, slammed away from my body, far, far, and *far*. Everything went black.

Minutes . . . hours . . . passed. I struggled awake, fighting the lethargy, the lifelessness, the penetrating and powerful fatigue. I was underground. I was . . . not in Soulwood.

I reached out, trying to find it. But I was lost, deep underground. Worse, I was blind. Disoriented. I flailed, trying to find up and down, trying to find my land. I called to it, but it didn't answer.

Had Ephraim killed my land? Had he killed me, then stripped my soul away and tucked it into a pocket, like the pocket he had made for himself? I struggled harder, panic filling me.

Then I heard . . . something. I stopped. Holding my panic still. Forced calm into my spirit, breathing, though there was no air, resting though I had no body to calm. *Okay,* I thought. *Okay.*

"Neeeellll?" The voice was too slow, too distant. "Neeeellll?" it called again.

This time I found where it came from and angled my consciousness toward it.

"Neeell?"

I raced toward it, through the darkness, through the impossible distance, straining, struggling. Fearing I was losing parts of myself to the expanse of darkness. Struggling on nonetheless.

"Nell. Please come back." T. Laine's voice, calling me with her witch magic.

There. It was *there.* I slung my mind, my spirit, my very soul at the voice.

Back to headquarters where my body lay. And up into the soil of the potted plants.

I sucked in a breath, and my lungs made a now-familiar rubbing, flapping sound, as of air-deprived tires chafing against smooth asphalt. I coughed. Tried to force my eyes open. They were still sticky from the fire, gummed shut, the lashes sealed. Someone placed a warm, wet compress over them. I could hear the distant murmur of voices. Feel the softness of the blanket over me. An air mattress beneath me. I had been taken to the new sleeping room, my fingers still in the potted Soulwood soil that someone had wet down with fresh water. Cool air moved over my lower face and it didn't hurt to the touch. I was healed. I was whole. Minutes passed as I mentally searched my body. Finding myself restored, recovered. Though rather more leafy than I might have wanted.

"How long have I been out?" I whispered. "How many of my plants did I kill?"

"Two hours, give or take. Ten plants. Two more that look a little wrinkled but will probably live. Another batch are fine. Are you . . . all here? Feeling better?" It was T. Laine, her voice calm and even-toned.

I pulled my fingers from one clay pot and clutched the edge of the compress, easing it off my face. My eyes opened and the first thing I saw was a hand, my hand, with green leaves curling out of the tips of my fingernails. From my thumb, a thin brown vine coiled and curled, tiny green leaves unfurling. "Grapevine," I murmured. "I'm sprouting."

"No shit, Sherlock," Lainie said.

I breathed out a laugh at the crudity. "I'm healed, though, I think." And saved from Brother Ephraim's assault. He had waited until I was already in some kind of danger to attack. I wondered what he had done to Soulwood but was too much a coward to drop back into the land and look.

"Yeah," she said. "But things went to hell in a handbasket while you were growing leaves. You need to talk to Occam." I didn't respond, and she added, "When you first got hit, he went catty. We got shredded clothes and cat hair everywhere. Place is a mess."

"No hairballs?" I managed.

T. Laine barked a surprised laugh. "God no."

I chuckled with her, a breathless, strained sound. "Is Devin okay?"

"Yeah. Still asleep. The senator had flown to DC with his brother, Justin, and so we're waiting on someone from the child protective services and the kid's nanny to get here."

"I hate not being human." The words startled me.

"If you had been human, the blast might have killed you. Or disfigured you forever."

"If I'd been human, I wouldn't have been reading Devin."

Lainie was silent for a few moments and I managed to focus on her face in the dim light. Pugnacious chin, dark brown eyes and hair. Her mouth wrinkled in a pursing frown, as if something tasted bad. "Okay," she said. "I got nothing."

I laughed again. "Help me sit up. Then water. Then you can debrief me about Occam's problems." T. Laine pulled me to my butt on the inflatable mattress. While I drank the room-temperature water that I remembered asking for earlier, she filled me in.

"You know the guy's nuts for you, right?"

She meant Occam. I shrugged, an embarrassed noncommittal response that said, *Yes, but . . .*

"He lost it when you got hit. Shifted. Ruined a perfectly good pair of boots and a break room chair. Went at the kid. Pea came at him out of nowhere and cut his face up. Then Rick went catty, pulled into the shift by werecat magic. Talk about ruined clothes. And blood. Pea and Bean . . . well, all I can say is that those little things can freaking move."

"And Soul?"

T. Laine hesitated. "Not as cool as a cucumber, but she kept it all together. She and the grindys kept the kid safe and threw the cats into the null room to deal with dominance issues in the only way their cats know how. They're still alive, if a little bloody."

"And Devin?"

"He's a pyro of some kind. A firestarter. There's a couple dozen different kinds of firestarter species in mythology. We think the assassin is a pyro too. So our entire investigation is . . . officially, let's call it askew. It's either closer to being solved, because we stand a better chance now of figuring out what the assassin is and the Tollivers are, or it's really totally bollixed up."

I frowned. I had heard the word *bollocks* in a film or two and had looked it up. It was from a German word for testicles, though I had no idea what they might have to do with this investigation. "Bollixed up?"

T. Laine rubbed her forehead with a hand. A slash of blood was dried across it. Blood Spatter 101 class at Spook School had taught me that the droplet had been moving laterally at speed when it hit her. Her hand fell to her lap. Fortunately my bloodlust didn't rise. She said, "I was trying to find a word that was acceptable to you. I was trying to say the investigation probably just took a major wrong turn and dumped all our potential conclusions into a ditch."

"Fubared?" *Fubar* was Rick's term. I was used to hearing it.

"That works better than bollixed up, I guess. Though I'm surprised to hear you say it." Her expression was sly.

My face relaxed at the teasing. "Yeah. Well. Bollixed up is fine. We routinely castrated animals in the compound." I leaned to her and said with a straight face, "That means cutting off their bollocks. Want to know how it's done?"

T. Laine made a face. "Remind me not to try and shock you."

"Okay," I said.

She shook her head as if I had misunderstood her request.

"And the situation with the case isn't really that bad," I said. "We knew all along that it was either homegrown terrorism, familial infighting, or business. So now we've narrowed it down to family. Pyro against pyro. We just need to figure out how many of the Tollivers are pyros, what kind of pyros, and then which pyros have done the attacking and why. And if the attacking is a para-war."

"Right. That's all. And then we have to decide what to *do* about the pyros. The current legal system can't deal with a pyro. If the senator or a member of his family is a pyro, what happens to his career? What will the public think about it? What happens in Congress and to the bills the senator has in place when it all comes to light?"

Lainie was right. A pyro wasn't a witch, to be jailed by her own kind in a null room. Not a vampire to be chained in his sire's basement or destroyed by a vampire killer. Not an insane werewolf or a *gwyllgi* to be killed on sight or sent to the Montana Bighorn Pack for training. A pyro was a totally new paranormal creature that could set a courtroom on fire. Explode a courtroom. That could use fire to kill. "Oh," I said, sounding lame.

"Until today there were three kinds of paras." She lifted a finger with each class: "A mutation of basic human stock like you, the Welsh *gwyllgi* devil dogs, and witches; vampires and were-creatures who start human and are infected and then can pass along the trait to their offspring; and *arcenciels* and whatever the fangheads' Misericords are." She dropped her hand. "And now we have this thing. It doesn't seem to fit in anywhere. We don't know what it is. And Soul's really worried. She hasn't said a word since Devin shot fire at you."

Lainie extended a hand again and I took it, letting her pull me to my feet. I said, "I have to go to the locker room and shower and . . . ummm . . . clip my leaves."

"Good plan. I have kiddie guard duty. See you in a bit."

She left me alone and I went in search of my gear bags. I hid in the locker room, shaving my legs and clipping my leaves and studying my face in the mirror. My eyes were greener, a leafy spring green with flecks of evergreen. My pupils were larger, or maybe that was just a temporary adaptation to the low light. I hadn't turned on all the switches when I entered. My hair was longer. Brighter. A richer nut-brown with reddish tresses. Was I becoming a plant? I smiled at my reflection and it smiled back, so that part was still good. It was long after two a.m. and I should have been exhausted, but I felt pretty decent considering my several days with poor sleep and nearly getting burned to death. I repacked my gear bags and went in search of information. First up, and most important, were my plants. Someone had placed the live ones on my desk. Ten dead, two sick, eight still thriving. I placed all ten in my window box and bolstered them with a little love. Once they were okay, I headed for the conference and break rooms.

Devin was on the couch in the break room, sleeping the sleep of the spelled. Someone had pried up the blistered flooring and pulled the table over the bare underflooring. A chair had been removed. I could still smell the stink of fire over the fumes of vinegar that had been used to clean up the mess. I was glad I had been out for that one.

Soul tapped on the wall at the door behind me. "Are you well, Ingram?"

I shoved my hands in my pockets and turned to her. "Well enough."

"This child's nanny and child protective services just drove up. I had Jones set all internal cameras to record every moment." Jones was JoJo. I tilted my head to show I understood. "I want you watching the transfer with Jones and Dyson." Dyson was Tandy. Soul was doing everything by the book, her face utterly expressionless. I figured Clementine was active.

"Are the cats still catty?"

"Yes, though they have calmed down greatly and seem to have sorted out their burgeoning dominance issues."

I didn't ask how that had turned out. "You know Jo has to be going on twenty-plus hours with no sleep."

Soul narrowed her eyes at me and let a silence build between us, probably at my temerity to speak to the assistant director in such a manner. I might have sounded just a bit judgmental. I probably should have apologized, but I didn't. I had been stared down by a group of shotgun-armed churchmen in a righteous religious fury. A peeved light dragon was nothing by comparison. "I do," she said at last. "I'll see she gets a full twenty-four off starting in the morning."

"Thank you."

Soul studied me as if I were a specimen under a microscope. Again, no problem. I just stared back. "Hmmm," she said and went to the stairwell to greet the nanny and the social worker. I slipped into the conference room, which was lightless, the overhead screens dark, and shut the door. I leaned over Jo's shoulder. Tandy was sitting close to her so they could share screen views. Their positions had nothing to do with the romance between them. Uh-huh.

We watched as the two women followed Soul up the stairs, the social worker in the middle of the short column. She was a frizzy-haired woman wearing a frowzy sweater, a scarf that had to be twenty feet long wrapped around her neck in rolls, and comfortable snow boots. She was easily identified by the official name tag and the overlarge purse she carried. The nanny was an odd duck. She wore an ugly orange-brown pantsuit, a color never intended for her gray hair, which she wore slicked back, to expose a sun-damaged forehead and cheeks marked with light and dark pigmentation, especially dark beneath her eyes and spotted on her cheeks.

"Is it the screen or the lighting or the clothing or is she sick?" Tandy asked softly.

"Maybe the clothing?" I said, doubtfully.

"No. I think she's . . . gray," Jo said. "My aunt looked like that when she was about to die from COPD. Just that color gray when her lungs filled up, just before she passed. Black woman with lung troubles wearing orange clothes is not a good look."

"You think she's African-American?" I asked.

"She sure ain't European," Jo said, exasperated.

On camera, the three women moved from the stairwell camera into the hallway camera. The volume was turned down on the security equipment to keep the visitors from hearing a delayed conversation and know they were being videoed, but we could tell they were introducing themselves to one another. The nanny didn't shake hands, just nodded to Soul, who said a few words and led the social worker down the hall toward the break room. The nanny followed and then stopped in the hallway. She lifted her head and sniffed, nose in the air, her head bobbing like a ferret's.

She raced into my office cubicle.

"What the—?" Jo said, changing camera angles quickly. The odd woman was standing, hunched over, in front of my plants and she . . . stuck her hands into the pots.

I whirled to go stop her, but Tandy grabbed my wrist. "No," he said.

"But she's *touching my plants*!"

"Watch. Let's see what she does."

It was an invasion. A personal and intimate violation. It was disturbing and I had no idea why it was bothering me so much. Unit Eighteen members used my plants all the time, cutting them, touching them. But this woman was doing something else. Something odd. Something *not right*.

The strange woman stuck her hands into all ten pots, dipping fast, as if tasting. As if she knew what I was. Or what Soulwood was. Or something worse. It was bizarre.

Seconds later, she whirled and raced after the other two women, arriving at the break room only a moment behind them. She rushed in and knelt, running grayish hands over the sleeping boy. She jerked her head to glare at Soul. She picked up Devin like a baby, though he had to weigh seventy pounds, and carried him down the hallway. The social worker had Soul sign some papers before she followed the nanny and her charge away.

"That was freaky," Jo said.

"I don't think that either of the women mentioned the stink of burned hair, flesh, and vinyl tile," Tandy said, still holding my wrist. "Neither reacted or even seemed to notice it."

"The nanny was aware of, and angry about, Devin's deep sleep," Jo said, "but she didn't do anything about it. She just got the kid out of the office pronto. They were in the building for four minutes, twenty-seven seconds altogether. Soul's coming back in."

The conference room door opened. "They are gone," Soul said. "Play the video, please, with audio."

Tandy released my hand and I went to my office to check

my plants. The soil felt fine. The plants seemed fine. But . . .
the strange gray woman had *touched* them. I didn't like that
at all but I didn't know what to do about it. But . . . dang it.
She had *touched my plants*!

I stopped by the null magic room, where the weres had
been herded by Pea and Bean, and where they would remain
until they were totally calm and ready to shift back to human.
T. Laine was sitting in a chair in the hallway, looking sick.
Even through the door, the null room affected her magics.

I pointed at the door and lifted my eyebrows, asking for
permission. She nodded and I cracked the door and peeked in.
The cats were stretched out on the long table and looked bored,
a spotted tail tip twitching slightly. The metal chairs had all
been tipped over, and one was bent like a pretzel, clearly having suffered from cat ire. Grindys were nowhere to be seen.

I said, "Devin's gone." The wereleopards ignored me, as
cats are wont to do. I shut the door, catching a glimpse of
Soul in Rick's office, talking on her cell, pacing. I patted
T. Laine's shoulder and left her to her null room misery.

JoJo and Tandy were in the conference room, sharing a quiet
moment over coffee, and probably thinking that no one knew
they were an item. There was an open tin of Christmas cookies on the table, half-empty. I sat and fingered my longer hair,
not willing to start back on the case, not yet. Soul came in
again shortly after and started a fresh pot of Rick's Community Coffee. We had recently discovered that Ingles gro-
cery stores carried the brand, and he no longer had to buy it
over the Net. Best coffee ever. By the scent, this was their
coffee and chicory mix, which was coffee with a flavor kick
I was coming to adore. The quiet moments passed and we
each accepted a cup of coffee from the big boss, letting her
serve us all. We sipped. Rested.

Before the cups were empty, T. Laine entered and plopped
in her chair. "Pea let the cats out and they started changing
back. The daytime crew needs sleep so let's please do a quick

debrief and let us get to bed. You can fill in the cats when they get back."

Soul inclined her head and said, "Summary. We have firestarters. Jones and Dyson have spent the last few hours going over, again, the Tollivers' past and current financial, political, and familial status. Kent has been looking at fire-starter species. Jones?"

Soul was still using a neutral, demanding tone and last names, which seemed to give this case a gravitas it hadn't had before, again suggesting that this case was no longer an easy-to-solve one but a dangerous one. I tapped my tablet on and opened the files waiting on my screen.

Jo said, "We've been searching through birth and death records and fire and arson records to see if Tolliver firestart-ers are new to this generation or have been around a while."

New? I asked, "How could they be new?" Was *I* new? Or had there been leafy people in my past family tree? *Family tree.* I repressed a grin, turning my lips under and biting them together, tucking my head so no one would ask what was amusing. But Tandy knew and shot me a look full of questions. I ignored him.

"Recessive genes," Jo said, "or mutated genes. Tandy's got the birth history research."

Tandy hit a key on the remote that controlled the big screens. "If pyro is a new trait, then the mutation started somewhere. So let's start with the parents. Justin was adopted but from inside the family. An older sister, Miriam Tolliver, got pregnant out of wedlock, which was a social crime in the day. The infant Justin was adopted by her parents, and a father's name was never put forth. This makes Justin and Abrams biological uncle and nephew raised as brothers."

Jo said, "Miriam moved away and hasn't been seen or heard from in more than three decades. I've started a search for her whereabouts. Until now, no Tolliver children or adults have publicly displayed pyro capabilities, but it was Justin's house that burned, so maybe Justin's kids are pyros or Devin got there somehow and started that fire too. Okay. That sounds stupid for an adult, let alone an eleven-year-old. Never mind. But maybe the appearance of a pyro ability is what started all this."

"If so, then we're postulating recessive pyro genes?" I asked, thinking about T. Laine's listing of the types of paranormal creatures.

"Jones and I are hypothesizing that firestarting is a natural ability that the young Tollivers have to be trained to control," Tandy said, "and that this isn't the first time it's appeared. Just after Justin was adopted, he and Abrams were staying with Abrams' paternal grandparents, who would be Justin's maternal great-grandparents, if I have the family tree right. There was a massive fire in their remote home in the mountains near Whittier, North Carolina. Justin and Abrams survived. None of the adults did."

He looked around the room to make sure he had our attention, his Lichtenberg lines glowing bright in my improved vision.

We all leaned in slightly. He had hooked us. "Arson investigators speculated that the fire started in the master suite, but it burned so hot and fast they were never able to pinpoint the exact location or cause, though arson was ruled out. This was almost thirty years ago, and even then the Tollivers had their hands in every political pie, so it's possible anything suspicious but unconfirmed was ruled accidental or unresolved, as a favor to the family."

Follow the money, Spook School taught. "Who got the estate?" I asked.

"Seven million dollars. Equally split between Justin's missing biological mother and Abrams' father. A week later, the elder Tollivers' car went off a cliff in the Appalachian Mountains in the middle of a snowstorm. It crashed into a gorge and exploded, killing both of Abrams' parents."

I said, "So the money went to the kids. That would be motive but it's not likely that the children killed their families, especially not by a car wreck in the mountains."

Tandy turned up a palm as if to say maybe, maybe not, and shook his head. His reddish curls quivered with the motion. "Abrams' parents deceased. Justin's mother disappeared, leaving the family fortune in the hands of the boys. If we follow the money, this feels suspicious."

"Speculation which we can't prove," JoJo said.

"Who was the guardian?" I asked.

Tandy said, "The estate lawyer, who hired nannies and sent the boys to military and boarding schools."

"And where's he?" I asked.

Tandy said, "Deceased. Natural causes at age eighty-nine."

I rubbed my arms. I had been burned. And now that we knew what to look for, pyrokinesis was everywhere, fitting T. Laine's human mutation theory. I said, "So we think that the Tolliver family has a dominant pyro gene? Justin's pillow smelled human, right? His wife, Sonya, who wears too much perfume, didn't smell human?" I worked it through my mind. "Sonya and Clarisse Tolliver *both* wear—wore—too much perfume; the men wear none. It's unlikely that the Tollivers are both scentless nonhumans and married smelly nonhumans of a different species."

"Not so unlikely," Jo said, "if the trait began prior to the dead great-grandparents. But then we've got problems tracking it down. Forensic arson investigations were pretty much nonexistent prior to 1950 and records were never computerized or even independently preserved to microfiche. And we don't have time to search through every single local newspaper on microfiche about fires going back for decades, for every small town in a hundred square miles."

I nodded agreement. I had done microfiche research. It was tedious and boring and very time-consuming when going through old papers for one county. The idea of searching through newspapers for two states and a hundred years was daunting.

Soul said, "The assassin had an 'other-than-human' scent. We're pretty sure Devin did too, though beneath the smell of the car fire it was impossible to tell. The fact that he threw fire is proof enough. We'll know more when the cats are back in human form and can tell us what *they* smelled. For now, speculation is running us in circles." She shook her head and twisted her hair. "This feels incomplete. We need more."

I looked up to see Occam standing in the hallway staring at me, his eyes glowing golden, his cat too close to the surface. He looked disheveled and predatory and tightly wound, like a cat tensed to strike. I gave him a slight smile to show I was okay. His shoulders dropped, relaxing slightly, and he nodded, his hair swinging almost to his shoulders, longer after his shift. He was dressed in sweat pants and a tight T-shirt, his feet bare.

Rick stepped around him, into the doorway, and leaned against the frame, black hair and beard shaggy and scruffy, but he looked vital and more healthy than hours past. Except for the silvering hair, each shift seemed to heal him more. "Devin is not human," he said. "He smelled . . . I don't know. Watery? Like algae in a pond?"

Occam pushed him aside and entered the room, pouring them both a cup of coffee. "More like a rock that's still wet from river water. Oddly mineral, fishy, wet, and very different from lizard or snake, otter or weasel family. I don't know what he is, but he doesn't smell exactly like his father *or* his mother."

"So are we now thinking that we're either in the middle of an intra- or interspecies conflict or a cross species mating?" I asked.

"The scents are confusing," Rick agreed.

"Speculation," Soul said, looking oddly introspective and still worried.

"Feud," Occam said. "It feels like a feud. A paranormal-versus-paranormal mini-war, either familial or a clan-versus-clan confrontation, like between vamp clans or between were-creature species. The scents might mean nothing. Or everything." Occam sipped, thinking, and I could see everyone nodding, putting pieces of the case puzzle together. "Like werelions against wereleopards or wolves against hyena. Vaguely similar paranormal species fighting over territory," he finished.

"Inside the family? Family on family?" I asked. "Miriam went missing. Maybe she's back?" That sort of thing didn't happen in the church. The patriarch's word was law and no one fought against it. And then I realized, it had happened. And it had started with me, which made me uncomfortable in ways I couldn't explain to myself, so I shoved it into the back of my mind for later consideration. But family against family, that was very common in the church. I just hadn't thought about things like that happening in the townie world.

"You've done well narrowing it down," Soul said. "Has anyone had sleep in the last sixteen hours? No? Then Unit Eighteen is now officially off duty. I want everyone to bed. I've kept the feds updated and will update them again in an hour or so. They can carry the ball for the next twelve. I'll monitor everything from here and see you all back here at six p.m., well rested and feeling lively. Dismissed."

It wasn't a request. I checked the time and found it was after six in the morning. I had no idea where all the hours had gone, but I was expected at Pete's Coffee Shop. To have breakfast with Benjamin Aden.

I stood, ignoring Occam, who stared at me as I slipped past him in the doorway. I got my bags and took the stairs to the outside. To discover that I didn't have my truck. "Well, dang," I said.

"Need a ride?"

My boots crunched on the sleet as I turned to see T. Laine. All I could think was, *Thank God it isn't Occam.* "Is Pete's Coffee Shop, downtown on Union, out of your way?" I asked.

"Totally, but I'm driving. I want to see this paragon of manliness and restraint that has Occam's panties in a twist."

"What?"

"Never mind. Get in." Lainie popped the locks and we climbed in. She glanced at me and away as she started her car. "Occam told me about your truck not being here. Sent me to drive you. Boy's got it bad." I didn't know how to reply to that. We drove off into the dawn, with the storm clouds blowing away and a golden sun climbing into the sky.

TWELVE

Amazingly, T. Laine found a parking spot on the street and pulled in. I looked at her from the corner of my eye. "You are not joining us for breakfast."

"Of course I'm not. I'll be at the bar. Getting food. Minding my own business." She slipped into the morning light and shut the car door. I realized that there was no way to stop her. That I had no car to get home. That I had no cash for an Uber. And that my option was for Ben to drive me to my house. I hadn't thought this through. I blew out a breath and followed T. Laine into the building, which looked a lot like an old-fashioned diner.

Muttering as I passed by her seat at the long stainless bar, I said, "You turn him into a toad and I'll be really mad."

Lainie snorted and accepted a cup of coffee from the bar waiter.

Ben was seated at the last booth in the back of the building. I moved through the morning crowd, removed my coat, and sat across from him. He was freshly shaved and dressed in an Old Navy pea coat and leather boots, Levi's, and a waffle Henley in a blue that made his eyes glow brilliantly. Not churchman clothing. Store-bought. Not new. Things he had owned for a while. I figured that his clothes might be an attempt to communicate something about his separation from the old ways of the church.

"Morning," I said.

"Morning, Nell. You look mighty pretty to have worked all night. Most people would be dragging, but you look wonderful. Your eyes are . . . really green," he added. "And your hair is . . . was it always so red? Did you . . . *color* it?" Coloring one's hair was a sign of vanity, a damning sin to the church.

"It's the light," I said shortly. "I haven't been to Pete's. I didn't know it was also a restaurant. What's good?"

Ben dropped his eyes to the menu and said, "Most everything. I eat here whenever I'm in town. It's a decent, inexpensive breakfast." Which was something my daddy would have said and was high praise for a churchman. And . . . that was what Ben was, no matter how townie he dressed. A churchman. Through and through.

I didn't know why that made my eyes fill with tears. I blinked them hard and smiled at the waitress when she brought coffee I hadn't ordered. "Extra cream and sugar," I said to her. "Thanks."

"You folks ready to order?" she asked.

I opened my mouth to reply but never got the chance.

"Yes," Ben said. "The lady will have the cinnamon French toast with sausage. I'll have a Greek omelet, sausage, bacon, and biscuits."

It was exactly what I would have ordered, but . . . but Ben ordered without asking me. Just like the weird nanny stuck her fingers into my plants. Without permission.

"With two eggs," I said. "And actually, I've changed my mind. I'll have hot tea instead of coffee. And bacon instead of sausage."

Ben looked nonplussed and I said, "And that will be separate checks."

"Got it," she said. She walked away.

I studied Ben. A faint blush had spread over his cheeks and down his neck as I spoke to the waitress. I figured he was embarrassed at my behavior in changing my breakfast order instead of being a docile woman. Churchmen might think that ordering a woman's food was a compliment instead of an intrusion. Carefully not using any church-speak, I said, "We were interrupted yesterday before we got to the meat of the discussion about you and me. I'm not a church-woman, Ben, not anymore, if I ever was. You say you know it, but you don't."

I leaned in and stared him down, dropped my voice like I'd heard the cats do, and said, "I'm not a child to be married off by my parents. I'm not a hillbilly backcountry hick, or too stupid to know beans from bunny droppings. I'm a law enforcement officer and a paranormal investigator. I don't want to spend my life spittin' out babies like an assembly line. I don't want to make my own clothes or cook for a huge family and live and die in the house and the church. Maybe . . . maybe if we'd met right after John died and before the churchmen decided to try and kill me, things mighta been different, but they aren't."

"I heard you fought back. I like that in a woman. I don't want a woman who—" He stopped.

"A woman who lets a man order her food for her? A submissive little doormat?"

The waitress set our plates in front of us. Pete's cook was fast. My tea went to the side and my coffee cup was whisked away. I poured tea from the small pot and added cream and sugar as Ben and the waitress chatted about us needing more of anything. The tea was a little weak yet, but the warm mug felt good in my cold hands. I held it close to my face so the steam would warm me.

The waitress walked off and Ben turned back to me. "I asked your brothers and sisters what food you liked best. It didn't occur to me that I'd come across as bossy. So I propose we start over." He held his hand across the table. "Hi. I'm Ben Aden. I like walking in the rain, singing in the shower, working wood, and making things grow. I'm not always real bright about women, but I'll never lie to you, hit you, or make you be anything you don't want to be."

His hand hung across the table. I stared at it, thinking over what it meant if I accepted it. Thinking about Occam's kiss. Slowly I reached out and clasped it. "I'm Nell. I'm independent, got a big mouth sometimes, and like living alone. I'm a cop of sorts. And a farmer. I like making things grow too. Mostly vegetables and fruit."

Ben released my hand. "See. We got something in common already." He dropped his head and closed his eyes for a moment. I realized he was praying over his food. And that he didn't expect me to pray with him the way a churchman would. I seldom prayed anymore—the church had put me offa praying—but I closed my eyes and said a silent word of thanks for the food and the company and the strange handshake, which surely cemented a deal of sorts. And for Occam. And asked God if he had put them both in my path, and what I might learn from the presence of two such different men in my life. When I opened my eyes, my unplanned prayer over, Ben's blue gaze was on me. He nodded and we dug in.

The breakfast was pretty good. The company was better. Ben was charming and kind and told me about his first year of school and classes and how he was a fish out of water in the normal world. He asked me about getting my GED and going to Spook School. He told me about his ideas for sustainable farming with ancient aquaculture, specifically, integrated multitrophic aquaculture, a method devised in ancient Asia. I'd read about it, but Ben's degree in agriculture gave him a deeper and wider understanding of the pros and cons of the farming methods. I brought up permaculture principles of farming and what animals he might suggest for a half acre of dedicated land. His answers made me want to try permaculture on Soulwood.

The conversation was light and cheerful and fun. And it wasn't a discussion I could have had with Occam.

At nine o'clock Ben checked his cell and said, "Nellie, I gotta go. I got a shipment of well dried manure being carted in from Daddy's land, now that the weather's eased up. You can get home on your own? Your watchdog took off about half an hour ago."

I twisted around in the booth and saw that T. Laine's seat at the bar was now occupied by someone else. "You saw her? I'm sorry."

"I think it's nice that you got folks who'll watch out for you."

"I'll be fine," I said.

Ben tossed a twenty and a five to the tabletop, looped his jacket over an elbow, and slid from the booth. He leaned down and I tensed, near horrified at whatever he might be about to do. In public. He hesitated, his mouth only an inch from me. I didn't turn. I didn't breathe. He crossed the distance and gently kissed my cheek. His lips were warm and moist. He pulled back a fraction of an inch and, when he spoke, his breath feathered across my face, smelling of coffee. "I know you said you'd pay for your meal. And that's fine. It just means the waitress gets a mighty fine tip. I'll see you later, Nellie."

I didn't look around, didn't move for a good two minutes. And then I gathered up my coat and left Pete's, allowing Ben Aden's two crisp bills to buy my breakfast too.

A date. I'd had a real date.

Outside, I spotted T. Laine's car. The overworked witch was asleep in the driver's seat with her head leaning against the window, her mouth open a little. I tapped on the passenger window and she snapped awake and unlocked the doors. I got in and buckled up, saying nothing, ignoring her steady gaze. A few seconds too late, she turned to the front and pushed the start button, easing into traffic, heading toward the hills that marked Soulwood. More minutes passed.

"Okay. Fine," she said at last, taking the turn toward Oliver Springs. "I wasn't going to ask. I was going to let you volunteer. But I have to say, that boy is a fine specimen of manhood. Dark hair and creamy skin, blue eyes to freaking die for. And you made him blush. Deets. I want to know everything. And before you say no, just remember that it's a damn long way to your house from here, on foot."

I had begun to smile as she spoke and when she finished her harangue, I said, "You waited for me."

"Of course I waited. Unit Eighteen rule number one. No one goes in alone. No one gets left behind."

It was the single most important reason that I had joined PsyLED. "He kissed me on the cheek before he left."

"Day-um, girl! *Dish!* Start at the beginning!"

For the first time in my life, I had what Lainie called a "girl talk" about men. And it was pretty wonderful.

* * *

Back at the house, I unloaded my gear from the car and waved T. Laine away. She was so tired, I feared her eyes wouldn't stay open for the drive to her place, but she refused to "crash at your pad," as she put it, and pulled back down the hill at speed, her mouth moving. I figured she had waked up JoJo to tell her about my breakfast date.

I took care of urgent housekeeping chores, like heat and water, and mixed up some no-knead bread for later baking. I had venison stew, but it needed corn bread to go with it, so I set the Dutch oven on the cooler part of the stove to warm, and the skillets on the hot part of the stove top for later use. Let the cats out and then back in, and fed them. Washed a load of clothes. Put on my pajamas. Turned on the electric blanket. And went out to the married trees with my faded pink blanket, raided from my big gobag. I sat on the blanket on the damp ground, my palms flat, and blew out the stress of the last few hours. I eased my mind into the earth, down and deep, into the warmth that was Soulwood. I had drawn on it pretty hard and wanted to make sure it was all right. And it was, energies humming quietly through the ground like pulses of pale light. I gave it a small bump of energy, like a scratch behind the ears. Had it been a dog, the sentient thing that was my woods would have rolled over and given me its tummy. Satisfied, I glanced Brother Ephraim's way long enough to ascertain that he wasn't doing anything naughty. His area looked cold and dark and appeared to be free of electric snakes. I figured he had used everything he had for his strike at me. If I was lucky he was well and truly dead. I wasn't usually lucky where Ephraim was concerned. Slowly, I eased back to my body.

The air was warmer than any day in the past week, but I was still cold. I raced for the house and the bed that was snuggly and warm and wonderful. And fell asleep. Only to wake at four p.m., stirred from whirling, confusing dreams about Ben Aden and Occam. About bravery and cowardice and lifestyles and the future. And not being human.

I was ready for work by four thirty, when I felt an unknown vehicle on the road up the hills to my land. And realized that I hadn't felt Ben or Occam when either of them drove onto my land. That was worrisome and I didn't know what it might mean.

I put my gear by the front door and waited until I saw Daddy's truck turn into the gravel driveway. Sam and Mud got out, and Soulwood perked up, aware and drowsy and happy to have them here. Which was disturbing in its own way. I opened the door and let my true sibs in, offering the church welcome of hospitality, keeping the good things from my past. "Welcome to my home. Hospitality and safety while you're here."

Sam chuckled and pulled off his bright blue toboggan. It looked brand-new, it wasn't Mama's favorite paler blue shade, and I assumed his new wife had crocheted it for him. "I hope you'un have something on the stove, sister of mine. Mindy says you two are having an early supper."

"We are?"

"Yup," Mud said, plopping on the couch and pulling an afghan over her.

"Woman stuff," Sam informed me.

"I have to leave for work in an hour."

My brother's face flashed surprise, quickly shuttered. "Oh. Right." Churchwomen didn't work out of the home. Cultural bombshell—I did. But neither of us said any of that. "I heard about the rainbow wig," Sam said teasingly, his expression so much like the young boy he had been that I laughed and shook my head.

"Ben told you."

"Ben told everybody. I'll pick her up in sixty minutes." He slipped out the door and closed it.

"Grilled cheese okay?" I asked my sister.

"And somathat lemony tea, if'n you'un got any?"

I remembered the cramps of my first cycle. Mud must be hurting. "My feminine relief mixture coming up. Lemon, ginger, and maybe some fennel this time?"

Mud shrugged and snuggled deeper, the cats walking over her, investigating. Jessie curled on Mud's shoulder, purring. Cello, the scaredy-cat, crawled under the afghan, peeking out. Torquil leaped to the kitchen cabinet and sat, staring at me, her black head looking like she wore a helmet—Thor's helmet, for which she was named.

I put butter in the skillet and started the sandwiches, heated water in the microwave, and ladled up some stew into bowls. I spooned my honey lemon preserves into the new infuser cup, then added a small spoonful of fennel seed, some dried black cohosh, dried raspberry leaf, and some black tea. When the microwave dinged, I poured boiling water over the mixture and brought a tray with tea and stew to the table.

Mud had pulled the afghan up to her cheeks and was watching me over the edge. The silence between us had grown but was still somehow comfortable. "I don't like being a woman grown."

"Oh?" I put her stew bowl, teacup, and the infuser near her.

"Brother Aden come by this morning. He said he was there to take breakfast with Daddy, but he was there to look me over. Gossip says, his son Larry is looking for a second wife. Gossip says, Brother Aden wants you'un to marry Ben and me to be affianced to his second son, Larry, Mary's boy, to cement relations in the Nicholson faction."

I went cold and still, even as a heated rage flushed through me. Brother Aden was a church elder and Ben's daddy, and had been a family friend for years. He was older than the hills, and he was important in church hierarchy. Usually he was a progressive sort of man, though he did have two wives of his own, Sister Mary and Sister Erasmus. And Larry had one wife already. Voice steady, I asked, "What do the Nicholson womenfolk say about the gossip?"

"Mama asked me what I thought about Larry. I told her'un he smells like gun oil and spent ammunition. I told her'un I ain't interested in getting married. She said, 'Pshaw. All women want to get married. Even Nell. She likes Ben.'" Mud cocked her head at me. "You getting married to Ben? 'Cause if'n you are, I'd rather be Ben's second wife than Larry's. We'uns could all live here and be a family together."

To hide my shock, I spun to the stove and flipped the sandwich. My hands were cold and shaking. I added a log to the firebox and adjusted the dampers to create a faster-burning fire. I turned on the overhead fans to distribute the heat. Keeping busy so I didn't say any of the awful things that I wanted to.

"You'un'er thinkin', ain'tcha?"

Face blank, I nodded slowly.

"You'un's mad, ain'tcha?"

I nodded, the motion jerky. I moved the hot skillet off the hottest part of the stove and put the sandwiches on pretty plates, with roses around the edges. Wiped the skillet. Found some pretty folded napkins in the linen drawer and brought them to the couch. Placed them on the tray. Arranged it all so Mud could reach it. Pulled Leah's favorite rocking chair over close and sat in it. The choice of chair was subconscious but telling.

Leah had not been entirely truthful to me when she and John had asked me to marry them, but she had been wise in lots of ways I never had been. And . . . I was twelve when I agreed to marry the Ingrams. That was how I'd always thought of it. That I'd affianced them both, a package deal, to tend to Leah as she died, and to marry John after that. *Twelve.* The same age as Mud, though I hadn't had to come to John's bed until I was fifteen and that had been far too young.

My breath was coming too fast and I felt light-headed. I wanted to sock something. Or shoot something. I folded my hands and studied them as Mud ate. When the tea had steeped enough, I strained and decanted it into her mug and pushed it close to her. "This is a different blend, but it's good." I nibbled on my sandwich though I was no longer hungry.

When I thought I could communicate my thoughts without screaming, I said, "Last time we talked, two days ago, you said you didn't want to get married. Didn't want to have children until after you were twenty-four."

Mud sipped the tea and made a face that said, *Not bad.* Her fingers wrapped around the mug for the warmth, the same way I held my own, for the comfort. "I might not have a choice. Life don't always hand a woman pancakes and blueberries. Sometimes it's oatmeal and raisins. Or even cold pea soup with grease on top and stale bread. And if'n I got to marry and you'uns gonna marry, I'd rather be here on Soulwood. With you."

My little sister was wise in the ways of the church. Wise as I had been, when I made a choice for safety. When I chose to marry John and Leah and move here, to avoid a worse fate. I managed a breath and said, "Or you could just come live with me."

Mud stopped with the mug halfway to her mouth. Her eyes went slowly wide. Her mouth dropped open. The mug tilted, forgotten, and I grabbed it before it spilled. Her eyes were far away, focused on something only she could see. Then they snapped to me. "You'un gonna marry Ben?"

"I admit I like Ben. But there's problems with Ben. With any churchman."

"There's always problems with churchmen."

"True." I handed the mug back to her and said, "Don't spill it. You know how I told you about claiming land?" She nodded. Sipped. "You remember how the church wanted to burn me at the stake?"

Mud went still as dirt and swiveled her eyes up to me. "Yup."

I took a breath. "Beings who can claim land like I can, like I think you can, aren't human. And a sizable number of church folk want to burn all nonhumans at the stake. That means you too. Maybe our sisters. Mama and Daddy. Sam."

Mud sipped. Sipped again. Picked up the sandwich with one hand and slowly ate half of it. Her forehead was scrunched with thought. "Can we kill the witch killers first?"

I thought about that. About feeding the earth with their

blood. Or even sending the vampire tree to kill on church land. No court would ever convict me because no court would understand how I had done it. But more important than getting caught was the morality of not committing murder. "Probably, but I won't kill unless I'm attacked. Or you or the Nicholsons are attacked.

"I can read the land like . . . like Daddy can read the Bible. I can commune with it. It can heal me if I'm hurt. Save my life if I'm dying. And if I read the land too long or too deep it grows roots into me as a way of claiming me back."

Mud's eyes went so wide I was afraid they'd pop out of her head. I hadn't told her that part yet.

I held out my hands to show her. "I have to be cut free and that makes the land angry sometimes. And then there's the foliage that grows out of my fingernails and my hairline." I touched the nape of my neck, finding a tiny sprig there, curled and twisted, newly sprouted, faster than usual, perhaps as a result of the burning. I pulled my hair aside and showed her the leaf, as if maybe she had forgotten my leaves from last time. I put my hand to my belly, feeling the hardness there, from roots that had grown into me and left their mark. I seldom thought about them, unless reminded. And I decided I had told her enough for now. Roots growing inside me might be too much for my sister.

Mud picked up the stew bowl and started eating, thinking. I waited. Nibbled on my own sandwich, smoothing my pants with my free hand. I was wearing black today, with black office shoes and a black jacket, a soft and flowing navy shirt over a black T-shirt, to protect my skin from the weapons harness. I was thinking of stupid things. My heart was racing and my fingers tingled. I cleared my throat.

"You'un ain't said exactly. I know we'uns not fairies. Is we'uns plants?" Her voice was calm, not excited or panicked. Calmer than I was.

"No. We bleed blood, not sap. We're meat. Mostly."

"Would Ben Aden burn you'un at the stake if'n he found out you'un wasn't human?"

A *knowing* skirled through me like a dancing wind. "I don't know," I whispered, accepting fully what I had just said. "Even if he knew what I am and he still wanted me, I'd be putting him in danger to marry him. I'd be putting all my babies in danger. So . . . No matter how much I might like Ben Aden, I won't be marrying him." I placed the sandwich on the plate. It tasted like sawdust. "And if *you* are the same creature as *me*, then you need protection too."

As I spoke, tears had gathered in Mud's eyes. She put the mug on the tray. And threw herself into my arms. Hugging me so tight it was like being strangled by roots. I hugged back. Realized we were both crying. Rocking. She had grown in the last months and weighed more than I anticipated. The chair was moaning beneath us. I stood and lifted Mud and myself to the couch. Grunted more than I expected. I was getting soft working at PsyLED.

I shoved cats out of the way and pulled the afghan over us, holding my sister, not sure if she was happy or horrified or something too complicated for a single word. Time passed. I felt the car on my road again. Surely an hour hadn't gone by.

"How you think we'll get them to let me live here?" Mud asked.

"I'll have to work on that. But maybe the mamas can be persuaded. Maybe we'll have tea. Talk. Show some stuff."

Mud giggled into the warm space between my neck and shoulder. "Leaves?"

I laughed with her, a single note of shared hilarity. "If necessary."

Her merriment faded. "Is Sam one of us?"

"I don't know. He knows I'm . . . different, though. And he knows he's different, though he never mentioned growing leaves."

"Esther? Priscilla? Judith?"

"I don't know. But it's genetic, so even if they're human, their children might be like us."

Mud pushed away and stood, smoothing down her skirts and smoothing back her bunned-up hair. "You let me know when you'uns is gonna have that tea. I reckon I'm gonna need to be with you'un for it."

"I will." I stared up at Mud as Sam parked and got out of the truck. She had to be nearly five feet tall now. Growing like a weed, though that would stop since she had started her feminine cycle. Mud was going to be a short woman. Which brought a soft smile to my face. "You scared?"

"No. I'm not scared at all. I got you. And you got me. Will I have to go to public school?"

"Yes. And we'll have to talk about you riding the school bus. Get legal papers so you can stay with me. You'd be a latchkey kid."

"I don't know what that is. Can't be no stranger than grow-ing leaves."

"We'll figure it out."

"Good. I gotta go now. Thank you for the hospitality."

"Peace as you leave my home."

Mud nodded and raced out the door, banging it closed behind her. I curled my legs on the couch, feeling the warmth from her still in the cushion. Wondering what—by all that was holy—I was getting myself into.

I stopped off at the Rankins' place of business and caught Thad Rankin in the office. "Mr. Rankin?" I asked softly, tapping on the door.

"Sister Nell Ingram, get yourself in here." The big man stood and enveloped me in a hug. He had taken to hugging me since I went to church with him a few times. Quick, gentle hugs, as if teaching me that hugging a man was an okay thing to do. They hugged a lot at his church. Laughed a lot too. It was a very different church from God's Cloud. If I ever decided to attend a church again, it would be one like Brother Rankin's, one full of honest friendship. He let me go. "Take a chair, Sister Nell," he said, sitting behind his desk in the only other chair. "What can I do for you?"

I took the single spindled wood chair and held out a list of fires that might have been suspicious. "You know I'm with

PsyLED. I've been looking at some of the recent fires and wondered if you were on-site at these."

Thad didn't take the list, just watched me across the expanse of his desk. "Do I need a lawyer, Nell? Black man with an officer of the law in his office?"

"Oh." I dropped my hand and let a breath go in shock. "Mr. Thad, I would never come to you'un—to you—my friend, with you as a suspect in anything. First of all, I would know you hadn't done whatever crime it is. Second, I'd be standing with you, shotgun in hand to defend you and yours. And last, you do not need a lawyer unless you tell me you can start fire with your mind."

Mr. Thad threw back his head and laughed, accepted the sheet of paper, and asked, "What can I do for you on these fires?"

"Did you see anything odd? Smell anything odd? Have any thoughts about a guilty party? Did any of your fellow firefighters act strange at these fires? Any orange flames with purple tips?"

"No, no, no, and no, to the first four questions. Everything was pretty normal. As to the color of the flames, you see all sorts of colors as houses burn, what with all the synthetics and man-made furnishings. So I see orange flames all the time. That's the most common color of fire, you know." His eyes dropped to the sheet and scanned up and down, his brow creased as he thought.

"Yeah. I know that. The purple flames?"

"Over the years, I've seen green, purple, a strange metal-flake blue, an iridescent rainbow color, though nothing I can recall at any of these fires."

I deflated and accepted the list back. "If you think of anything odd you might have noticed, will you give me a call?" I handed him my card. "I have a cell phone now." I waggled my cell at him, showing it off.

"Well, would you look at that. It's good to see you joining the world, Nell. It's real good. You coming to church soon?"

"As soon as this case is closed," I said.

"We're having dinner on the grounds every Sunday this

month. We're smoking a whole hog each week, with all the trimmings. Raising money for the Baker girl, the one with leukemia."

"I'll make a donation even if I can't come," I said.

"The Lord's work is never done."

I went around the desk and hugged him, which seemed to freeze Mr. Thad solid for a moment before he hugged me back. I had never taken the initiative with him. I wasn't sure I had ever been the hugging originator with anyone except family. It felt good. "Later, Mr. Thad."

I was only a few minutes late to work. Dusk was the usual time for the EOD—end-of-day meeting—and current case summary, but with us all off for twelve hours, it was more like SOB—start of business. I slid into my seat at the conference room table only moments before Soul took her place. The smell of eggnog and sugar cookies rode on the air. The little tree's lights were on.

JoJo opened without preamble. "Clementine. Note date and time. Present are all members of PsyLED Unit Eighteen and the assistant director. As of seventeen minutes ago, we have discovered Justin Tolliver's biological father. His name is Charles Healy."

I sat up straight. Soul looked surprised. She had been on duty and she clearly didn't know about Healy, so JoJo must have been working from home instead of sleeping.

"In 1973," JoJo said, "Healy was incarcerated on weapons charges, for selling stolen military weaponry to third-world companies through contacts he made in the Vietnam War. An undercover ATF officer died in the takedown, and when the ammo was traced to Healy's weapon, the feds threw the book at him and he was convicted on all charges. He should be eighty years old and still in federal prison, but he disappeared during a prisoner transfer eleven years ago."

"Where?" I asked.

"United States Penitentiary in Beaumont, Texas."

Occam winced. I guessed that meant it was a particularly bad prison.

"Interesting," T. Laine said, her fingers flying over her keyboard. "Yeah. I thought I remembered this. The Tolliver family has connections to a weapons factory. Did the stolen weapons come from the family factory?"

"Ask for the old court records," Soul ordered. "Did Healy have a steady cellmate in federal prison?"

"Yeah," JoJo said, clicking and swiping, working on three electronic devices at once. "Guy called Bradley 'Boom Boom' Richards. He's still there, serving twenty to life."

Soul said, "PsyLED doesn't have a unit stationed in Texas. The closest is Mobile. Or maybe Arizona, with Special Agent Ayatas FireWind." She frowned, thinking. "I don't think we can make either one work. Dyson and Kent?" she commanded, addressing Tandy and T. Laine. "Fly out to meet with prison officials and talk with Mr. Boom Boom. See if you can interview the guards who lost Healy on the transfer."

T. Laine said, "Whoot! Our first official flight! Overnight?"

Nose in her tablet, her earrings swinging, JoJo said, "It'll have to be. There's a flight out of McGhee Tyson Airport to Jefferson County, Texas, in two hours but no flight back from Jack Brooks Regional Airport until tomorrow. Booking now. If you run lights and sirens you can get there in time to make it through security."

The two disappeared down the hallway, and we could hear them shouting back and forth about supplies, gear, electronic devices, and timing. JoJo's face was tight, and I realized that her boyfriend . . . lover? some better title? . . . was leaving town with her best friend. She wasn't jealous. She just wanted to be the one to go away with Tandy on an investigatory jaunt.

"You'll have to check your weapons in your baggage," Soul called to them.

"You booking us a hotel too?" T. Laine yelled back.

"Done!" JoJo shouted. "Confirmations for flight and hotel sent to your cells."

And then they were gone. Soul and Rick exchanged a
look that was full of something almost parental, as if to say,
Aren't the little ones cute at this stage? She slid her wide
flashing black eyes to me. "Nell. It will be fully dark out
soon. Would you feel up to reading the land near the
DNAKeys research facility?"

My instant mental reaction was, *NO!* but my mouth said,
"I thought we had ruled out DNAKeys as part of the problem.
What do you have in mind?"

Soul shook her head. "I don't know exactly. Everything
about the case changed when we discovered that some of the
Tollivers were pyros. We still don't know why a pyro shot up
the Holloways' party and the Old City restaurant. We could
have more than one thing going on and I don't want to drop
any strands just yet. I want to keep everything in the weave."

"But the adult Tolliver males smell human. It's the wives
who smell nonhuman. None of this makes sense yet."

"Unless—" Soul stopped. "Perhaps the males can mask
all scent traces as they age. We don't know enough and I
have a bad feeling that we need to move quickly, need to tear
the fabric of this case apart and knot it back together again."
Soul slowly twisted her hair into a coil, an unconscious gesture of self-soothing while she summarized. "The Tollivers
own DNAKeys. DNAKeys is doing genetic research on paranormal beings to accomplish some amorphous goal. We
don't know what that goal is, so we have to consider the
possibility that it pertains to this case. Brainstorm, people."

"Okay," I said, following her reasoning and guesswork.
"What if the testing at DNAKeys has to do with some genetic
problem the pyros have, or a falling birthrate, or a predisposition to some dire illness? Maybe the attacks lead back to
that research."

Coiling her hair tighter, she frowned, staring into space.
"I want us to go back over everything we've done to this
point and get a fresh perspective."

Rick spoke for the first time, with what might have been

amusement. "There's no evidence for any connection between the pyros and DNAKeys except that it's a business the Tolliver family owns. There's no logic, in a world full of paranormals, to suggest that, if we have pyros, then we must have vampires and werewolves involved on the periphery of these crimes."

"And mad scientists," JoJo said with a straight face.

"True," Soul said. "I agree we have no hard evidence other than the presence of known and unknown paranormals scented there and the Tollivers owning this medical research facility; however, a pyro is coming after the Tollivers and the Tollivers may be pyros. We have circumstantial evidence pointing to this facility and want to leave no stone unturned." She seemed to realize she was coiling her hair and placed her hands at her sides instead. "I know it isn't safe for you to read deeply," Soul said to me, "but if you could read specifically for the traces you picked up in the ground at the crime scenes, it might help."

"What do special agents with children at home do when they have a case like this, that requires long hours?"

Soul looked perplexed at my non sequitur. "Woolgathering again, Ingram?"

I said, "Yes, I'll do the reading. No, not shearing sheep. What do people do with their children?"

"They have family. Spouses. Or day care," Soul said.

"Day care is for babies. What about a twelve-year-old who can't stay alone at night. What about that?"

Occam was watching me with sharp eyes. "Nell, sugar, you talking about Mindy?"

"Maybe," I said.

"You're gonna adopt that girl to keep her safe." His mouth spread into a smile, his dimple peeking out on the side. "I'm proud of you, Nellie."

I scowled. What he said was nice, but I wasn't sure I wanted anyone to be proud of me for something I should have started months ago.

"We would have to make concessions with your schedule," Rick said.

"In an emergency, a child of twelve or older could sleep here while you pull paperwork hours," JoJo said. "I'd never tell."

Rick and Soul exchanged a look that I couldn't interpret. As a child raised in God's Cloud of Glory Church, I had gotten pretty good at reading body language, but some things were beyond me. Rick said, "We'll chat once you know if this will be a conflict or a problem. For now, I'd like you to go read the land near DNAKeys."

"I'll go with," Occam said, too casually, too offhand.

JoJo coughed into her hand, burying the words, "Captain Obvious," in the fake cough.

Without looking at him, knowing my face was flaming, I got up and left the conference room, and then HQ. Outside, the weather was dry and warm. It would get up to sixty tomorrow as the cold front moved off and a front from Southern California moved in, desert dry. Weather in the South—you don't like it today, wait a couple days and the entire season will change.

I threw my gear into the space behind the seat and climbed in. Gunned my C10 out of the parking lot and out toward Rutledge Pike. Within a few minutes, I spotted Occam's headlights in my rearview mirror. My cell rang. I glanced at it, not surprised to see Occam's number. I punched answer and put it on speaker. "Ingram," I said, setting the tone for conversation.

Occam hesitated at the name. "Ingram. I apologize for anything untoward I may have said or done. Sometimes I'm jist stupid. And my cat is stupider."

I smiled out into the night, remembering him sitting on the floor, blocking the hallway. Remembered his cat scent-marking me, claiming me. "Apology accepted."

"I was trying to find a time when we could chat, face-to-face. In private."

"We're pretty private right now."

I heard him sigh. "I reckon we are." He sounded mighty Texan in that moment. "You going to date Ben Aden?"

"No. Ben's human. Ben needs a human wife. I'm not human." I scowled out at the world through the windshield. "I plan on having a chat with my parents about being not human."

"And Mud ain't human either? So you figure you might have to shelter her."

"Correct."

"I'm good with that. You gonna date me?"

Was I? I thought again about what that might mean. It made my insides clench. But that was fear talking and uncertainty and distrust that hadn't been earned. "Dinner and a movie," I said softly, "in a theater. The first night we have off at the same time."

"Steak?"

"Pizza. And a comedy."

"Chick flick," he said. His tone was only slightly scathing.

I smiled and changed lanes. His headlights followed. "If you don't like comedy I'll go for historical drama or even something like *Star Wars*."

"Okay. I can make that happen." His tone was smiling. That might not be a real thing, but I could hear it nonetheless.

"And, despite the approval already given by Pea, what if an older, more experienced grindylow is against us . . ." I didn't know what to call it, but settled on, ". . . dating. Pea's a baby still."

"That won't be a problem, Nell, sugar." He sounded pleased, maybe a tad smug.

"Yeah," I said. Because I wasn't human and so might be unable to contract the were-taint, the prion that caused wereism. "Hey, Occam. I put in for a car ages ago. How do I get it approved and make sure it has heated seats?"

"JoJo can make that happen."

"Yeah? JoJo can do anything."

"JoJo is the queen of making things happen, sugar."

THIRTEEN

I pulled off the narrow private road on the far side of House Mountain and backed into a weed-covered drive, about half a mile from the place where Rick and Occam had parked last time. Maybe the distance would give us some protection from spying eyes who might remember the cars or surveillance equipment that the cats might have missed. Occam pulled in behind me, his car facing out too. There would be no time-consuming three-point turns to slow down our escape route if we needed out fast.

The lack of streetlights and the cloudy skies left the night darker than the armpit of hell—a saying of Daddy's that seemed appropriate. I got out, carrying my gobag, in which I had placed the psy-meter 2.0, a bottle of water, and a protein bar. I slung my pink blanket over a shoulder, seated my weapon, and took the flashlight in one hand, but off. I should have brought the low-light/IR headgear. I'd surely remember next time. This was one reason I was still a probie. I didn't always plan ahead.

In the dark, I crossed the road into the woods. Occam would be along in cat form when he could, and with his cat vision, I'd be easy to find. Pressing the light against my belly, I turned it on.

Shielding the beam, I found a rabbit trail into the woods, thankful that most barbed and poisonous plants would be dormant. A thin fog was growing up around me, created by the cold earth and the slow-moving, warmer weather front.

Deep in the woods, the scent of pine needles and dead fir trees and loamy soil strong in my nose, I spread my blanket and sat, cross-legged. Without the flashlight, my eyes adjusted and I could see the distant lights of the DNAKeys compound. On my cell phone map, I had thought the area was all uphill, but the lights seemed to come from below-ground, so the compound was in a hollow—what I had grown up calling a "holler," a fold in the mountain, visible only from this angle.

I tested the psy-meter to the four compass points, getting a baseline normal, then pointed it at the lights. I got baseline normal again and pushed a button to put the unit to sleep. Holding it on my lap, I relaxed and put one fingertip on the earth, easing into the land in the way T. Laine had suggested not so long ago. Like on Soulwood, the land here was dormant, sleeping, but it seemed weak and . . . maybe *stupid* wasn't a nice word but by comparison to Soulwood it was both. My woods were growing more powerful, more aware, and therefore more intelligent year by year. This place was not even half-aware. The land was no threat to me, and so I placed my palm flat, reading deeper, wider. I searched through the trees, finding so many dead that it gave me pause. There was a disproportionally high number of dead pine and Douglas fir trees, and a lively army of bark beetles hibernating just below the surface of the trees' outer skins. I moved among the trees, letting my consciousness touch here and there, giving a bump of energy to a tree that was still on the brink of death but hadn't crested the hill. And another tree. And another. But there were so many trees on that cliff face of dying that I would never be able to save them all. Half of this forest was dying and there was nothing I could do short of claiming the land and . . . well, I wasn't going to kill a human to save the conifers.

Unsettled, I turned my attention elsewhere and searched the shape of the land, reaching out for the creatures moving upon it, sleeping on it, or hibernating below it in dens. I reached out and out. There were bear and lynx and dozens of deer. Skunk in a den. Squirrels high in trees. Birds sleeping in trees and thickets. I moved through the ground, looking for buried electronic devices and electrical lines, and then up, into the air, searching for the same, plotting out the electrical and water that supplied the corporation. I found four places with minute changes in the electromagnetic ambience that seemed likely locations for cameras or alarms. And there was the larger incongruity that would be DNAKeys.

I was sensing things I hadn't before. Or maybe identifying things that I hadn't recognized before. The burning by Devin and healing by Soulwood had done something to me on a deeper level than just leaves and twigs and sprouts.

I marked in my mind where the compound was and explored its outlines, its parking lots, walking trails, and outdoor pens. The pens were massive, with tall mesh fences and taller mesh roofs. The building had basements, two deep. There was a familiar but fuzzy sensation in the basement levels, as if something was interfering with my perception. Rebar? The thickness of the basement walls? I pulled away for now. I'd need to get closer to be sure my impressions were correct.

Changing direction, I pressed my awareness out and down, into the heart of the small mountain. I found rock and water, the shattered stone of an ancient mountain, slab upon fractured slab, broken and splintered and rotting back to sand. The water table was higher than I might have expected and the earth's crust thinner. The water in many places was hot and rising through cracks in the earth, as if struggling to become hot springs. I eased back to the surface, clasped my hands together, and thought about that.

Hot underground water was produced when water came into contact with magma (molten rock) and was heated. It became hot springs when that hot water rose to the surface. The town of Hot Springs, named after the heated water that boiled up to the surface there, was only a stone's throw from Asheville, North Carolina, which was a short distance as the bird flies from Knoxville, so the wider region had geothermal activity.

Most geothermal systems were near volcanoes that had been active in the past, or were still active, but there was no known volcanic activity in this immediate area. Soooo. What had caused this thermic change?

Soulwood had recently forced heat through the ground when I was hypothermic. Had magma risen closer to the surface under the command of Soulwood, just to warm me? If so, had allowing magma closer to the surface caused some kind of unexpected instability? Should I—could I—do anything about it? If I had caused the change in the earth's temperature, had I also caused the death of the trees by making the environment a better place for the beetles to live? Robert K. Merton's thoughts about unintended consequences danced through my mind.

Disconcerted and uncertain, I got up, turned on my flash, and carried my blanket deeper into the woods. I read the land by the psy-meter 2.0 again and got the same levels. My personal, less scientific reading confirmed the readings as well. I wondered if I should walk deeper in the woods for a closer reading, if I could do so safely, and decided that I'd know if a stranger came toward me. But the thought of being caught was distressing. I had been given a basic class on what to do if I was ever held captive by a dangerous subject, but the lesson at PsyLED Spook School had done little to salve my fear of attack. Not that I was afraid of being hurt while in the woods—any woods, anywhere—but I didn't want to kill anyone just because they were stupid.

Taking my own fears in hand, I gathered up my supplies and walked deeper into the woods, the trees catching stiff branches in my hair, as if reaching out to me as I passed. I knew they weren't doing that. I knew it. But it still felt a little spooky as the fingers of dead trees touched me.

As I was detangling a branch from my hair, I heard a sound like a breath behind me, and I whirled to look back. Occam, in cat form, was crouched on the narrow path, leopard paws giving him a silent approach in the dark, his eyes glowing a golden brown. He wasn't stalking me like food. Not exactly. I knew not to give in to the shiver that raced up my back like a dash of little spiders. I also knew not to run, not from an apex predator, even one with a human mind. Instead I aimed the flash at him, all forty-eight hundred lumens, right in his eyes, and hissed at him, "I don't like being stalked even in fun, you dang cat. If you'uns gonna track me, you'd be a heap better in the trees."

Occam turned his face away, squinted, and huffed.

"I need to get a little closer to the compound." Much closer than Rick and Occam had gotten.

Occam looked toward the distant lights and back to me. He shook his head slowly back and forth, telling me getting closer wasn't a good idea.

I ignored him. "Where's Pea?"

He huffed again and looked up, over my head. I shifted the light that way and caught a glimpse of a tiny, neon green critter before she jerked away from the light. She chittered and leaped down, landing on Occam's back. The big-cat dropped and rolled, the two wrestling and play-fighting with hisses and spits and slashes of claws. I shook my head, rolled my shoulders to get rid of the nonexistent spiders, and moved on down the pathway to the crest of the hollow, where the compound lights trailed through the barren and dead trees.

I spread my blanket out again. It was damp from contact with the ground, but I sat on it anyway and hugged my knees. I was cold and wished I had brought my mug with me, though the scent of coffee might have alerted any possible canines in the compound. Coffee is strong and might carry far on the night air.

I sighed quietly and tested the land with the psy-meter. Level three psysitope measured into the high midrange. Psysitope one rose about half that much, and psysitope two was erratic. Psysitope four—the one that indicated the paranormal creature burning the grass—stayed nearly at zero. The numbers were off for any specific paranormal creature, but seemed fine for a mixed bag of them.

Not knowing what this might mean, I turned off the machine and pressed the tips of both index fingers onto the ground. I slid through the land, closer and closer to the compound, careful to search out the telltale hints of the presence of magical danger, magical attacks, magical anything. There was nothing. No witches had set a working or curse into the ground. No plants or trees were burned and dying. This close, however, I could discern what had made me think of fuzzy familiarity among the presence of guards. There were four humans and a were-creature patrolling the grounds, and I thought the were-creature might be a wolf. Something dog-like at any rate.

There were more were-creatures in the basements. And the maggoty feel of vampires. The vampires were on the move, first in one room and then in another. I wasn't able to tell if they moved by choice or by force. And then I caught the sensation/presence/feel of blood. My bloodlust woke with a start. *Blood.* So much blood. Enough blood to feed the land, to heal the land, to—

I yanked myself back to the surface, breathing deeply, reining in the need to take blood and feed the land. Forcing it down, gulping it back. Why would there be that much blood? Gallons of it. And not safely within bodies, but loose and free and . . . I hugged myself again, forcing down the need to take it all. When I had it under control, and the sweats had passed and left me chilled, I put one finger on the ground and checked the position of the guards again. Still in the same area. They hadn't sensed me or smelled me or come hunting for me. It was taking too long. Too long. But I needed to be sure we were safe before we moved back to the vehicles.

I eased out of the land to sense warmth at my side. My elbow hit Occam's ears. He had pressed up against me, the way wolves might in the alpha's den. His body warmth was higher than mine and while I often came back to the surface to find myself feeling deeply chilled, this time I was warm. I rested my hand on his head and he snuffled my fingers, licking once. I petted his ears. Occam sighed and pressed against me. "Thank you'un for keeping me warm," I whispered.

The wind changed, blowing harder up the hill and directly at us. Occam was on his feet in an instant, sniffing, nose in the air. He began to growl, the sound a vibration I could feel through my backside on the ground. I pulled myself to my feet and gripped the cat's ear tab firmly to get his attention.

He whined softly and tilted his big head up at me. "You smelling weres?"

Occam dropped his head and raised it in a nod that was all too human on the big-cat.

"Okay. Let's get back to the vehicles. You lead the way. I'll follow," I said, to give him a job that would keep his cat brain occupied. With the flash on but shielded, I kept him in sight as we wended out through the dying woods. Minutes later, Occam jumped away from the path and I stumbled onto the road, where I spotted our vehicles.

Standing in the edge of the trees, I watched as Occam leaped over the hood of his fancy car and I felt the magic of his change start. I was tired. More tired than I expected to be. I was often full of energy after reading Soulwood, but here, I was enervated. I had to wonder if my recent healing, the dying trees at the crime scenes, the rising boiling water, and the presence of all that blood in the compound had affected my body as much as they had my psyche. And I had to wonder what kind of torture room had let so much blood pool.

I yanked my thoughts away from the possibilities and forced my feet to lift and carry me forward, knowing I wasn't safe, not yet, not until I was back at HQ. *All that blood . . .* I stowed my gear, fell into my truck, and drove into the street before putting the Chevy in park to wait. I laid my head on the headrest and closed my eyes, the engine rumbling quietly up through the seat, soothing.

Some ten minutes later, Occam pulled out behind my vehicle and I led the way back into town and to HQ.

Occam passed the sugar for my tea. "I expected to smell blood on silver," he said, "but the mesh pens weren't silver-plated. They could get away. Why don't they?"

"Maybe it's all that blood in the place. Maybe they've all seen it and are scared. Maybe they're all weak from blood loss." I'd seen a starved vamp once and it was pitiful. Until she got free and came after me. "Or maybe their loved-ones are in danger and that keeps them from howling to the winds about the torture room."

"Are you sure it's a torture room?" Rick asked.

"No. I ain't sure about nothin'," I said. "Except there's blood, at least three or four gallons of it, and not a drop in a body. That I know for sure."

Over a cell connection, from the airport, Tandy said, "I should have been with you. I might have picked up something from the werewolf on the surface. Or his humans."

"More likely you would have gotten overwhelmed by Occam and me," I said, thinking about my exhaustion and the bad feel of the lab and the disembodied blood.

"Proximity and all that," Occam added, agreeing.

Rick said, "There's no point in stressing any of your gifts. So why would werewolves stay in a cage they could tear through in a heartbeat?"

"I don't get it," Occam snarled. "I got away from my cage the first second I could. Took me twenty years, but I did it."

I carefully didn't look at Occam. The werecat never talked in detail about his years in captivity or his escape. Just unadorned statements of basic fact. There were rumors. There was scuttlebutt. There had to be files stored somewhere on Occam and the details of his background. But nothing was verified. I realized I knew next to nothing about Occam. How was I supposed to date him if I didn't know anything about him? Unless that was the purpose of dating, to learn.

I looked down at my hands, one holding a slice of pizza, the other gripping a mug handle. My own experience had similar captivity overtones, and I too had gotten away the first moment I could, yet not all my sisters wanted freedom. I said, "They might want to stay, like a caged bird not wanting to fly into the wild. Maybe they feel safer there. Maybe to them it isn't a prison after all." I took a sip of tea, feeling all sorts of unnamed things flowing through me. "Maybe they've been tamed, like a dog to the hand. Maybe they're being given vampire blood to drink and it does something to them. Maybe having something done to their genes, research, like the two employees, Candace and Mary, said. Or

maybe it's just something that makes the weres believe they
have to or want to stay." Like my sister Priss. Like Esther.
But not like Mud.

Occam said softly, "Like you, thinking about going back
into your cage."

A protest flashed through me. But until today, he had a
point. "Programming can be hardwired into a body," I said,
not looking up. "It's something that has to be fought, day in
and day out, forever. Like an addiction one hates, has de-
feated, yet still has to battle." I took a bite of pizza and
chewed. It tasted spoiled, as if the pepperoni had gone bad.
I swallowed and set the remaining slice down on the paper
plate in front of me.

"We're sorry, Nell," Tandy said, his voice tinny over the
cellular connection, maybe picking up on my emotions, despite the distance between us.

"No," I said. "You aren't sorry. You all seem to think you
need to push and prod and remind me constantly what I was
and what I came from." Tandy let out a sharp breath, startled. A barb of anger speared up in me, hot and sharp. I was
mad, not spitting mad, or throwing-things mad, but some
other kind of mad, and I was holding it in like a . . . like a
good *churchwoman*?

At that thought the anger burned hotter for a moment, struggling to blaze free. My anger would never be a churchwoman's
anger, something chaste and controlled, or pot-throwing
mad. My very own anger was different from all others I knew.
Because when I stood up for myself, people died and were fed
into the earth. I was a killer with too little control. I didn't get
to let loose and howl.

I was both a victim of my past and a victimizer through
my gift. That thought stopped me.

Turning my lips in and back out, thinking, feeling the
winter-chapped skin chafing on itself, I nodded. Yeah. I had
good reasons for not getting mad when others might, not
fighting back or arguing as a human might. Because I knew
how easy it was to lose myself to the bloodlust. So very, very
easy. And there was all that blood on DNAKeys' compound.

I was overreacting because I wanted—no—because *Soulwood* wanted that blood.

I said, "I want you all to stop pushing me. I have a right to work through things on my own terms, in my own time." I lifted my chin, knowing it was a confrontational gesture. "And if you don't grant me that time and space, I'm gonna get . . ." *Furious?* ". . . unhappy. I don't like who I become when I'm in a bad mood. I don't think *you* will like me in a bad mood." I looked up at Rick, who had an inkling just how dangerous I could be. "Understood?"

Rick inclined his head. Occam was watching us, his eyes shifting back and forth.

Softly, Tandy asked, "When you're in a bad mood, is Soulwood in a bad mood?"

Sometimes Tandy was too dang discerning. I stood. "You all going in to DNAKeys' compound and checking out that blood or not?"

"We're going in," Rick said softly. "You have blood on-site. We have two reports of prisoners on-site. The county tactical team is on the way. I want Nell, Occam, T. Laine. Vests. Service weapons only. SWAT will carry the big guns. Let's ride."

We took Unit Eighteen's van to the site, up the mountain and then down into the holler, riding the bumper of the county SWAT team, moving fast so DNAKeys' security cameras wouldn't have time to warn the employees. We flew past the site where I'd parked recently. Then the drive where we'd parked before, then an empty parking lot. Closer to the lights of DNAKeys. The pavement developed speed bumps that Unit Eighteen's van was not equipped to handle. I held on to the grab handles, what the others called the "oh, shit" handles, feeling the van roof brush my head on one particularly high-speed bump.

And then the van doors slid open and things got confused.

The guards at the front of the compound were taken out by SWAT. The werewolf was shot with a beanbag that knocked him down. His handler was hit too. No blood. Thankfully, no blood.

The door went down, no match for the battering ram wielded by the team.

Occam muttered, "Dumb-asses."

It took a moment, but then I realized the steel door had been held in place with wood strips. I might never use the word *dumb-ass*, but I had to agree it was poor security. Someone screamed, "Flashbang!" Instantly a flashbang went off inside. Light and noise and smoke. Then another. And a third. Smoke bombs filled the entrance with gray-white smoke.

Then I was inside. Fighting my way through the low light and the smoke. As probationary agent I was near the back of the personnel entering the building. The SWAT guy pulling the six position pushed me with his weapon. Probably not standard behavior, but then I wasn't standard-issue either. I sped up and nearly ran into the SWAT woman in front of me. The team cleared the first floor. I followed the woman and tried to take it all in, but it was a jumble of smoke and flashbangs and lights going off and coming on and DNAKeys' employees screaming. That was the worst.

Vampires screaming. That awful, high-pitched wail of fear and death.

Wolves snarling. Grindylows jumping and cutting, steel claws slashing. Blood, scarlet splashing. But my bloodlust was muted by the speed and violence.

A witch throwing defensive spells that made my teeth and the roots in my belly hurt, until T. Laine's null weapon took her down.

Wolves howling in fear and grief. Stairs leading up and down.

What might have been a juvenile *gwyllgi*, raging in his cage. Another were-creature I couldn't identify.

Laboratories. Green color scheme. Machines and machine noise.

Storage rooms. Dull gray. Boxes. Old, dusty jars containing liquid and fetal humans and creatures with genetic abnor-

malities and horrible deformities, like things confiscated from
a traveling carnival of the fifties and sixties. Newer jars full
of sea creatures, starfish, jellyfish, small sharks. Strange
things. Strange creatures.

Offices, pale stone color scheme. Desks. Computers.

Then the laboratory on the lowest level. And the glass
doors. And the blood inside. In bags. Like a blood bank.

In bags.

Blood bank.

For research.

A vampire wearing a lab coat looked at me and demanded,
"Call Ming of Glass. Call her. Now!"

"Ming?" I whispered, looking around, taking in everything. The lack of caged were-creatures. The lack of vampires
in silver cuffs. Blood in the refrigerator in plastic bags. Gallons of it. No torture room. Just a *blood bank*. I was an idiot.
I had messed up badly. The fact that Soul and Rick had
pushed for this raid didn't make that knowledge any better.

Rick and the PsyLED team met back at the entrance and the
broken door frame. "The paras are on the DNAKeys compound willingly," he said, his tone wooden. "They are co-
operative and well-paid test subjects or are employed here
in research projects. And the lab has all its animal research
paperwork up-to-date. Everything here is legal and moni-
tored by the proper authorities."

He didn't look at me as he continued. "This was a waste
of time and resources. You all have your orders for the rest
of the night. I'll see you in the morning."

Shoulders hunched, I went to the van and took a seat in
the back. I was immeasurably happy that Rick hadn't fired
me on the spot.

Much later, I drove to the senator's place on the river, stopping by Starbucks just before it closed, where I picked up a
leftover banana bread loaf, a carton of coffee, and a short

stack of foam cups. It was a probie move, meant to create a warm and fuzzy feeling in the agents already on duty. I didn't have to do it. I didn't have to spend my hard-earned money. But I was feeling stupid . . . really, horribly, abysmally stupid.

No, the raid itself wasn't on my shoulders. But . . . the stupidity sat heavily on me.

I parked on the shoulder of the road and got out, carrying a hefty load of food and gear. Warm air blew past and, overhead, clouds scudded through the sky, racing in ragged tails, lit by the moon. The wind was strong enough to overpower the scent of coffee and I caught other smells on the night air: burning tobacco, wet dogs, the ozone of something electrical.

I set the coffee up on the hood of my truck and people began to meander over, as if they were psychic to the presence of fresh coffee. A dark-skinned woman in a jacket and pants, her hair cropped close, got to me first and I held up my ID at the same time I handed her a steaming cup. She barely glanced at the ID and drank the scalding brew like her life depended on it. When she was rescued, she blew out a breath and said, "You must be my telepathic new best friend." I nearly flinched until I identified her amused tone. "Special Agent Margot Racer, FBI. Coffee addict, going on a four-hour withdrawal."

"Special Agent Nell Ingram, PsyLED, probie and all-around coffee gofer."

She offered her hand and I was surprised when she shook mine. Not all feds were willing to treat well with other agencies, especially the "magic wands and broomsticks" agency. Two ALT uniformed guards reached the truck and I passed out cups and offered sweeteners and creamers and the banana bread. They each put money in the banana bread box, paying their way, which was nice. I nodded to P. Simon, Peter, the security man from the Holloways' and Justin Tolliver's house. Simon gave me a quizzical look before he seemed to recognize me. He lifted a hand and turned away. Margot tossed in a five and took a piece of the bread.

I felt an unusual something approach and somehow knew it was my cousin. Chadworth Sanders Hamilton strode up, an expression of dissatisfaction on his face. He took a cup and tossed a dollar at me. I caught the fluttering bill even as he spun on a heel and walked away.

"Charming," Margot muttered.

Before I could ask her about my cousin, the others gathered around. Two sheriff's deputies and two more people in suits took cups and food, said their thanks, and returned to their quadrant. Everyone tossed a dollar or two into the box to offset expenses. I was quickly alone with Margot, who poured herself a second cup and leaned against my old truck. The weather had warmed, and she didn't look chilled, her jacket enough for the temps.

I thought about asking after Hamilton, but decided against it. "Anything interesting tonight?" I asked.

"Not a thing. Nothing's biting."

It was a fishing metaphor and I said, "Maybe we're using the wrong bait."

Margot laughed, her eyes moving across the dark, taking in where every flashlight was, as if counting them off. I had served seven people and I saw only three lights, so some were likely using low-light lenses. "Politicians," she said, "so, yeah. Bait might be a problem, for better or worse."

"I have a psy-meter 2.0," I said. "I was sent to take readings. You mind?"

"Fine by me. You mind if I watch? I've heard about them, but never have seen one in action."

That meant she would be watching me read the earth too, and I wondered if I could hide my communing. I shrugged, uncomfortable at the thought. "It's pretty boring, but sure." I finished off a cup of coffee and carried my gear to the far front edge of the property. I spread the blanket and sat on it, opened my cell to take notes. Turned on the psy-meter and took basic readings to the north, east, south, and west. "Mind if I read you?" I asked. "I need a human standard."

"What makes you think I'm human?"

"Oh. I'm so sorry. That was rude."

Margot shrugged. "Mama's mama was a witch. Mama's got some knacks, small gifts. She can tell if the weather's going to turn. If a woman is pregnant and what sex the baby is, with about a ninety percent success. She called the night I was nearly shot and told me to be careful, to wear my vest on my entire shift, even when I was at my desk, and not turn my back on anyone. Saved my life."

"Really?" I thought about Sam, and his ability to tell exactly what the weather was going to do and what cows were going to have trouble calving and when to plant and when to hold off. "Someone shot you at your desk?"

"Elevator, actually. No idea how she got a weapon inside, through security."

"Inside help?" I asked.

"Had to be. Never figured out who. But I will. I have a feeling about it."

"So can I measure you?" I asked, frowning, trying to put her statement together with her family narrative.

"As long as this doesn't go on the record. I haven't disclosed my family history to HR, and no one was looking, back when I was hired. Then Gramma died and . . . evidence died with her."

"I'm sorry. Losing people you love hurts. And I promise to keep my mouth shut and all readings off the record."

"So what do I do?"

"Just stand there and drink your coffee?"

"Totally doable."

I reset the compass readings and then turned the rod to Margot. She read a low positive at two and three, but level one rose higher. I shrugged up at her. "You're human, but yeah, you got some energy. You told me what your mama can do. What about you?"

Margot looked back out over the lawn. "Small things. I know when someone is thinking about breaking the law, working it through, building up the nerve. Usually I can stop them. I know when someone's lying." She was watching Hamilton as she said the last words.

"What's he lying about?" I asked.

"More than one thing, fewer than five. Can you read him?"

"When I get over there. I'm too far away now."

"Tell me what you find?"

"Yes, ma'am."

"And this stays between us. I'll catch up with you shortly." Margot carried her steaming brew into the dark.

I read the land with the psy-meter 2.0 and then, quickly, touched the land with a fingertip. Hurt and pain surged up into my hand and I jerked away, shaking it. Something had injured the land where the senator lived. More gingerly, I touched the ground again. The pain was still there, but it was bearable and I was able to identify the specific and familiar sensation. The plants on the senator's big lot were dying. Every single one of them. I didn't have to move to a different place on the grounds; from this one spot I could tell that it was the same in each area. Dying, death, fire. I was pretty sure a pyro had been here in the last day or so and had covered the grounds. But it could be anyone—a groundskeeper, an employee. A law enforcement officer. I frowned and looked at P. Simon, standing in the shadows, his back to me.

Carrying my blanket, I walked toward the river, access to which was blocked off by a three-rail fence. On the far side of the river, I could see lights. Here there were no lights, just a frigid breeze blowing off the water.

I slipped between the rails and approached the Tennessee River. The senator's land was deceptive, higher than I expected, almost on a bluff, the river flowing at the bottom of the sharp bank, rocks piled to keep it in place. The water was surging smoothly, a black ribbon in the night. A tiny deck was upstream, visible in the nearly full moonlight. From the deck, a set of steep steps led to the water, zigzagging down the cliff to a scant beach, the shore littered with driftwood, an entire tree, broken pale gray rocks, and whitish sand in small piles.

Among the wood and stones, black and white and striped and patched forms moved, leaped, hunted. Feral cats, everywhere, some in silent hunting mode, others mewling in what sounded like excitement. I searched out what might have attracted the cats, and finally saw dead fish floating on the water. Hundreds. Caught in the slow current, lying in low piles on the shore, white bellies swollen. I had thought they were piles of white sand, but the river sand in this area wasn't white.

I was reminded of the slime mold that had grown from a curse, but there was no shimmer on the water, no evidence of a mold or a spell. I sat and tried to read the earth once more. It shocked fear and pain up into me and I shook my hand again. This time my fingertip was hot and painful to the touch. The land had burned me. I stood and yanked my blanket off the ground, swooping under the fence rail and toward the house.

"What do you have?"

I nearly jumped out of my skin. Margot was standing in the shadows. "You'un scared three years of gray into my hair," I said. She had seen me read the earth. Seen me shake my hand. Rather than hide it, I reshook my hand.

"Something hurt you?" she asked.

Truth. Margot could read lies. "Yes. It feels like it's burned."

"Something stung you?" she pressed, her tone slightly different now, even and low and controlled.

I thought about that. *Truth. No lies.* "That's what it feels like."

Margot clicked on her flash and gave me a *Let me see it* gesture. I held my finger up in the beam of light. "Burned," she said. "Blistered."

"Really?" I leaned in, surprised that my pain came with a real cause. I looked back at the steep bank and then jiggled my blanket. Nothing fell out. Not that I expected it to. Lying by omission. I felt guilty as all get-out. To distract her, I said, "Something's on the bank below. Dozens of feral cats and piles of fish. Any chance you could get one of your men to bring in some of the fish, send them to a lab for sampling?"

"Looking for what?" Margot asked, her tone still too uniform and too unemotional. She suspected something, knew I was hiding something. Her gift at work.

"Poisons? Parasites? Bacterial or viral infection? Industrial contamination? Magic?" I hazarded.

Margot walked past me, ducked under the rails, and shined her light down to the water. She made a sound like, "Humph." She swept the light back and forth. "Look at that." I heard a click and realized she was wearing a mic and was attached to a comms system. She said, "Probie, get over to the shore. I got a job right up your alley." She clicked off the mic and muttered, "Collecting dead fish. Perfect."

Hamilton jogged over and Margot adjusted her flash, creating a small personal light. I had never seen a flashlight that would do that, but it was a brilliant idea. I wanted one. Margot told my cousin what needed done.

"You gotta be kidding me. Do you know how much these shoes cost?"

"Don't know, don't care. Put on your field boots and get down there."

"I didn't—" He stopped.

"You didn't what, Probationary Special Agent Hamilton? Please don't tell me you packed your field boots in your gear bag and then left it at headquarters."

Hamilton's face contorted and then smoothed out. "I'll be right back, ma'am."

He vanished into the night and when he reappeared, he was wearing waders up to his knees. I vaguely remembered seeing waders with the fishing gear. Probie had borrowed the senator's wading boots. He had a small evidence kit in one hand, and he dipped under the fence and jogged upstream, to the small deck and the stairs that led down.

Margot and I watched as he made his way by the light of a small flashlight down the steps, which seemed to be slippery and filthy, to the shore below. He kicked the grayish rocks out of the way and kicked at the feral cats as well. They jumped in the way of cats, spinning in midair, and raced away so that none of Hamilton's kicks landed, but it didn't appear that he tried very hard to miss them. Hamilton had some serious anger and self-control issues.

I didn't like people who were cruel to animals, and I felt the bloodlust start to rise. Margot flashed me a look, one that was oddly familiar, enough so that it helped the desire to feed the land to wither. "You're part empath," I said. "That would explain your gift."

"No empaths in the family tree. Just Gramma the witch."

I nodded, but she was wrong. Empathy was a rare gift. Somewhere in her family tree an empath had hidden, and if Margot had the proper stimulation, that gift would roar to the surface. There wasn't time to suss out the genetic trait. Footsteps rang, dull and muted, on the stairs. "I'll get a reading from Hamilton when he reaches the top." I pointed to some heavy shadows. "I'll be there. Make sure he walks alone."

Margot moved toward the small deck. "What did you find?" she called to her probationary agent.

"Fish dinner," he said as he reached the top of the stairs. Hamilton was filthy, his suit grubby, soiled in streaks, his pants and shirt cuffs and the senator's waders smeared with slime and crusted with sand, his hands grubby. He didn't mention his clothing, but held out a fish, its white belly exposed, where a cat had bitten deep and torn through. "The fish are half-stewed. All the white parts, the bellies, are cooked."

I thought about the hot water boiling toward the surface on the hills near DNAKeys. What if the magma was still reaching toward the surface, heating even the river water? I had a feeling that I had done something dreadful.

"I used to fish with my dad," he added. "This is cooked flesh, not raw."

Margot said, "Take them to my SUV. Make sure the COCs are properly filled out. And set one aside for the PsyLED agent."

"You're going to— Never mind. Yes, ma'am."

Hamilton headed my way and I woke the psy-meter 2.0, quickly checked the ambient readings, and aimed the reader wand at my cousin. It lit up on psysitope one. A perfect reading for a witch. Hamilton hated paranormals, yet he carried a witch gene himself. He had to know, on some level, that he was gifted. Fear or training at the knee of a witch hater had taught him to loathe what he was, to bury it so deep that only fear and hatred were left. He passed me in the dark without seeing me, the stink of spoiled fish dank on the air, and he disappeared into the shadows near the pools.

In my hands, the machine lit up again, a dim glow. I still had the reader rod out and it was picking up something. Psysitope number four redlined. Something was here. And then, in an instant, before I could find its direction by turning in a circle, changing my position in the yard, it was gone. I spotted P. Simon in the shadows again and I turned the wand to him. And got a full human reading. Humans everywhere.

Frustrated, I walked back and forth, trying to pick it up again, before giving up and closing the device. As I worked, Margot came up in the night. Margot who wanted to know what Hamilton was. Margot who would know if I lied. "Don't ask," I said. "I can't answer."

"Which means he's a paranormal."

And because his being one of the rare male witches meant he was a PsyLED problem, and I had to report to Rick before I told anyone else, even his immediate supervisor. "Don't. Ask." I moved through the dark, back to my truck. I loaded up and drove off into the night.

FOURTEEN

It was later than late when I got back to the office, trudging up the stairs, keying in my code to enter. Half the lights were off, in nighttime mode, and I didn't bother turning on my cubicle lights while I unpacked and repacked my gobag, thinking. T. Laine and Tandy would be airborne by now, and the remaining day team—JoJo—would be sleeping somewhere, leaving only the night-shifters on duty, only our cars in the parking area: Rick and me. I didn't know if I was delighted by Occam's absence or something else.

I took off my weapon, letting my belly relax when the waist strap slid away. Too many pizzas and not enough greens had put a few pounds of weight on me. I hadn't liked being beanpole thin, but I wasn't thrilled with the small muffin top I was developing. I locked away my weapon and was about to leave the office when I caught a glimpse of the plants in the small window box. They looked slightly wilted. I stuck my fingers into the soil and yelped, leaping back. Almost instantly I heard footsteps approaching at a run.

"Nell!" Rick rounded the corner, weapon first. "What?" he demanded.

I shook my head, trying to piece together what I had just sensed.

"I'm okay. No intruders. I'm not in trouble or hurt. Not exactly."

"What does *not exactly* mean?" Rick growled, holstering his service weapon.

"The plants," I said. "They're all sick." I stepped back to the planter and ran a rosemary stem through my fingers.

"Dying," I amended softly as several of the small stiff leaves popped away from the green stem.

"And that means?" Rick asked.

I didn't answer. Cautiously I reached into the box, letting my fingertip—the unblistered one—brush across the surface of the soil. It felt like the earth at the Holloways'. At Justin Tolliver's. At the senator's.

The nanny had touched my plants.

I turned from the dead herbs and strapped my weapon on.

"Nell?" Rick said, warning in his tone.

"She killed my plants. I'm gonna shoot her."

"You're not shooting anyone," Rick said, standing so that I'd have to shoot *him* to get out of my cubicle. "Tell me what happened," he said, with that tone people use when they think they got a crazy person on their hands.

"I ain't—I'm *not* insane," I corrected. "The nanny's what happened." I gave Rick a fast debrief. "And she's the only new person to touch my plants. She killed them."

"I get that. But shooting people for killing plants isn't nice," Rick said, laughter hiding in his words. "And it's a bit of overkill."

"That isn't funny," I said precisely. "The nanny may have killed the people at the Holloways' party, and Sonya Tolliver in the limo. The nanny may be our shooter. And she is at the senator's house with all the remaining Tollivers."

"I've seen the video of her in the office," Rick said. "She doesn't look like the shooter. Doesn't move like the figure we've caught smudged images of on video. Body mechanics are all wrong, and most people can't hide body kinetics."

"I don't know about that. Maybe she isn't 'most people.' But she's the same kind of creature who killed the plants everywhere we've been. If she's the same kind of creature as Devin—"

"Then that clarifies this as a turf war or intraspecies war," Rick said. "I have some calls to make. You"—he pointed at me—"are not to go after the nanny." He turned and nearly bumped into Soul. "We need to dig into the nanny. Hell, we don't even have a name. How did we miss her?"

"We're near the full moon. Are you okay?" she asked Rick.

"I'm fine," he snarled, clearly lying. "Come with me."

Soul followed Rick toward the conference room, Soul saying, "We might have to interfere in a war that would out the senator's family"—she hesitated—"or the senator's extended family, as paras." The two left me alone with my gear and my dead plants and my thoughts.

If more of the high-powered Tollivers were paras in hiding, that could mean a divorce, loss of the senator's job in DC, and a lot of other bad things for them. People who hid parts of themselves from a spouse, from the public, often paid the consequences in the deaths of both marriage and career.

I had considered, for a moment that was as small as a hair split three ways, hiding what I was from Ben. I had considered going back into the church because it would have been easier—on the surface—than living in the real world. We would both have suffered something awful.

Occam, who knew what I was, or mostly so, still wanted me. And yet, he had called me *churchwoman*. I dialed his number and it went straight to voice mail, as I had expected. I said, "I'm a little bit ticked at you, cat-boy. I am not a churchwoman going backward in life instead of forward. You can apologize to me over that dinner." I ended the call and a strange feeling swept through me, something almost joyful, to be speaking to a man in such a manner. In the church, I'd been punished for such forward speech. Here, in my new life, I was safe, and safety was making me bold.

"Nell," Rick called. "If you're finished reacting to whatever you're reacting to, get in here. We need help."

Laptop and tablet in hand, I followed LaFleur and Soul down the hall into the conference room.

By dawn, as the day shift—JoJo and Occam—were dragging back in, Soul and I had uncovered a small hill of new evidence on the Tollivers and the nanny. The others gathered in the conference room, placing a box of Christmas-tree-shaped pastries on the center of the table, the smell of fresh coffee in various flavors riding on the air. Travel-weary images of Tandy and T. Laine were up on the big screens. They had arrived safely in Texas and were present via Internet. I didn't look at Occam when he came in, but I didn't have to be an empath to know my message had snagged his attention. I could feel his eyes on me from the moment he entered, with full-moon werecat intensity. We were in the time frame of the three days before the three days of the full moon. Occam was cat-itchy.

"Clementine," Rick said to the software, "record morning meeting." He gave the date and time and listed everyone's name. "Soul. Summarize the night's intel. Please." The *please* was added as an afterthought, as if he just remembered that Soul was the assistant director of PsyLED and not one of his crew.

Soul said, "You all thought the nanny looked a little strange. Now we know she is the same kind of creature who is stalking the Tollivers, though evaluation of body locomotion mechanics suggests she's not the shooter. The nanny's name is Connie Bulwer, and she was originally fully vetted through a service that plays matchmaker between certified nannies and potential clients. She was re-vetted through the government service when the senator first went to Washington, then she was re-re-vetted when Senator Tolliver became part of the Senate Intelligence Committee. She passed with flying colors with only a mention or two of her skin color, which was described variously as dusky or grayish. Now we have to consider the possibility that her skin color is indicative of species, not a human ethnic trait."

Rick said, "Her file is listed under her name. You should each have a copy by now. I want everyone to go through it, see what was missed, because we clearly missed something." Rick changed the subject and swiped new info onto the screen. It appeared between the images of Tandy and T. Laine. "We discovered evidence of an old, failed, financial takeover attempt of four small local industries owned by the

Tollivers. The businesses did not include DNAKeys, as we might have expected. We may have gotten fixated on DNAKeys because of the paranormal aspect. Go on, Nell."

I put the financial network file up on the screen. "The buyout attempt was by a man named Wilder Thomas Jefferson. Jefferson owned and still owns a munitions company, one that the Tollivers' plants produce parts for. He wanted to merge the companies together for a chance at a government contract, one that would have required all the plants be under one corporate heading. The Tollivers refused a merger. They also refused a buyout. Things were tense between the companies. Until . . . well, Jefferson also happens to be the father of Abrams' wife, Clarisse."

"Where's Jefferson now?" Rick asked.

"He's in an upscale nursing home in Nashville," I said. "Diagnosis is advanced dementia."

Rick sipped eggnog, thinking. "So Jefferson negotiated or approved a marriage between his daughter, Clarisse, and Abrams Tolliver." Which sounded a lot like some church marriages, arranged and miserable, though I didn't say so. "Now he has dementia," Rick said, musingly. "Tells us nothing."

JoJo was pulling on her earrings with one hand; her other hand was flying over keys, pausing so she could read, and then flying again. T. Laine was frowning on the overhead screen as she swiped through whatever file she was reading. I still didn't look at Occam.

Rick said, "To summarize, the buyout attempt was eleven years ago and the financial takeover was dropped when Clarisse married Abrams and the companies merged. Eleven years is around the same time as the disappearance of Charles Healy from prison, and Clarisse getting pregnant with Devin. A lot happened that year."

"So what does it mean?" JoJo asked. "The families married off the children like two kings consolidating countries against mutual enemies?"

"That isn't as uncommon as you might think," T. Laine said, "even outside of Nell's church." I started to say it wasn't my church, but she went on. "Offspring of wealthy families marry into wealthy families. They meet each other at debutant balls or Ivy League schools, discover they have things in common, and fall in love." Lainie's tone went dark and caustic. "Their families sanction the union and then do business together after the knot is tied. The babies are named after grandparents and great-grandparents and are presented with trust funds and a future to marry—again into the right circles and for the right reasons. Money. They don't marry grocers or car salesmen or schoolteachers or nurses or preachers or veterinarians or other ordinary people. They don't marry paras. Only the *right people*." Her mouth turned down and her eyes never lifted off her tablet. Tandy was watching her, but it didn't take an empath to know that T. Laine, the moon witch, had not been the right sort of person for a rich man to marry. At some point in her life, she had been hurt.

Rick said, "Well, that generations-long tradition of intermarriage isn't what happened here. There are no family records of the Jefferson family before 1950, when the elder Jefferson was delivered to an orphanage, at about three days old. Fifteen years later the children's home burned to the ground in a massive conflagration."

JoJo looked up at that one and grinned. "So the kid, Devin, is a pyro from his *mama's* side? Not his daddy's? We been concentrating on the wrong family name. And the nanny is gray because . . . why?"

I shook my head. No one had an answer. Yet.

I asked, "Is the PM on the body burned in the limo fire complete? Do we know *for certain* that it's Sonya Tolliver, Justin Tolliver's wife, the cousin-in-law of Senator Tolliver? And why was she with Devin instead of her own kids?"

"I asked that," T. Laine said. "Security and Sonya had picked up the kids at school. They had dropped off Sonya's children at ballet and soccer practice and were heading home."

Rick leaned in to his laptop and punched a button. A form flashed up on the overhead screen, the words *Preliminary COD* at the top. "Cause of death for Sonya Tolliver is burn-

ing at extremely high temperature. There wasn't enough
liquid left in the body to do toxicology screening the usual
way and liver tissue has been sent to a reference lab for
special testing. The results aren't expected back for ten working days. I doubt they bothered with ordering DNA comparisons. Why should they, when multiple witnesses know
Sonya Tolliver was in the limo."

"Can we get samples sent off for DNA?" Occam asked.
The first words he'd spoken.

"You can check," Tandy said, "but line seven says the
body was burned so badly that the family requested immediate cremation." He tapped his screen. "The forensic pathologist released it to the funeral home at two a.m. That's
five hours ago."

"That's awful fast," JoJo said.

"The Tollivers have a lot of political pull," Tandy said,
wryly. "They usually get what they ask for, and there was
no reason to hold the body."

Rick said, "We don't have probable cause to request that
the remains be DNA tested. And I'm sure rich-as-sin Justin
Tolliver and the senator would resist an invasion of privacy
that might imply anyone was somehow culpable in Sonya's
death or that they were hiding something."

Soul said, "Jones, put in a request to have extra samples
taken and held for possible future DNA comparisons. If the
body hasn't been picked up and if the techs or the pathologist
is in a receptive mood we might get our wish. But I won't
hold my breath."

"Any tissue left after toxicology testing would be held for
a time in the lab before disposal," Rick said. "If we find probable cause, we'd have a narrow time frame to get a warrant
and then claim the tissue. We need to talk to Justin. And the
senator and his wife. And Devin, if the father approves. And
the gray-skinned nanny. Because it's possible we're looking
at this all wrong. We're still thinking paranormal turf war.
What if it's simply nonhuman lineage and paperwork? A way
to keep the money in the family. Like vampires do."

T. Laine said, "So they burn Sonya to death? You're suggesting that they're long-lived and are covering their tracks by killing people? If so, then the body in the limo wasn't Sonya Tolliver. It's a body they picked up to arrange a legal death certificate. But that would indicate the *possibility* that they murdered someone in the fire. And what happened to the real Sonya? Where is she? And what about the kid? No one could have foreseen that Devin would be saved by Soul. Was he supposed to die? This theory doesn't work."

"I'm not suggesting anything," Rick said. "I'm saying we haven't dug deep enough."

"Too many unanswered questions," Soul said. "Our goal right now is to apprehend the unknown subject who's been shooting up Knoxville. Second order of business is to determine what paranormal species all four of the Tollivers and the Jeffersons are. Not vamps. Not *gwyllgi*. Not were-creature. Humanoid? Something that produces fire and might live a long time. That might have gray skin." Soul wasn't meeting anyone's eyes; she was wearing her working-worried-emotionless face.

JoJo said, "Pulling up my search files. A number of creatures—including Hephaestus, who was the Greek god of blacksmiths, craftsmen, artisans, sculptors, metals, metallurgy, fire, and volcanoes. Roman equivalent of Hephaestus is the god Vulcan."

Occam said, "You think we have gods here? In Knoxville?"

"No," JoJo said, shoving long braids over her shoulder with a clicking of beads. "But what if we have descendants of some creature that was once worshiped as a god? Sending you all my list. Go over it and see if you can make any connections. There are even a couple of Hindu gods that were traditionally depicted as being blue-skinned."

Rick said, "Nell, update on your night out."

I said, "There isn't much to tell except the thing we're looking for has been all over the senator's property. Every single plant on the entire acreage is dead or dying. The psymeter 2.0 gave me a level four reading. Whatever we're looking for has recently marked territory there and showed there

in the night. If the nanny is one of the creatures we're looking for, then maybe she let another one or more onto the
property. Maybe they had a party there. It's a big piece of
land and every single plant on it is dead, when they were all
fine only a day or so ago."

"Which means the senator is either colluding with her or
is in even greater danger," Rick said. "Occam, get back there.
Stay on the senator like white on rice. Do not let him out of
your sight, even in the shower."

Occam sighed, a sound like a cat blowing, and added the
senator's schedule to the overhead screens. "His entire day
is booked with appointments with his constituents. The first
one is breakfast with the Small Business Association. The
man treats his voters right. Even with a death in the family,
he's keeping appointments."

Rick said, "Get over there. E-mail an updated schedule
to us as soon as it's confirmed. JoJo will update you via text
or e-mail on anything new that comes up before we conclude
the meeting and anything we find during the day. Keep your
eyes open. Do some good."

"On it, boss." Occam stood and swung a leg over the back
of his chair. He had been straddling the chair, his arms
braced on the back. I carefully didn't look his way, but I was
completely aware of him as he left the room. And I felt some
odd unexplained tension leave my body when he was gone.

"Nell," Rick said.

I jerked at my name, as if I'd been caught daydreaming
in church.

"Every single appearance of the shooter has been at
night," he said. "I want you at the senator's property with
your hand in the earth every single night, all night, until this
is solved. I know it's a lot to ask, but we need to get ahead
of this guy and you're the only one who has even half a
chance to find the shooter before he strikes."

I dropped my chin, indicating that I understood what he
was saying, but it was also the most dangerous job on this
case. It put me right at the most likely location of the next
crime scene. "Backup?" I asked.

"You'll have it. I know I'm asking something that's difficult. Energy draining. Unlike the others, I don't want you pulling sixteen-hour shifts. I want you home and in your bed, to recuperate between shifts. Twelve hours on, twelve off. Go home. Get some sleep."

But I didn't make it home. I was within a mile of the turnoff toward Oliver Springs when JoJo's call came in. "Getchur butt back to town. The senator was just attacked on his way into the breakfast meeting of the Small Business Association. I got no deets. Texting you the address and the GPS. *Move!*"

"On my way," I said, pulling into a corner gas station, where I braked and checked the location, pulled up a map, and eased back into traffic, heading for the Just Yolking Around breakfast café, on East Summit Hill Drive.

I could see the smoke miles out, a black cloud rising straight up into the still air. Fire trucks and medic units were everywhere. Flaming ash fell from the sky, burning everything it touched. And all I could think was, *It's daylight. The shooter, if it was the shooter and not a grease fire, just changed his MO.* And, *Occam was with the senator.* My fingers trembled and my breath came too fast.

I remembered seeing John's old hard hat in the back. It was too large for me, but it would keep my hair from going up like fireworks. As I drove I reached behind the seat and felt around until I found it. I banged out a dusty spiderweb, slid the yellow plastic hat on my head, and caught an unexpected whiff of my husband, from when he was hale and hearty, and not the sick smell from the months he was dying.

Memories flooded over me and I hesitated an instant. His laughter, which had been soft but vigorous enough. His small smile when he brought me a bouquet of daisies from the edge of the woods. His work-roughened hands smoothing a length of wood as he made a cedar chest for some townie. Kindness, a dour composure, and a steadiness of purpose were mingled into the remembered scent of his sweat and, for reasons I didn't understand and didn't have time to analyze, it stopped my fear cold.

John had never been cruel to me. According to the church rules and guidelines he had gone far beyond expectations in his care and treatment of me. And he had died and left me protected and wealthy enough, rich in land if not in monetary funds. And now there was Occam. A man as different as it was possible to be from John Ingram. And not really a man, but a cat-man. Who might have been inside the restaurant when it went up in flames. I gunned the engine and turned on the emergency lights and siren.

Just Yolking Around was mostly gone. The brick walls still stood, but the roof had fallen in, the windows had blown out from the heat, and glass on the ground glittered with the reflection of the orange and red flames. Two high-powered water streams jetted into the cavern of black smoke and hungry fire. Anyone who had not gotten out was dead. A sense of loss gripped me, which was stupid because Occam wasn't mine. Never had been. Such a thing was only a possibility and one fraught with obstacles. Yet, I felt grief, a wailing, raving, furious grief.

I couldn't shake the strange feelings away. I carried them with me like a survival pack, insulating me from more possible hurt. Getting out of the truck, I was instantly assailed by the heat and the smoke and the incredible noise of flame, shouting, sirens, water pumping, and generators. A uniformed officer ran to stop me and I held up my ID. "Command center?" I shouted over the din.

He pointed across the street from the fire and I held up my thumb before trotting toward the conflagration. An ambulance pulled away; another followed; both were running lights and sirens, which meant they carried the injured and the dying. The strange feelings clasped me tighter, and then I saw Occam on the far side of a table littered with gear, his eyes glowing the brownish gold of his cat. There was blood on his white shirt, and his blond hair was whirling in the fire-wind. His clothes were black with soot. But Occam was alive. Relief shot through me like some kind of drug, melting my bones.

Occam looked up as if he scented me. He met my eyes and the glow of his cat went brighter. My relief was so intense that my knees nearly buckled.

I hadn't lost him.

As if he knew what I was feeling, Occam placed a hand on the command center table and leaped across it, to land with balanced precision. He stalked across the street, dodging equipment without really seeing it, relying on his cat senses. My heart was beating so fast it felt like a drum in my chest. And I feared he might shame me by doing something overt in front of other people. "Special Agent Occam," I called out as he reached me. "Special Agent Ingram reporting in."

Occam stopped so fast his feet ground on the broken glass. His fists were balled as if to keep him from doing whatever he had been about to do. "Thank you, Nell, sugar. This kinda kiss don't need to be out in the middle of a crime scene."

This kinda kiss . . . "Crime scene?" I asked instead of what I wanted to say: *This kind of kiss* . . . What *kind of kiss?*

"The fire started in the kitchen about three minutes after the senator entered. Flames exploded outward, from the kitchen. Smelled of natural gas and grease and something earthy, like mushrooms. The first flame caught the senator. A direct hit. He's badly burned. Third degree on his face, head, and hands. Second degree on his torso and abdomen, with his clothes stuck to him like glue. One of the kitchen help, a human, was injured at the scene, and both of the Secret Service assigned to the senator were killed. I couldn't get them snuffed in time."

Occam took my arm and guided me back the way I had come. "LaFleur is here and interviewing witnesses. Soul is hobnobbing with the brass, talking arson and grease fire and accelerants. Rick wants you and me to follow the senator's ambulance to the hospital and try to talk with him before he's airlifted out to a burn center, and my car is back at the senator's office."

I raced back to my truck and got in as Occam entered on the passenger side. Our doors closed and the noise died to a low roar. The stink of smoke and fire and burned flesh didn't go away but filled the cab from his clothes and hair. I started the engine and Occam pointed to an ambulance that was just pulling out. I still didn't ask what I wanted to: *What kinda kiss?* "Which hospital?" I asked. If the senator was human he could go to any hospital, but UTMC was the only one in the area with a paranormal unit and fully trained paranormal practitioners.

"St. Mary's Medical Center is closest. Something about his airway means he needs immediate surgical attention. The only burn centers in Tennessee are in Memphis and Nashville, I think. He can't wait that long."

I activated my emergency flashers and pulled in behind the ambulance as it sped through a red light. "Are you hurt bad?" I asked, hearing the strain in my voice. "You've been bleeding. And I smell burned skin." It was a smell like no other.

"Burned myself and got cut pretty bad"—he held up his arms to expose seared, bloody sleeves—"wrapping the senator up in a woman's overcoat and jumping through the front window." He shrugged and belted himself in. "I'm fine now. Werecat healing. Becoming a leopard was a life stealer, but at least the taint has a few benefits."

"Walk me through what happened," I said, to keep my mind on the case and not on the man beside me.

"Early breakfast meeting. The senator and two Secret Service men walked into the restaurant at six forty-two. I was directly behind them. At six forty-six, while the senator was still glad-handing his voters, someone yelled. I heard a noise from the kitchen that went *whump*. A wall of orange and purple flame shot out through the service window and caught the senator and his men, dead-on. I threw three people to the floor, yelled for everybody to get out. Grabbed a woman's coat off her back and smothered the senator. Picked him up. Jumped through the front window. Finished snuffing the flames. His men were dying when I left them. On the floor. The fire was abnormally"—he paused and I heard him swallow even over the siren—"unbelievably hot. It spread like it was fed by kerosene. A flash fire that far away from the stove should have missed anyone except kitchen help. Instead it ate to the bone on the senator's face. His eyes are gone. His lips." Occam shook his head, his voice shaking. "His men were pretty much the same but over a larger body area. I never saw such a thing."

I took off my hard hat and tossed it behind the seat, then reached behind into a gobag and brought out a room-temp bottle of water, which I gave to Occam. He drank it in three massive swallows, crushing the bottle fast as it went down. "Thanks, Nell, sugar."

"The senator. You were holding him and he was bleeding. Is he human?"

"Flame that hot? Burning so many things at once? Including me? I don't know, couldn't tell, don't remember anything standing out as nonhuman."

We were silent the rest of the way to the hospital and reached the ambulance bay at the same time as the medic unit. I parked in a No Parking zone and put my shield up in the window to avoid getting towed. We bulled through into the emergency department behind the senator's gurney as the paramedics shouted vital signs to the doctors and shoved their patient into the trauma room. We held up ID when the nurses tried to make us leave, shouting to be heard over the din in the trauma department, "PsyLED. Official business!" Not knowing what else to do, they let us stay.

A short, stout trauma doctor began working on the senator's airway and I got my first view of Tolliver. His face was charred away, with blackened and red weeping edges. His chest was working, trying to draw in air. He was gurgling and gagging. It was the most horrible thing I had ever seen.

People ran back and forth cutting off his clothes and sticking things into the senator's scorched body. He was badly burned from the hips up, only his legs still pale and hairy and growing gray from oxygen loss.

"Upper respiratory system is fried," the doctor said, her

gloved hands at the senator's jaw and throat and a headlamp on her forehead. "Suction! He's aspirating."

"Probably inhaled flaming air," another woman said. Her name was Madeline, with the word *Respiratory* below it, on her name badge.

"I need a trach kit," the doctor shouted.

Because there was nothing else to work with, and they needed multiple lines, they started inserting IV lines with screws into his thigh bones, which I had no idea could even be done.

Two people were monitoring the senator's oxygen status and trying to get blood pressure readings off his lower leg. It was a haze of action that I couldn't even begin to follow.

The doctor at his throat grunted out the words, "Who's taking notes? We have acute inhalation injury. Acute pulmonary edema. Lungs are scorched."

Madeline said, "Not sure the tissue will hold for a trach. His trachea is cooked."

All that happened in the first two minutes. By the third minute, three doctors were working on the senator, along with two respiratory therapists and four nurses and techs. I recorded as many of their first names and departments in my cell as I could, in case I needed them later. It gave me something to do rather than staring at the senator's ravaged body.

My cell dinged in the middle of the medical resuscitation attempts and Occam and I read the news that JoJo had texted to our cells. Clarisse, the senator's wife, had been on the way to a meeting in her official car, with a driver and a full security detail. The driver had gone off the Alcoa Highway and into the river. The car had been only ten feet offshore and had been recovered quickly, along with the bodies of the driver and her security—two women and a man.

The senator's wife wasn't inside. When the car was pulled out, at about the same time that the senator was flash-burned, it was discovered that the windows were all broken out. The car was riddled with bullet holes. There were no witnesses to the shooting, and the shooter was believed to have driven up beside them and opened fire with a high-powered automatic rifle. Casings were being recovered from the street where the attack took place. The same ammunition as had been fired at the Tollivers on each of the other occasions. Clarisse Tolliver was presumed dead.

Occam and I huddled against a wall, silent and ignored. Useless.

Twenty-seven minutes after we arrived, the senator's heart stopped. They tried to resuscitate him for another half hour. Then they pronounced Senator Tolliver dead. The sudden silence was profound. The team working on him backed away. It didn't last long. They had seen this kind of thing before. They began to clean up paper and plastic packages, to count discarded needles.

Occam and I informed LaFleur. Took names and told the doctors that we'd be sending papers to get copies of the medical report. Half an hour after the senator died, the day shift Secret Service agents, who had been stuck in traffic on the way to take over for night shift at the senator's meeting, finally caught up with their quarry. We left the hospital.

The air outside didn't smell like burned human, though the scent clung to our clothes and hair. Instead, the air was warm and the sun was shining. A dog trotted across the parking lot. An ambulance was pulling in. Cars followed it. Occam stepped off the curb into the street.

"You okay?" I asked Occam as we left the emergency entrance.

He didn't answer until we were back in my truck, the cab an oasis of wakeful normalcy after a nightmare. "No. Not really," he said. "I've seen a lot of awful things in my life. Never seen a cooked piece of meat still trying to breathe. I don't know how medical people do that kinda thing, day in and day out. It was . . ." He paused as if trying to decide how to phrase what he was feeling and seemed to settle on the inadequate, ". . . pretty horrible."

I reached over and took Occam's hand in mine. There was an instant of resistance, or maybe just surprise, before he laced his fingers through mine and gripped my hand back.

His skin wasn't rough or calloused like John's. Or like mine, for that matter. Not the hand of someone who had labored too hard for too many years, working the land with tools that abraded the skin and damaged the joints. The flesh of his palm and fingers was firm and solid, like the paw of a young dog or cat. Healthy. Reborn every time he shifted forms.

He said, "The shooter went after Clarisse. If the flames in the restaurant were from a pyro, then we have two killers now. Maybe we did all along."

Occam's cell pinged and he swiped it with his other hand. Without emotion he translated what he was reading. "The senator's postmortem has already been scheduled. It's at four p.m. It'll be performed by a forensic pathologist. According to the feds and the arson squad, the cook at the fire saw a strange-looking man in the kitchen just before the fire. She swears the man's skin was blue."

"We got to go to the PM?"

"Looks like *I* do. You got your own text."

"I'll check it after we get to HQ," I said.

From the corner of my eye, I saw a small smile pull at his lips, and his dimple deepened. His shoulders relaxed. "When your hand isn't busy being held, Nell, sugar?"

"That's my plan," I said, feeling unaccustomedly bold.

"I find I'm right fond of that plan." His fingers tightened on mine and I squeezed back.

FIFTEEN

"The senator's PM is scheduled for four p.m. today," Rick said, "and Occam and I will be there, along with two feds and two members of the Secret Service. Meanwhile, JoJo's been digging sideways and has discovered that the daughter who produced Justin Tolliver—Miriam—and who fell off the map right after Justin was adopted by her parents, was never reported missing."

"So we don't know if she disappeared as in ran away or disappeared as in presumed dead," I said. And then realized how dreadful it was that I could say such a statement in a calm and rational and unemotional tone of voice. I didn't know what I was becoming as a special agent, but it wasn't the woman I had been.

Rick said, "Disappeared as in there's been no sign of her since—no leads, no official search, no credit report, no death certificate, and she isn't on any missing persons databases—nothing."

"That's odd," Soul said, "especially for the family member of a public official, who could pull strings and find her, get her case special attention."

JoJo said, "We have an incoming call from T. Laine and Tandy."

The overhead screens flickered and Tandy's face appeared, his lips moving, his eyes to the side. T. Laine appeared beside him, and she was clearly looking at him, listening. Rick said, "We have visuals. Why don't we have audio?"

Oh. Sorry, Tandy's lips said, without sound. He punched a button and looked at the screen, saying, "Starting over.

Healy's prison cellmate died in an infirmary fire last night. We were just shown in and saw the place. It looks like either he was attacked with a flamethrower or he suffered self-immolation."

"But there is no accelerant smell," T. Laine said. "One of the warden's trustees said it was spontaneous combustion. That's what we got. A dead witness."

Rick cursed inventively and rubbed his head. His eyes were glowing slightly green, the color of his cat. We were getting too close to the full moon. "So now we have three players? And one's in Texas? Get home," he said to Tandy. "We'll see you late this afternoon."

"Okay, boss," Tandy said. "Out." The screens went black.

Rick swiveled in his chair to the partial team in the conference room. "Clearly we have more than one killer. It's highly unlikely that a killer managed to get inside a maximum security prison, find and fry a specific prisoner, and then get back here in time to locate and fry the senator, *and* shoot up Clarisse Tolliver's car."

"Unless he could fly," I said softly.

Rick cursed again and threw himself out of his chair. Pea, the grindylow, appeared at his side and leaped onto Rick's shoulder, chittering madly as Rick stormed down the hallway, calling for Soul.

A flying, fire-throwing, gun-shooting paranormal. Which would explain how the shooter got away each time. He/she/it shifted shape and flew away. Like an *arcenciel*?

There were no other known species that could do all the things we had seen and that had been attributed to it. If it could fly or even teleport . . . how would we stop it? Without commenting further, I went home to shower off the stench of fire and death and to sleep, a feeling of failure riding on my shoulders, and later, into my dreams.

T. Laine and Tandy were in the conference room when I got back to HQ, both wearing fresh clothes, hair still damp from showers, and the EOD meeting was in midswing. On the screens was a new case file. What had been a protective investigatory case was now an examination of data and evidence with national importance: the investigation into the extraordinary and bizarre death of Senator Tolliver by unknown means and under unusual and possibly paranormal circumstances.

A stranger stood in the corner, a man with a face like a piece of oak and a suit that had to cost a month of my wages. He was a Secret Service agent, one of the ones who had come to the hospital after the senator was blasted with fire. And he was staring at Occam.

I didn't have to be Tandy to know why he was here. Occam was a wereleopard. Occam had been in the presence of the senator at the time of the bizarre and unexplainable fire. Occam had survived that fire when the senator and his security detail had not. And Occam the wereleopard looked fine. Occam was a suspect. I looked around the table as I took my seat and saw from their body language I had missed some important stuff. I pulled up the files that were open on the big screens, scanning to catch up on the intel.

An irritated burr in his voice, Rick said, "Clementine, record the attendance of Probationary Special Agent Nell Ingram. Time is six twenty-seven."

I flinched and whispered, "Traffic." And then I flushed with anger, cleared my voice, and said, "I was caught in traffic. There was an accident on South Illinois Avenue." Rick looked at me blankly. "On Sixty-two near Tuskegee Drive," I clarified. Unit Eighteen was composed of out-of-towners, not local people, and for months now, I'd had to refer to roads by their number instead of the pike name or street name.

Rick said, "Okay, so why aren't you at the senator's place, reading the ground?"

"Ummm." I flicked my eyes around the table, meeting Tandy's. "Because the senator's dead?"

Tandy gave me a slight nod telling me that Rick was not himself, but that he was working to share his own calm with the boss. The full moon was close. Rick was antsy. I put a sugar cookie shaped like a gift box tied with a bow onto a paper plate and passed it Rick's way. He didn't take it, instead looking even more annoyed.

Calmly, Soul said, "Nell is where she should be. In fact, I think Nell should concentrate on a timeline. We have murders to investigate. This is now our case. The FBI and Secret Service will still be involved but on the periphery."

"Fine," Rick said, his voice tight, his green-glowing eyes on me. "Read the file notes, Ingram. T. Laine, continue."

T. Laine said, "I spent the last half of the day and the flight back working on the legislation angle. The senator had three bills before Congress: one that would make all paranormals born in this country equal citizens with all protections under the law; one that provides regular law enforcement equal power over all paranormals; and the last one unrelated, that requires much deeper background checks on all gun buyers and a three-week waiting period. All this is totally out of character for a Republican senator, especially since several of the Tolliver companies contribute to the production of weapons."

Tandy said, "I've been talking to his aides. They say he'd been acting strange for the last three months, taking breaks and disappearing, missing meetings, postponing trips to DC, abstaining from votes he normally would have strong feelings for or against. It means nothing by itself, but taken together with a possible paranormal turf war, it might eventually make sense."

"Occam," Rick snarled. "Update us on the senator's PM."

Occam didn't raise his eyes from his computer screen, eyes that were glowing the golden brown of his cat, but his lips lifted in a snarl of his own. The tension in the room was suddenly too high, the air feeling too hot. The werecats were acting catty, not human. It could be from the stuff I missed before I arrived. Or because when it came to cat shifting, Rick was a brand-new were and had little control over his emotions. Or because the dominance games in the null room had been unsuccessful. Or because, when I helped Rick shift back to human during the last full moon, breaking the wereleopard curse he was under, maybe I didn't succeed all the way. I had tried not to think too much about that event, but I had never broken a curse, let alone one applied by a cat-woman. Maybe I just partially solved his problem and he was still in trouble. Or maybe the tattoo magic spell on and in his flesh was the problem. Whatever it was, Rick acting hotheaded or out of control would be bad for him and for all of us in Unit Eighteen. Rick tilted his head in a catty, nonhuman manner.

At the gesture, the Secret Service guy slid his hand inside his jacket, moving like former military, instincts on high. I glanced to Tandy, and he looked spooked.

Out of nowhere, Pea landed on the table, chittering madly. She leaped over the little Christmas tree, dropping onto Occam, landing like a cute kitten, a grindylow reacting to the rising violent were-pheromones in the room.

Tandy stood, his Lichtenberg lines too bright, too red on his white, white skin. His face was caught in a rictus of fear, his eyes on Rick, his hands reaching, as if to hold the SAC in place. And failing. Something was about to happen. Something bad.

There was only one grindylow. Where was the other?

The Secret Service guy was drawing his weapon. Occam's eyes flashed golden fire. Rick reached for his service weapon.

I barked, "Rick!" I pulled on Soulwood. Pulled peace and calm from the sleeping trees and bound them around Rick's cat. I had claimed Rick soon after I met him, claimed him for the land, to heal him, to heal his were-magics. Now I used that, and reached out to Tandy too, hoping he could help calm the cat. But the empath was panicked himself, picking up the wereleopards' territorial anger.

I used the tools I had and wrapped Soulwood around all of them: the cats, the grindylow, Tandy, the government warrior. More quietly, I said, "We're all happy here."

Rick blinked. His eyes lost the green leopard sheen. Pea looked up from Occam and leaped all the way across the table to land on Rick. Stuck her nose into Rick's face and chittered. It seemed everyone in the room took a breath. "Everything is okay," I said. I looked at Tandy and said again, softer, "Everything is okay." Tandy nodded and closed his eyes, his body language wilting. The empath had learned that in times of extreme stress and fear he had the ability to share his own emotions, to change other people's reactions, but he hadn't managed to do that, instead falling back on old patterns of being controlled by the rages and passions around him. Now he too drew on Soulwood, pushing the calm of the land that lived inside me into the room. It was a bizarre sensation, similar to the touch of a slow spring rain pattering down on the earth. I liked it.

The tension in the room went down fast. The Secret Service agent blinked in confusion and replaced his weapon with a soft click of hard plastic holster.

Rick's weapon disappeared; he took a breath and released it. "Where were we?" he asked.

The glow in Occam's eyes died and he said, "I'll skip the weight of the senator's liver and brain and heart and conditions of his internal organs to give you the English translation of the COD. Cause of death is listed as third-degree burns and inhalation of superheated air, resulting in the shutdown of his respiratory system. It's transcribed in medicalese, but that's the gist. They were starting on the security guys when I left, but prelim results were the same."

"But he was human," Rick stated.

Occam hesitated, glancing at the Secret Service agent as if weighing what he wanted to say, and it was clear he had held information back. "His organs were . . . off. His digestive system wasn't normal." He looked at Soul and she tilted her head, telling him to continue. "He had no kidneys, no gallbladder; his liver was bluish. His blood smelled weird and it was darker than expected. The unburned parts of the senator's skin turned a deep bluish color that looked nothing like livor mortis after death. The forensic pathologists sent patches off for DNA workup and they'll be processing it through chemicals and dyes to look at it under a microscope in twenty-four hours. We should have a report in forty-eight hours or so. But no. The senator was not human."

* * *

The meeting lasted too long. When it was over, the Secret Service agent left and the others went home or to their office cubicles. I printed out a dozen files and spread the pages over the conference room table, to put together a timeline and a possible family tree. I worked for hours, as the moon passed by outside the windows, marking the night's progression. I drank eggnog right out of the carton. It wasn't near as good as Mama Grace's nog. I ate cookies. Also not as good. When I was done, I organized it into a new file with bullet points.

- Wilder Thomas Jefferson, infant, taken to orphanage— 1950.

- Burns it down at age 15 (entering puberty, which is when many paranormals come into their powers).

- Numbers of potential paranormals in Jefferson/Tolliver family: Wilder Thomas Jefferson? Jefferson's wife? (Note: No details on her. Determine status.) Justin's mother Miriam Tolliver (actually sister to Senator T) missing? Sonya Tolliver, deceased? Clarisse Jefferson Tolliver, missing presumed deceased? Charles Healy (Jail 1973. Missing 11 years). Nanny. Devin. Unknown which family line trait descended. Both? Unlikely.

- Theory: Long-lived pyro shape-shifters, able to assume human form. No kidneys. Nonhuman digestive tract. Gray skin. Dark blood postmortem.

- Possibility: Flight?

- Possibility: Ability to hide/camouflage scent patterns? Males only?

- Need/want way to reproduce safely.

- Need/want way to transfer holdings.

I did a little more research and added to the list:

- Note: Wilder Thomas Jefferson never married, but starting 30 years ago, he was photographed often with his young daughter, Clarisse. Went into business with Tolliver upon three things: marriage of Sonya to Justin, Clarisse marriage to Abrams, and birth of Devin.

- Possibilities of pyro types: phoenix (would fit flight), hellhound (a fire-based type of *gwyllgi*?), dragon (different from *arcenciels*?), efreet (multiple spellings; can be caught or killed with magic), cherufe (reptile humanoid; may not be true shape-shifter), salamander (born in volcanoes).

As I pulled together the timeline and possibilities, I found something that T. Laine had entered into the files just before she went to Texas. Soon after the birth of Devin, there was a huge fire at then-state-senator Tolliver's mansion and two bodies were found in the building, an adult female and a child. Fire investigators determined that a servant and her child died, and death certificates were issued in the names of Monica Smith and Marcus Smith. Which was interesting, but not particularly useful information. Unless . . . I sat back in my chair, watching Soul, who was standing still as a glass statue, both of us thinking.

"Soul?"

She turned from the window and the brightening sky, which had held her unfocused attention. She raised her brows in a gesture that said I could continue.

"What if someone killed the real-life real wife Clarisse and the real Devin, and replaced them with shape-shifting pyros?"

"If so, then why burn up Sonya in the limo?"

"Hmmm. Unless Devin accidentally set off the fire. Or unless Sonya was a problem and she had to die for some reason, say, to protect them, or Sonya was like them and it was time to replace Sonya's pyro identity?"

Soul gave me a head-shaking shrug that suggested I was guessing and my guesses were getting too complicated to make sense, and she was right. I sent my lists off to JoJo and went back to work. But something kept nagging at me. Something about the timeline and the sequence of the deaths through three generations.

Rick put a cup of coffee at my elbow, the steam curling up. Hot enough to burn my mouth.

I stopped, my fingers motionless above the tablet. I remembered the burned and dead plants at the senator's house, and the cooked fish in the water below. My mouth came slowly open. "Ohhh," I said. "I need to go to the senator's at dawn."

"Why?" Rick asked, the question low and concerned. I'd heard my cats use that specific interrogative tone.

"Something I saw. It was dark. It might be nothing so I'd rather not say. But I want to see it again, in the daylight."

"Fine. Work on the timelines and try to narrow down the species of pyro. Take off near the end of your shift. I'll send Occam with you." I wasn't sure that I wanted Occam with me, not with so many things unknown and undecided between us, but I shrugged. There wasn't anything I could do about my wants.

I spent the night in the conference room, the Christmas tree and a sleepy grindylow keeping me company. Just before dawn, I heard Occam come in and I left the conference room to pick up my gear bag. We headed out, Occam behind me, his gait limber, supple, and flowing, more so than other days, as his cat rose with the lunar cycle. Small hairs lifted on the back of my neck, the way they might if I was being pursued, tracked by an apex predator. Which, of course, I was. But I didn't give in to that awareness, instead carrying my gear down the stairs to my truck. Standing out in the warm air— winter in the South was changeable at best—I said smartly, "You got Pea with you?"

"Yep. In my shoulder bag. Why you asking, Nell, sugar?"

"I'd rather *she* kill you if you go off leash. The paperwork for shooting a teammate has gotta be a pain in the backside."

Occam started laughing, a purring chuff of sound that brought a smile to my face and made me tease further. "You cat-boys are hard to get along with in your time of the month."

"Time of the— Nell, sugar, that is an appalling insult." Occam was still laughing as he got in the truck beside me and we drove off together.

"You didn't tell me we'd be climbing down a couple thousand slippery, slimy, and stinking stairs to the river," Occam said to me.

I'd known about the stairs but not their condition. They were vile, sticky beneath my field boots. Even the handrail was sticky and slimy and I couldn't make myself touch it. It was no wonder my cousin's clothes had been so filthy when he came back up. In the dark, Chadworth Hamilton had to have touched everything. I bet he had to throw his expensive suit away. "Didn't think I needed to. What do you smell?" I figured his senses would be heightened in the moon-time.

"Dead fish. Some cooked, some raw. All of it rotting."

"Mm-hm." We reached the bottom and I looked back up. The stairs were the only way down or up without some kind of parachute or a rappelling rope. The vegetation at the top was brown, desiccated, dead. Below the deck, there was greenery in spots, rooted in the rocks.

On the beach, the sun was warm, casting short shadows on twisted, broken driftwood. The water was placid, reflecting back the sun. There were fewer dead fish and a lot of animal tracks from raccoon to 'possum, to bird tracks. There were crows perched nearby on the rocks and the scant vegetation. Seagulls calling, flying overhead, watching. There were also a lot of flies on the rotting fish, all of them showing the effects of scavenger predation. The sand was a dun color here, the bank narrow, the gray rocks in small piles, each rock ovoid, about the size of a basketball, but . . . cracked, and broken. I walked to the water's edge, bent, and picked up a broken piece. It was pale gray with small white and brown specks, lightweight, thin, and hollow. The inside was white, with a dried film stretched around the concave curves. "Shell," I said softly. I looked out over the water. "Salamander eggs."

"What's that?" Occam asked.

"One of the potential pyro paras was a salamander. According to mythology, salamanders were created in volcanoes but live in freshwater environments." I looked around. "We got freshwater. Water that was heated somehow, enough to parboil the fish swimming in it. We got eggs. Someone—something—hatched babies here." I looked up at the cliff face and the slimy steps. Slimy from salamanders coming and going? "The entire yard above is dead, burned at the roots, though still greenish in places. The trail of dead vegetation leading to the river is a lot more dead, as if it was injured more often, for a longer time, as something went back and forth to the river." Still holding the shell, I bent and placed my fingertips in the water. "The river water's heated. Warmer than good dishwater." I shook my head as disparate and formerly unrelated bits of evidence began to settle in place. "Perfect for keeping eggs warm to hatch? Or maybe the eggs hatch on the shore and the warm water is just a result of their physiology? Pyros who live in water at least part of the time. Pyros who are attacking the Tollivers. Maybe trying to take their places. Maybe already took their places, long ago."

I walked up the beach. On the sand, I found a matching part to the shell in my hand and pieced them together. The creature that had been contained in it, assuming it was boneless like a tadpole, shaped like one, and could curl up tight, might be a slender five feet long with a small, narrow head, or three feet long with a wider head and body. I could imagine it weighed anywhere from ten to twenty pounds, but if it wasn't an Earth creature, then weight-to-mass ratio might be different. If the substance from which its body was composed was more dense than an Earth organism, then gravity, while still a constant, might make it heavier than similar-appearing material.

Weight-to-mass ratio. I was surprised I remembered that. I had tried to educate myself on mathematics while Leah was dying, but a lot of it was hard to understand without a teacher. I had given up on lots of learning for just that reason.

Out in the water, about two feet deep, I spotted something pale. Ovoid. Solid. An unhatched egg? I handed Occam the broken shells and my jacket, then pulled off my field boots and socks, tossing them to the beach. Rolled up my sleeves. Pea leaped from Occam's gobag and raced up and down the beach, chittering at me as if she found me amusing or alarming.

"Nell, sugar, what the Sam Hill you doin'?"

I rolled up my pants legs above the knee, conscious that no one had seen my knees since I was twelve. Even John hadn't seen my naked legs. I felt embarrassed, shy, and daring all at once. "Getting that." I pointed at the shell. "It might be whole. And what's inside would tell us everything we need to know." I stepped into the water. Warm, bathwater warm.

"Nellie, stop," Occam said. No. Demanded.

I flashed him a look. Pretty sure it was Mama's look when one of her young'uns got uppity. I took a deeper step, the water to midcalf, then deeper to my knees as I walked out.

"Nell, let me do this."

I ignored him. This little woman did not need protection from a little water. The river temperature rose to uncomfortable as I stepped deeper. Then one more step, the water just above my knee. The egg was only about a foot away. With the toes of one foot, I scooted the egg closer to me, the warm water wetting my pants where they were rolled. Pea chittered again, sounding less amused now.

"Nell!"

"Don't bark at me like a dog," I said, ignoring him otherwise.

"I smell something. Something bad."

"It's rotting fish." The egg was heavy, twirling in a circle instead of inching closer. I wriggled another inch out, my foot now buried in the sandy bottom, my pants legs quite wet. But I got a firmer toe grip on the shell and pulled it toward me. Stepped back and pulled it again. "Got it," I said, easing it closer to shore. I stood on two feet and bent to pick it up.

Something sliced through the water, fast as a fish. I felt it touch my wrist and I jerked away. Splashing the water. I held up my arm. My wrist was bleeding. Three distinct, but not linear slashes.

"What the . . . ?" Occam growled.

The water splashed and swirled. I turned to race from the river.

My feet flew out from under me. My ankles in a vise. I hit bottom on one hip. Was dragged under. Deeper. Into blacker, hotter water. The current caught me as I flailed. Fighting. Pulled deeper. Blacker. Hotter.

Something gripped my wrist, slicing, multiple times at once. Something else caught my short hair. Pain cut at my abdomen. Above me, a three-fingered hand slashed down. I jerked back my head. Claws caught my collarbone. Different sizes of clawed tadpoles.

The need to breathe strangled me. Water burned. *Need to breathe. Breathe. Breathe!*

Deeper. Hotter.

I pulled my gun. Shoved it hard against one of the things that held me. Squeezed the trigger. Heard a *thump*. Saw nothing.

Suddenly the things let me go. They were just gone, in a frenzied mass. I whirled in the water. Face-to-face with glowing eyes and killer teeth. The fangs reached out and snagged my shirt at the shoulder. Tugged me upward.

Breathe. *Breathe. Breathe!* I needed to breathe! I swallowed water. More water. Gagged.

I kicked hard. Harder. Desperate for air. Caught in a current that pulled me down. I swallowed more water fighting *not* to breathe the water in. The teeth pulled me upward, toward the light.

I broke through.

Coughing. Gagging. Vomiting water.

The fangs broke through beside me. Took my bleeding wrist between them, fangs clasping and meeting on the other side. *Occam.* Occam had saved me. His sleek spotted body, as supple and graceful on the water as on land, bumped my side as he swam me to shore while I coughed and gagged and spat. When we were knee-deep he let me go and splashed back into the water and under. Where the egg was.

Something long and quick swirled through the water and grabbed for me. I spun in the shallows and scratched it, my fingernails catching it on the . . . face? Its blood boiled into the water and over my hand. Blue blood. Heated. Bubbling. Metallic and sour. It felt *wrong* on my hand. Wrong under my nails. Wrong, wrong, so very *wrong*.

But it was *blood*. Bloodlust gripped me. I reached out and the blood spewed over my hand and I . . . I fed it to the water. Drained it. *Knew it.* Salamander. Flaming being. Very nearly immortal. Fishy. Scalding. I killed it. Broke it into its composite parts. The cells floated away. Disintegrated. Others of its kind were caught in the bloodlust. I pulled them apart and broke them down, taking as many of them as I could. The rest of the tadpoles took off for deeper water, leaving us safe. The water cooled.

I pulled away and back to the shore.

Occam's head emerged from the water, his nostril flaps opening and blowing, breathing and closing, and dipping back underwater. Shock zinged through me, followed by relief so intense it made me shiver. He hadn't noted my killing the salamander tadpoles. My bloodlust had bypassed him. He was batting the egg across the bottom to the sandy beach. I crawled on my hands and feet out of the water and far up the bank against the rock wall. I threw up again, losing all the water I had swallowed. Heaving, losing everything I had eaten in the last hours. Dry heaving when that was gone.

Exhausted, I rolled over and sat where I could see the water. Now heaving breaths. Nothing had ever felt so good. Air. Blessed air. Pea curled up beside me and made worried moans.

I had thought I didn't need Occam—a man—to do this thing for me—a woman. I needed to listen more and not let my preconceived notions make me do something stupid. I lay on the sand in the sun and breathed.

I was still holding my gun. Guns aren't designed to shoot in water. Normal bullets aren't fabricated to fly true through water. Useless underwater except for the one shot, which I had somehow missed. I pulled the holster to me, around my waist. I needed to service it, give it a good cleaning and oiling. I holstered the Glock. Bloody water squirted out of the hard plastic holster. I was bleeding freely from so many places I didn't know what to put pressure on. And I didn't care. I breathed. Just breathed.

Occam came out of the water, pawing the egg before him, up onto his clothes, his pants and jacket and shirt that were scattered in a small area. They appeared to be in ruins. Occam had shifted. Faster than I thought possible. That had to have been an agony.

He had tried to stop me. In the way of cats, he had scented danger on the air. He had saved me when the things—the young salamanders—had taken me under. Had tried to drown me. Occam had saved me. Tears spilled down my cheeks.

The spotted leopard trotted across the sand, dripping, splashing, padding, paw to paw, a sleek, killing machine. He fell at my side and dropped his huge head on my lap. Chuffed. His golden eyes met mine. He squirmed his jaw over my thigh, back and forth, scent-marking me. It wasn't the first time he had done so. And Pea didn't seem to care. She rolled over and turned her belly to the sun, closing her eyes.

I lifted a hand that now felt as if it weighed a ton. Placed it on his head. His wet hair was silky smooth. My blood flowed over his pelt. He sniffed. Growled. He sat up and held my eyes with his golden ones. Growled again. "I know. I'm still bleedin'," I said. "Not having werecat healing abilities, there's not much I can do about it."

Occam looked surprised, tilted his head, pushed to his feet, and pawed down the shore and around a huge rounded, pitted rock that appeared to have fallen there long ago. He disappeared. "You better not shift and walk back here all nekkid," I said. And smiled at the image of Occam, the way I imagined he would look, human and naked, stalking along the beach.

He chuffed from around the rocks. And trotted back to me, half carrying, half dragging a small green plant in his fangs. It was an evergreen, with leaves, roots, and all, pulled alive from the ground. It looked like a boxwood shrub, yanked from the dirt, but it wasn't. I didn't know what it was. A waterweed or rock-face weed of some kind.

Occam padded up to me and extended his claws, digging in the soft sand until he had scooped out a hole several inches deep. Water rose in the hole, but he shoved the roots in and then pushed the sand back over it. He looked at me and chuffed, saying clear as English, *Draw from the land. From this little tree. Heal.*

"You're a smart kitty cat." I reached to the small plant and placed my hands on the leaves. Dropped into the earth. And into Soulwood. Not that far away. I closed my eyes. Laid my head back. And felt pain I hadn't consciously noted flow out of me. I dropped deeper into the earth. And breathed. Just breathed.

When I opened my eyes, the sun had moved and I was in shadow. No. Not the sun. The little shrub was a tall tree, maybe fifteen feet high. There were other trees and water plants growing all over the beach, which had been bare of greenery only moments before. I inspected my arms and ankles and bare feet. My abdomen. I was healed. I was also growing leaves from my fingertips and my toes. I reached up and felt leaves and twisty little vines, like grapevines, growing from my hairline all around.

"I didn't know if I should trim you or let you grow," Occam said wryly. I looked around at the voice. He was sitting on a rock, in the shade of a lower branch of the sapling, dry, dressed in ripped clothing.

"I grow leaves and vines now, when I . . ." I made a small flapping motion with my hand. Noticed my fingers were brown and wrinkled like the bark of a young tree. The leaves trailing from my fingers swirled with my motion. I sighed softly. "Oh dear."

"So I see. Your hair grew out about six inches, Nell, sugar. It's brighter, like the heart of a cedar tree." His voice dropped, a caressing sound. "Your skin is still soft and smooth, but the color of bark. With my cat nose, your leaves smell of lavender and cedar and just a hint of eucalyptus, but also, just before I shifted to human, the scent was threaded through with catnip. My cat wanted to roll around in the leaves, the way he might if you *were* catnip." There was a laugh in his voice. He sounded happy. I met his gaze, which had gone catty golden again. "And your eyes . . ." His voice trailed away. "Oh, Nell, sugar. Your eyes are emerald and tigereye and just a little blue fire. You are, without a doubt, the most beautiful woman I have ever seen."

I blushed hotly and could think of nothing to say at all, thinking back to my mental image of Occam walking along the bank of the Tennessee River, naked and glorious. I shook the thought away. Pea rolled over and blinked at us. Unconcerned.

"I'm not gonna wait till that dinner to kiss you again. I know the men in your life to this point have taken what they wanted and not asked. I want to kiss you again, a possibly improper kiss. I'm gonna back you against a wall and hold you still, gentle and rough all at once. I'm gonna put my mouth on yours and I'm gonna take my time exploring."

With my background I might have been, maybe should have been, horrified, but . . . this was Occam. And I felt my face flame and a zing of electricity flash through me at the thought of him holding me just so.

"I'm gonna kiss you until you're gasping for breath and begging for more. Fair warning about that. But I'll wait until you say yes. You gonna say yes, Nell?"

I was breathing too fast, my pulse tripping. But I let a small smile cross my face. "Oh yes, Occam. I'll be saying yes. Just . . . warn me. Okay? So I don't shoot you by accident."

Occam laughed, a chuffing rush of sound.

SIXTEEN

I made it to the top of the stairs without touching the icky handrail. By the time I reached the top, I was shivering. The day's heat had been nice, but the chill of early evening was blowing in on the river breeze, following the course of the Tennessee like the breath of the world. My clothes were soaked and bloodstained, making me colder. Occam was behind me, carrying the egg that nearly cost me my life.

We reached the truck with no interruptions, even from the security types. There was a wreath on the front door and dozens of cars up and down the road and parked in the yard. People wearing black walked from the cars to the front door, looking away from us, the way they might if we were homeless, not wanting to engage. Official word had been released that the senator was dead and his wife was still missing and presumed dead. The crows were flocking in.

What a tragedy, assuming the burned-up senator and his shot-up wife and his charred sister-in-law were really dead. But if some of them were shape-shifters, maybe they weren't dead at all. What if they had each traded off with some dead body and burned it? How did we even find out? DNA, fingerprints, dental records. All had been falsified before, altered, replaced.

Occam opened the passenger door and I climbed in the truck, not too tired to drive, but not wanting to drive anyway. He got in the driver's seat and I found my keys in a pocket of my jacket, slightly damp and sand encrusted. Occam placed the egg in my lap and started the Chevy. Pea clawed out of the gobag and onto my lap with the egg. I cradled them both and sent a quick report to HQ before I laid back my head and closed my eyes.

I must have dozed off because suddenly we were back at HQ and my eyelids were stuck together, forcing me to rub them open. I had gotten insufficient sleep for days and the catnap did me good. I chuckled quietly at the thought. Catnap. The movement of my laughter caused a reek of rotten fish to waft into the air. My clothes were ruined. There was no way I could get the stink out of them. "What's so funny, Nell, sugar?"

"I was attacked by . . . salamanders? I was saved by a cat. I took a catnap. I smell like rotten fish. I'm growing leaves. I have to laugh or I might cry."

Occam smiled and opened the door for Pea to scamper out and away. Occam leaned over. Closer. His voice the low rumble of a cat, he said, "I'm gonna kiss your cheek, Nell."

I held very still. "Even though I stink?"

"My cat likes the way you smell." He put his nose and mouth against my jaw and rubbed along it. Like a cat. Scent-marking me. There was something that felt . . . safe in his touch. I burbled a laugh that sounded almost real, almost free. His lips touched my cheek, held for a moment, and then withdrew a fraction of an inch. He was still so close that I could feel his breath on my face as he said, "My cat likes you just as much as I do. Let's get you inside so you can clip and shower."

"Occam? You talk about your cat as if it isn't you. But then so do I. Is that strange?"

He hadn't moved away, his breath still on my cheek. The leaves in my hairline moved with each exhalation. "It is and it isn't," he said. "Cats don't have brains that work or reason the same as humans. Limited frontal lobes. Greater vision, faster reflexes, quicker aggression instincts. So I'm me and not me when I shift."

"I thank you both for saving me."

Occam kissed my cheek again. "Don't forget that improper kiss I got planned."

"I don't think I *can* forget that improper kiss. Occam. I ain't—I *never* had an improper kiss."

"Must remedy that. Soonest."

I shoved the egg at him. Grabbed up my gear bags and got out of the truck. Aware that my color was high and I was overwhelmed with sensations, images, improper thoughts. Occam behind me. I let us into the stairway and climbed to the second floor. And walked alone into the locker room. I stepped fully clothed under scalding water and let the shower wash away the stench and gore and the river water. And my blood. I stripped, then wrung out and bagged my clothing. Then started in on grooming myself. Or landscaping myself.

It wasn't funny. Not at all. But I was laughing quietly as I started clipping. I used the mindless landscaping tasks to let my brain go free to ponder and ruminate and reason, trying to see how all the unmatching pieces might fit together. They didn't. Not yet.

Twenty minutes later, my longer, straggly hair still wet, but my leaves and vines all clipped away, I joined the rest of the team in the break room: Occam, Rick, T. Laine, Soul, JoJo, Tandy, and me. The egg was in the small sink and they were discussing what to do with it. I stepped into the room and spotted a box of donuts on the table. The Krispy Kreme jelly-filled pastries looked almost fresh. I took one and stuffed half of it into my mouth. It was raspberry flavored and so good and so sweet that my mouth ached as the filling squished into it. I might have moaned, just a little, because Occam whipped his head my way.

He was dressed in clean blue jeans, field boots, and a T-shirt the same color gold as his eyes. His hair was dry, but too long, and his beard was scruffy, telltale signs of a shift to his cat. His expression was severe, stark, and he was staring at me with eyes that carried the faint golden glow of his cat, reminding me that we were very close to the full moon. Rick was looking at Occam, and his gaze swung to me, his nostrils widening as he scented, probably taking in the smell of my blood, tadpole blood, the stinking water, and the egg. His eyes too were glowing, that green that signified the coming phase of the moon. Pea was sitting in a corner, cleaning her nether regions, just like a cat. Not something I needed to watch. Occam passed me a metal travel mug of coffee, pale with cream and smelling of sugar. It was prepared the way a cat might like coffee. I drank half the mug empty. It was delicious. Someone passed around a platter of cold hoagies; Occam took three, and started eating like a starving cat.

"If the egg is still viable," T. Laine said, breaking the silence as we ate, "then cracking it might kill the creature. If it's sentient, that's murder."

JoJo added, "It would be handy to have it alive, whatever it is, to study."

"That's keeping a sentient creature against its will," Soul said. It didn't sound like disagreement, but more like information added to the discussion. "Civil rights and protections of paranormals haven't yet been addressed by Congress or the Supreme Court or the UN and are not protected by the Geneva Conventions."

"Special Agent Ingram," Occam said, his voice slow and growly. I whipped my eyes to him and saw his dimple appear and deepen. "What do you think?"

"'Bout wha'?" I said through the sweetness.

"About the viability of the egg."

"It's not alive. The creature inside's dead."

Soul leaned in so she could see me around the others. She reached up and coiled her hair, which she did when she was deliberating. "And you know this how?" Her tone was arch, as if she might be ticked off. Or doubting me.

I shrugged. I was pretty sure I'd said all this to someone once before. "I know it. I knew it when I touched it the first time." I scowled at her and then at the others. "You people really can't tell when something's alive or dead when you touch it?"

"No," Soul and T. Laine said together. Soul asked, "Are you always correct in your evaluation? Your judgment?"

I shrugged and stuffed the rest of the donut in, chewed, and eventually swallowed. The others were all looking at me, waiting. I drank more coffee, thinking back. "I don't remember being wrong, but then I don't remember always proving it to myself that I was right either. So I guess I coulda been wrong and not known it." I licked my fingers to get the last of the sugar. "I knew when Leah died. I was out of her room and I felt her going. I ran in and she was mostly gone. I shouted for John and we were both there when her pulse stopped. Same with John." I shrugged. "But that was on Soulwood." I took a second donut. I sipped more coffee. "Tandy, you agree?"

"I do," he said softly. "But I must admit that my lack of familiarity with the egg species and your conviction may be overriding my judgment."

Occam freshened my cup and adjusted the creamer and sugar. I pretended not to notice him serving me, but the room was awfully silent. "Thank you," I said. He gave me a dimpled smile, one that felt warmer than it should have.

"So we open the shell," Soul said, "and see what we have."

"What about PsyCSI?" JoJo asked. "They're supposed to do all necropsies on paranormal creatures."

"On my authority," Soul said. "I want to see this *thing* now. This thing"—she glared at me—"that is most assuredly *not a salamander.*"

The words were laced with venom and that brought my head up fast. Mostly because I'd sent in the report that we might have found a salamander egg. "Why not a salamander?" I licked my sugary fingers again.

"I know of a certainty, for three reasons." She held up one finger. "Their eggs were said to be white, with a pearly iridescence and small brownish spots. This one is dull and gray with white and brown spots." She uncurled a second finger. "Salamanders were killed off to the last egg, in the year 4000 BCE." And a third finger. "Because *arcenciels* killed them."

I went quite still, only my eyes flitting around the room. Everyone looked as surprised as I felt but for different reasons. The information about an *arcenciel*/salamander war was not in the databanks. And Soul hadn't yet released the intel that she wasn't human to the group at large, so not everyone knew. She was skirting the truth about her species, and releasing that information could change the dynamics within our unit.

Drawing the same conclusions I had, Rick asked softly, "*Arcenciels* and salamanders? At war?"

Soul dropped her fingers. "It was six thousand years ago. Long before my time," she said wryly, as if inferring a human age. "There are no *arcenciels* on Earth who lived then, but the oral accounts and tales persist and the songs continue to be sung. This is not a salamander egg."

Interspecies war and genocide, I thought. And what was I supposed to do about it? For all of two seconds I considered texting my mentor at Spook School for advice, but the thought died.

"Ingram, is it rotten?" Occam asked me, breaking a silence that was fraught with potential, none of it good.

I frowned, thinking. "Sorta. A little bit. It won't stink too bad. Not near as bad as the dead fish did."

Occam held up a bit of grayish shell, pulled from a pocket with finger and thumb. "Shell's this thick. Maybe use an icepick to chip it open."

Soul took the shell and worked it in her fingers. "Brittle but stronger and tougher than a chicken egg. More like ostrich egg."

T. Laine pulled open drawers in the small cabinet, slamming them one by one. She came up with a bottle opener. "This is the only metal thing I see." She handed it to Occam.

"What?" he asked. "Because I'm a man you expect me to do all the dirty work?"

"Because you handled the shell," Soul said, "and are familiar with it."

"And because you got all those big strong man muscles," T. Laine added, putting her hands over her heart and batting her eyes.

JoJo faked gagging.

T. Laine added, "And because I do not want to get rotten egg all over my nice office clothes." She exhibited herself by moving a demonstrative hand up and down her form. "You, on the other hand? I don't care if you stink."

I could tell by Tandy's expression that the tension in the room had lessened.

Occam shook his head. "Uh-huh. It's fine for the dumb cat to get slimed, if Nell's wrong about the extent of the rot. I'll remember this." However, he elbowed the others away from the sink and put the sharp tip of the bottle opener on the shell.

"Wait," I said. I looked at Soul and asked, "And if it is a salamander?" Because I had seen them underwater. I had a feeling Soul was very, terribly wrong.

Soul glowered at me and said, "Dyson or Jones, record this for the records, please." But she didn't answer my question.

JoJo punched and swiped her cell and balanced it on a chair back for stability. She gave the date and time and named all of us in the room.

"Go ahead," Soul said to Occam.

He brought his palm down on the metal bottle opener three times. It *tap-tap-tap*ped, and the egg cracked. Occam moved the point to the side about four inches and repeated the tapping. This time it took four taps and the cracks both spread but didn't meet. He repositioned the tip at a triangle point, tapped again, and this time a chip broke free. A sour fishy smell filled the room as Occam pulled the shell shard away. A long line of goo followed the fragment out and dripped down into the sink. The others leaned in. Studied the exposed part of the creature. It was a clawed hand, of sorts, three odd-shaped fingers curled in a tight fist. Mottled gray-brown skin. Spots on the wrist that seemed to grow larger as they rose up the arm.

At the sight of the flesh, Soul stopped dead, a look of dread on her face. For an instant her body seemed to flicker with light. Bells clanged softly, clear and ringing, but the tones dissonant. Then the light and bells stopped, and Soul stood again, but in the hallway. I had seen her shift into her dragon, and the light was all the shades of color, but the off-key tones—that was new. And the expression on her face was new. Fear.

Tandy's eyes went wide and shocked. He had seen her

move and felt her terror. This egg had struck a chord in her and Soul was not as cautious as she should have been.

His eyes on the assistant director, Rick asked quietly, "So, tell me. What is a salamander?" And I realized his voice was soothing and soft, so as not to startle a wild creature. Soul.

Just as quietly, JoJo, reading from her tablet, told us, "Other than the lizard-shaped thing that likes rain and lives near water, reports allude to their ability to turn their bodies so cold they can extinguish fire. They have both medicinal and poisonous properties and excrete toxic, psychologically and physiologically active substances." Her eyes flicked to Soul and back to her tablet. I was sure she too had seen Soul flicker and reappear in a different place. There was no hiding Soul's nonhumanness now. "The Talmud says salamanders are creatures born in fire and anyone who is smeared with salamander blood becomes immune to fire. Muhammad said salamanders are 'mischief doers' and 'should be killed.' Other myths say they are hatched and live in volcanoes."

"Mythologists have some of it right," Soul said, her voice too lyrical and ringing, again giving too much away. She seemed to glide across the room and sat at her accustomed place, her gauzy skirts buoyant on the air, her silver hair lifting and floating. T. Laine was watching her too closely, one of the handheld psy-meters in her hand, reading Soul's magical signature.

"Fire salamanders came through to this dimension from inside active volcanoes. They were evil, twisted things, shape-shifters who could take on human forms, who could take the place of kings and moguls, and, if they chose, could take to the air, as winged dragons."

I thought about Jane Yellowrock, the Cherokee skinwalker who could take the shape of animals if she had enough DNA to work with. "They absorb or use the genetics of the beings they want to replace?" I asked. "Including *arcenciels*?"

"Salamanders," she said, her lips curling in a snarl, "do not have genetics as humans understand them."

Which wasn't an answer. Did that mean that they were like

light dragons? Like Soul? But no. The look on her face suggested that they were very different and had indeed been mortal enemies. Her expression said the war had been horrific.

Tandy closed his eyes and I could feel the gentle calm the empath was sending out. As if to encourage what should have been a normal debrief, Occam broke off more shell pieces. I ate another donut and drank coffee. JoJo was updating something on her laptop, oblivious. I'd seen enough of the slimy ugly critters underwater.

Rick watched Soul the way a cat might a snake crawling nearby—cautious, concerned, and warily respectful. "What else can you tell us? Habitat requirements? Life span? Reproduction?"

Soul reached up and pulled down her floating platinum hair, twisting it into its long spiral, her fingers threading through as she coiled it tighter. "They were said to reproduce like lizards, living in harems of four females to each male, with the primary leader being the eldest wife. That female chose the other wives first, and then selected a mate strong enough to protect the harem. They were said to mate within families, with no regard for lineage or blood ties. They did not—*do not*, as the tales of their demise seem to have been grossly exaggerated—bear live young but lay a clutch of eggs in fresh running water, with the hatchlings unable to breathe air. They live the first five years in the water, tailed, like a tadpole, but with arms and hands with one clawed finger and two clawed opposable thumbs." Soul looked down at her hands twisting her hair and stopped the motion. "They were—are—amphibians, not reptiles. According to the histories, there was one that lived over five hundred years. But then, the shells were supposed to be beautiful. Much of what I think I know may be wrong."

"Shakespeare's historical plays prove that history is written by the victors," I said. "Churchill said so too." I pulled my tablet to me and began to add all her comments to my bullet point file. "It's been six thousand years. Some things might have been forgotten or changed in that time span."

JoJo said, "I'll need those histories to update our *arcenciel* file."

While we had been speaking, Occam had tapped and removed shards of shell, placing them in a small pile to the side of the sink. The tapping and removal of shell went faster now, bigger pieces set to the side, revealing the creature within.

"Salamander," Soul whispered, her face blank.

T. Laine cleaned off the break room table and opened out the ad section from the *Knoxville News Sentinel* across the top, covering the surface. I scooted my chair into a corner just as Occam carried a lump of slimy blue flesh to the table and placed it in the center. "We shoulda thought about scales for weighing it and devices for measurement," he said.

"All we want is to get a feel for it and then overnight it to PsyCSI in Richmond," Soul said.

As she spoke, a long line of goo slid across the papers and dripped to the floor.

I had seen enough of the salamander, and I hadn't slept enough in the last few days. I needed a nap. I made another trip to the locker room for my clean blanket and pillow, found the room with the mattresses, fell on one that looked unused, and was asleep about the same moment I got the pillow in place.

It was fully dark outside when I woke, starving and smelling something with a strong protein base. Beef maybe. Hopefully not roasted salamander. I got up, checked for leaves and vines—none—and pulled on my boots. I had kicked them off at some point. Stumbling to the locker room, I folded the blanket, stuffed my linens back into the locker I had chosen, and staggered into the break room.

They had finished with the autopsy and cleaned up the goo. Now there were paper cartons and bowls all over the table, with packets of soy and duck sauce, and chopsticks, which I had not learned how to use. If I hadn't been so hungry I might have felt icky about sitting at the recently disgusting table. As it was, I accepted a bowl and let JoJo ladle Chinese soup into it. The broth was thin and clear and had lumpy things in it that I was unfamiliar with, but it smelled and tasted wonderful, of onions and herbs I didn't recognize.

"This is fabulous," I said, slurping it down, drinking it straight from the bowl.

"Yeah, yeah. Eat up," JoJo said. "Soul wants you and Occam back at the senator's mansion to talk with the guests—Occam to get a good smell of Justin and any other Tollivers and Jeffersons he can find, and you to shake Justin Tolliver's hand and get a feel for him. Human or not human? That is the question."

"*Hamlet*," I said, checking my cell for the time. "It'll be after eight before we can get there."

"Good enough. Occam will be driving. You two okay together?"

She had a strange tone, one I'd heard in the church, when a new pairing was being considered. *You'un thinking about becoming Obadiah's second wife?* Or, *You'un and Luke thinking 'bout marrying in a new wife? It's always harder the first time.* Or, *You'un and Zebadiah really marrying Isolde? She's got a temper on her.* The tone was kind but nosy.

I slurped again and, without looking up, asked back in a similar tone, though maybe a little more provoking, "You okay with *Tandy*?"

JoJo flinched, visible in my peripheral vision. "I'm not . . . How did . . . How did you know?"

"I got eyes in my head. And yeah, I'm fine with Occam. We're working through a lot of things."

"He saved your life today. It's in the report."

I smiled. "Yeah. He did. And I gotta tell you. When you're used to fighting for your own life, it's nice to have a man help out. Or a leopard." I shrugged.

Occam flew into the break room like a cat with his tail on fire. "I smell Chinese. Fried rice? Beef with broccoli? Oh yeah. Feed me, Mama."

"I ain't your mama, white boy." JoJo swatted the back of his head. Occam laughed and filled a plate. The others who were still in HQ filed in and joined us.

I tried three different Chinese dishes I had never heard

of: lo mein noodles with shrimp, beef with broccoli, which seemed to be everyone's favorite, and chicken with cashews. It was all good, the sauces thickened with cornstarch and as gooey as the slime from the salamander egg. I tried not to think about that comparison as I ate.

The traffic at Senator Tolliver's home was not as bad as I expected, though there were a lot of cars. Many of the vehicles had DC plates, marking the occupants as Washington bigwigs. Occam and I sat in his fancy car and drank coffee as the moon rose and the crowds thinned more. Occam's eyes glowed too bright, and Pea (who had not been in the car when we set out, I could almost swear, not that I ever swore—that was one church teaching I hadn't left behind) was *mwor*ing and chittering and exploring every square inch of the interior, moving and sounding like a kitten. Only her neon green coat and the rare glimpse of her ridiculously long steel claws gave her away.

Occam said, "We never did identify the shooter. Or recover his weapon."

"No, we didn't."

"Search and rescue teams never did recover Clarisse Tolliver's body."

"No."

"We still got no DNA on Sonya or Abrams."

"No. But we know Abrams isn't human."

"So two women salamanders, three if we count the nanny, may be on-site."

"Could be," I agreed.

"We could get shot tonight." When I didn't reply he added, "And I still ain't given you that improper kiss."

I blushed in the dark and dropped my mouth to the sealed lid of my travel mug to hide my smile. "Drink your coffee," I said.

"Yes, ma'am."

We sat, not talking, spending the minutes catching up reading reports and files from the interagency investigation.

When there were only two visitor cars left, we got out and spoke with the private security types who were trailing around the property. They were packing up gear and writing reports themselves, having been informed by their boss, P. Simon—Peter—that their services would no longer be needed. Which seemed a tad strange to me. Simon was there, in charge, sending his men away, staring out over the house and grounds. His body language seemed particularly angry, tense, and something else. Something odd, like, maybe possessive. I touched Occam's arm and nodded toward Simon.

Occam made a rumbling noise in his chest, a catty sound of interest.

Inside, we spotted Justin in a formal dining room, talking to two Washington types, one younger, one older. The older, gray-headed man said, "Whenever you're up to it, we'd like to begin substantive talks on the possibility of your taking over the office and then, next year, your run."

"Your family name would be a strong bonus in any campaign," the younger man said. "We know it isn't something you had ever considered, and it's far too soon, but the feelers we've put out suggest that the seat is yours if you want it. But don't wait too long to decide. People forget too soon."

Occam and I eased away, into the living room. He leaned down and put his mouth to my ear, murmuring, "Motive? Kill your brother—who isn't really your brother—and your wife—who wasn't human and maybe you just figured it out—and your brother's wife—who might be offered the Senate seat—and take over his high-powered political position?"

I said softly, "Stretching a lot. Why kill them now? We don't have an instigating event for that line of reasoning to fit the parameters of the crimes."

Occam reared back and gave me a look that said he hadn't expected me to talk cop-speak. Which was mildly insulting. I scowled at him and he grinned and shrugged. "Sorry, Nell, sugar."

"We need to get a look at all the Tollivers' wills. Double-check who might have seen a divorce lawyer. Go over the financials again."

"I'll text HQ," he said, pulling out his cell and tapping with his thumbs.

The grieving Tolliver showed out his last two guests. We approached Justin, offered IDs, and shook hands. I could see Occam sniffing the man out—literally—and I held Justin's hand a moment too long, feeling for the metallic, sour scent and feel of blue blood, now that I knew what it felt like.

Justin Tolliver felt human. I could tell from Occam's body language that he still smelled human too, maybe more human, now that his salamander wife was no longer in the picture, sharing her scent with him. We offered condolences, asked the proper grief-talk questions, and said the appropriate small-talk things. Then Occam asked if we could talk to Devin.

"I'd rather not," Justin said. "The children are all in bed. Devin's a little boy and he's been through some horrible things." He looked at us more closely. "May I ask why PsyLED wants to talk to him?"

Occam lied smoothly, his Texas accent stronger than usual, as if he deliberately brought it out to put people at ease, the way I sometimes did with my church-speak. "Our boss at PsyLED feels there might be a paranormal angle to the method of his parents' deaths and we want to see if he remembers anything new about his aunt's death. Witnesses, especially children, tend to recall things later, after traumatic events."

Justin's eyes went bigger. "I thought that was a gas tank explosion or something mechanical. You mean it was a magic? Why didn't someone tell me?"

I said, "The car is still in forensics, Mr. Tolliver. Our greatest concern is to catch the killer and to protect little Devin."

"Wait," Justin said. "You think Devin is in danger too? At the recommendation of Peter Simon of ALT Security, I'm sending the crew home at midnight. He didn't think we would need them again."

"We're not sure about anything," I said. "We're just covering all the bases." I realized that I had just lied, without lying but with obfuscation and prevarication, speaking a truth but in such a way as to hide the real truth behind the words. In other words, I had lied. Lied well. I frowned.

Thomas Jefferson's quote about the truth came to mind, as it often did when I was working. He had said, *He who permits himself to tell a lie once, finds it much easier to do it a second and third time, till at length it becomes habitual; he tells lies without attending to it, and truths without the world's believing him. This falsehood of the tongue leads to that of the heart, and in time depraves all its good dispositions.* Last time I thought about that quote it had been in regard to Rick LaFleur. Now it applied to me. Lying was a slippery slope and I was sliding down that slope into hell mighty fast.

"It's against my better judgment, but I'll get Devin. Please have a seat." Justin indicated the matching sofas in the living room to the left, and then stopped, the cessation of movement jerky. Without turning to us, he said, "I shouldn't be here, letting guests into my brother's house. He should be here. Sonya and Clarisse should be here. This is . . . a nightmare." His shoulders hunched and he left the room quickly, his leather shoe soles slapping across wood floors and up a set of stairs.

Occam said, "My nose says he was speaking the truth every time he spoke."

My frown got darker. "Speaking the truth is sometimes still a lie."

Occam looked puzzled and then slightly insulted.

"I was talking about me, not you," I said.

"Even worse, Nell, sugar." But he entered the living room through a wide, cased opening and sat on one of the sofas to wait. I took the seat across from him.

"You got Pea?" I asked.

A green and black nose poked out of Occam's jacket pocket. Pea chittered and vanished into the pocket.

"More like the grindylow's got me," Occam said, disgusted. "So. Tell me what kind of food you like best."

I frowned at him.

"It's called small talk, Nell, sugar. The kind people use when they're trying to get to know each other."

"Oh." My frown got deeper. "Fresh?"

Occam dimpled. "As opposed to spoiled?"

My frown softened at his tone. Leaving the church when I was twelve hadn't given me much time to learn how to converse in the getting-to-know-you or teasing conversations that most people courted with. Marriage and relationship discussions had been more like business negotiations. And this seemed like a dreadful time to engage in such peculiar chatter. "Why you asking me this now?"

"Because any other time might seem too threatening. I'm trying to put you at ease, Nell, sugar."

"Oh." My frown came back. "Part of me likes it when I don't have to cook. Part of me only wants to eat food I've cooked so I can be sure of the freshness and the ingredients. I like trying new things. Like the Chinese food today. Like pizza. That was amazing the first time I tasted it. Like Krispy Kreme donuts. I could get fat on those alone and I'd never be able to replicate the donuts. I tried a time or two and had no luck at all. But I think I could make a better pizza if I put the time into it. I've been working on a recipe for crust." Occam was smiling at me, as if I had said something fascinating, when all I'd done was tell him how food had changed my life. I scowled at him. "What do you like to eat?"

His dimple went deeper and his blond hair swung forward as he dropped his elbows to his thighs and leaned toward me. "When I'm a cat I like raw venison. When I'm a human I love pancakes. I know this woman, lives in the hills, likes to garden? She makes the best pancakes I ever tasted."

I had made him pancakes. I was that woman. My breathing sped up and Occam focused on my throat, where my color had to be high and my pulse had to be pounding. "What kind of farm animal do you like best?" I asked.

Occam laughed as if the question surprised and delighted him. "When I'm cat I like to hunt wild boar. Pig if not boar. The big old males are mean and good hunting. When I'm human I like to eat chicken. Your favorite farm animal?"

"I like fresh eggs and fried chicken, so, chickens. Second choice would be either milk goats or meat goats, for the milk or the meat, and also to sell the meat and the hides."

We shared a good ten minutes of casual and sometimes unexpected food and critter conversation before we heard feet on the stairs again, this time slower and heavier. We stood and faced the entry as Justin carried Devin into the room. The boy was towheaded and sleepy-eyed, wearing blue pajamas with Marvel heroes printed all over them. His feet were tucked into white socks. He looked pale and fully human, though small for his age.

Occam's nose wrinkled slightly as he took in the boy's scent. And I remembered Devin hitting me with a ball of fire. Occam's left thumb went up slightly as he stood, telling me that Devin did indeed smell like the fireball-throwing salamander we knew him to be. I didn't smell anything one way or the other, except that the child no longer reeked of smoke and flame and death.

I smiled at the little boy. "Hi, Devin. My name is Nell. We met a couple days ago."

"You talk funny."

"Yes, I do. I was raised in the hills. It's a hillbilly accent. Kinda hard to let go of." I let my smile grow wider and held out my hand. "It's nice to meet you again."

"Are you retarded?" It came out "wetauted."

"No." I kept my smile in place by force of will. People who thought accent was an indicator of intelligence or lack thereof, and people who used the *R* word, were not real high on my list of favorites. People who taught children to think and ask such things were even lower on that list. And then I wondered if the slur had been used on him, since he was eleven and had a slight speech impediment. I kept my hand out, waiting, and Devin put his hand into mine. I didn't read him—I knew better. I had no intention of getting burned again. Instantly I felt/tasted/remembered the blue blood from the salamander I had fed to the river. I shook the kid's hand and let go as quickly as I could, resisting wiping it on my pants.

Occam said, "Devin, I'm sorry about your parents."

The little nonhuman child looked up at Occam and tears filled his eyes. His nose wrinkled up and his mouth pulled down, his breathing ragged as he fought tears, making me want to cry with him. "Me too. I'm so . . . sad."

"I know what you mean, little man."

Devin reached out and gripped Occam's hand tight. "Are your mama and daddy dead too?"

"Yep. They are. And I know they're gone, every single day. Let's sit over here," Occam said, "and talk. Just for a minute or two. I know you need to get back to bed."

It was clear the child had latched on to Occam. We all sat on the couches, me across from the men in the same seat I had taken before. I let my partner do the talking and thought about the feel of the salamander's little hand. He was small, not much bigger than the tadpole forms in the river, but his hand had felt . . . different from their touch. Older. Not ancient exactly. But not young. I wondered how quickly they achieved physical growth, and at what age they could take on a human form. And then I wondered what correlations I could draw between them and any Earth creature. Probably not many. Maybe none. But for sure the kid didn't feel like his tailed, swimming, and murderous . . . siblings? Cousins?

I let my attention wander from the conversation and drift around the warm-gray-toned room. It was fancy. Traditional style. Neutral color palette. Dark hardwood floors. Lots of crown molding. Beams in the high ceilings in the style architects called coffered. On the air I smelled cleaning supplies, a hint of fresh paint. Art objects on shelves and on tables illuminated by strategic lighting. Asian rugs set the limited color scheme of blue and deep red, carried out by pillows and a lamp and the backing on framed prints. Two small ornamental chairs at a small Oriental-style table matched the rug's colors. A vase on a shelf in the dark red, another very large vase in blue on the floor, full of red and blue flowers. Heavy drapes puddled on the floor. They looked like they'd be hard to keep clean; dust catchers for sure, not that the senator or his wife had ever personally cleaned this house. They had a staff for that or a cleaning crew.

I'd had a continuing education computer class in Spook School on reading people by the style of their decorating. This room indicated only taste and money. A decorator had set-styled the room and there was nothing in it of the inhabitants. This was a public place, not living quarters. There was probably a great room or family room elsewhere, a room the Tollivers actually lived in.

"Mr. Tolliver, it's Devin's bedtime."

I almost flinched. I hadn't seen or heard anyone enter. The nanny stood in the cased opening, which I realized had pocket doors that could be closed to separate the room from the rest of the house. The nanny was wearing a deep-grape-purple velour jogging suit and orthopedic shoes. Her skin was less blue today, more gray in shade, an ashy color that I could almost place within normal human parameters. But she wasn't human. Now that I knew what I was looking for, the air was laced with a trace of the strange metallic and sour scent I recognized as salamander. A bit like a stack of old quarters and a pair of old leather loafers.

"I'm sorry, Connie," Justin said. "Here. Take Devin to bed." He transferred the boy's hand to the nanny, and the little gray woman trotted off, Devin half dragged back up the stairs.

I wondered why Devin was human-colored and the nanny wasn't. I wondered what I had missed while I was woolgathering.

"Thank you for your time, Mr. Tolliver," Occam said. "You been mighty kind to let us take up so much of your time and Devin's."

"The funerals have been all held off," Justin blurted out, "until they find or recover Clarisse. The services for Abrams and Clarisse will be held concurrently." Justin shook his head and ran shaking fingers through his hair, which stayed sticking up in a disheveled mass. His fingernails looked a little blue.

Was Justin human or salamander? Had we messed that up too? Or were the male salamanders better able to fake human? Or maybe he was ill.

"My wife's services . . . will be handled after the others.

A more private ceremony." He closed his eyes to cover his emotions, which were raw and fractured. He cleared his throat. "What should I do about the security team? Do you think I need to keep them on?"

Occam said, prevaricating, "Security is always important."

A security team on the grounds was a waste of time when the danger might be inside already. And when the danger could throw flames hot enough to sear a man to the bone. I kept all that to myself.

"I hope you will keep me informed about your progress on the investigations," Justin Tolliver said, in an obvious dismissal. He walked to the door. We followed. "If I can help in any way, please call." He extended a card to Occam. He didn't offer one to me, in unconscious sexism. Or maybe he had forgotten me, sitting so silent on the other sofa.

And then we were outside in the cool night air and, though it wasn't freezing, I was glad I had worn my coat. Together we made our way to Occam's fancy car, got in, and drove away.

"I wasn't listening all the time," I said. "What did I miss?"

"Not much. The little salamander doesn't remember anything. And he's a little snot. Needs a good tanning."

"You talking about him asking me if I was retarded?" I asked, amusement in my tone. "And you talking about spanking the recently orphaned son of a deceased senator? Corporal punishment? Child abuse?"

"My daddy beat me with a belt, buckle to the skin," he growled. "I don't remember much about my life before the cage, but I remember that. And I learned my manners."

Occam had said he didn't remember much about his younger human life. Maybe he simply hadn't been ready to share.

"No," I said as he pulled out of the neighborhood. "You learned to be afraid of your daddy."

"Didn't say I was or wasn't scared. Said I learned my manners."

"Mm-hm."

"You disapprove."

"Your daddy leave bruises?"

"Every dang time."

"You think you mighta learned manners without the bruises?"

He made a turn, thinking. Made another turn. "Probably," he said grudgingly.

"Then he was venting his rage and violence, not teaching you manners."

Occam thought about that for a while, shifting lanes, his speed inching up. "Werecats fight their sons. It's the only way to teach them manners. 'Manners' in this case means not to eat or bite or harm humans. It's a bloody lesson."

"Different situation," I said. "If a human child is rude, no one dies. If that human child takes a few dozen reminders to be taught a lesson, then the parent learns a little patience. Werecats are completely animal when they first shift. Their human is buried under the were-brain. If werecats don't learn manners, and accidentally spread the were-taint by infecting a human, they get killed by a grindylow. What an adult cat does to teach them not to kill is different from teaching a human manners. Was your daddy a werecat?"

"No."

"Your mama?"

"No. You really wanna do this now, Nell, sugar?" he demanded.

"Yes."

Occam squinted into the distance. "I don't remember much. Stuff is still coming back to me in bits and pieces." His voice softened. "I was bit the day after I turned ten. My daddy was a minister in a hellfire-and-damnation church and when I came home from playing in a gulch with friends, with tooth marks from a big-cat, he locked me in a cage. The full moon came. I shifted."

Were-creatures hadn't been out of the closet then. His daddy had known what had happened to his son. Somehow. Or guessed. Or just took a chance on myths being real. "What happened after?"

"I woke up partially, found myself in a cage. Couldn't shift back because somebody had put a silver-threaded mat in the cage with me. But the silver didn't stop me from re-membering, slowly, that I was human. It took me twenty years to get free and I did. Shifted back and found the near-est police station, telling them I had been hit on the head and had no memory. Got lucky and had a chance to go to school. Graduated from Texas Christian University with a degree in ranch management. I survived."

"Your mama and daddy?" I whispered, my hands clench-ing on each other.

"Dead. Died in a car accident five years after I went 'miss-ing.'"

"You think your daddy sold you?"

"I know he did. I remember."

"When were you going to tell me this?"

"When you finally admitted that you were in love with me."

I flushed. *In love* . . . I had no idea what that even meant except from reading a rare romance book and living the skewed life of a God's Cloud wife, neither of which was probably normal. "Ummm." I wasn't sure what I was sup-posed to say or do now.

"I didn't want no pity getting in the way of us . . . becom-ing whatever we're becoming."

"I don't pity you, Occam," I whispered.

"Damn good thing."

I fought a smile.

Occam said, "So. Back to our original subject. You're saying you're against spanking?"

I thought about a child reaching to touch a hot stove. A child ignoring a parent's caution and running for a swift-moving river. A child scaring a horse or a mother pig even after being told of a danger. Worse, and more of an issue when it came to abuse, an older child, one old enough to know better, deliberately hurting another, younger child. Was there a difference between a swat and a beating? Was there ever a time to hit a child, even one growing up evil?

Was Brother Ephraim beaten when he was a child? Most likely. It hadn't helped him a lick. If I hadn't been whupped, would I have grown up mean and evil? Probably not. "Lots of the church folk beat their young'uns. But ninety-nine point nine times out of a hundred, a whuppin' isn't necessary. It's the adult's emotional problem, not the kid needing a beating."

"I'll concede that. Are we having a philosophical discussion about corporal punishment in child-rearing, Nell, sugar?"

I ducked my head and looked out the window. We didn't talk again until we were in HQ, and giving Rick and Soul our impressions of the Tolliver household. It didn't take long. I finished my part with the words, "I'm worried that things are about to go to hell in a handbasket at the Tollivers'."

Rick put his head down, studying his hands on the tabletop, thinking. "I hate to send you back out, but I want Unit Eighteen on the grounds tonight," Rick said. "With the private security and the feds gone, it's the perfect time for an attack. Also the perfect time for us to look around."

"We don't have a warrant," I said.

"We also haven't received a call from Tolliver relieving us of responsibility for the welfare and protection of the family. And I don't listen to third-party claims—like those of ALT Security."

"Occam and me aren't exactly a third party."

"No. You're not," Rick said. "And you told me you were worried about the salamanders and what was going on there."

"Sneaky," Occam said. "I like it."

SEVENTEEN

It was just after two a.m. We were wearing night-gear camo unis in shades of gray with *PsyLED* in huge white letters across the back. The unis were combined with high-tech bullet- and stab-resistant personal armor and dark field boots. I wore a low-light monocle lens on one eye. Occam had cat eyes that could see in the dark. We both had vest cams running and comms headsets. An RVAC was giving us flyover protection and eyes in the sky. We were carrying our service weapons just in case.

T. Laine was off duty, getting some rest. JoJo was in the passenger seat of PsyLED's old panel van, all her electronics fired up and running. Tandy was belted in behind her, looking sick from the excitement he was surely picking up. Rick had been driving, but now he slid open the doors and we stepped from the van, watching as we slid into the shadows, Occam more graceful and silent, me uncoordinated and noisy by comparison, shuffling in the fall leaves behind him. We walked from shadow to shadow down the road and entered the property. I heard the van door shut, Rick now safely inside with the others.

Back at HQ, Soul was watching the whole thing on the big screens. Having the assistant director observing was difficult. If the probie screwed up, I might be out of a job. Worse, if I screwed up, people might die.

Someone had lit a bonfire in the backyard, near the pools, and smoke blew on the uncertain river wind. Shadows and light danced through the night as we circled the house to approach on the river side. We stopped in the protection of a dead spruce, hearing splashing and grunts and soft laughter, the sounds advertising that people were there. Someone was swimming in the heated pools.

I touched my communications gear. "Ingram here. RVAC?"

"Coming in now. Stay put. I see you," JoJo said.

"Copy," I said.

"We have a swim party," Rick said. "Looks like humans and salamanders in their natural forms. Mostly eel-looking things, some three feet, like our egg at HQ, some five feet, some longer. In physiology and morphology, they match our dissected egg salamander. What?" Rick's voice moved away from the mic. "What? Soul? What the—" His voice returned to the mic. "Soul is incoming from HQ," he said, irritated. "Looks like there will be three of you."

"Copy," I said again, trying to control my breathing. Ops training said that whenever our side moved away from agreed-upon strategy and tactics, without that action forced by provocation from the enemy, it indicated things were about to go south. Fast. I checked my weapon and fingered the extra mags through the ammo pockets in my camo pants.

"Meanwhile," Rick said, "the water of the pools is steaming and it looks like boil bubbles in places."

I remembered the heated river water. If pyros could heat moving water, then maybe they could bring contained water to a boil.

Soul appeared beside Occam and he whirled, spitting like a cat. Soul had covered miles in ten seconds flat. At HQ, she had been dressed in gauzy skirts. Now she was wearing field armor in what looked like shades of purple. *Soul, the shapeshifting, style-conscious light dragon reporting for duty, sir.* I didn't say it, but she might have known what I was thinking because she cast me a suspicious glare. I smiled sweetly, an easy thing for a former churchwoman to do. We were taught to smile through most anything.

Soul said, "According to the RVAC, we have salamanders, at least a dozen tadpoles, four adult fire lizards, two human adults, and two human children, who appear to be Justin Tolliver's children. Our strategic goal just changed from 'protect the Tollivers' to 'rescue the humans.' Who happen to be Justin Tolliver, his kids, and one of the staff."

"Moving in," Occam said, and he jogged like a big-cat closer to the house. Soul and I followed. "Something's wrong with Justin," Occam said, inching even closer beneath the trees. His cat vision was better than my human vision. Soul's vision must be too, as she hissed softly.

"I smell death on the air," Occam said. He raced away, along the perimeter, to the back of the property. I followed and we came up behind the guesthouse, the three-bedroom house behind the pools. We stood under cover of the stand of firs, where we could see the entire backyard. I was breathing deeply. Occam looked fresh as a snoozing cat. Soul appeared to our left. I tried not to jump or to look at her.

I had guessed wrong. The smoke didn't come from a bonfire. The pool area was lit by three fire pits, each blazing with dry wood, sparks rising on the wind like living sprites in the smoke. The concrete and tiles were wet with water, and winglike arcs of splashing water and small waves lapped over the sides of all three pools continuously. The pools were full of dark bodies, leaping like dolphins, swimming fast. Salamanders for certain, so many of them; most were small, but five, or maybe seven, were bigger, ten feet long. Squealing, blowing, and making sounds like reed instruments. I had a moment to wonder how they got the tadpoles up from the river, and then that thought wilted away.

"Do you mean Justin Tolliver is dead?" I clarified quietly to Occam, speaking into the mic, studying the man on a lounge chair beside the largest pool with all my senses. He was only some thirty feet away, reclining, stretched out, but he wasn't moving. His head was lolled back. I bent and put a fingertip on the earth, but my senses were obscured by the smoke, the tadpoles, and the concrete between him and the ground.

"Dead," Occam growled.

My heart ached as I asked the next question. "What about Justin's children?"

"Dead," Occam growled lower, the sound a vibration of fury in his chest. "The human woman there"—he pointed—"is alive, but only barely."

The heir to the entire Tolliver fortune was on a lounge chair beside Justin. Devin, the eleven-year-old boy, was swathed in a towel, staring at his uncle with wide eyes. His expression was one I couldn't decipher in the flickering illumination, but maybe revulsion or intense excitement. To either side stood humanoid-shaped salamanders, including the ashy-skinned nanny, who stood closest to the child, facing us. She was naked, with her human face on a slope-shouldered body, her odd skin slick and blue in the wavering light, spotted with phosphorescent starbursts in gray fading to purple. She had no breasts or other external indications of genitalia, her abdomen pale and smooth. Her eyes were a bright, iridescent, phosphorescent blue. Except for her face, she might have been any of the other full-sized salamanders because they all had the same blue skin and spots and sloped shoulders.

Occam whispered, "I see something else, there." He pointed into the darkness.

Rick said over comms, "Another adult salamander. He's wearing the uniform of ALT Security."

"Peter Simon," I said. "The security guy who was at the Holloways' house."

"They replaced him," Soul hissed. "They ate him and made his body their own."

Devin slowly reached out a hand to his uncle. The humanoid salamanders to either side didn't stop him. Devin took his uncle's hand and cried out, a childish sound of agony, and I almost raced up to save him, but Soul put a hand on my shoulder. Her grip was strong, bruising, holding me in place.

She murmured, "The RVAC is getting all this on infrared and according to it, Justin is already dead and cold. We have no one to save."

Devin's face changed. Shifted. It grew older. His skin darkened to a gray-brown, golden blotches emerging. His limbs grew longer. Developed joints where humans had none. His skin purpled, blued, and then went golden. And finally the color faded to Caucasian pale. A five-o'clock shadow grew on Devin's face, now his uncle's face. There were now two Justin Tollivers. The new one lifted his uncle's hand and put the fingers into his mouth. Bit down with a crunch I could hear even over the sounds of water splashing. Justin didn't react, and I knew he was well and truly dead. When Devin pulled the hand away, his uncle's fingers were gone and Devin—Justin, now—chewed them up with a crunch of bone.

I had secretly thought Devin a child pyro sociopath. Instead he was really a fully grown, older salamander. As we watched, he changed shape again and became his missing grandfather, Charles Healy, the one who had escaped from the prison, eleven years ago, when Devin was born. Was Devin really Healy, hiding in the form of a child he had killed? And then Devin shifted back to Justin. The face and form settled and firmed. Simon slid to the ground nearby, watching, his own form wavering into indistinct features and blued skin.

One of the women at Devin's side shifted into Clarisse, Devin's mother, and shook herself like a dog as her form settled. Another leaned down, sat, and curled up in his lap. Her face altered and she became Sonya, who supposedly died in the fire. Sonya, who was Devin's aunt. I realized that the creature who had lived for years as Devin had a life and a culture far beyond anything I could imagine, and it appeared that he had been taken as mate to a harem.

I went back through my bullet point timeline. Devin had never once been on-scene at a shooting, though he had been present when Sonya supposedly died. Devin, the child Soul had saved from fire, was our fire assassin. And I was almost willing to bet money that the nanny could shape-shift into a male, and that she was the shooter.

Occam rumbled, "I need to shift."

"No," Soul said, putting command into the word. "You need to be able to fire the AR-15 and take out as many salamanders as possible."

"Why take them out?" I asked. A flash of bloodlust raced through me. *Salamander blood, all that rich blue blood.* I swallowed the bloody thoughts down, away, but they were there all the same, eager. I finished, "Especially the juveniles. The tadpoles."

"They are having a *party*," Soul said, her tone biting, "around the *dead body* of Justin Tolliver, whom they are eating. I accept full responsibility for this raid and the salamander deaths."

Light burst around her body and was snuffed. Her body wavered from human to something nonhuman and back. A sound like bells ringing in the distance sounded before being abruptly cut off. Then Soul stood there again, wearing her armor, though this time it was in shades of blue camo, not the purple of before. Soul was about to lose control of her *arcenciel* shape. Bells rang again, soft and tinkling. "The human woman we will save," she said, "if she is truly human and if she lives. But anyone who shifts to lizard will die." Her words sounded odd, tinkling and chiming, not at all human.

Soul, assistant director of PsyLED, had just condemned sentient beings to death. And then small things came together for me. Soul, who should have been in DC or at Spook School, training new agents, was in Knoxville, on what should have been a relatively simple case. Soul, who nearly shifted when she first heard the word *salamander*. Soul, who was acting out of character. Soul, whose ancestors had fought a war that decimated the salamanders. Genocide.

I said, "*Arcenciels* and salamanders hate each other, don't they? You're *still* at war with them."

Soul's eyes narrowed. "No. The war ended six thousand years ago. The salamanders were wiped out." Lights illuminated her face and pearled teeth began to grow from her mouth, long and serrated and wicked-looking. "There *can be no salamanders*," she hissed.

"But there *are* salamanders," I said. And then I understood. Soul's worldview had just changed, like what would happen to the members of God's Cloud of Glory Church when life was found on other planets. Soul had been taught that her ancestors had wiped out the salamanders and yet, here they were in her own backyard and she hadn't even recognized what they were. "That makes this case personal to you. When it's personal you have to withdraw. PsyLED regulation . . . I don't remember which one, but it's a regulation."

"I will not withdraw." Her body began to lose its human contours, drifting and wavering.

"Senior Special Agent LaFleur," I said, wondering if I was in danger of having my head bitten off by the assistant director of PsyLED. It was probably not very smart, but I went on. "I formally request that Soul be removed from command position and sent back from the front lines."

"You dare," she snarled.

"Tomorrow is the first day of the full moon," I said, holding my ground. "Are *arenciels* moon-called?"

Soul reared back, her body glowing, elongating, shifting to her native light dragon form. Wings spread to either side. Her face was terrible.

"Problems," Rick said over the comms system.

"I noticed," I said. I was holding my service weapon on the assistant director of PsyLED. Though it was likely that she could bite me in two before I could squeeze the trigger. Occam was trying to shift, or struggling to not shift, stumbling into the shadows, probably pulled into the change by magics in the air and the nearness of the full moon. I was alone with Soul in a tizzy and salamanders riled. "I really noticed."

"They must have heard you or seen the light show," Rick said. "Baby salamanders are crawling out of the pool and heading your way. The ground is smoking behind them. Soul. You are formally relieved of command. Probationary Special Agent Nell Ingram, you are now in charge of Mission Salamander."

"Oh. Oh. Dagnabbit," I cursed.

Soul shot into the sky, bellowing a challenge.

From the pool, flames surged.

The dead trees above us, offering us scant shelter, burst into fire. I ducked away. Soul whirled and dove. Light blared out, blinding. Her dragon wove itself in the space between trees. Occam was on the ground, also shifting. Over the comms, Rick was growling, rumbling.

Things occurred to me in overlapping images of understanding. We were about to have a bloodbath. Soul and the cats were losing whatever humanity they possessed. JoJo was getting all this on film from the RVAC overhead. The werecats were catty and contagious. And I was now officially, though nominally, in charge—nominally because the chance of anyone listening to me and following my orders was pretty much nil. I was on my own.

Fir trees, dead and dying, exploded in fire, purple-tipped orange flames licking and leaping from tree to tree. Heat blasted over me. I ducked and ran. Wrapped an arm around my head, racing back toward the road, my flesh scorching. The wooden siding on the guesthouse burst into flame. Slender slick forms sped from the pools, crawling like racing snakes. I lunged between the remaining trees as they flared into flashfire. Fire devils whirled into the air. Wind leaped high, roaring with the flame tornadoes. JoJo was shouting in my earbuds, but I couldn't hear the words over the howl of the fire.

From the sides of the property, the woods awoke.

Fire. Fire. Fire. Fear. Fear. Fire. Fire. Fire, they whispered. The winter-dormant trees and grasses that had survived the salamanders came aware. Their old enemy was among them. Fire, the destroyer, attacking. Fear raced through the earth.

A naked Justin Tolliver—Devin—trailed after the young salamanders. I caught a glimpse as he raced through flames and wasn't burned. Where his bare feet touched the ground, new flames shot up. He was hunting me. I dashed around the front of the house. The cool air shut off the extraordinary heat and noise, though cold air whistled past me, feeding the fire. Overhead, I saw a flash of light, but when I looked up, Soul was gone. She reappeared, and dove at the pool area, blasting light. JoJo was yelling about fire departments and Tandy and getting my white ass back to the truck. I peeked out from the brick wall.

Devin was striding toward me. He threw out his hands. Fire, orange and soot-dark, shot at me. A spotted leopard leaped in front of the fire.

"Occam!" I shouted. "No!"

The fireball hit him.

The werecat screamed. Fell.

Fury leaped inside me. Leaves burst from my fingertips.

From the trees, Rick LaFleur, in black leopard form, hurtled, dropped down, landing just behind the pyro. He leaped and hit the salamander with front and back feet. They went down, landing hard. Rick bit down on Devin's neck and he shook the creature like prey.

Blue blood splattered. The thing on the earth rolled, knocking Rick away. Blasted Rick with fire. The werecat screamed and fell, silent.

Knowingly or not, he had given me salamander blood. A great deal of the blue blood. Bloodlust merged with the fury. *Needing.*

I dropped and shoved my hands into the earth. Breaking nails, digging deep. I caught the droplets of blue blood as they landed. My gift. My curse. I caught the blood and caught the creature it came from. It wasn't human. Its blood was *wrong*. But I hungered. I *wanted*.

The craving for that strange metallic blood roared up in me like the wildfire that consumed the wood. The soil sucked at the blood, the awareness of the trees awakening, turning to the fire but seeking me, ready, impatient. A quiver of power zapped through the trees across the road and through me. I claimed the land with the strange blue blood. The forest was awake and full of fury, seething with need, with blood-hunger, the strange sour metallic blood of the pyro creature. The salamander was mine.

This was my magic, my dark power. To take the life of

anyone who bled onto land I claimed as my own. My gift—
to feed that life to the woods. The trees pulsed through me.
The heat of the fire scorched me as it rounded the corner of
the house. Evil air that breathed and burned and killed.
Killed Occam. Killed Rick. *Killed Occam!* I screamed in
fury and grief.

I called to the blue blood on the earth, pulling on it, on
the life it represented, drawing the burning life force to me,
gathering it as if fire webbed between my fingers, buried that
life in the dirt. I felt Devin writhing on the ground, his life
force disentangling from his body, shuddering through the
ground. My magic caught it, pulling it to me and across my
flesh, an embrace, a vow, and a threat, burning and scorching and killing.

I shoved Devin's life away from me, deep underground,
dismantling it as I worked, ripping, tearing. The process was
slow and purposeful as I fed him to the earth, my mind focused. Aboveground, I burned. The pain my body was ex-
periencing, I ignored. I was on fire, but I couldn't care. I
pulled other salamanders to me, breaking them, bleeding
the adults and the tadpoles into the earth. Pulling each body
to pieces, each bone and muscle and tendon. Undoing each
cell. The life force, alien, strange, fed the land. The flames
in the dark slid below me, scratching at me as they went,
screaming deep into the dark beneath. Feeding them deeper.

My awareness spread out, to the trees and grasses and
shrubs all around. I claimed them, feeding the creatures of
fire into them, awakening them, giving them life. What was
left of the blue-blooded things, I pushed all deep. *Deep.* Into
the magma I had called to the surface by accident. The
salamanders screamed, reached back. They fought. All of
them in a single concerted assault. But the magma and the
earth wanted the heat that was salamander. *Salamanders.*
All of them. All that rich, strong, potent blue blood and alien
life. I fed them to the earth. I fed them to avenge Occam. To
avenge his death. I fed and fed. And I learned how feeding
truly worked. It was a gift of myself, as much as a sacrifice
of blood.

When the salamanders were gone, I reached back to Soul-wood and found the walled-off prison that hid and protected Brother Ephraim. I fashioned a blue spear out of the remaining life force of the salamanders and I thrust it into the cell that hid and protected and imprisoned Ephraim. Pointed and sharp, edged and spiked, like a two-edged sword, it slid through the cell wall. The Bible verse came back at me as I pulled back and rammed the pointed edge again into the protective wall. *For the word of God is quick, and powerful, and sharper than any two-edged sword, piercing even to the dividing asunder of soul and spirit, and of the joints and marrow, and is a discerner of the thoughts and intents of the heart.*

That was what I needed. Something that would divide Ephraim's soul and spirit and joints and marrow. I hadn't prayed to God very often, not since I'd killed the first man on Soulwood. Not really. Not with need. But now . . . Now I was avenger and death come calling, and I refashioned the spear into a sword of light and heat. I shouted to the heavens, "Death to Ephraim for the evils of his heart! I claim him for the earth! Death! Death! Until nothing is left for heaven or hell!"

Ephraim gathered the scarlet and black energies into himself. The snakelike power whipped and whirled and began to form a point, a weapon.

The blade of vengeance sliced back and forth through the walls of Brother Ephraim's prison. I stabbed and cut and ripped into the cavern. Into his snake-energies. Ephraim tried to resist, tried to pull power from the earth, from the church and the tree that shared my genetics. But the sword of vengeance was faster and hotter. Heated by the earth and by the magma that was mine to call. And I sliced into the foul old man's soul, cutting, cutting, dissolving each sliver of life into separate components—individual thoughts, needs, hopes, memories—and fed them to the heart of the world. This time I didn't stop too soon. This time I gave myself as I tore and cut and ripped and fed, fed, *fed* Brother Ephraim to the land until there was nothing left.

Then I tore apart the cavern he had made for his life force.

Dismantled the walls, the emptiness, the death he had surrounded himself with. And I cut through the tendrils he had once again sent down into the church land. To the vampire tree. I sliced and destroyed the vine-like coils and shoots of himself that he had sent into the tree. Not hurting the tree itself, but destroying the roots and vines where Ephraim's life had touched it, had shaped it. He had taken over the tree, turning it into a death tree. He had done this and I hadn't noted it, hadn't understood.

When nothing was left of Ephraim or his prison or his control of the vampire tree, I turned my attention back to the land where my burned body lay.

Entwining my energies with the roots and trees nearby, I fed them. Pulled their energies in, replacing the death of the land around me with life. Soulwood stretched out and joined in the battle against the fire, sending groundwater up toward the surface, engulfing the roots, protecting them. The warmth and love and joy of my land entwined with my own soul. Together we communicated goodness and health and strength to the trees all around me, bringing the burned land and all that still contained a spark of life to fecund, flourishing, abundant health.

Life, green and full of all good things, burst forth.

Feeding it, I claimed the land.

I felt it when roots grew into and from my body and plunged deep. I felt it when they rose again and burst through the crust of dead grass and sprouted new trees. Felt it when the trees sprouted leaves out of season. Felt them grow tall and strong. Grass and vines and flowering plants followed. The land came alive. It pulled me into it. It enfolded me. And the pain of burning I hadn't even noticed vanished. I leafed out. I grew.

Yes, I whispered to the land, to the trees. *Grow. Live.*

Much, much later, after the full moon had waxed and waned, I felt the vibrations of footsteps, footsteps I had once known. And . . . ahhh. Soul. Soul, in human form, walked across the new leaves and grasses growing atop the crisped and charred land to me. I felt her kneel beside me. Felt her touch on my side. But I couldn't come back to her. I was part of the earth now. I was part of this land. Here there was no fear or grief. No worry or pain. Here I would stay. I felt Soul move away.

Sun fell upon me. Rain watered me. Moon rose and fell, waxed and waned and waxed again. Birds perched on me. My forest grew. My trees grew. Grasses and shrubs and deer and rabbits. Foxes. A family of bear. I was alive. I was the land and it was me. Soulwood was part of us and roots thrust deep. The land was alive with me.

Moons later, when the days had grown longer and the earth had warmed with spring, I again felt Soul return, this time not alone. There were others with her, tromping on the earth, between the saplings and mature trees that were my land. There were humans and were-creatures and a witch and they gathered about me. And . . . there was a creature like me.

Some part of my understanding woke. I understood what Soul had done. She had brought with her the sentient creatures that my former self knew. There were two in animal form, one which belonged to me, which I had claimed. *Rick LaFleur.* That was what this one was called. Black were-leopard. He had died. But he had died on land I claimed. And I had . . . I had given the land a great portion of the salamanders' life force, but I had kept something back. With it, with the help of Soulwood, he had been healed.

Rick draped himself across my body. Purring. His claws extruded and pressed into the wood that I had become. He milked the wood, claws in and out, pricking me as a wood-pecker might, though there were no insects within me.

Occam pressed beside him. Occam had died as well, and I had shared the land with him. I had claimed him as I had claimed the trees. He was mine. He laid his cat across my roots and he shifted into his other form. His human form.

He was different, disfigured, scarred from the salamanders' fire. I had not been able to save him from all the damage.

T. Laine, moon witch. Soul herself. Tandy, empath, whose thoughts were clear to me. He missed me. He wanted my old self back. JoJo, who was human and silent and perhaps . . . appalled at my new form.

And Mud, sister of my mother's body. She was like me. She was part of the land.

Mud placed her hand upon my form and said, "Nell, come back. I'm callin' you'un back." She pressed her fingernails into the wood that had once been my shoulder and said, "Come back. Come back *now*." She shoved Rick out of the way and pressed herself onto the wooden shape that was all that was left of the human I had never been.

Mud's strength. Her life. Her *greenness* reached out to me. Her life force was strong and dancing, the way buttercups danced in a summer wind. The way tree limbs beat against the sky in a spring storm. And she watered my wood.

"You'un need to come back," she wailed. "You'un need to teach me. And you'un got to deal with the vampire tree. It's growing to your'n land. It's lookin' for you'un, putting up sprouts everywhere, between the church's gate and the cliff to Soulwood. If'n you don't come back, Sam's gonna set something he calls C-4 on the tree and explode it. Or poison the land to stop it. But I don't want it to die. It's special, or it can be, if'n you'un'll finish what you started." Softer, she said, "I need you, Nellie. I'm scared. And I'm alone. And I'm afeared they's gonna give me away, no matter what I do." Wetness fell upon my bark and my bare wood. She watered me. She watered my wood.

Tears. Mud was crying. For me. For herself.

Daddy had been sick. Daddy had been failing and growing close to death. Daddy might be dead . . . If he was gone, then no one stood between the churchmen and Mud. They would force her . . . force her to marry one of them.

I tore my arm, with its roots, out of the earth and reached around. Clasped Mud's body to me. With my other hand, I reached up and tore my jaw free of the roots that bound me to the earth. "Cut me free," I said, the words grinding as sand on stone. "Cut me free of the land. Take me to Soulwood."

I felt the blade cutting me free, hacking me from the earth, tearing me out of the soil. The air felt strange on my roots and limbs, and my bark shivered and ached as I was moved. And then I was resting on Soulwood, on the land behind my house. I dug my fingers into the earth and slept. Days passed.

But every day there were the humans and a predator cat, talking, talking, talking, making me listen. Making me care for them, for the things they had to say. And every day, more of my bark slipped from me, fewer leaves grew upon me. And I stood from the earth and walked upon my land.

The humans and a predator cat came and went and fed my mouser cats and brought me food and water. I woke and I ate and I drank. I listened to the noises of the humans as they spoke and told me tales. With them and alone, I walked around Soulwood, silent, touching my trees, knowing the earth. I slept in the woods, sinking deep, communing with the resting power beneath the ground.

And finally, one day I looked at the predator cat and I said, "Occam?" He chuffed and shifted to human and held me in his arms. He was scarred, missing part of his hand, most of his roots. Not roots. His hair. I closed my eyes and wrapped my limbs about him, sad that he was still so damaged.

Three weeks after I was cut from the earth, I woke in my bed. The sheets felt strange beneath me. The mouser cats felt strange beside me. The house was too enclosed, too empty, and too full. I crawled out of bed and pulled on clothes. My sister Mud slept on the couch. I didn't understand why, but she was safe so it didn't really matter. When the sun rose I was sitting on the front porch, my face to the east and the pale dawn sun. And I realized that I was nearly human again. Or could be, if I chose.

Like a flowering plant, a morning glory trying to bloom,

new leaves and some kind of odd, tight blooms were all over
me, trying to open. I ripped the flowers away and watched
them disintegrate into ash and vanish into the land below
me. I sat on the porch swing, unsettled and despondent as
the sun rose, before I went back inside and sat on the couch,
where Mud directed me, to sit and to think. To decide what
I needed to do. I hadn't gotten very far in my plans, beyond
some amorphous ideas and visual images. Words were still
hard.

I was still sitting on my couch, a blanket over my knees
and cats prowling across the furniture. Mud had been banging around in the kitchen for two hours now. The scent of
fresh bread was warm on the air. And I felt a car pulling
slowly up the hill to Soulwood. No. Not a car. A van. Familiar. This was the first time I had felt and understood sensations that I once took for granted. Unit Eighteen was on the
way up. I looked out the front window, wondering what this
might mean.

Birds were fighting in the oaks out front. Deer were pawing and eating the grass in the lower part of the yard. Squirrels were picking out nesting sites. The ground in the three
acres of yard was warming, the grasses and herbs reaching
for the surface and the pallid heat of the sun; the cold temps
were gone. Spring had arrived.

And people were coming up my hill. I thought it might
be okay for them to come.

Inside, the woodstove had heated the house. The dust that
had accumulated while I worked the case was gone. The
dishes were washed and put away. The house was neat as a
pin. I felt a small measure of pleasure at being able to remember that saying, one of Mama's, though I'd never understood how a pin might be considered neat.

I had been home for weeks, Mud staying with me, taking
care of me. I had no idea why Mud had been allowed to stay
with me for so long. She assured me that T. Laine had handled it and Mama and Daddy hadn't seen me, which was a
good thing, as I had changed a lot.

Mud had been busy with more than housecleaning. She

had caught up the winter chores in the garden and it felt hopeful and ready for spring. She had also scraped much of the bark off of me, down to the skin below it. Had hacked my roots away. Clipped and cut my leaves. Except for the pale white blooms this morning, and the leaves I sprouted here and there when I slept, I looked almost human again, though my joints were still dark brown with bark-like flesh on elbows, knees, feet, and knuckles. But that was fading, softening, vanishing as Mud rubbed them down with my winter emollient every morning and evening. Overall, my skin was browner. Not tanned, but nut-brown all over, though paler skin was visible at my underarms and in blotches on my torso. My eyes were the glittering green of spring leaves and emeralds. My hair was rougher, curlier, redder and browner in streaks. Most mornings when I woke, it reached the middle of my back and wild curls sprang out around my hairline like rootlets or vines about to burst into leaf. Mud kept the plant parts clipped and I hadn't told her about the flowers this morning, thinking—hoping—they were just an anomaly.

I believed that in a week or so I would look and sound human to the casual observer. I'd look human, but I was different.

For the last week, as she groomed me like a topiary animal, I had begun to talk with Mud, to understand her words. To remember my human life. My pasts, all of them. My youth. My family. My marriage. Unit Eighteen. And with each memory that returned, Mud and I celebrated. Today, Mud had invited people over. That was why the van was climbing the hill. Company was coming. Ahhh . . . I remembered.

I felt the car stop. Felt people, sentient beings, get out and walk to the porch. Rick. T. Laine. Tandy. JoJo. Not Occam. I didn't know how I felt about that. Rick knocked on my door.

"They're here," Mud sang out, racing in from cleaning the bathroom, which often meant carrying leaf trimmings to the yard. I smiled at the thought. She sped to the front of the house and threw the door open. Let them in. Chattered at them. I studied their faces, which were carefully neutral and noncommittal. JoJo's head was wrapped in twisted vines—no, they were braids—adorned with beads that sparkled like sun on water. She wore green and black, the color of leaves and dark wood. I liked it. T. Laine was wearing black pants and a thin jacket with a white shirt. She had cut her foliage—her hair. Tandy was wearing browns. Good tree colors. Rick was wearing the same colors as T. Laine, even in his foliage, which was white and black in ribbons of color. It didn't mean anything that they were dressed alike. And Rick's leaves— No. His hair. His hair had new white streaks in it. Accomplishment shot through me at the thoughts.

They said hellos, to which I said nothing. They sat. They stared at me as if waiting for me to speak, but I had nothing to say.

Mud had made tea and coffee and now placed a bread plate on the coffee table along with a jar of my homemade jelly. On the plate was a loaf of bread she had made herself and sliced. A stack of plates and forks were nearby. I remembered that Leah had traded a townie for the plates when she was first married to John. She had been proud of the barter and told me about it every time we used them.

Mud went to the kitchen and my eyes followed her. She brought back a cup of coffee and gave it to Rick as if she was his personal servant. Repeated the trip and gave Tandy a cup. But she offered nothing to the women. *Church training.* I hated it. I felt a spark of disgust and fury, though it fizzled and disappeared. Fury and disgust were human emotions. I hadn't felt them in a long time.

Rick started talking. "We're here to debrief. You know what I'm saying?"

A debrief was a summation. I remembered. Mostly. Though it seemed a long time in the past. I nodded again, silent. The front door opened and Soul walked in. She hadn't been in the van. Soul was a light dragon, an *arenciel*. She had flown. I remembered that too and felt a momentary satisfaction that the memory was still inside me somewhere.

She took a seat in the rocking chair, watching me, her gray clothing floating with her movements.

Abruptly, Soul said, "The flames at the home of Senator Tolliver were abnormally hot. Yet they went out all by themselves after you dropped into the earth. The fire department did its job, but the houses and the fir trees were mostly smoking ruins by the time they got there. Smoking. Not flaming."

I continued to stare at her. She had the most amazing eyes, black with faint tints of purple and green and blue that caught the light at odd moments.

T. Laine said, "The body in the limo, the one that should have been Sonya? You remember?"

I nodded once, remembering.

"It hadn't been cremated. The FBI held it at the morgue pending further testing. It was fully human and turned out to be the body of a missing local woman. Mother of three. PhD in nursing. She had been drugged and placed in the limo to burn to death in Sonya's place. They murdered her to carry on their bloodlines and the transfer of real property."

JoJo said, "We captured four salamanders: the female who had played the part of Sonya, the nanny, and two other females who were hiding inside the smoking walls of the house. We also caught four baby salamanders who had stayed in the pool and not attacked you. The others disappeared, presumed burned in the fire."

I tilted my head, not disagreeing. I had killed all the ones I could find.

Soul said, "We put them in the null room. Then we transported them to PsyLED, where they died. The null room stripped them of their magic. It was . . . tragic." Her tone said otherwise.

I frowned. Or thought I did. I wasn't sure. Soul had wanted all the salamanders dead. So had I, and I had finished the battle for her. I had fed dozens to the land. I had murdered even those not yet guilty of a crime. Even so, the human law would call it self-defense if they ever thought to try me for a crime. But . . . all the salamanders were killers. They poisoned the earth and the trees and the land. They killed the plants that I loved, that I was here to protect. PsyLED's job was to police paranormals who couldn't be kept in check by any other means. And that too, I had done. And perhaps Soul had done by placing the salamanders in a null room. Again ending her war.

Tandy said, "Once we knew what to look for, the explanation was all there in the family's financial papers. Jefferson/Healy/Devin wanted the family money back in his hands and under the control of him and his bloodline—his mates and progeny. All the shootings and fires were about money and the transfer of property out of the hands of humans and into the hands of the salamanders. They had been living below the human law enforcement radar for decades. They took each other's places as needed for the last two centuries."

Rick said, "We still don't know if the nanny was actually trying to kill Abrams."

"Worst shot in the history of serial killers," JoJo said. They made a noise. It was laughter.

My eyes tracked the speakers, but I still had no desire to say anything. I just listened and thought. Mud poured me a cup of super-sweet lemon ginger tea, which I had developed a deep desire for, though it didn't taste exactly the way it had before. I accepted the cup and sipped, instantly soothed by the tart sweetness. No one spoke. I realized that I really needed to say something; most anything would do. I thought back over the days of the case, and one thing seemed important. Occam hadn't come. Occam wasn't here. But I couldn't say that. I said instead, "Did you bring Krispy Kremes?"

Tandy laughed, his odd reddish brown eyes on me, the sound of his laughter relieved and excited and joyful. JoJo put a hand on his arm and he quieted. None of that made sense to me.

Rick looked down and I realized he might be upset. Part of me wanted to water his roots and I smiled at the urge. Tandy smiled with me.

JoJo took up the narrative again. "The raid on the DNAKeys compound didn't reveal what we thought or feared. There were vamps and witches and weres there, just like we thought, living and working on the campus. That's what they called it. The campus."

Rick glowered and said, "They were on-site by choice. The were-creatures were hoping that someone at DNAKeys would find a cure for were-taint, and the researchers claim to have been making some progress on it."

"Prions cause were-taint. Prions can't be killed," I said at last. "Not by fire, heat, radiation, freezing. They never, ever die."

Bitterly, Rick said, "No, they can't be killed. The claims were false."

JoJo pulled at her earrings, a nervous tic, one I remembered. She said, "The witches were on contract. The vamps were there on contract too, to provide blood as needed for experiments on diseases that cause bleeding—coagulation diseases, from the new form of Ebola to platelet problems to one called DIC. Don't ask me what it stands for. It's a bunch of syllables."

"Disseminated intravascular coagulation," T. Laine added. "And that part of the claims was true. They found some new treatments that are amazing." I remembered that Lainie had a lot of degrees and partial degrees and her breadth of knowledge had made her attractive to PsyLED.

With that thought, all sorts of memories, full and partials, came back to me, piles of images and smells and sounds, landing on me like a kaleidoscopic avalanche. My lips stretched into a smile and Tandy rose, crossed the room, and sat beside me on the couch. He put his head on my shoulder, which felt peculiar and comfortable all at once. "She's remembering," he said. I was pretty sure Tandy was watering me. Like Mud had watered me in the woods. No. He was crying on my shoulder. That was it.

I lifted a hand and patted his shoulder. I said, "You stopped eating. You lost weight."

"I've been worried about you turning into a cord of firewood," he said, his voice shaking. "I've been worried that Occam wouldn't heal from his scars. It's hard to eat when I'm worried."

That was interesting. "Mud, make Tandy some of this tea"—I lifted the mug—"and fix him a jelly sandwich."

Mud stood, heading for the kitchen, saying, "Okay. Can I hold a gun on him if he tells me he ain't hungry?"

"Yes," I said.

"No," Rick said to Mud. "You are way too much like your sister for my comfort level."

"Thank you," Mud said.

"Occam?" I asked. "He's . . ."

"Scarred," Rick said, something odd in his voice. "PsyLED sent him to Gabon, twice now, to a colony of were-leopards to heal." I said nothing and Rick added, so very gently, "He came back from the first visit to make sure we moved you safely from your . . . your rooted state to Soul-wood. Then he had to go back."

"Oh," I said, my fingers picking at my skirt. I wondered if he'd ever come back here. To have dinner with me. But I didn't ask.

My sister ended up fixing them all jelly and bread and making them eat it, though not at the end of a gun. My baby sister was quite forceful, all without the need for weapons. I liked her. And I had things I needed to do for her. If I could remember what they were.

The members of Unit Eighteen stayed for an hour, talking. Memories opened like the blooms of flowers and what might have been feelings began to unfurl inside me as they talked and shared and ate Mud's bread. It was pleasant. Confusing but valuable. The memories were settling inside me. Enough for me to know that Occam's not being here made me very sad. I remembered the disfigurement and the scars. Perhaps I hadn't healed him well enough after all.

EIGHTEEN

Within forty-eight hours after the visit by Unit Eighteen, I had regained the last of my human form, though I had to trim my leaves and the vines in my hair several times a day. My hair was still growing awfully fast, needing to be trimmed every morning to keep it near my shoulders. The reddish tresses were riotously curly.

My returning memory had suggested that I had let some things go too long unresolved, undealt with, unfinished. Before I went back to work, in a week or so, I had a lot of relationship housekeeping to catch up on. With that in mind, Mud and I were heading to the church in my old Chevy C10. I was driving for the first time, taking the roads slow and cautiously.

"I think this'n's a stupid idea."

"I heard you the first time. And the fourth," I said mildly.

"I done asked." She stuck a finger in the air, shaking it with each statement. "Mama and Daddy ain't gonna let me live with you'un." Shake finger. "They ain't gonna let me go to no public school to learn the lies of evolution and science." Shake. "They ain't gonna let me wear no pants or cut my hair. They ain't—"

"I didn't trim my leaves," I said.

Mud stopped. Her raised hand shot out and she lifted my hair. Green leaves sprouted in my hairline at my nape. A few small vines tickled there. "Why?"

"Because if you don't get taught, if you don't learn how to use your gifts, you'll likely make the same mistake I did and grow leaves and vines and take root. You can live with me and not make the same mistakes because I'll teach you."

"Mama will never, ever in a million, billion years agree."

"We're invited to have tea with all the mamas and Daddy."

"All of 'em?"

"All of them."

"His surgery's tomorrow. The surgeon made him wait until his liver was in better shape and his blood was built up enough to cut him open. And he wanted to wait till you were back from undercover."

Undercover. That was the lie PsyLED had told my family about my absence. "I know. That's why this is the perfect time to hit them with the truth."

"Why now?"

"Because when Daddy was shot, I wanted him alive. I might have . . . accidentally . . . told the land to keep him alive."

"Did he grow roots?"

The laugh that escaped me had a gurgle, but it was the first that came close to my own, previous, human laugh. It sounded strangled, but it gave me hope. "Not that I saw," I said, "but he needs to be aware and unsurprised if they pull a passel of leaves and roots out of his belly."

Mud giggled.

I showed my ID and, together with my true sib, drove through the gate onto the grounds of God's Cloud of Glory Church. We slowed as we passed the barbed and vicious-looking trees on the inside of the twelve-foot fence. It looked like something out of *Snow White*, a cursed world that turned on itself and its humans, spindly saplings with long thorns, pulpy deep green leaves with red petioles and leaf veins, dark, wet-looking bark that looked as if blood seeped out. On one of the spikes of thorns a squirrel squirmed, making piteous noises. A vine was wrapped around it like a snake, contracting, constricting, squeezing. The tree was killing it.

I looked away and drove on. I had done this. I had to stop it. I didn't know how much blood it might take to take the tree back over. I didn't know what I'd be when it was done.

We parked at the Nicholson house, a three-story cube in the saltbox tradition, with few architectural elements to add style. "You let me talk unless I need you to confirm or deny. Okay?"

"Not okay." Mud had her stubborn face on, eyes squinted, mouth firm.

"Mud . . ."

"I want it on record that I'm against all this sharing about what you'un is. About what we'uns is. Are. About what we are," she said, speaking proper English for the very first time.

"So noted," I said gravely, and I pushed open my truck door.

We knocked and entered. Mama called from the kitchen, "Welcome back home. Hospitality and safety while you'rn here."

"Peace and joy upon all who dwell here," I said, in one of several appropriate responses.

As I spoke Mama Grace and Mama Carmel bustled in and hugged us both. Hugs were a rarity in my life and might become even more of a rarity after today. I hugged back extra hard.

Mud extended a basket filled with loaves of bread. "I been bakin'. Three loaves. Raisin cinnamon, sourdough, and herb bread. The herb bread is good to dip in olive oil."

"Well, ain't that sweet. Nell, you'un settle. Mindy, you go on upstairs and put away your'n things, and get on to class," Mama Carmel said. "We'uns need to hear about our Nellie's undercover life."

"She needs to be here," I said. "She's part of why I'm here."

All three women turned to face me and stared. They were wearing dresses in various shades of blue and pink—colors said to make women look prettier. I was wearing jeans and a navy jacket, my shirt untucked and my hair down and flowing to my shoulders in all its curly multicolored shades of brown and red. Pointedly, Mama looked Mud and me over and said, "Mindy's bunned up, but she's too young to . . ." Mama stopped, firmed her mouth, and said, "Too young to marry. We won't be letting our girls marry young no more."

Mama Carmel said softly, "You'un ain't here to talk undercover. About coming back to the church."

I took in the good china cups and linen napkins on the
table. Gently I said, "No, ma'am. I'm sorry I wasn't clear on
the phone. I'm here to talk about what we are. Mud and me.
And maybe Daddy. Or Mama."

All three of the mamas blinked, taking in my statement,
standing motionless, like dead trees in still air. Panic flooding
the air, they looked at each other, communicating silently,
the way people who have lived together for a long time can.
Mama shook her head, saying she had no idea what was happening. Long seconds later, she looked down and wiped her
hands on a towel. "Well. You'uns come on in then. Set a
spell."

Mud and I sat on the long bench at the kitchen table, side
by side. Mama poured us each a cup of coffee and passed
the creamer and sugar for us to fix to our tastes. Today I took
it black, straight up, and bitter, like the meeting we were
about to have. From the back of the house I heard shuffling
steps and a cane, and Daddy rounded the corner to take his
place at the head of the table. He looked awful, gray-faced
as the salamander nanny, skin sagging where he had lost
weight, his hair disheveled. He accepted a mug of coffee and
drank a while, the lines on his face easing. "Forgive me for
overhearing, Nellie," he said, "but we'uns had hoped you'un
were coming to tell us good news. Am I to understand that
was a mistaken impression?"

"Yes, you were mistaken. I'm here to talk about witches
and magic."

"We had you'un tested," Mama said, her voice sharp.
"You'un ain't no witch."

"No, ma'am. I'm not a witch." I took a slow breath and
let it out, jumping in with both feet and praying I wasn't
gonna drown. "I'm something else. And Mud is like me."

No one replied. No one looked up from their coffee cups.
It was so quiet, I could have heard angels dancing on the
head of a pin, to mix two of Mama's sayings.

"Some months back," I said, "'round a year or so ago, a

Cherokee woman came to my house looking for a way onto church property to rescue a vampire." Still, no one moved. I wasn't sure they were even breathing, except for Mud, whose eyes were darting from face to face so fast I was surprised her head didn't fall off. "That was when the Department of Social Services raided the church and took away so many children. I never hid the fact that the vampire hunter came across my land to raid the church. What I didn't tell you is that she told me I'm not human."

Mama closed her eyes and her lips moved, praying silently. Probably for strength, or maybe for protection from my evil.

"Her name is Jane Yellowrock and she's a vampire hunter. Lives in New Orleans. I called her today to get the names she called me, the Cherokee words for what I am or might be. She called me a *yinehi*. Or *yvwi tsvdi*. Or *amayinehi*. I'm not pronouncing them right, but that's close. They're Cherokee for fairies or wood nymphs or brownies. Maybe dryads."

I stopped. Mama stopped praying. Daddy said, "But not a witch."

"Not a witch," I agreed.

"And your'n sister ain't a witch either."

"No, sir."

"She's one of what . . . whatever you are."

"Yes, sir."

Daddy's brown eyes latched on to me. "Bible don't say nothing about none of those things. Long as you'uns both not a witch, you jist keep it to yourself and we'uns'll all be fine."

Beneath the table, Mud grabbed my hand and squeezed. I patted hers with my free one and eased my fingers away. I stood. "It isn't so easy, Daddy. Whatever I am, it shows."

All four of the Nicholsons shot covert glances at me. "How so?" Daddy barked. "The color of your'n eyes and hair? Them contact lenses and hair dye, or a wig like you'un was wearing when Ben come to visit?"

"Not contacts. Not dye. Not a wig. I'm changing physically. I grow leaves."

Daddy reared back in his chair.

I approached the head of the table and knelt at Daddy's knee. I pulled my hair to the side and up to expose the nape of my neck to the patriarch of the Nicholson family. To do that, I had to bow my neck, which meant I couldn't see his face, couldn't see any of their faces. I was staring at the underside of the table and the floor. "You can touch them," I said. "Pull on them. I cut them when needed. Lately, I trim them every day."

I felt Daddy's fingers on the back of my neck. Felt him tugging and pulling on the vines and leaves. Felt the mamas all move closer and tug and pull. Mama said, "When you trim them, do they bleed?"

"No, ma'am."

"Mindy's gonna grow leaves?" Daddy asked, his tone disturbed.

I dropped my hair and moved back to my seat. "I think I can keep that from happening. I think I made mistakes because I didn't know what I was and those mistakes caused the leaves and vines to grow. If Mud—Mindy—lives with me, I think I can keep her from making the same mistakes."

"Lives with you'un?" Mama said. "No. I forbid it. It was hard enough with her staying with you while you healed. Mindy is too young to live away from home for good."

"She's too young to move out," Daddy said.

"But she's not too young to have churchmen hovering around her like bees to flowers?" I asked. "Not too young for a churchman to ask for her?"

Mama's mouth went firm and I recognized one of my own expressions—stubborn and boxed into a corner. Mama said, "We'uns protecting her."

"For how long? How well?" I didn't add that Mama had been taken by Brother Ephraim (may he burn in magma forever), raped, and punished. I didn't ask after my half brother, who was part Ephraim. I didn't have to ask after him because the fact of him was there between us all, like a pack of playing cards spread, faceup, on the table. "Mindy can't marry into the church," I said. "You know that a husband would disown her if she grew leaves. Some might even burn her at the stake, if it was discovered after she married that she wasn't human."

"Where'd it come from?" Daddy asked, one hand lifting toward my leaves. "One of us is carrying that trait?"

"Probably," I said. "Probably more than one of you. Probably you and Mama both got the trait in recessive genes. Probably Priss and Esther and Judith got it too in one form or another."

"My other girls ain't grown no leaves," Mama said.

"No. I'm thinking it needs a specific stimulus in the teen-aged years. Fear. Danger. Fighting for your life. All my other sisters are older or well established in good and happy marriages. As young women, teenagers, they never had to fight for their lives. Fighting for your life seems to start the process of change into whatever I am."

"You had to fight for—" Mama stopped. I hadn't told her about the man who tried to rape me years ago. "Esther was raped," Mama said, the words bald and unadorned by the usual prevarication of a churchwoman talking about sexual abuse. But Mama had been raped too. Maybe she was tired of putting a good face on an evil.

"I know she was," I said. "But not one of us knows if she grew leaves. It's possible that she and Jedidiah Whisnut are hiding it." The mamas looked at one another fast, and back to their mugs. "Jedidiah loves Esther to the moon and back. He'd hide most anything to protect her." I didn't add, *And she hadn't been on the ground when she was attacked. She hadn't scratched the attacker and found his blood on her hands. She hadn't fought back. She was too well trained to fight. She had taken whatever was dished out.* I didn't know what kind of woman Esther had turned into since the attack. This conversation made me want to find out.

I said, "I don't know enough about genetics to figure out how it might work. But Mud—Mindy—is the same kind of creature I am. And she's at risk." I took a big breath and said all at once, "I want her to come live with me. I want you to give me custody."

Mama burst into tears.

Daddy patted her shoulder.

Through her tears, Mama demanded, "You'un think it's my blood that's bad, don't you'un?"

I scowled at her. "You stop that right now, Mama." At my tone Mama's head jerked up and her eyes went wide. So did Daddy's. "Being whatever I am isn't bad or good. It just *is*. And *no*. I really think it's a combination of you and Daddy together." I looked at his middle. "It's possible that's what is wrong with his belly. He might know tomorrow. After the surgery."

"Who all knows this?"

I scowled. If Daddy was thinking to control the information he was being foolish. "I told Sam."

Daddy scowled back. "That tree in the compound. That part of this mess with you growing leaves?"

The man was entirely too smart. "Maybe," I said. "Probably."

"You'un gonna be fixing that tree?"

"I'll be trying as soon as I leave here. Now. You all talk it over and decide. I need to get Mud moved into my place soon so she can start public school."

"Public—" Mama's words cut off sharply.

"Public school," I emphasized. "Mud will need a proper education to fit in the human world. In the townie world."

"What about church services?" Daddy asked.

And I knew I had won, because this was Daddy's negotiation tone. Some of the tension left my shoulders, though I didn't let that show.

I pretended to think about his words for a while, trying to decide what I could give up and what I wouldn't. I tapped my fingertips on the table and then clenched my fist, knowing I had given something away to the master negotiator. I scowled and glared at him. "We'll both come to Sunday services once each Sunday. We'll come to weekday morning devotions *or* evening devotions once a week. The exception to this rule is if I'm on a difficult case, or Mud has exams, in which situation we'll make up for half of missed services."

"Exams?" Mud said, startled. I kicked her under the table.

"Twice a week to devotions," Daddy bargained.

"Twice a week," I agreed. "But we only make up one missed service per week if we have to miss due to a case."

"You'll bring a note from your boss."

"I'll do no such thing."

Daddy squinted at me and my bossy tone.

"I'm your child. I don't lie."

Daddy nodded slowly. I noticed he was rubbing his belly, where the medical problem was, the one that might show him to be nonhuman in tomorrow's surgery. "No note. Clothing?" he asked. "I insist on my daughter being properly and demurely dressed."

"Dresses to below her knees or pants. No bare legs and nothing tight-fitting until she's eighteen."

"Who sits with her when you'rn on a case?"

"She comes to headquarters with me. Plus, I take off and do computer work at home. I already spoke to my bosses. They'll work with me on this."

A silence thick with tension filled the space between us. Daddy drummed his fingertips on the table and I realized where I got the nervous habit. He stopped instantly and shot me a look. I stared back at him with a *Gotcha* look.

"The mamas and I'll talk it over. You'uns get on outta here." Mud and I stood. "And Nell? You'un take care a your sister."

"Yes, sir. Always."

"I want her to have a dowry, or whatever townie women get when they don't marry. I want all my girls protected."

"I'll see that she's protected. I'll see that she gets land. And education. And money. And while we're negotiating, I need a rooster."

"A *what*?" Daddy asked.

"A rooster. A big one."

Daddy shook his head at the vagaries of womenfolk. "Mud, you know which one to give your sister." He dropped his chin and pointed a single finger to the door. Mud and I took off, stopping by the chicken coop on the way down the road. "You sure it's the one?" I asked, watching the huge rooster strut around.

"That rooster ain't nothing but trouble. He starts yelling at three in the morning and he pecks the feathers offa the small hens. Mama's been threatening to feed it to us in a stew pot for weeks now. I'm surprised it's still struttin' and still has its head."

Good enough. I put my hand on the earth and reached. Small vines stretched up and snared the rooster's ankles. Mud gasped and then laughed. "I need to learn how to do that."

I held out my fingers to show her the leaves that were already sprouting from my fingernail beds. This was a demonstration, and worth any long-term effects of working or reading the land. "I can teach you, and you can grow leaves. Or you can *not* learn and stay human."

Mud's expression fell and she said, "Ohhh."

I opened the door of the chicken coop and slipped a bit of cloth over the rooster's head like a hood, wrapping the ties loosely. Then I tied off the rooster's feet, tore away the vines that had imprisoned him, and carried the huge bird to the back of my truck. It musta weighed twenty pounds.

Guilt swept through me. I wasn't sure about any of this. I was feeling my way through it all. I had talked it over with Jane Yellowrock and she called it flying by the seat of her pants, which made no sense to me at all. But . . . now I had a plan. And a rooster.

"What we'uns doin'?" Mud asked. "It might kill us, just sittin' here."

"It might try." I got out of the truck and picked up the rooster. Carried it closer to the tree, watching it. Feeling the tree through the ground. It was aware. It was angry. And it was my fault.

From behind me Mud said, "That ol' tree's mean as a snake."

"You feel that?"

"I feel it."

"I feel it too," a soft voice said.

I smiled without turning. "Tandy. Thank you for coming. You know my sister."

"I do," the empath said. "What is my job, precisely?"

"This is the vampire tree. It's sentient. It needs a place to grow, a way to reproduce, and a job. I tried to make that happen and it didn't listen because of . . . well, because of an interference problem. That problem has been resolved, but the tree has taken over a good two acres of the compound and it's started killing pets."

"That will never do," Tandy said.

"I want you to help me tell it to behave."

"I see." Tandy's tone suggested that he didn't see at all and didn't know how to go about talking to a vampire tree.

"You think you can get close to the tree?"

"It likes me," Tandy said. "So yes."

"Okay. You get close. I'll sit right here. With your keeping it calm and my hands in the earth, I'll tell it the facts of life, survival, and death. Then we'll sacrifice a rooster."

Tandy was silent a moment. He said, "We'll do what?"

"When I claim land I use blood. I want to claim the tree and all its saplings, and the land they live on. Jane Yellow-rock said it may take blood to accomplish that."

"I see," he said again. But it was clear he didn't. Tandy stepped to the vampire tree and put his hand on the bark. He leaned his head in and touched it. Then he laid his entire body against the tree. Minutes passed. "Now," he said quietly.

I dropped my dirty pink blanket to the ground and sat, the rooster squirming in my lap. I pulled off my shoes and put my bare feet flat on the ground. Instantly vines burst from the ground and twined around my feet and ankles.

"Nellie?" Mud asked, worry in the word.

"No thorns. It stopped at my ankles. I'm good."

"Okay." But she didn't sound as if she was okay. She sounded scared. Good. If she was scared she might not try the things I had. She might stay human. Longer than I had.

"You sure you want to be part of this?" I asked her.

She heaved a breath. "Yup. Move over." She sat beside me on the faded pink blanket and crossed her legs, pulling her dress down to cover her knees. "I don't gotta be barefoot, do I?"

"No. I just want you to have the chance to see and feel what this is like. But if it goes wrong, you pull out and get away. Fast."

"Okay." She grabbed my hand and we interlaced our fingers, holding tight.

"I'm dropping into the earth now," I said. I closed my eyes, concentrated on the link in our hands, felt the land through the soles of my feet, and dropped into the earth slowly, easing Mud with me. Into the dark, into the deeps. She gasped in delight, her fingers tightening on mine.

I reached out and found the tree, a green, green, *green* being with a mind full of curiosity—curiosity about Tandy, who it liked, and me, who it didn't. About Mud, who it considered only a twig, of little importance. About Brother Ephraim and why he was no more. The tree had noted his absence as it might a lull in the rains.

I had no language to share with the tree, no common . . . ground. Mud laughed at the thought, and I nearly laughed with her.

Instead I remembered what it had felt like to be a lump of root and limb, tethered to the land, part of it, but not. Healing it, growing the trees. And I sent the vampire tree the feeling of rain falling upon me. The warmth of the sun filtering through bare branches to caress my wooden form. I showed it Soulwood and the extension of Soulwood on the banks of the river at the two Tollivers' homes, on the bank of the Tennessee River, the few acres that now contained mature trees. Land that now really and truly *lived*.

The tree followed me, absorbing the impressions, the presence of life and death. The tree understood. It turned its full attention to me. Without words, it thought at me, sharing concepts, meaning, all without words or pictures. *Seeding, rooting, fruiting, reproducing.* Mostly that. *Reproducing.*

I empathized, as Tandy did, understanding, comprehending, accepting. The tree was the only one of its kind. Like all trees, it needed to make more of its species. It wanted to spread into the land. It was *compelled* by Nature herself to reproduce. And it had no place that was safe to live in. No sexual opposite that would allow it to reproduce.

Humans wanted it dead.

It was . . . lonely.

I thought back, showing it the rootlets at the gate. Springing up, leafing out, becoming saplings. Uncut. Unmolested. Allowed to grow. The land dedicated to it alone. But not allowed to kill or seek blood. Not allowed to thorn or trap with vines. It considered this, but its loneliness was acute. It was isolated, solitary, abandoned, lost. It wanted what I had. Unlike other trees, it wanted . . . family.

Mud's mouth opened in awe. "Nellie," she whispered.

I promised the tree that . . . that I would claim it and keep it as part of my woods.

That it could become part of Soulwood, part of the trees there. But it had to live in harmony with the other trees and animals, wherever it grew. And it must no longer kill. If a human cut it down, it could come back from its roots, but it could not attack or resist. It must live in harmony with other trees in the wood. It must allow humans dominion. It must serve, not fight back. If the tree did these things then I would claim it as family.

The tree went silent. The concept of harmony and servitude was not foreign to it. Trees and the land had lived in servitude for ten thousand years. It understood. It agreed.

It agreed to being claimed as part of Soulwood.

It agreed to harm no human, no mammal, no bird. No vertebrate of any kind.

One last blood feeding, I thought at it. *Then no more.* One-handed, I placed the rooster on the ground, an offering. The tree pushed rootlets up through the ground. Found the chicken. It wrapped its vines about the rooster's struggling body, but then it hesitated. Paused.

The vines around my feet tightened. It didn't want the

rooster or its blood. It wanted me. It wanted a willing sacrifice. It was asking permission. Waiting patiently, in the way
of trees.

I studied the tree's consciousness, the tree I had mutated
and brought to sentience with my blood. *If you take only a
drop of my blood,* I thought at it, *fine. But if you take too
much, I'll . . . I'll be most unhappy.*

The tree extended a single barb. It pierced my toe. Pain
and shock jetted up my leg. Drops of my blood welled and
trailed down, to drip onto the ground. The tree sucked up
my blood. Ate it. The thorn withdrew, leaving a sharp pain
in my flesh. I felt the leaf that spooled out of my wound and
closed it.

I felt the vampire tree's rootlets uncoil from my feet. Uncoil from the rooster.

I felt the interest of the tree turn to Soulwood. Knew when
it shifted its attention away from me and to the land.

I opened my eyes to meet Mud's eyes.

"Whoa, Bessie," she said. "That was . . . That was . . ."
She shook her head, not having words.

"You growing leaves?" I asked her.

Mud released my hand and felt her hair, studied her fingers. "Nope."

"Good." I pulled away from the land. Standing, I gathered
my blanket into a ball at my waist.

Tandy walked from the tree to stand in front of me. "That
was . . ." He shook his head. "Oh my God. That was amazing," he murmured. "Beyond wonderful. Not anything I
could ever have imagined." His eyes were shining bright red.
His Lichtenberg lines feathered down his face and neck,
scarlet against his too-white skin. "Thank you for letting me
be part of that."

"I don't reckon *you'un* grew leaves?" I asked in church-
speak.

"Nary a one," he answered back in church-speak.

"Thank you for coming. I know it's made you late to
work."

"I wouldn't have missed this for the world."

"Me neither," Mud said. "Let's go home."

"Mama and Daddy haven't said you can move in with me."

"If'n they don't let me move in, I'll jist grow me some leaves," she said, mischief in her eyes. "I think I know how to do that now."

"Oh, Mud." I hugged her for a moment before releasing her. "Well. Okay. What are we gonna do about the rooster?"

"Let it go? Someone'll claim it and when it wakes them up at three in the morning they'll get a good meal outta it."

Together we released the rooster. The mean old bird scratched the earth, giving me the evil eye, as if trying to decide if he was going to attack me, but then he reconsidered and raced away, crowing. I put on my shoes. Tandy in our wake, my true sister and I walked to my Chevy truck and drove back to Soulwood. Back to home.

EPILOGUE

I sat on my porch swing, warm spring breezes dancing across the lawn, brushing newly leafed plants, pale green trees waving in the wind. Birds were singing and squirrels were racing around wide trunks, playing tag and catch-me-if-you-can. A brave lizard raced across the house wall and into a space it believed the cats couldn't reach. Had they been awake, one of the cats would have caught and eaten him, lizards being a very fine dinner to a mouser. But they were snoozing on the front porch, stretched out in the sun, unmoving, except for Cello's tail tip twitching every now and then.

Mud was at home, packing for her move here. I didn't know if it would be a permanent move or not. That would be up to the state's social services department and a judge.

My cell phone rang. It was on the swing seat beside me. It was Occam's number. Something leaped in my chest, like a wereleopard into a tree. I answered. "This is Nell." Nell. Not Ingram. To set the tone.

"Nell, sugar." His voice sounded rough and coarse, like the voice of a chain-smoking old man. "I didn't know if you'd answer."

"I didn't think you'd call. Seems like we both were wrong." He didn't reply, but I could hear the soft purr of his fancy car. "What happened? Why haven't you—" I stopped, not able to ask why he hadn't called me.

"I've been out of work. Healing."

"From the fire?"

"You brought me back from death, Nellie. And I thank you for that. But . . . well, the healing wasn't complete. It's taken a lot of shifting to heal from the burns."

I nodded, even though he couldn't see me. "I took some time to turn back from being a log." I risked a small joke. "A truly vegetative state."

Occam laughed. I laughed with him.

"Nell, sugar, can we have that date?"

"I'd like that."

Occam said nothing. And I decided to be brave. "How about now?"

Silence stretched between us. "Now is good," he said after a while, his voice so hoarse it sounded torn.

"You gonna tell me about your life, the things you re-member?" He stayed silent. I went on. "From before the cage and the traveling carnival, and the time from your leopard imprisonment?"

"I will. You going to tell me about your family? About John Ingram? About the Nicholsons?"

"I will."

"Good. 'Cause I got things to say about how I nearly died. And how Soulwood healed me. As well as it could. I been out of work for just as long as you. Burned. Badly burned, with lots of scars that not even shifting to my cat has helped. But healing and still alive because of you and your land. This will be our 'getting to know one another' first date."

"I like the sound of that."

"And at the end of this date, or maybe at the middle, I promise that I am going to kiss you, Nell, sugar."

Warmth spiraled through me and settled in my belly. My breath came faster. "A properly improper kiss?"

"The most improper kiss I can think of, Nell, sugar. What do you want me to pick up to eat?"

"You just come. I'll have a picnic ready when you get here."

"That sounds right nice, Nell, sugar. I'll be there in an hour."

* * *

The weather was comfortable enough to allow me to wear a long-sleeved shirt and a silky skirt, my feet bare. At my side was a basket, one with sandwiches, a plastic bowl of fresh fruit, a bottle of Sister Erasmus' wine. And my pink blanket, clean and neatly folded.

It was early yet, but I felt it the moment the fancy car began the drive up the hill. My fingertips ached, as the small leaves that grew from there tried to quiver in nerves or excitement or both. Occam and I were going to have a picnic on the hill of Soulwood, overlooking the distant skyline of Knoxville and the even more distant mountains. And he was going to kiss me, a very improper kiss. I thought it was time and past time for me to have my first very improper kiss.

The fancy car turned into the drive. I stood and walked down the steps to Occam.

Read on for an excerpt of the first book
in Faith Hunter's *New York Times*
bestselling Jane Yellowrock series,

SKINWALKER

Available wherever books are sold!

I wheeled my bike down Decatur Street and eased deeper into the French Quarter, the bike's engine purring. My shotgun, a Benelli M4 Super 90, was slung over my back and loaded for vamp with hand-packed silver fléchette rounds. I carried a selection of silver crosses in my belt, hidden under my leather jacket, and stakes, secured in loops on my jeans-clad thighs. The saddlebags on my bike were filled with my meager travel belongings—clothes in one side, tools of the trade in the other. As a vamp killer for hire, I travel light.

I'd need to put the vamp-hunting tools out of sight for my interview. My hostess might be offended. Not a good thing when said hostess held my next paycheck in her hands and possessed a set of fangs of her own.

A guy, a good-looking Joe standing in a doorway, turned his head to follow my progress as I motored past. He wore leather boots, a jacket, and jeans, like me, though his dark hair was short and mine was down to my hips when not braided out of the way, tight to my head, for fighting. A Kawasaki motorbike leaned on a stand nearby. I didn't like his interest, but he didn't prick my predatory or territorial instincts.

I maneuvered the bike down St. Louis and then onto Dauphine, weaving between nervous-looking shop workers heading home for the evening and a few early revelers out for fun. I spotted the address in the fading light. Katie's Ladies was the oldest continually operating whorehouse in the Quarter, in business since 1845, though at various locations, depending on hurricane, flood, the price of rent, and the agreeable nature of local law and its enforcement officers. I parked, set the kickstand, and unwound my long legs from the hog.

I had found two bikes in a junkyard in Charlotte, North Carolina, bodies rusted, rubber rotted. They were in bad shape. But Jacob, a semiretired Harley restoration mechanic/Zen Harley priest living along the Catawba River, took my money, fixing one up, using the other for parts, ordering what else he needed over the Net. It took six months.

During that time I'd hunted for him, keeping his wife and four kids supplied with venison, rabbit, turkey—whatever I could catch, as maimed as I was—restocked supplies from the city with my hoarded money, and rehabbed my damaged body back into shape. It was the best I could do for the months it took me to heal. Even someone with my rapid healing and variable metabolism takes a long while to totally mend from a near beheading.

Now that I was a hundred percent, I needed work. My best bet was a job killing off a rogue vampire that was terrorizing the city of New Orleans. It had taken down three tourists and left a squad of cops, drained and smiling, dead where it dropped them. Scuttlebutt said it hadn't been satisfied with just blood—it had eaten their internal organs. All that suggested the rogue was old, powerful, and deadly—a whacked-out vamp. The nutty ones were always the worst.

Just last week, Katherine "Katie" Fonteneau, the proprietess and namesake of Katie's Ladies, had e-mailed me. According to my Web site, I had successfully taken down an entire blood-family in the mountains near Asheville. And I had. No lies on the Web site or in the media reports, not bald-faced ones anyway. Truth is, I'd nearly died, but I'd done the job, made a rep for myself, and then taken off a few months to invest my legitimately gotten gains. Or to heal, but spin is everything. A lengthy vacation sounded better than the complete truth.

I took off my helmet and the clip that held my hair, pulling my braids out of my jacket collar and letting them fall around me, beads clicking. I palmed a few tools of the trade—one

stake, ash wood and silver tipped; a tiny gun; and a cross—
and tucked them into the braids, rearranging them to hang
smoothly with no lumps or bulges. I also breathed deeply,
seeking to relax, to assure my safety through the upcoming
interview. I was nervous, and being nervous around a vamp
was just plain dumb.

The sun was setting, casting a red glow on the horizon,
limning the ancient buildings, shuttered windows, and
wrought-iron balconies in fuchsia. It was pretty in a purely
human way. I opened my senses and let my Beast taste the
world. She liked the smells and wanted to prowl. *Later*, I
promised her. Predators usually growl when irritated. *Soon*—
she sent mental claws into my soul, kneading. It was uncomfortable, but the claw pricks kept me alert, which I'd need for
the interview. I had never met a civilized vamp, certainly never
done business with one. So far as I knew, vamps and skinwalk-
ers had never met. I was about to change that. This could get
interesting.

I clipped my sunglasses onto my collar, lenses hanging
out. I glanced at the witchy-locks on my saddlebags and,
satisfied, I walked to the narrow red door and pushed the
buzzer. The bald-headed man who answered was definitely
human, but big enough to be something else: professional
wrestler, steroid-augmented bodybuilder, or troll. All of the
above, maybe. The thought made me smile. He blocked the
door, standing with arms loose and ready. "Something
funny?" he asked, voice like a horse-hoof rasp on stone.

"Not really. Tell Katie that Jane Yellowrock is here."
Tough always works best on first acquaintance. That my
knees were knocking wasn't a consideration.

"Card?" Troll asked. A man of few words. I liked him
already. My new best pal. With two gloved fingers, I
unzipped my leather jacket, fished a business card from
an inside pocket, and extended it to him. It read JANE
YELLOWROCK, HAVE STAKES WILL TRAVEL. Vamp killing is
a bloody business. I had discovered that a little humor went
a long way to making it all bearable.

Troll took the card and closed the door in my face. I might have to teach my new pal a few manners. But that was nearly axiomatic for all the men of my acquaintance.

I heard a bike two blocks away. It wasn't a Harley. Maybe a Kawasaki, like the bright red crotch rocket I had seen earlier. I wasn't surprised when it came into view and it was the Joe from Decatur Street. He pulled his bike up beside mine, powered down, and sat there, eyes hidden behind sunglasses. He had a toothpick in his mouth and it twitched once as he pulled his helmet and glasses off.

The Joe was a looker. A little taller than my six feet even, he had olive skin, black hair, black brows. Black jacket and jeans. Black boots. Bit of overkill with all the black, but he made it work, with muscular legs wrapped around the red bike.

No silver in sight. No shotgun, but a suspicious bulge beneath his right arm. Made him a leftie. Something glinted in the back of his collar. A knife hilt, secured in a spine sheath. Maybe more than one blade. There were scuffs on his boots (Western, like mine, not Harley butt-stompers) but his were Fryes and mine were ostrich-skin Luccheses. I pulled in scents, my nostrils widening. His boots smelled of horse manure, fresh. Local boy, then, or one who had been in town long enough to find a mount. I smelled horse sweat and hay, a clean blend of scents. And cigar. It was the cigar that made me like him. The taint of steel, gun oil, and silver made me fall in love. Well, sorta. My Beast thought he was kinda cute, and maybe tough enough to be worthy of us. Yet there was a faint scent on the man, hidden beneath the surface smells, that made me wary.

The silence had lasted longer than expected. Since he had been the one to pull up, I just stared, and clearly our silence bothered the Joe, but it didn't bother me. I let a half grin curl my lip. He smiled back and eased off his bike. Behind me, inside Katie's, I heard footsteps. I maneuvered so that the Joe and the doorway were both visible. No way could I do it and be unobtrusive, but I raised a shoulder to show I had no hard feelings. Just playing it smart. Even for a pretty boy.

Troll opened the door and jerked his head to the side. I took it as the invitation it was and stepped inside. "You got interesting taste in friends," Troll said, as the door closed on the Joe.

"Never met him. Where you want the weapons?" Always better to offer than to have them removed. Power plays work all kinds of ways.

Troll opened an armoire. I unbuckled the shotgun holster and set it inside, pulling silver crosses from my belt and thighs and from beneath the coat until there was a nice pile. Thirteen crosses—excessive, but they distracted people from my backup weapons. Next came the wooden stakes and silver stakes. Thirteen of each. And the silver vial of holy water. One vial. If I carried thirteen, I'd slosh.

I hung the leather jacket on the hanger in the armoire and tucked the glasses in the inside pocket with the cell phone. I closed the armoire door and assumed the position so Troll could search me. He grunted as if surprised, but pleased, and did a thorough job. To give him credit, he didn't seem to enjoy it overmuch—used only the backs of his hands, no fingers, didn't linger or stroke where he shouldn't. Breathing didn't speed up, heart rate stayed regular; things I can sense if it's quiet enough. After a thorough feel inside the tops of my boots, he said, "This way."

I followed him down a narrow hallway that made two crooked turns toward the back of the house. We walked over old Persian carpets, past oils and watercolors done by famous and not-so-famous artists. The hallway was lit with stained-glass Lalique sconces, which looked real, not like reproductions, but maybe you can fake old; I didn't know. The walls were painted a soft butter color that worked with the sconces to illuminate the paintings. Classy joint for a whorehouse. The Christian children's home schoolgirl in me was both appalled and intrigued.

When Troll paused outside the red door at the end of the hallway, I stumbled, catching my foot on a rug. He caught me with one hand and I pushed off him with little body contact. I managed to look embarrassed; he shook his head.

He knocked. I braced myself and palmed the cross he had missed. And the tiny two-shot derringer. Both hidden against my skull on the crown of my head, and covered by my braids, which men never, ever searched, as opposed to my boots, which men always had to stick their fingers in. He opened the door and stood aside. I stepped in.

The room was spartan but expensive, and each piece of furniture looked Spanish. Old Spanish. Like Queen-Isabella-and-Christopher-Columbus old. The woman, wearing a teal dress and soft slippers, standing beside the desk, could have passed for twenty until you looked in her eyes. Then she might have passed for said queen's older sister. Old, old, *old* eyes. Peaceful as she stepped toward me. Until she caught my scent.

In a single instant her eyes bled red, pupils went wide and black, and her fangs snapped down. She leaped. I dodged under her jump as I pulled the cross and derringer, quickly moving to the far wall, where I held out the weapons. The cross was for the vamp, the gun for the Troll. She hissed at me, fangs fully extended. Her claws were bone white and two inches long. Troll had pulled a gun. A big gun. Men and their pissing contests. *Crap.* Why couldn't they ever just let me be the only one with a gun?

"Predator," she hissed. "In my territory." Vamp anger pheromones filled the air, bitter as wormwood.

"I'm not human," I said, my voice steady. "That's what you smell." I couldn't do anything about the tripping heart rate, which I knew would drive her further over the edge; I'm an animal. Biological factors always kick in. So much for trying not to be nervous. The cross in my hand glowed with a cold white light, and Katie, if that was her original name, tucked her head, shielding her eyes. Not attacking, which meant that she was thinking. Good.

"Katie?" Troll asked.

"I'm not human," I repeated. "I'll really hate shooting your Troll here, to bleed all over your rugs, but I will."

"Troll?" Katie asked. Her body froze with that inhuman stillness vamps possess when thinking, resting, or whatever else it is they do when they aren't hunting, eating, or killing. Her shoulders dropped and her fangs clicked back into the roof of her mouth with a sudden spurt of humor. Vampires can't laugh and go vampy at the same time. They're two distinct parts of them, one part still human, one part rabid hunter. Well, that's likely insulting, but then this was the first so-called civilized vamp I'd ever met. All the others I'd had personal contact with were sick, twisted killers. And then dead. Really dead.

Troll's eyes narrowed behind the .45 aimed my way. I figured he didn't like being compared to the bad guy in a children's fairy tale. I was better at fighting, but negotiation seemed wise. "Tell him to back off. Let me talk." I nudged it a bit. "Or I'll take you down and he'll never get a shot off." Unless he noticed that I had set the safety on his gun when I tripped. Then I'd *have* to shoot him. I wasn't betting on my .22 stopping him unless I got an eye shot. Chest hits wouldn't even slow him down. In fact they'd likely just make him mad.

When neither attacked, I said, "I'm not here to stake you. I'm Jane Yellowrock, here to interview for a job, to take out a rogue vamp that your own council declared an outlaw. But I don't smell human, so I take precautions. One cross, one stake, one two-shot derringer." The word "stake" didn't elude her. Or him. He'd missed three weapons. No Christmas bonus for Troll.

"What are you?" she asked.

"You tell me where you sleep during the day and I'll tell you what I am. Otherwise, we can agree to do business. Or I can leave."

Telling the location of a lair—where a vamp sleeps—is information for lovers, dearest friends, or family. Katie chuckled. It was one of the silky laughs that her kind can give, low and erotic, like vocal sex. My Beast purred. She liked the sound.

"Are you offering to be my toy for a while, intriguing nonhuman female?" When I didn't answer, she slid closer, despite the glowing cross, and said, "You are interesting. Tall, slender, young." She leaned in and breathed in my scent.

"Or not so young. What are you?" she pressed, her voice heavy with fascination. Her eyes had gone back to their natural color, a sort of grayish hazel, but blood blush still marred her cheeks so I knew she was still primed for violence. That violence being my death.

"Secretive," she murmured, her voice taking on that tone they use to enthrall, a deep vibration that seems to stroke every gland. "Enticing scent. Likely tasty. Perhaps your blood would be worth the trade. Would you come to my bed if I offered?"

"No," I said. No inflection in my voice. No interest, no revulsion, no irritation, nothing. Nothing to tick off the vamp or her servant.

"Pity. Put down the gun, Tom. Get our guest something to drink."

I didn't wait for Tommy Troll to lower his weapon; I dropped mine. Beast wasn't happy, but she understood. I was the intruder in Katie's territory. While I couldn't show submission, I could show manners. Tom lowered his gun and his attitude at the same time and holstered the weapon as he moved into the room toward a well-stocked bar.

"Tom?" I said. "Uncheck your safety." He stopped midstride. "I set it when I fell against you in the hallway."

"Couldn't happen," he said.

"I'm fast. It's why your employer invited me for a job interview."

He inspected his .45 and nodded at his boss. Why anyone would want to go around with a holstered .45 with the safety off is beyond me. It smacks of either stupidity or quiet desperation, and Katie had lived too long to be stupid. I was guessing the rogue had made her truly apprehensive. I tucked the cross inside a little lead-foil-lined pocket in the leather belt holding up my Levi's, and eased the small gun in beside it, strapping it down. There was a safety, but on such a small gun, it was easy to knock the safety off with an accidental brush of my arm.

"Is that where you hid the weapons?" Katie asked. When

I just looked at her, she shrugged as if my answer were un-important and said, "Impressive. You are impressive."

Katie was one of those dark ash blondes with long straight hair so thick it whispered when she moved, falling across the teal silk that fit her like a second skin. She stood five feet and a smidge, but height was no measure of power in her kind. She could move as fast as I could and kill in an eyeblink. She had buffed nails that were short when she wasn't in killing mode, pale skin, and she wore exotic, Egyptian-style makeup around the eyes. Black liner overlaid with some kind of glitter. Not the kind of look I'd ever had the guts to try. I'd rather face down a grizzly than try to achieve "a look."

"What'll it be, Miz Yellowrock?" Tom asked.

"Cola's fine. No diet."

He popped the top on a Coke and poured it over ice that crackled and split when the liquid hit, placed a wedge of lime on the rim, and handed it to me. His employer got a tall fluted glass of something milky that smelled sharp and al-coholic. Well, at least it wasn't blood on ice. Ick.

"Thank you for coming such a distance," Katie said, tak-ing one of two chairs and indicating the other for me. Both chairs were situated with backs to the door, which I didn't like, but I sat as she continued. "We never made proper in-troductions, and the In-ter-net," she said, separating the syl-lables as if the term was strange, "is no substitute for formal, proper introductions. I am Katherine Fonteneau." She offered the tips of her fingers, and I took them for a moment in my own before dropping them.

"Jane Yellowrock," I said, feeling as though it was all a little redundant. She sipped; I sipped. I figured that was enough etiquette. "Do I get the job?" I asked.

Katie waved away my impertinence. "I like to know the people with whom I do business. Tell me about yourself."

Cripes. The sun was down. I needed to be tooling around town, getting the smell and the feel of the place. I had errands to run, an apartment to rent, rocks to find, meat to buy. "You've been to my Web site, no doubt read my bio. It's all there in black and white." Well, in full color graphics, but still.

Katie's brows rose politely. "Your bio is dull and uninformative. For instance, there is no mention that you appeared out of the forest at age twelve, a feral child raised by wolves, without even the rudiments of human behavior. That you were placed in a children's home, where you spent the next six years. And that you again vanished until you reappeared two years ago and started killing my kind."

My hackles started to rise, but I forced them down. I'd been baited by a roomful of teenaged girls before I even learned to speak English. After that, nothing was too painful. I grinned and threw a leg over the chair arm. Which took Katie, of the elegant attack, aback. "I wasn't raised by wolves. At least I don't think so. I don't feel an urge to howl at the moon, anyway. I have no memories of my first twelve years of life, so I can't answer you about them, but I think I'm probably Cherokee." I touched my black hair, then my face with its golden brown skin and sharp American Indian nose in explanation. "After that, I was raised in a Christian children's home in the mountains of South Carolina. I left when I was eighteen, traveled around a while, and took up an apprenticeship with a security firm for two years. Then I hung out my shingle, and eventually drifted into the vamp-hunting business.

"What about you? You going to share all your own deep dark secrets, Katie of Katie's Ladies? Who is known to the world as Katherine Fonteneau, aka Katherine Louisa Dupre, Katherine Pearl Duplantis, and Katherine Vuillemont, among others I uncovered. Who renewed her liquor license in February, is a registered Republican, votes religiously, pardon the term, sits on the local full vampiric council, has numerous offshore accounts in various names, a half interest in two local hotels, at least three restaurants, and several bars, and has enough money to buy and sell this entire city if she wanted to."

"We have both done our research, I see."

I had a feeling Katie found me amusing. Must be hard to live a few centuries and find yourself in a modern world where everyone knows what you are and is either infatuated with you or scared silly by you. I was neither, which she liked, if the small smile was any indication. "So. Do I have the job?" I asked again.

Katie considered me for a moment, as if weighing my responses and attitude. "Yes," she said. "I've arranged a small house for you, per the requirements on your In-ter-net web place."

My brows went up despite myself. She must have been pretty sure she was gonna hire me, then.

"It backs up to this property." She waved vaguely at the back of the room. "The small L-shaped garden at the side and back is walled in brick, and I had the stones you require delivered two days ago."

Okay. Now I was impressed. My Web site says I require close proximity to boulders or a rock garden, and that I won't take a job if such a place can't be found. And the woman— the vamp—had made sure that nothing would keep me from accepting the job. I wondered what she would have done if I'd said no.

At her glance, Tr— Tom took up the narrative. "The gardener had a conniption, but he figured out a way to get boulders into the garden with a crane, and then blended them into his landscaping. Grumbled about it, but it's done."

"Would you tell me why you need piles of stone?" Katie asked.

"Meditation." When she looked blank I said, "I use stone for meditation. It helps prepare me for a hunt." I knew she had no idea what I was talking about. It sounded pretty lame even to me, and I had made up the lie. I'd have to work on that one.

Katie stood and so did I, setting aside my Coke. Katie had drained her foul-smelling libation. On her breath it smelled vaguely like licorice. "Tom will give you the contract and a packet of information, the compiled evidence gathered about the rogue by the police and our own investigators. Tonight you may rest or indulge in whatever pursuits appeal to you.

"Tomorrow, once you deliver the signed contract, you are invited to join my girls for dinner before business commences. They will be attending a private party, and dinner will be served at seven of the evening. I will not be present, that they may speak freely. Through them you may learn something of import." It was a strange way to say seven p.m., and an even stranger request for me to interrogate her employees right off the bat, but I didn't react. Maybe one of them knew something about the rogue. And maybe Katie knew it. "After dinner, you may initiate your inquiries.

"The council's offer of a bonus stands. An extra twenty percent if you dispatch the rogue inside of ten days, without the media taking a stronger note of *us*." The last word had an inflection that let me know the "us" wasn't Katie and me. She meant the vamps. "Human media attention has been . . . difficult. And the rogue's feeding has strained relations in the vampiric council. It is *important*," she said.

I nodded. *Sure. Whatever. I want to get paid, so I aim to please.* But I didn't say it.

Katie extended a folder to me and I tucked it under my arm. "The police photos of the crime scenes you requested. Three samples of bloodied cloth from the necks of the most recent victims, carefully wiped to gather saliva," she said.

Vamp saliva, I thought. *Full of vamp scent. Good for tracking.*

"On a card is my contact at the NOPD. She is expecting a call from you. Let Tom know if you need anything else." Katie settled cold eyes on me in obvious dismissal. She had already turned her mind to other things. Like dinner? Yep. Her cheeks had paled again and she suddenly looked drawn with hunger. Her eyes slipped to my neck. Time to leave.

Ready to find
your next great read?

Let us help.

Visit prh.com/nextread

Penguin
Random
House